# One Too Many

Also by Maureen Anne Jennings
*Bartender Wanted*

# One Too Many

## A Rose Leary
## Mystery

Maureen Anne Jennings

Copyright © 2014 by Maureen Anne Jennings
All rights reserved. Published in the United States by
Tough Prose Press.
www.toughprose.com.

Cover design by Randy Comer
ISBN 978-0-9852835-9-9
October, 2014

To Patrick Vincent and Rita Margaret Jennings,
who taught us the glories of a strong story
and a good laugh.
And to Michael, Patrick, Margie,
Rose, Kevin, and Sharon,
who perfect those lessons every single day.
Professional comedians pray for such wit.

# Chapter One

Her blood dripped into the ice. Slender crimson ribbons twirled around and over the cubes, tinting the shimmering mix with darker shades of red. Rose Leary stared at her injured hand, surprised at the amount of blood. The chipped top to the damned Absolut bottle had barely nicked her middle finger, but big drops still stained her cuff and tainted the ice in the martini shaker. Vampire cocktail, straight up, hold the tissue. She splashed well vodka on the cut, blotted it with a napkin, and threw the ice into the sink.

"That's it. Last call." She held her cuff under cold water, surveying the bar to see who'd want just one more. Customers who'd come to My World to drink and escape the heavy heat of an August Saturday might plan to linger for another half hour of air-conditioned relief on this early Sunday morning.

"Finally. Waiting for you to pronounce last call tonight has been like waiting for the city to sleep."

Rose lined empty liquor bottles on the bar in front of the tall man in the navy linen jacket. She didn't look at him while she grouped the bottles into liquor types and then brands. If she didn't meet his eyes, she wouldn't smile into them.

Even the faintest smile would ruin the poker face she wanted to bluff. A stern expression now might make Detective Frank Butler listen the next time she refused a ride home from work. Ignoring her insistence that she detested being fetched from her job like a child from daycare, he had timed his departure from the Sixth Precinct to the end of her bartending shift again. He'd walked in the door ten minutes and five customers before the bar closed, muttering about being in the neighborhood.

The extra minutes she'd talked to Nick must have bothered Butler into ignoring the blood staining her sleeve. Green wasn't going to be one of his best colors, and jealousy was the main reason she didn't want him hanging out at her bar.

Impatience already rumbled in his voice as he cocked his head toward the man sitting at the far end of the bar.

"Who's that lurking down there?"

"Lurking, Frank?"

"The fun-with-razors kid you've been chatting up since I got here. Did he just keep shaving until his mirror unfogged? Who's the guy whose conversation was so interesting you took notes?"

"You've met Nick before. He lives with Yvonne, the bookkeeper here who gives me those home-baked goodies you inhale. Please try to remember his face, since we're going to dinner at their loft tomorrow. He was giving me directions."

Rose returned the olives, onions, and cherries to their jars, hesitated over the fresh fruit, then dumped everything but the lime wedges into the garbage. The lemon twists and orange slices looked as tired as the speech she expected Butler to repeat about the idiocy of wasting cab fare when he had a perfectly good vehicle at her disposal. Frank Butler didn't give any favors freely, not even those he demanded she accept.

Butler scrutinized Nick again. "Here I was thinking Nick looked familiar from a mug shot. Dragging me into the depths of the Lower East Side for a dinner isn't enough? We're going somewhere in Manhattan where you need directions? What—are we going to take a left after the third hooker? Then I'll have to eat some artsy slop while I watch that overexposed head salivate at you all night? If it's tofu, I leave."

"I'll call them in the morning with a special request for something at the pinnacle of the food chain. Dinner will be great: he cooks as an art form, and she bakes like a grandmother. They're both bright. We've agreed we should socialize more. I'm always so gratified when I listen to you."

Looking down to see if her blood had turned to water and disappeared, Rose drenched her cuff with club soda and scrubbed the rusty splotch that would doom this blouse to the dire-emergency reaches of her closet. The tightly tapered sleeves that had resisted her attempts at the classic bartender's roll wouldn't hide this stain.

"You know, every time you wear something that good to work you might as well sport a 'Kiss Me, I'm Vain' button. Bartenders aren't supposed to aim for the best-dressed list, although I suppose the pretty stuff inspires more guys to drool."

"I wrote for an extra hour before work tonight instead of picking up my laundry. This was the lightest silk I could stand behind this hellaciously hot bar. Thanks for obsessing about it. Distracts me from regret about ruining a good blouse for the sake of literature."

Nobody who nursed cocktails at an air-conditioned

bar ever appreciated that the server behind it worked in a microclimate at least twenty degrees hotter. The motors and compressors behind the bar threw off so much heat that Rose often wanted to dive into the bins of ice.

Butler still wore his jacket. "At least you didn't waste your sacrifice. Nick appreciated your silk's sheer qualities too."

"I never wear sheer clothes to work. I could tend bar in a negligee for all Nick would care. He doesn't salivate over any woman but Yvonne. Your evening could end up pretty dry, too, if you don't drop the cop act." Rose met Butler's eyes, but she didn't smile.

She turned her back on him and started punching the subtotal keys to ring out the register. In the mirror above the back bar, she watched Butler decide not to interrupt her accounting. They could continue the argument in the comfort of home. Her home, where he obviously assumed he'd stay again tonight. Their agreement was no more than four nights a week together. Tonight would make six. If she ever got out of here.

Rose emptied the drawer into her cash box, thankful again to be reading a register's tape instead of a monitor's display. Her bosses hadn't computerized My World yet, and she didn't expect them to introduce a POS system here. A computer terminal behind My World's bar would serve as public notice that the Victors family had sold the place.

Since buying My World in the 1940s, the Victors had watched its clientele shift as newer village residents and visitors from other zip codes replaced the longshoremen and meat wholesalers they'd originally served. Along with the combination to the safe, the family bequeathed an instinctive suspicion of fixing the unbroken to the next generation. The Victors family knew their strengths.

She wished Joe and Bob Victors would come back from Italy soon.

Rose put the last of her bar checks in numerical order and folded her register tape around the stack. Ten minutes of counting downstairs, a final swab of the old wooden bar top, and she could walk out the front door. She'd cleaned and restocked everything but the very last-minute supplies while she'd talked with Nick. None of the remaining people at the bar looked scared to go home to Sunday's first hours. Tonight would end early for a Saturday shift. With any luck, she could be home drawing a cool bath by 4:45.

Butler lifted the thick Sunday *Times* from the barstool next to him and dropped it onto the bar. Digging for the magazine, his arm knocked over the stack of ashtrays she'd just washed. Two ashtrays fell into the bar sink and shattered. She couldn't leave the tiny shards of glass for the porter's tired hands to find.

Departure became less imminent.

Two minutes earlier, and the mats in the sink would have cushioned the drop. Five minutes earlier, she would have had the shards picked up and herself safely downstairs counting cash before Terri and Ken Apted strolled in.

"Impeccable timing, Frank." She raised her voice to greet Terri and Ken. She'd scream if they insisted on blended drinks. She'd scream twice if the blended drinks featured heavy cream. Butler would finish the *Times* crossword and read all the classifieds before she rewashed the blenders and scrubbed a thick scum out of the sink.

"Hi, sweetie, how was your night? You look real cute in that blouse. Hello, Frankie hon, terrific shirt." Terri sprinkled compliments into her greetings the way most people shook hands. Butler mumbled his thanks, excused himself to make a phone call, and hurried downstairs.

Rose searched for a return compliment on Terri's salmon jacket and matching shorts. She'd learned the difficulties of complimenting Terri last week, when a casual remark that a new hairstyle made her look so young had driven Terri into the ladies' room for fifteen minutes of apologetic tears.

Terri had thought Rose's remark meant she didn't look young all the time.

"Honey, what would be fun to drink?" Terri pulled her husband's arm away from the paper he was riffling through, no doubt for the sports section. "Frankie might not like you going through his paper like that. He can be real particular. Now think a minute and tell me something fun."

The moment when Terri's pastel sleeve brushed against her husband's lime green jacket looked like a bad example of underwater photography.

Rose almost giggled at the lengths of truthfulness she'd have to traverse in order to praise anything she'd ever seen Ken wear. The brightly colored and playfully synthetic clothes he sported looked as if he'd ordered them from catalogues where all the models posed on the beach. His clothes' colors were so bright and their cut so childish that only seaside days filled with bleaching sunlight and constant sport could excuse them on anyone over seventeen. She'd never met anyone else she could imagine wearing dayglo zinc sunscreen.

"Hi, Ken, what would you like?" No point in mentioning that she'd already closed the register. The Apteds hadn't paid for a drink in My World since Terri had agreed to "watch the place" while the owners visited family in Italy. Ken never left a tip, although Terri occasionally slipped a single under her emptied glass.

Ken's drink choices bothered Rose more than his failure to tip. He liked drinks made from several sweet and brightly colored ingredients.

You drink what you marry?

In the three weeks Ken and Terri had substituted as My World's managers, Ken had taught Rose over thirty new drink recipes she'd never wanted to learn. She suspected he read the informative little tags that hung around the necks of liquor bottles. Rose knew he pored over restaurant and hotel magazines the way chefs pored over *Larousse*, taking notes in the brown pleather daybook he carried with a junior executive's pride.

"Darn it, you've ruined that scrumptious blouse. Look, honey, Rose has some yucky stuff on her cuff. And you still haven't told me what to order." Terri tapped Ken's elbow to divert his attention from the sports section. He shook his wife's hand off his elbow with a sharp jerk, too engrossed in the first-draft choices to search through his growing repertoire of what he called "drink concepts."

Terri gave Rose a those-men giggle before she tapped one of her intricately painted nails against her cheek to pantomime the difficulties of ordering her own drink. Maintaining Terri's nails might contribute a sizable sum to some recently immigrated family's income. She also suspected the half-dozen products applied to Terri's hair to achieve the just-hopped-out-of-the-convertible look prevented her from scratching her head to illustrate her dilemma.

"Terri, have you had a gin rickey lately? They're just perfect for the end of the evening. Want to try one?" Rose filled two chimney glasses with ice.

That penetrated. "Yeah, make me one too. Top shelf, right? I'm in the mood for a fancy dessert." Ken turned the page to follow a story, roughly folding the paper as if it would never be used again except to line a bird's cage.

Fishing the lime slices out of the plastic container without removing it from the cooler was the fanciest thing involved in producing the two glasses of Tanqueray, club soda, and lime wedges. No blender, no cream, no parasols. Rose waited to see how Ken would choke it down, pretending to relish it rather than admit he'd ordered something he didn't recognize.

Ken dropped the sports section on the bar. "Good rickshaw. Remind me to special them some night next week. Maybe I can get some of those little plastic monkeys and elephants to hang off the side of the glasses. What do you think, hon?"

Rose tried not to imagine putting menageries in a glass.

"It's real nice, hon. But look at poor Rose's blouse. She's spilled grenadine or something on it. Now it needs dry cleaning. Think about how much money everybody will save if we go ahead with the uniforms before Joe and Bennie get back. It must get expensive for you all, huh, Rose?"

Uniforms?

"Dry-cleaning doesn't cost that much. The guy on Abingdon Square gives me a deal. We have to buy clothes anyway, don't we? What kind of uniforms are you two considering?"

"We don't know yet, really, just something fun. Fun and cheerful. Just between us girls, I think it's a little dull and gloomy in here sometimes. All this wood, and so many people wearing black. It looks like you're all still in mourning. Some nice bright uniforms would be more fun." Terri looked to Ken for suggestions about fun.

He shrugged and took another small sip of his drink, "No use talking about that till we're ready to position it, hon. Although of course we're always ready to hear suggestions from everybody on the My World team. You know how committed I am to employee input."

Rose wished again that she didn't envision footnotes from the Management 101 textbook ballooning above Ken's head when he spoke. "Since you're here, Ken, is it okay if I go downstairs now to count out? Unless you want another rickey?"

"No, this is plenty. Go count, babe, and I hope you have plenty to count, too. I'll lock the doors and let our last few guests out." Ken pulled the office key off a ring heavy with baubles promoting six or seven liquor brands and slid it along the bar to her.

As she'd expected, Jimmy waited for Rose at the top of the stairs to the basement, which housed the office, storage rooms, phone booths, and restrooms. After what had happened downstairs in February, Jimmy tried never to let Rose enter the lower level by herself. She'd seen through his ruse by March but had never challenged him. She didn't want to go downstairs here alone ever again, if she could help it.

Or in silence. "Explain it to me on our way downstairs, will you please, how Ken calls customers who pay for everything they receive in a restaurant he doesn't even own his guests? Guests don't pay. When did 'customer' become a dirty word around here? What's he going to call the new uniform—staff sartorial solidarity?"

Jimmy stopped his descent, as if immobilized by horror. Stupid to mention uniforms at the top of the stairs. She gently nudged her favorite waiter down to the next step. He could emote while they counted money in the office.

"Say it isn't so; say no, no, no. Tell me I didn't hear those two talking about fun uniforms even before you mentioned it. Pretend that Joe and Ben are really in Italy talking to Mr. Armani about dressing us all, instead of attending dreary memorials. Tell me lies, Rose, beautiful lies." Jimmy was tall, skinny not thin, and insisted on wearing starched white shirts and pressed black pants to a job with no dress code. So far.

"I beg you. Do not let 1986 be the year that annihilates my sartorial reputation."

Putting Jimmy in a fun uniform would torture him more than making him work a shift when everyone sported mullets, ordered white zinfandel, and didn't tip.

"Let's not worry about it yet. Ken and Terri don't know what they want, and they shouldn't institute a major change without Ben's approval. Those two making changes around here would be like a babysitter deciding to remodel the house." Rose swung the office key in front of Jimmy's eyes like a hypnotist. "Let's count out downstairs and go home."

"Yes, but I'm afraid to go down there till your cop gets off his phone call. I don't want him to think I'm eavesdropping as he calls his bookie, or the FBI, or whomever he needs to talk to at this hour. He does have the most awful glare, almost like the Chernobyl of frowns. I was going to hurry past the pay phone into the office, but his look almost scorched the bottom off my shoes." Jimmy shuffled his softly gleaming Italian loafers.

He spoke in a stage whisper, "What do you see in him? How long is this little foray into the down-and-dirty world of law enforcement going to last, darling? If you need stories for your books, I'd think you could find a better Scheherazade than Sergeant Silent. Hush, here he comes now, creeping up the stairs on his rubber soles. Is it those awful shoes that does it? Got a thing for high polish, dear?"

She'd stopped defending her affair with Butler months ago, no matter how much Jimmy goaded, although she'd just bitten her lip at Chernobyl.

She squeezed past Butler when they met on the stairs, ignoring both Jimmy's smirk and Butler's innocent smile when he patted her ass. His smile would disappear soon enough when he saw he'd have to wait for her in the company of Ken, Terri, and a very crumpled Sunday *Times*. She'd cleared his half-full wine glass, too.

"Obviously, Jimmy. My love for high polish is why I cultivate your friendship. Bet you three gold stars on the new employee-incentive chart I'll finish my check-out before you do. The last one done has to chat with Ken and Terri till they're ready to leave." Rose struggled with the lock while she balanced her cash box and a pile of checks in her left hand. Once in the office, she sat at the smaller of the two desks and began counting her bank.

Jimmy dumped his cash on the desk. He shuffled through the bills with a croupier's speed, singing his subtotals to the tune of "Like a Virgin."

His Madonna imitation didn't slow his counting one single beat.

# Chapter Two

Rose and Butler walked out of My World and into hell. Two hours before dawn, the street hung in a murky grey. Humidity hovered around the lampposts in a haze too cynical for fog, while the Hudson River sprawled at the end of the block like a swamp. The heavy air hoarded all the efforts exhausted on tonight's work and play. August in New York punished the city's worst offenders for crimes they'd yet to imagine.

"Let's go to the Cape, Frank. Let's hop in that big boat you drive and sail up to someplace with chilly mornings. Let's eat fried foods instead of inhaling greasy air. Or the Berkshires—we could cruise to Catherine's place and eat blueberries for breakfast, tomatoes for lunch, and corn for dinner. We'd see fireflies instead of these damn lights spotlighting every piece of garbage on the street. Where's the car?" She twitched her sweaty blouse away from her back.

"Sshh, we already have dinner plans tonight, remember? Now stop pretending you're mad and let's go to your place. I bought strawberry ice cream."

Butler gave her one of the quick hugs he considered

the outer limit for public displays of affection, then grabbed her right hand and started walking west toward the river. "We'll try to get away next week. Cops aren't really shrinks, you know. Precincts don't generally close in August."

While the etiquette of a gentler time had dictated the man walk on the street side, danger often came from doorways these days. Perhaps Butler kept his right hand free for the emergencies he always expected.

The three inches of newspaper he held under the biceps of his left arm weren't quite as bad as a bundling board. She felt too hot to walk intertwined anyway. And the ice cream should soften to the perfect consistency by the time they reached her apartment.

She could see his beat-up old Bonneville in front of the hydrant on the corner. The surprisingly comfortable, not so surprisingly speedy, old hulk wouldn't tempt any thief interested in sound systems more advanced than eight-track tapes.

"Come on, Frank, this car should make quite a splash in Lenox. They love historical things up there."

"Don't insult my car. It's the perfect copmobile. I can take it anywhere without worrying. Plus, it's like an ad for my integrity. One look at this baby and they know I don't take payoffs. Now let's get home before the ice cream melts. The guy at the deli only gave me a little ice."

Home? It was too hot to argue about dropped possessives. A cool bath, wandering ice cream kisses, and wrinkling the fresh sheets she'd changed before work could save this summer night yet. She quickened her steps toward Butler's car and tightened her hold on his hand.

It really was too hot to spat.

The bright streetlamp lit Butler's waiting car in a harsher light than its owner might desire. The crumpled rear bumper and rust splotches over the trunk formed part of what Butler called the car's character. At least the old monster had air-conditioning.

Butler dropped Rose's hand as he stepped in front of her to unlock the passenger door. He dropped the *Times* when he saw the car's shattered windshield and defaced hood.

Someone had tried very hard to destroy the windshield, hitting it over and over with a heavy tool. A spider web of cracks showed where the blows had landed, right in front of where the driver's head belonged. Long cracks stretched toward the passenger's side, but the primary target was unmistakable. Chips of glass glittered up at Rose from the front seat and mixed with the paint flecks on the car's hood, where a more precise instrument had etched smaller strokes.

"Fucking kids. Where's the kick in wrecking a car like this? What the hell did they use, anyway? Nothing lying around here could have done this much damage." Butler searched the sidewalk and bent to peer under his car. Rose looked behind them, sure she'd heard an engine start. When no headlights appeared, she picked up the paper he'd dropped and walked around the front of the car to stare at its scarred hood.

"Did you read this?" She studied the marks.

"Read what? No, I was saving the *Book Review* for later. Jesus, you'll be reading the fiber content on the lining of your coffin while they lower you down." Butler straightened.

"The hood. It says something."

"Yeah, it says that the patrol car that should have cruised this block tonight was somewhere else and that whoever lives upstairs here is hard of hearing, anti-authority, or both. My luck to park my car in front of some deaf old radical's house. Don't try to make sense out of some punk's tag."

Rose used the *Times* to sweep the glass particles off the hood. "Look. These aren't just random scratches. They tried to gouge a message in here. The letters are different sizes and too angular, but they're definitely letters. I think these fainter ones are e's. They didn't do as good a job on all of them."

"As good a job?" Butler glared.

"Yeah, you can still see the primer under some. It's easier to read the ones where they dug down to metal. But I still can't decipher it."

Rose walked around the front of the car, hoping a different perspective would clarify the marks. None of the angles worked until she leaned over the left side of the car and bent her neck into a contortionist's stance.

"It makes sense now. You have to look at it from the driver's viewpoint. They wanted you to see this from inside, if you could read anything through this windshield. But I can read it this way."

"What's it say?" Butler pressed against her and craned his neck until his head imitated her stance. They bent over the car like Kama Sutra models.

"'Leave my girl alone.' I guess that's supposed to be an exclamation point, then 'right now,' except he spells it r-i-t-e. Whoever defaced your car uses phonetic spelling, Frank, if that's a defining characteristic these days."

"Let me see. Still looks like wild scratching to me."

She grabbed his hand and used his forefinger as a pointer to trace the letters. Annie Sullivan probably enjoyed the job more. Her pupil certainly showed more gratitude.

Butler muttered the six words of the message enough times to make Rose fear he'd adopted a mantra.

She interrupted him after the thirtieth repetition and the seventh time he'd circled the car, "Come on, let's go to my place. Standing here while our sweat drips onto the hood won't help. They probably didn't sign it in a secret code visible only under drops of cop sweat. You can stare at the thing in daylight all you want tomorrow. Think of the car as a movable crime scene."

"Rose, I don't want to ask you this, but I better. You have any idea who the author here could be? Anybody slouching around who might consider you his girl? Beside me?"

The eternal detective. "No, Frank, we've done all that tales-of-the-city bit already. My dance card is clear."

Butler smiled as he inserted his key into the passenger door, then cursed as the key revolved in a full circle, "Shit, they jimmied the door and broke the lock."

She walked around the car and bent beside him to stare at the useless lock, as if looking at a mechanical device would tell her anything. He twirled his key in more unimpeded circles.

Her thighs ached. Squatting on the sidewalk after working behind a bar for eight hours wasn't one of the exercises in the bartender's relaxation routine. When Rose started to stand, Butler grabbed her shoulder to stop her. She fell backward, sprawling onto bits of glass and other unidentified trash. He held her down when she tried to stand again.

"Damnit, this hurts. My cheeks are getting tenderized. I don't even want to think about the state of my new skirt. Let me up."

An approaching car's loud rumble almost drowned Butler's quick bark to be quiet. The absence of headlights warned Rose to stay down. The darkened car slowed and stopped nearly parallel to the Bonneville. She slid closer to the car and waited.

Rose crouched onto her knees, feeling more tiny slivers bite her skin. She felt stupid cowering on the gritty sidewalk next to her grittier boyfriend, as if either of them could pass as frightened woodland creatures. Some tourists unused to the city's bright streets had probably forgotten to turn their headlights on after a long night. She was too exhausted to hide from vacationers gawking at real graffiti and exciting urban vandalism. Time to stand up.

The driver of the other car beeped a friendly "shave and a haircut" and the car door opened.

"Frank, this is—"

A shower of tepid muck silenced "absurd." Filthy liquid poured over Rose and Butler in three viscous waves. Drips and globs slid off her hair and down her face. Rose tasted oil, and salt, and flavors she didn't want to identify. A man laughed and three dull thuds followed by three lighter clunks sounded from the Bonneville's far side before the other car roared away. Rose stood in time to see a brown van without a license plate round the corner.

Slimy rivulets led from the roof of Butler's car to three five-gallon buckets with shredded labels resting in puddles in the street. The buckets' plastic lids sprawled nearby.

"River water, Rose, water from the Hudson. The bastards just lowered the buckets down off a pier, hauled it up, and delivered the slime. They must have hoped we'd stand up as better targets when they honked. Shit, I'll bet this is that damned Greene case. It's dumb enough for that guy." Butler slicked the thick liquid off his hair.

Dumb but thorough. Rose was drenched. The nasty water saturated everything she wore. She scrubbed at her face and tried to spit the disgusting taste out of her mouth. Frightened of the filthy water in her eyes, she squeezed them tightly and dug her knuckles into her lids. She'd grab Butler's gun and shoot him if he mentioned a word about raccoons. A bartender's shift shouldn't require waterproof mascara.

The water oozing down her back and arms deposited a slimy residue the humid air wouldn't hurry to dry. "Home, Frank. Please take me home to my shower right now. I can't stand this."

Butler groaned as he collected the buckets and lids. He unlocked the rear door and crammed them onto the litter of papers and clothes in the back, then opened the driver's door, spread the paper over the front seat, and gestured to her to slide in. The steering wheel jabbed a tiny glass fragment into her thigh as she slithered under it. She hoped she'd have time to get the newsprint off her skirt before a dire infection paralyzed her entire body.

A taxi had never looked so good.

Butler outlined the Greene case as he drove home, hanging his head out the window instead of trying to see through the shattered windshield. "This is like trying to drive a goddamned disco ball. Least there's not much traffic. Ms. Euphelia Greene was caught straight out signing the UPS receipts for three stereo sets, two televisions, five grand worth of clothes, and twice that in flashy jewelry. She'd ordered the loot with credit cards belonging to customers from her job at an Eighth Street shoe store. Then she got confused and signed the wrong names to the wrong deliveries. Threatened the delivery guy with a gun when he pointed out the discrepancy. Chased him into the street with it and killed a bike messenger who got in the way." Butler honked to warn two leather-clad men who'd just stepped off the curb. A hangman's mask covered the taller one's face.

"Simple case? Piles of evidence in the apartment,

good long paper trail, and a delivery man who quit and moved to Minnesota but promised to fly back and testify anytime. Seems Ms. Greene was stealing the stuff to impress her boyfriend. That charmer's still arguing he believed she'd made a fortune in commissions. He knows we don't have anything on him, so he never looks real serious when he says it. That's a hell of a lot of twenty-nine dollar shoes, right?"

"So why would the boyfriend pull a stunt like this?"

"He wouldn't; the husband would. Poor fool refuses to believe any of it. The credit card companies made the mistake; the driver tried to rob his wife with the dead kid's help; and then that evil driver grabbed the gun from her and killed his accomplice in a moment of what Mr. Greene calls 'temporal insanity.' Forget trying to convince him about the boyfriend. Facts and witnesses don't bother Mr. Greene unduly. He calls every day with a reason why 'my girl' couldn't have committed a crime."

"Great, love is blind and we're dripping with the results. Could you drive a little faster? The *Times* feels like it's turning into slimy paper maché on my skin." Rose squirmed in her clammy clothes, squishing into the layers of wet paper below her while she stomped her feet to rid her shoes of the water squelching between her toes. Not as much fun as puddle stomping, but better than playing swamp thing.

Maybe the loud stomps would encourage Butler to apply a little more pressure to the accelerator. Talking to her while trying to see out his side window had him swinging his head back and forth like a two-year-old at bedtime. God forbid any of his words should be lost to the sidestream. The six blocks to her apartment seemed like a continental trek.

Rose stomped her right foot in front of her two

times, then changed the angle and stamped straight down, detonating a small explosion of something cold on the floor. Sticky wet slush splashed on her legs and into her lap, with just a few drops splattering onto her face.

She screamed. Butler slammed on the brakes. The cab behind them screeched to a halt. The driver shouted curses when he swerved around the Bonneville.

"What, Rose, what happened? You okay? Tell me now." Butler gunned the motor as if about to give chase.

"I'm not hurt."

"Then what the hell are you screaming about? Jesus, you could have caused an accident here."

"Sorry. Imagine the hours we could have spent at the emergency room if my head made a nice starburst in the windshield to match the one on your side. Hard to imagine a more fabulous ending to this romantic night." She squished cool granular bits between her toes.

"I'm not starting the car again until you tell me why you screamed."

"Ice cream. I found the ice cream, and now I'm wearing the ice cream." She fought the temptation to lick anything off her face. "Try to park in front of the hydrant on the corner again. You'll need it to clean this thing tomorrow."

Butler laughed and started the car. "Should we stop for more ice cream? The deli by the hydrant's still open."

"Why not, at this point? Chocolate, please."

Rose wished she'd refused the offer while she waited in the car outside the deli. She couldn't wait to get out of the soggy clothes clinging to her skin. The filthy river water still oozing down her neck killed any temptation to invite Butler to lick off some of his favorite flavor. Swamp sauce did not a sundae make.

Butler yanked the car door open. He handed her a

fresh Sunday paper, a tall bunch of fragrant stock, and a cold brown paper bag. She leaned over and kissed him as he started the car, then regretted the impulse when she tasted his skin.

The bag held two cartons, chocolate chocolate-chip and strawberry. Rose knew she still had the vanilla bubble bath her sister had sent for Christmas. She'd show Butler the grown-ups' version of Neapolitan before they went to sleep.

# Chapter Three

Manhattan seethed six stories below, but furled white morning glories and scarlet runner beans twined over the barbed wire surrounding Nick and Yvonne's roof. Four lemon trees hovered behind the picnic table, their blossoms' sweet smell softening the city's bitter night breath. Herbs growing in a raised circular bed spiraled their perfumes into the escapist mix. Kerosene lamps etched the shadows of flowers and stems, while the glossy lemon leaves reflected the flickering light that substituted for the stars hidden behind the night's haze. The two couples sat at a picnic table holding ironed cotton napkins, heirloom roses in a willow-ware teapot, and platters of bluefish grilled with summer vegetables.

Butler crossed his knife and fork on his plate. "So I'm standing down there trying not to watch the crack passing hands two doorways away. I'm looking at your box and trying to figure out how you'll be able to hear us with the receiver torn out and the wires dangling like they do. Don't see a functioning phone booth anywhere on the block. Like most city blocks, of course," Butler qualified quickly, as if unwilling to suggest he didn't consider the

Lower East Side a perfect neighborhood. She'd have to remember the soothing effects of preprandial mint juleps.

"So then Rose says you gave her the security code last night. 'Work,' she announces. I tell her I hope it will and ask her once more what the code is. She says 'work' again, staring at me like I'm the black hole of brains when I say the buttons only have numbers. Then she steps in front of me and pushes some buttons. When the door opens, she gives me the look and asks me why I didn't believe her.'"

"Writers. You translated 9675 into 'work,' Rose?" Nick grinned, shaking his head as slowly as he'd spoken.

The movement drew Rose's eyes to the silver stubble of his hair. Under the severe haircut, thick dark brows dramatized the deep blue of his eyes and the nose he'd broken early. Tremendous sculptor's shoulders stretched his black t-shirt; his callused hands looked too large for the silverware. Rose guessed he was at least 6'4" and knew that dragging her fingers across his head would trace smooth trails in his hair.

She hoped Nick's grin signaled admiration.

She never knew how to read a quiet man.

Rose plopped her bare feet into Butler's lap. He pushed his chair back to give her more legroom and absently rubbed her feet.

"I remember words better than numbers, so I translate them sometimes." She stretched and sighed. What Butler was doing felt better than worrying about her callused heels.

Yvonne stacked the dinner plates. "Did you ever use consecutive numbering for the letters instead of the phone configuration? That's how I'd do it. I like numbers in order."

The bowl of Yvonne's brown hair framed a broad face with golden skin and eerily pale blue eyes. She wore a white shirt tucked into old jeans that flaunted her unstylishly wide hips and thighs, giving her body twice the grace than the boxy suits she wore to work after her accounting classes at Baruch College. Vermeer would have begged her to pose.

Nick handed Yvonne his plate. "It's true. Yvonne talks about the beauty of numbers, but I work with shapes, with materials I can touch."

"Someday we'll convince each other, after we talk for enough years." Yvonne placed a café filter and a golden pie on the table. She told Nick the coffee needed two more minutes and squeezed his neck briefly. He held her hand to his head for a moment, then released it.

"Do you two have topics like that? You ever just get tired of talking about something and decide to accept your differences until you're too old to worry about disagreeing?" Yvonne walked around the roof, lighting the votive candles perched on the branches of Nick's sculpted copper birches.

Rose and Butler laughed, but Rose spoke first. "Silence seems to be more threatening to us. We'd worry if the talking stopped." She saw Butler's tiny grin at the plural pronouns.

Yvonne relit a candle the breeze had extinguished. "My ex talked all the time. Nick doesn't talk half as much, but he says more than Barney ever did." She drew a silver knife through the pie as if dividing up spoils.

Nick's large hand pushed the plunger on the twelve-cup pot as if he were sticking a pin into a cushion. "Yeah, Barney talked and you worked. Yvonne held down three jobs and kept a big garden while that blowhard almost flunked out of law school. He'd talk for hours to blame her for not doing enough, accusing her of causing all his failures."

"Nick, don't." Yvonne stopped cutting the pie but clenched the knife as if she wanted to pierce the heavy glass pan.

Nick swirled the coffee in the pot. "He bothers you again, I'll show him how much it hurts when somebody bigger pounds on you."

Yvonne gasped and dropped the knife.

Rose handed the knife back to Yvonne. Time for a topic switch. "Yvonne, this pie would make Martha Stewart jealous. Tell me you didn't grow the peaches yourself. I'm starting to feel guilty for not owning an apron, much less gardening gloves."

Butler joined in, praising the pie and the garden. He asked Yvonne and Nick where they liked to get away. The conversation veered into the merits of upstate, Long Island, the Berkshires, and Cape Cod. Yvonne shot Rose a grateful look, which she answered with the perfect guest's smile.

Ten minutes later, while Butler and Nick still compared favorite routes to avoid traffic out of the city, Rose stood and asked how to find the bathroom.

"The light's on and the door's open. See?" Yvonne pointed to the silhouetted doorway at the opposite end of the loft, past the living and bed areas and behind Nick's workspace.

*Brides* and *Details* rested in the wicker basket next to the clawfoot tub, along with *ArtNews* and *Rolling Stone*. An antique straight razor hung from a leather strap next to the sink. The whole room smelled of peppermint soap. Rose wondered if Yvonne kept her hope chest in the living or sleeping area.

The loft seemed even larger as Rose returned through the dim space. Only the streetlamps illuminated the big forms looming over her in Nick's studio. He made large pieces, some towering almost to the twenty-foot ceiling. The works cast dense shadows in the room. Rose walked around them slowly, as if tiptoeing through the Museum of Natural History after hours.

She stopped when one of the shadows shifted. A dark form separated from the sculpture ten feet ahead and approached her.

Rose didn't move. Had somebody climbed in the loft's open windows while they sat outside? The lights in the garden seemed too distant now. She peered ahead, willing herself not to scream.

She recognized Nick just before his hand gripped her wrist. He slid his arm up to her shoulders when she gasped, pulling her too close. "Did I scare you, Rose? Sorry. I worried you'd have trouble finding your way back with the overheads off."

She stepped away and asked if he wanted to turn the lights on so she could see his work better.

"Yvonne and Frank already planned a return visit. I'll give you both the full studio tour then, if you still want."

"We'd love it. You two have made such a refuge here. My apartment's going to feel awfully urban later." No aprons dangled from hooks in her kitchen. All her flowers arrived wrapped in cellophane. Garbage left under the sink an extra day didn't qualify as compost.

"Yvonne deserves to feel safe every minute of her life. I shouldn't have said anything at dinner, but Barney hurt her too much when they were married. Now he's sleazing back around. He says he's changed, because she provoked him all those years. She still feels sorry for him somehow."

Nick gestured at the shapes surrounding them, "Yvonne's a real muse to me, but she'd never take any credit. She shouldn't take any of the blame for Barney's abuse, either. I don't want to ruin Frank's night, but you think I could call him at work tomorrow about a restraining order? Barney needs to go away. Would Frank mind?"

"I'm sure he'd be happy to help as much as he can." Butler could also repeat his theory that restraining orders worked like red flags to bulls as often as they protected.

Nick looked like damn good protection himself. He'd felt like it, too. The studio did seem darker after the bright bathroom.

She let him take her hand to lead her through his workspace. Ducking under the edge of some scaffolding, Nick moved his arm around her shoulders again to guide her past the obstacles. The brief protective gesture felt like an embrace, a surprisingly welcome embrace. When they'd passed the scaffolding, he stopped and whispered to her to look at the moon through the skylight. She felt the length of his thigh against her as she spotted the blurred crescent pressing through the hazy night. He bent down as if to share a secret, shook his head, and straightened again. Nick's silvery head looked like another phase of the moon.

"Rose, I didn't mean—" His arm slid off her shoulders. She missed his touch when he pulled away.

"Ssshh, let's go back outside now." She held his hand lightly again. Trying to navigate through the darkened space without it might be dangerous.

After the initial month of infatuation and five closer months together, Rose knew that she loved Frank Butler. He was smart, funny, passionate, and kinder than he wanted anyone to see. Handsome in the craggy way she liked, Butler combined cynicism and romance in just the proportions Rose wanted.

But Yvonne wasn't the only woman bothered by a former husband. Even distantly alive, an ex could haunt from any side of the grave, howling about the foolishness of trust, clanking dire warnings about looking, not leaping, and shrieking the gospel of impermanence. With the past's pall fluttering overhead, love letters threatened more than ransom notes. The knight on the white charger might try to run her down. Sheltering arms might hide a cudgel. Rose wanted Butler too much to let the ghosts win, but the safety he offered had its own fears.

Nick wasn't the kind of protection she needed. She dropped his hand. His arm around her wouldn't have felt so welcome without the momentary fear just before his touch. She knew better than to confuse adrenaline with excitement. She hoped.

When they returned to the garden, Butler was regaling Yvonne with stories about the painter he'd once been married to, commiserating about the difficulties of loving an artist. He'd looked into the loft while he spoke, though.

"And then there's our Ms. Leary, who doesn't want me in the same borough, let alone apartment, while she's writing. I clomp around on eggshells all the time, never knowing when I'm encouraged to ask about her work or when an innocent question might cost me a night's peace. Then there's that look she gives me. It makes me wonder if she's casting me for a murder victim in her book and considering a very grisly death." Butler chased the last crumb of flaky crust across his plate.

"Sometimes I get nothing but mutters from Nick for days at a time. I used to cry over it, but now I just distract myself with my own work or baking. And I really do love him, don't I, honey?" Yvonne poured Nick more coffee and cut both men another piece of pie.

Rose smiled at Yvonne. Exceptional cook, exquisite gardener, and now extravagant in her emotional declarations. Good thing Rose liked her.

"You sure do." Nick's North Dakota roots showed in his slight blush at the verbal valentine.

For a moment, Butler looked hungry for something sweeter than his second dessert. Maybe she'd offer him a third piece of pie before Yvonne did.

"There's just something about creative women that gets me. All the shit I see in my job, on my own time I like to be around someone who's making good things, even if she does get moody. Crazies at work, crazy at home, good to have some continuity, anyway." Butler grinned.

"That's so great. I didn't know you two had finally moved in together." Yvonne beamed like the patron saint of domestic bliss.

"I meant home in a general sense, Yvonne. Rose and I still keep separate domiciles, which may be how we avoid homicide. We do spend a lot of time together, usually at her place. She says my place is too brown. I can't deny her apartment looks better. It's also where her books are." Butler circled his fork around his empty pie plate.

She'd have to remember the truth-serum effects a second piece of peach pie produced.

Yvonne slipped another sliver onto Butler's plate. "Whatever works for you two is good. Sometimes Nick says I see the whole world like one of those Noah's Ark toy sets, and that I want to be the one to match up all the pairs. He's right in a way. Now that I've found somebody so good, I want all my friends to have the same thing."

"You mean you want to share me?" Nick stirred more sugar into his coffee.

"Of course not. Sharing like that is stupid. It's a mistake." Yvonne's voice sounded very determined.

Butler stared at Nick. "She's right. Sharing doesn't work."

Nick looked right back. "It does with the right people.

I mean sharing dreams, sharing a future. Shit, I sound like a high school yearbook. Yvonne knows what I mean."

Butler's laughter started after everyone else's.

Rose spoke through her giggles, "It's true, though. Sitting outside like this turns conversation into campfire talk. Frank's going to be suggesting Truth or Dare in a minute."

Butler hugged her close. "Dare this, darling."

Yvonne beamed. "I love thinking about our future. Nick's going to make art, and I'm going to make money. When his art makes big money, I'll know exactly what to do so it can make more money. We'll both be building something, and we'll both be happy."

"Yvonne always talks about when my work makes it, not if. She gives me faith." Nick started to pour more wine into Butler's glass but stopped when Butler shook his head.

"How do you two combine your work, Rose? I mean, with Frank a, um, police officer and you a mystery writer, do you get material from him or anything?" Yvonne looked very interested in her own question. "Isn't it easier to write about stuff that really happened?"

"Not always." It was one of the reasons Rose had abandoned journalism for fiction. It was also a topic that could keep them here until dawn broke over the rooftops.

Butler stretched. "Right. The day Rose uses me as a source for material hasn't happened. I still think about the dedication all the time, 'To Frank, who taught me everything I know.' Any day now. Actually, one of Rose's pet peeves is how many people want to tell her stories they think she can use in a book. Right?"

"True. I like to pick my own stories." Rose finished her wine. "But what's really funny here is the total cliché of a woman mystery writer having a cop for a boyfriend. I keep waiting for the cosmic editor to delete Frank with a scribbled 'trite' in the margin."

Butler laughed. "Cops' wives and girlfriends always worry about our safety, but this may be the first case I've heard of where the threat is an editor in the sky. Wait till I tell—"

"Tell anybody and watch your name disappear from my cast of characters. You know I detest that kooky-writer routine you and all your buddies think is so funny." She checked Nick and Yvonne's faces, pleased to see neither of them had mistaken the teasing she and Butler relished for anything serious.

Butler checked his watch and sighed. "Speaking of work, it's almost 1:30. I have to fight the bad guys early tomorrow. How about a quick look at your studio before we leave, Nick?"

"Next time. Once I get people in there, I want them to stay a long time. I'll have a new piece ready to show in about ten days. Can we plan the next dinner in two weeks, Yvonne?" Nick smiled at Yvonne like a man who'd never heard the word no.

"Perfect. I'll turn in my big paper that Friday, so let's celebrate with Sunday dinner." Yvonne stacked the dessert plates. None of them needed scraping.

"We'd love to see your work, Nick, but the next dinner should be at my place." Rose hoped two weeks would give her enough time to scrub the place down and find her baking pans. Installing a window box might be pushing it.

"No, please. While the weather's this warm, we love to eat in the garden. The loft is so drafty in winter that we try to have friends over as much as possible in the summer. As soon as it's fall, we'll take you up on every invitation you offer." Yvonne's easy assumption that the four of them would still socialize next season relieved Rose. She'd already been planning a menu of cold fruit soup and salads to disguise her kitchen's inadequate air-conditioning. She didn't know any recipes that would make the room appear bigger.

"Sounds terrific. We'll gladly come here. Sometimes meeting friends in restaurants feels too much like another night at work. But now I think Frank's gentle nudges to my ankle mean that he wants us to say our good-byes and leave. Thanks again." Rose gave Butler a light reciprocal kick in his shin as she stood.

Butler's thanks turned effusive when Yvonne insisted they take the remaining third of the pie. He cradled the pan on the taxi ride home, without one complaint about the driver's jouncing them over every pothole and roadwork sheet on their route. When a three-block stretch of Houston Street threatened to puree the pie and their spines, he merely told the driver to slow down or risk having his car impounded. Nicely.

Rather than his usual diatribe about learning the city if you were going to drive it, Butler gave patient directions to her apartment, calmly agreeing how odd the corner of Fourth and Eleventh Streets was as a destination. She waited for an outburst when the driver pulled up two doors past her building, but Butler paid and tipped generously before he left the cab holding the pie in both hands. If he'd told the driver to have a nice night, she would have had the filling analyzed for drugs.

# Chapter Four

Friends who pitied Rose for working weekend nights didn't recognize the joys of leisurely Monday-morning coffee. The luxury of squandering the workweek's most dreaded hours in her nightgown compensated for whatever festivities she missed. Sleeping late on Monday mornings flavored her coffee with a special illicit pleasure.

She and Butler, perhaps inspired by the connubial bliss at dinner, had kept each other happily awake until 5:00 this morning. He'd left at 7:15 to leave his car at the body shop on his way to another twelve or sixteen-hour workday. She'd managed to stay half-unconscious while she stumbled to lock the door behind him and then fell back into bed for another three hours of sleep.

The coffee Butler brewed earlier had evaporated into an undrinkable sludge. He'd forgotten to pour it into the thermos carafe again. Rose started a new pot before she read the note on the pie pan he'd polished clean for breakfast.

He'd probably work late and wouldn't plan on seeing her because he knew she wanted to write tonight. But he'd call to say good night and see how her work had gone. She should call earlier if she felt like a break. And would she please call Nick and Yvonne to say thanks for dinner? He loved her, even though she had scratched his back a little.

Rose added milk to her fresh coffee and walked toward the living room. She would reread the new chapter of her novel, then take a walk before settling in to write at 4:00 this afternoon. Mondays might start slowly, but they had to end with at least eight hours of writing. She still worked best at night.

Her second mystery would be published next spring. Her agent expected the third by the end of this year.

"One a year, sweetie, one a year," Sophie repeated every time they spoke. No matter what Rose said, her agent insisted that the real murders at My World earlier this year should help Rose's writing. She'd even suggested that the bodies Rose had discovered might provide a good publicity angle for her next book launch. Rose had ignored that suggestion, but she couldn't ignore how the memories of real corpses sometimes paralyzed her fingers when she tried to kill imaginary people for fun and profit.

Dead faces didn't haunt Sophie's keyboard. Rose couldn't let them haunt hers either.

She gasped when she reached the living room, then exhaled like a yoga fanatic. Her living room smelled like the hallway of a tenement too foul for Dickens. She held her breath against the heavy stench filling the room.

Rose rushed to open the windows, almost gagging when she leaned over the vase of stock on the windowsill. Pennies in the vase hadn't kept the water clean in this heat. She should have changed it yesterday. The flowers still smelled sweet and sharp when she put her nose next to their soft blossoms, but the water holding them could have birthed monsters. She hurried to flush the foul water down the toilet, then scrubbed the vase, rinsed the stems, trimmed their ends, and added three new pennies to the fresh water before returning the flowers to the living room. She put the vase on her desk so the sun wouldn't hit it.

She'd air the room while she bathed, then close the windows and crank up the air-conditioner. She could read her latest chapter after a restorative stroll.

Showering with the cucumber soap that reminded her of freshly cut lawns and summers where the heat was welcome, Rose tried to decide where to walk. She wanted exercise after last night's huge dinner, but the open windows had warned of a day well into the nineties. A brisk stroll in this high humidity would quickly feel like underwater ballet. She dusted herself and half the bathroom with talcum, then left white footprints down the hall as she ran to answer the phone. Long phone chats were another Monday indulgence.

"Rose? It's Yvonne. I hate to bother you, but I was stupid to send that pie home in its pan. I need Grandma's pan today for a pie I promised to bring to my study group tonight. It makes the best crusts. She gave me her old rolling pin too, and I swear it's magical."

Rose told Yvonne the pie had cast a spell on Butler and described his uncharacteristic attitude last night. She offered Yvonne thanks for more than dinner.

Yvonne laughed. "Maybe I should have kept an extra slice here, too. Will it bother you if I come get the pan this afternoon? I can't ask Nick to do it. He's going to Long Island City. He needs to find some materials and try to cool himself down."

Rose volunteered to deliver the pan herself in a few hours, assuring Yvonne she'd planned a walk anyway. Instant destination, although Christie Street wouldn't have been her first choice for an afternoon promenade.

Yvonne argued for a minute, then admitted she

could use the extra time to study.

Hanging up, Rose looked forward to seeing the loft, and Nick's sculptures, in the daytime. She could swing past B&H on her way home to buy some cold borscht for dinner. If she hurried, she might even be able to wander through the Strand's miles of used books for a little while. She could call it research, and the extra blocks to Tenth Street exercise.

She closed the windows and virtuously set the air-conditioner at medium cool. She gulped her tepid coffee, poured the rest of the pot into a pitcher in the fridge, and drew the kitchen blinds against the sun.

Rose dressed in a thin black cotton blouse and a short white skirt, then remembered her destination and changed into a long pleated black skirt. No point in inviting catcalls. After skewing her hair into a loose topknot and applying two coats of mascara and a sunscreen she hoped not to sweat off, she shoved money, lipstick, and keys into her pockets. No need for a purse in this heat, or that neighborhood. A prudent woman wouldn't take credit cards near the Orchard Street fashion discounts or The Strand.

She held the heavy pie pan up to the light, surprised to see that Butler had washed it so it sparkled. Mom said never to return any borrowed container empty. Truffles or pastries from Lanciani's Patisserie down the street would melt by the time she delivered them. She'd wait till she got closer to Yvonne's, then pick up some little treat.

The heavy air descended as soon as she stepped outside. The shade trees on Eleventh Street couldn't offer any relief in this thick haze. The sky looked metallic, with the sun just a more burnished spot. Her hand started to sweat onto the handle of the plastic bag holding the pan before she reached the corner of Bleecker.

Adopting a slow tropical pace, Rose headed east on Hudson, tempted for a minute when she passed Leroy Street and its pool. She watched the basketball players at Sixth and Houston in disbelief at their energy and ignored their invitations to join the game as completely as she'd ignored three truck drivers' less innocent invitations. She ducked into Raffetto's for a pound of spinach ravioli to fill the pie pan and asked the waiter in the Cafe Figaro to refrigerate it while she gulped two iced cappuccinos. Returning to Houston, she avoided a detour onto Broadway and its pseudo-chic stores. She gave a dollar to the bum who offered to wash her sunglasses on the Bowery, and stood at Nick and Yvonne's door twenty-five minutes later, drenched in sweat and wondering if she might ask Yvonne for a cold washcloth.

No matter how gentrified or artsy chic the Lower East Side had become, the streets still reeked of garbage too much for Rose to ever consider living here again. The five teenagers lounging in the doorway next to Yvonne's who suggested she come into the hallway with them and see what hot really was didn't make her nostalgic either. Five months on Avenue C when she'd first arrived in the city had been plenty, thank you. Too bad if she'd grown old and unadventurous.

Yvonne had said she'd leave their floor unlocked. Rose used 'work' to buzz herself into the building. The freight elevator took five minutes to clank its way downstairs. She spent another two struggling to raise and lower the heavy wooden gate. The elevator's slatted sides showed old bare walls and scarred steel doors on each floor she passed. She refused to look up or down at the cables, which sounded like one of the Industrial Revolution's first achievements.

Bird in a wrought iron cage, too hot to sing.

As promised, Yvonne had turned the key for their

floor. The heavy door slid open as soon as the elevator shuddered to a stop. Missing a door to knock on, Rose called for Yvonne as she stepped into the loft. Three huge ceiling fans and an industrial standing fan moved the air in the loft into a semblance of cool. Long white muslin curtains fluttered at the open windows. The loft seemed even bigger in the daylight.

"Yvonne? Nick?" No, Yvonne had said Nick was headed to Long Island City. "Yvonne? I'm here."

The door to the garden stood open. Maybe Yvonne was tending her plants or grafting her vines or something too horticultural to guess. Rose walked outside. A small sprinkler trained on the flowers nearest the door spun in her direction and sprayed her legs. No need to worry about her skirt staying damp in this heat. The sun's glare blinded her to the empty garden's loveliness. She hurried back to the inside's comparative cool.

How could Yvonne have contemplated baking on a day like this, and where had she gone? Yvonne expected Rose. If she'd run out for a quart of milk or a pound of lard for piecrust, she should have left a note. Rose hadn't seen one downstairs, or in the elevator, or by the entrance.

The coffee table displayed only the same objects and books she'd seen last night, while the large counter in the kitchen held an interrupted baking project. An aluminum colander filled with blueberries, a yellow box of cornstarch, and an empty white bowl holding a measuring cup and spoons waited next to the pastry board alongside crocks of sugar and flour. But no note.

Maybe Yvonne had gone first, and Nick had left a note. If he'd been working earlier, he might have stuck a message in his studio, assuming any visitor would check there.

He had already invited her into his studio, hadn't he?

Nick's workspace was full of messages, none of them meant exclusively for her. He worked in metals, bronze and copper and a silvery one she couldn't name. Rose examined trees and animals that only Nick had ever seen. His pieces were huge and full of a fascinating vital power. Their visceral appeal almost frightened her.

Rose wanted to spend more time looking than she could today. She wanted to touch Nick's work, too, feel its surfaces, its angles, and its curves. Wanting to touch his sculptures reminded her of their moments in the studio last night, moments that her long night with Butler should have erased. Time to get out of Nick's studio now.

On her way back to the kitchen, Rose saw the white gleam of a marble sculpture in the far corner of the workspace. She detoured to look at it, telling herself one more minute wouldn't hurt. It was a half-finished nude of Yvonne, as delicate as the metal pieces were forceful. Looking at this piece was like reading a love poem. The work seemed so intimate she wondered how Nick could ever offer it for sale.

Uneasy at spending any more time studying Nick's art without his repeated permission, Rose made herself leave the studio. Just because someone offered to show his art didn't mean you could look at everything he was doing. Her own offers to let anyone read her work were always very specific. She shuddered at the thought of someone casually rifling through her files and manuscripts before she'd chosen what they'd see.

The only place left to look was the bathroom. She knew better than that. A horrible memory of the last time she'd searched someone's seemingly empty apartment sent her hurrying toward the elevator. Stubborn curiosity made her retrace her steps to peer around the door into the clean bathroom. *Rolling Stone* lay on the floor and

*Brides* had tilted sideways in the wooden magazine rack.

She'd leave the pie pan, and the ravioli, and her own note. She should get home to work herself.

It was an immutable law: every time you ventured out without your purse, you needed something it always carried. Now hurrying to leave the loft, Rose found a notepad and jar of pens on a small end table next to the couch. She scribbled a note telling Yvonne she was sorry she'd missed her, thanking her again for dinner, and saying she should consider the ravioli a grossly inadequate thank-you token.

Yvonne couldn't miss the note if Rose left it on the counter with her baking project. She anchored the note with the pie pan, then decided to put the ravioli in the fridge.

She'd found the fridge and sink in an el at the end of the kitchen last night, only discovering them when Yvonne had asked her to take the julep glasses out of the freezer.

The chaos in this part of the kitchen looked as if it belonged in somebody else's home. Shattered crockery made a madman's mosaic on the drainboard and floor. A blizzard spotted the walls and floor, as if someone had wrestled with a monstrous flour sack. Yvonne must be a more temperamental cook than she'd appeared. Rose stepped across the mess and lost her balance but caught herself before she hit the floor. When she bent to put the ravioli on a lower shelf in the fridge, she saw how some of the flour had stuck to the bottom of her skirt when she slipped.

Almost sliding on the litter again, she waited till she found a clean patch of floor before she reached down to brush the flour off her skirt. This wasn't a neighborhood where you wanted to walk around sporting white powders. The flour felt heavy, probably from the humidity.

She leaned down and rubbed her skirt's hem harder, but the white stuff stuck stubbornly.

As she began straightening up, Rose saw it.

Her.

A hand reached through the striped cotton that skirted the base of the industrial double sink. The hand wore the same woven friendship bracelet Yvonne had worn last night. Rose bent down and touched the hand lightly.

The hand felt too cold for this hot day.

This couldn't happen again. It was a nightmare, repeating itself in new permutations. In only a second or two, Rose could move out of her terrified crouch. Yvonne's hand would wave while they laughed at this silly practical joke. Too many seconds passed. Nothing changed.

The bracelet didn't move.

Yvonne didn't wave.

The cotton hiding what lay under the sink slid smoothly along its rod when Rose finally pushed it aside. The sink was almost six feet long. She moved the fabric back to unveil the space beneath it.

No.

Yvonne sprawled under the sink, lying on her back with her legs bent at the knees. Her head and torso lay on a canvas tarp like the ones Rose had just seen in Nick's studio. Yvonne wore last night's faded jeans, now splotched with flour. The nails on her bare feet were painted pale pink, and another woven ribbon encircled her right ankle. Her lower body looked almost relaxed in its strange posture, like a kid who'd tired of hiding and fallen asleep.

Her face didn't look relaxed, though. It didn't look tortured either. Her face didn't look like anything.

Her face was gone.

Another face rested on Yvonne's body. A smooth white surface started at the top of Yvonne's hidden head and extended below her breasts, as if Nick's marble sculpture had been crudely vandalized, then transplanted here and grafted onto her body.

Yvonne wore her own death mask.

Unable to stop herself, Rose bent closer, holding the curtains back for more light. The mask wasn't marble. It was plaster, thickly applied plaster. A two-inch crust sealed the mask to the canvas underneath Yvonne's head. Extra plaster mounded over her nostrils and lips. No breath could have passed through those lumps.

It really was a death mask.

Rose really had found another dead body.

Corpse finding wasn't one of the skills she wanted to develop.

Oh, God.

She stared at Yvonne's torso in horror. The killer had done more than kill Yvonne. He or she had heaped two oversized mounds of plaster onto her chest and shaped them to transform Yvonne's breasts into a centerfold's parody. Doctor Death practiced plastic surgery.

Rose stood slowly.

Anyone in the loft would have made his presence known by now. Of course he would.

Crouching under the sink had made her feel faint. She needed water on her face right now. She could use a fork or other utensil to turn the faucet so Butler couldn't yell at her about spoiling fingerprints. Again.

Rose looked into the deep double sinks. A solid gunk filled the bottom of the left sink. An electric mixer stuck out of the hardened plaster at an impossible angle. Just whipping up a little something, honey.

She didn't need water on her face now.

Fuck what precinct this was, she called Butler from the phone in the living room.

"Frank, I need you right now. You won't believe this. I just found Yvonne. Dead. In her kitchen. How soon can you get here? I won't touch anything. Oh God, this is worse than the last time."

"Are you safe, Rose? You sure she's dead? Any point in sending the paramedics? Who's there? You alone?" He fired the questions in a burst she'd never wanted to hear again.

"She's definitely dead, Frank, cold dead. Forget the paramedics. It's way too late."

"Are you alone?"

Why did he ask her that again?

"No, I'm sitting down with the killer, discussing his childhood traumas over a cup of Earl Grey. Of course I'm alone, but I hate it. Could you please get here and interrogate me face-to-face? Please?"

"A patrol car will arrive in three minutes, and I'll see you in ten. You want me to put somebody on the line to talk to you until we get there?"

She refused his offer of a telephone babysitter, unwilling to sob out either what she saw or how she felt, and hung up.

Of course she was alone. Whoever had killed Yvonne was long gone. She'd already looked in every room. Nobody was crouching in the shower, or writhing behind the curtains, or certainly not lurking behind the largest sculpture at the far end of Nick's studio. Anybody hiding here would have attacked her already. Even the most maddened killer wouldn't wait till she called the cops to attack his second victim.

Of course she was alone.

Yvonne wasn't really here anymore. Even Yvonne's

face was gone.

The misshapen plaster mask hastened Yvonne's burial, as if a sarcophagus already entombed her. But resting under the kitchen sink was not lying in state. The dirty floor didn't make a ceremonial bier. Rose was still alone with the body of a woman whom she'd laughed with just a few hours ago. Again.

Rose started to walk back into the kitchen to close the sink curtains around Yvonne. Their cheery blue and white stripes weren't intended for funeral drapes. She knelt in front of the sink to look once more before the crime-scene unit's stoic frenzy began. Then she remembered her promise. She stood slowly, keeping her hands at her sides.

Not touching anything didn't include her own body. Rose hugged herself, trying to stop shaking. She felt horribly chilled, as if she shared the coldness of Yvonne's corpse. Feeling so cold mocked the August heat. As if she'd been stranded far from the noisy street below, the loft now seemed too quiet. Rose strained to hear any sounds of life from outside.

A pluckier heroine would have whistled.

The elevator's rumble finally broke the silence. Help was here. That pattern where killers returned to the scene of the crime only happened on tv. Rose looked around the loft in a panicked search for a place to hide. Or be trapped.

Then she heard voices and told herself how impossible it was that the killer would bring someone to admire his handiwork. Truly impossible. The voices grew louder.

"Great, another dead one today. Dispatcher said to go extra careful. The chick who found the body is Butler's girlfriend. Didn't they meet over some other cold one? Leave it to Butler to date somebody who has radar for stiffs. Damn, we're here." The two uniformed officers must have expected the elevator door to open into a hallway instead of directly into the loft

Butler's girlfriend? She hadn't signed up to be a topic for cop gossip. And she didn't want this kind of radar.

"Officers? I'm in here, with the cold one. She's under the sink. I'm just standing here scanning for death. Detective Butler is on his way."

It didn't make Rose feel any better when one of the cops blushed and the other cleared his throat. Embarrassing the first cops on the scene didn't do anything for Yvonne, either.

# Chapter Five

Waiting for Butler while the two humiliated cops attempted conversation expanded forty minutes into forty days. Rose already knew this heat wave should quit already, thanks. Both officers hovered at the edge of the kitchen. Rose didn't know if they were guarding her or the corpse. Overhearing the muttered comment that Yvonne's murderer had made the mortician's job easier didn't inspire her into conviviality. Nothing seemed able to distract her from trying not to cry.

When the radios hanging off their belts squawked Butler's imminent arrival, both men hurried to the loft entrance. Rose swallowed hard when she heard Butler's voice.

He rushed past the officers. "Sorry I'm so late, Rose."

"What took you so long?"

"Terri came by the station to ask if I knew what happened to some of the kids we knew back in high school. She and Ken rode the Staten Island ferry all afternoon, and the trip reminded her of old times." Butler shook his head.

"Like a fool, I told her where I was going. Poor Terri got so upset, she damn near flooded the sidewalk. I felt bad leaving her like that."

He reached to hug Rose. "You all right, darling?"

She stepped back. "All right? Sure, I've treasured every moment I've spend waiting here with the masque of the white death and two boorish cops. Not that finding Yvonne's body should distress me as much as hearing that the sad news upset Terri, of course."

She'd seen men do it a thousand times—turn their fear and sorrow into anger. The transformation held a strange comfort, only ruined by the approach of tears. Most men didn't fight tears when they were angry. Not only angry.

She couldn't let herself start crying. Best not to wonder if Yvonne had cried when the plaster descended.

Butler closed the distance between them. He held her tight. "Jesus, I'm sorry. I meant to get here sooner. I thought you'd be all right with Lou and Stan for a few minutes."

She pushed him away. "Five hundred cops in the room wouldn't have made me feel any better till you got here. Not that your arrival is turning into such a blessing."

The tears started in full force when she sat on a chair in the living room. Furious at herself for crying, at the cops for watching, and at Butler for trying to hold her again, Rose scrubbed her cheeks with her palms. She didn't even have a sleeve long enough to wipe her face. She didn't want any paper towels from the kitchen.

Butler reached into his breast pocket as if it always held clean handkerchiefs, then asked an officer for tissues from the bathroom. "But don't touch the box, okay, Lou."

Lou seemed quite happy to leave the scene. He brought Rose a bundle of blue Kleenex big enough to mop the floor. She used most of it.

"Forget about Terri. It's obscene for us to squabble

while Yvonne's body lies in the next room."

"That's better. Let me get this started, then I'll take you home. The lab guys should be here by now. Don't move around anymore, or touch anything else. You gonna feel able to tell me what happened in a minute?" He turned toward the kitchen.

"Certainly, Detective Butler. I'm ready to tell you everything I know right now." Rose dropped the soaked ball of tissue into her lap. What she had assumed was flour still dusted her skirt. But flour wouldn't have hardened into a death mask. Rose picked the wad of tissues up with the tips of her fingers and dropped it on the floor.

She heard Butler curse when he saw Yvonne's body. For a minute, it sounded as if he were cursing her for disturbing the room.

Any stupid thought beat dreading the interrogation she knew would start soon. She and Butler couldn't claim love at first sight. Instead, she'd spent the first several hours after they met unable to see anything except the body of the first dead woman she'd found. His relentless questions and her horrified answers had shaped their first conversation. She felt no sentimental attachment to the ritual, no nostalgia. An interrogation's rhythms shouldn't be their song.

Butler looked grim when he walked toward her. Of course, they'd talked last night about how much he liked Yvonne. It had only been last night.

Yvonne had cooked, and laughed, and planned another dinner. Now she lay in the same kitchen, dead. The mask transformed her corpse into a terrible object, even further removed from the woman they'd visited last night.

"Why are you here, Rose?" Butler's voice was all business. The interrogator replaced the lover.

"Yvonne called and needed her pie pan, so I volunteered to return it. She needed to study, and I had time before I started writing at 4:00." He didn't need to hear when she'd planned on working this afternoon. He already realized that, if the cop remembered the schedule her lover knew.

"When did she call? When did you get here? How'd you get in? See anybody? Anything look different when you got here than it does now?"

Her lover's voice sounded like the dentist's drill. No novocaine for this operation.

Time questions were the easiest. Time was factual. So was Yvonne's dead body. Rose took a deep breath and started answering Butler's questions. Then she anticipated more questions and described getting into the loft, looking for Yvonne, waiting for her, walking through Nick's studio, and finally finding Yvonne's body. She offered every detail she remembered.

"And I'm sorry I walked back and forth in the kitchen so much. I guess I tracked up all kinds of evidence, but I didn't know it at the time. I can retrace everything I touched if we try. I never touched Yvonne."

He pointed at her hem. "You didn't just track up the kitchen; you practically swept it with that damn skirt of yours."

"What?" She pulled the skirt up to her knees and stared at it. White powder had hardened into a terrible trim at the hem and crusted the other damp spots in an ugly appliqué. She wondered if he'd want her skirt for evidence. Either evidence or the trash—she'd never wear it again.

"Did you see any footprints when you walked in? Whoever did this must have made some tracks of his own."

"No. I didn't focus on the floor, but I think I would

have noticed a trail leading out the front door. Anyway, with the windows open and the fans on, couldn't the evidence have sort of sifted around?"

"That's a good one, huh, Detective? Evidence doesn't sift itself; that's our job." Lou's laughter sputtered out at Butler's frown.

"What did you notice, Rose? Anything look unusual? Stuff seem out of place or tossed around? You didn't move anything while you waited for Yvonne or for, uh, us, did you?"

"Since when have I straightened up when I was nervous,? I told you I didn't move anything except for the small things I told you I did move. The place looked perfectly normal until I looked into the kitchen alcove. I guess this is normal for Yvonne's and Nick's place. I've only seen it once before, you know." She tried not to sound defensive.

"Any sign of Nick? Yvonne happen to mention where he was supposed to be?"

"She said he was going out to Long Island City to buy materials."

She hesitated a minute, then remembered she'd promised to tell Butler everything she could remember. "It probably doesn't mean anything, but Yvonne did say something strange about Nick. When she said he was going to buy materials, she also said he was going to try to cool down. Long Island City isn't that much cooler than Manhattan, is it? Maybe she meant he was upset about something."

"Then he better hope he has all his receipts for those materials, especially if he was trying to cool off from some sort of scene. You sure she didn't say anything else about him? She sound upset? Scared? Angry? You hear anything in her voice?" Nothing in Butler's own voice indicated that he'd enjoyed Nick hospitality last night.

"No. Yvonne always claimed that baking calmed her down, so maybe she started the pie because she was upset. Or maybe she'd promised to bring it to her study group the way she said. Did it look to you like Nick and Yvonne were heading toward a big argument last night? I thought we had dinner with a very happy couple."

She remembered Yvonne's smile when she talked about her future with Nick.

Oh.

"Please don't tell me you actually suspect Nick."

"I suspect everybody, Rose. It's my job."

"God knows you're good at it. Forget the statistics about spouses and lovers as killers. I'd bet my life Nick couldn't have done something so ugly to Yvonne." She didn't think Butler had seen Nick's arm hover around her shoulder last night. Remembering the feel of his arm didn't push her into defending his innocence.

"Your life? Four, five hours of dinner with the guy and you're willing to wager your own life? What odds you giving?" She'd forgotten the ten years of heavy gambling in Butler's past when she'd spoken, years that he'd described as more about adrenaline than addiction. But he didn't bet anymore.

"I told you I glanced into Nick's studio. When you see the piece he was working on, you'll know he didn't do this."

Just like people who wrote children's books were always kindly, while thriller writers had horns.

"Anyway, Yvonne said Nick had already gone to Long Island City. If they did have a fight, it's not likely he would leave to calm himself down and then come back to kill her. If he did, don't you think he would have come up with a less incriminating method than using materials from his work? This is as if I bludgeoned somebody with my thesaurus, or strangled them with paper. It doesn't make sense." She studied Butler's face.

"Right, and artists are well known to be a highly sensible population group. Nick won't be the only suspect. He is the first. I liked the guy too, but I'm still going to ask him a whole lot of tough questions just as soon as he shows up or we go find him."

She didn't want to ask Butler why his friendly feelings for Nick fell into the past tense now. She knew all about professionalism and objectivity and all the other theoretical cop attributes.

He looked at his watch. "I'll know more after I've talked to Nick. Maybe he'll be totally in the clear. From what she said last night, it sounded like Yvonne's ex might deserve some scrutiny too. Or I could discover she was having problems with someone at school, or in some other part of her life."

"Like work, Frank? Like My World?" There couldn't be another murder connected to My World, not so soon. Not ever.

"Yeah, like that damn restaurant where you work. Hell, it's been at least six months since anybody connected with the place died, hasn't it?" Butler stood.

Rose nodded. Six months of nightmares and of struggling not to let the memories of other dead bodies haunt her. Rationalizations about good money, an interesting crowd, and plenty of time to write might not survive another murder. The horrors of looking for another job could pale.

"You feel up to taking another look around before we leave? See if anything jogs your memory? Then I'll run you home, but I have to come back. Can you handle being by yourself for a while?"

"Let me stay. Maybe I'll learn, I mean remember, something."

She could watch the crime-scene investigation, memorize what they did. Good writers always looked for useful detail. And distraction.

"You know I can't do that. If you're looking for material for your book, forget it. If you're afraid of being alone, say so. I'll work something out. Otherwise, we gotta go soon so I can be back when the crime scene guys go at it."

"I'm not scared of being alone. I told you everything I remember about finding Yvonne's body. Stay here; I'll get a cab home." He'd accused Nick too much already.

"Not on this block, you won't. I'll have Lou drive you, if you're sure. Just don't agree now, then hold it against me later."

"I'm fine. Do your job. I can get a cab within a block or two. I came here alone; I can go home alone." She walked to the door. A cab seemed infinitely preferable to a squad car. A weeping passenger could always salvage her dignity by over-tipping the cabdriver. Then she could cry as long as she wanted at home.

"Answer the phone when I call you later, please. I won't be calling to talk to your machine and I don't want you sitting there alone screening your calls."

"Right, Frank. I'll talk to you later. Call me as soon as you find anything."

Like a killer.

# Chapter Six

Walking. Walking should help. While Butler had insisted she take a cab home, she'd only said she'd get there on her own. That didn't constitute a promise to do what he wanted. Sunglasses would hide the mascara circling her eyes, and her ruined skirt could mimic a fashion statement on these streets. She could pass through the neighborhood like a robot just as soon as she adjusted her posture. Discovering a victim didn't excuse you for looking like one. Feel small; walk tall.

Plodding up to East Houston, Rose wanted the heat to melt her thoughts. The height of rush hour clogged the streets and sidewalks as she tried to focus on the approaching faces. At least they had features.

I wept because I had weak eyes, and then I saw a girl who had no face.

Negotiating the busy streets didn't demand as much mental energy as she'd hoped. Yvonne's twisted body and blankly deformed head walked with her. Me and my grotesque shadow.

Accelerating her pace, weaving through the crowd of tired workers heading for subway hells, Rose tried to obliterate the memory of what she'd just seen. She was walking too fast for the heat that a passing boom box announced as ninety-six degrees with ninety-eight percent humidity. She walked even faster, as if sweat could bathe her clean. Her blouse stuck to the middle of her back, while her skirt felt oddly heavy, as if designed to hobble her. She took deeper breaths and widened her stride. The image of Yvonne's corpse kept pace.

Questions. Butler had asked her a hundred. He'd undoubtedly think of fifty more. Her first journalism teacher had made it simpler. Who? What? Where? When? Why? Answer those five with the necessary information to begin every piece. Lead the reader into the story with those five essential facts. Count them off on your sweaty fingers and catch a killer. Make it into a story and pretend it's make-believe.

Who and why? She knew the rough outlines of what had been done to Yvonne, where she'd been killed, and when. Soon, Butler and his colleagues would know the details of what the murderer had done to kill Yvonne, where he'd started his attack, and when Yvonne had died. She'd torture Butler with her own questions until he shared the information.

Plaster required a certain amount of time to harden, didn't it?

Discovering who had killed Yvonne would take longer. Knowing why the murderer had done it would follow his identification. She couldn't imagine Nick obliterating his lover's face. It was too crude and too ugly. She didn't care what Butler thought. But she didn't have any substitute suspects to offer him, either. Not yet.

Stopped by a red light at Broadway, Rose turned south. Without a detour, her rapid pace would bring her home too soon. Too late and the wrong day for the museums. She didn't even cross the street to look at the window installation in the Museum of Contemporary Art. She'd seen enough new art today, thanks.

The windows of Broadway Panhandler made her stop. The cookware and serving pieces in the window echoed the baker's still life in Yvonne's kitchen in a more modern style. Cool metal gleamed in these windows, while Yvonne's counter had been warm with pottery, enamel, and wood. The cozy assortment of Yvonne's well-used domestic objects hadn't warned of any danger. These shiny new pans and bowls would have screeched alarms, stopped Yvonne's attacker, and then alerted Rose to the horror hidden under the sink. There could be safety in reflections.

Unless of course the reflection in the display window showed two wide men in their thirties wearing bad suits and nametags inscribed in big block letters. The juniper scent of late-lunch gin intensified as they both pressed too close behind Rose, walling her away from the sidewalk traffic.

The blond with the Orbison sideburns spoke, "Hey there. What's cooking with a hot babe like you? Where'd you get those stains on your skirt?"

Rose slipped around the redhead, whose attempt at blocking her failed when he stumbled, and faced the two. "Nothing, guys. Not interested."

Red regained his balance. "Why you wasting your time looking at kitchen crap? I could get you hotter than any stove in a minute." He grabbed for her arm.

She stepped back, wondering whether they accosted women this way back home in Topeka. "Fuck yourselves and your stupid nametags. One more word and I'll call Agriculture Information Services and tell them how much Mr. Gerberson and Mr. Neelman have to learn about civilized behavior."

Gin conquered sense yet again. Douglas "Red" Neelman pulled his nametag off his suit, rolled it into a cylinder, and threw it at Rose. He leaned closer and hissed into her face, "Keep this in case you forget my name, bitch. I own the freaking company, for Christ's sake. Complain all you want. You look like you been getting laid all afternoon, so we just thought we'd give you more of what want. Why else would a little New York whore be hanging around in front of a kitchen store?"

Enough. God help him, he might even believe his own venom. She'd been stupid to endure the encounter this long. The hours posted in the window said the store would stay open for another thirty minutes. Time to give the store's security guard something to watch for beside bulging pockets.

"Stroll on, gentlemen, or the police will be calling Mrs. Gerberson and Mrs. Neelman to discuss bail figures. Then I'll call the ladies back home and tell them about what kind of souvenirs you two were shopping for while you graced my city."

Hearing their wives' names erased the slack grins from both men's faces. Gerberson patted his nametag, and Neelman twisted his wide wedding band. Their wives would know how unlikely it was that the two men would actually be arrested for harassing a woman, however crudely. Rose doubted the question would arise. At least she hadn't said that her boyfriend was a cop.

The two men lumbered up the street. Rose watched them, still amazed at their mistaking her grief and shock for passion's aftermath. Mrs. Gerberson and Mrs. Neelman were not to be envied.

She wished the encounter itself surprised her, but such sexual arrogance wasn't rare. What did these men expect? Oh certainly, gentlemen, I've just been wandering around waiting to run into two suave hunks like yourselves. My doorway or yours?

Bedraggled as she might appear, Rose's outfit didn't resemble any neighborhood's variation of the Manhattan hooker look, ensembles designed to be obvious to even the dimmest tourists. As if it were only tourists who spewed unwelcome propositions.

As if grief were ever protection.

She wanted to be home now, right now. But home was a twenty-five minute walk away, and the subway would resemble the seventh circle. Trying to hail a cab on lower Broadway at rush hour would be as futile as expecting the heavenly hosts to swoop down and fly her safely home. A twenty-minute walk, if she rushed.

She felt sticky, weak, and near nausea. Of course she felt like hell because she'd walked too fast for the weather. Finding her friend's corpse had nothing to do with it. If the cold could make you shiver, the heat might make you shake.

Broadway Panhandler had air-conditioning, and cooling down should relieve some of her misery. Let the artificial chill raise goose bumps she could explain. She would wander through the aisles until at least her body felt physically normal, then slowly finish her trip home once she'd recovered from the heat's damage. Slowly didn't guarantee calmly.

Kitchen equipment crowded the store. Sharp knives with hundreds of uses glinted behind glass. Serious tools lined shelves and hanging grids. Obvious to mysterious implements offered themselves for every culinary task, from ribboning the most delicate strips of lemon zest to snipping a turkey's backbone. The professional store spurned the whimsical and cute, proffering its goods with confident authority. Only serious cooks needed to shop these aisles. She could have found the perfect wedding present for Yvonne and Nick here.

The rolling pin hit her over the head the second she walked into the pastry department, slamming into the back of her skill with a line drive's force. The blow could have crushed bone.

Weapons surrounded her.

Regiments of rolling pins lay on wire shelves. Rose saw marble rolling pins, pins in light and dark woods, and rolling pins that held ice water to keep dough chilled. She saw rolling pins for Norman Rockwell's mother and rolling pins for Barbarella. She'd never imagined so many rolling pins.

Nor had she seen another rolling pin earlier today. The piemaker's still life on Yvonne's counter had lacked its most essential tool, while everything else needed to finish the pie had been arrayed on the counter. A baker as dedicated as Yvonne wouldn't have resorted to the wine bottle wrapped in wax paper that Rose had once improvised for gingerbread men. Careful, methodical Yvonne would not have omitted the essential piece of equipment from her supplies. She'd arranged her ingredients and tools with too much care, too much anticipation.

Rose knew Yvonne had included her grandmother's rolling pin with her supplies. She was afraid she also knew how the heirloom had disappeared. Yvonne had been a big, healthy woman, her sturdy body capable of serious struggle, not a frail creature any assailant could have pinned one-handed. Whoever had applied the deadly mixture to her face had taken care, and time. Rose couldn't imagine Yvonne lying still while a plaster cast suffocated her. If a ruse had somehow convinced Yvonne to allow the mask to be applied, she would have fought hard and strong when she understood the danger. Her killer must have worked on an unconscious Yvonne.

Rose could hear hard wood thud against bone. The couple comparing baking sheets in front of her turned at her sharp gasp.

The baking sheets looked heavy, with edges sharper than necessary. The sturdy electrical mixers and large wire whisks on the next display appeared designed to puree flesh. She'd hurried past the knives earlier, but she now saw all the store's tools as torture devices, instruments to gouge and batter smooth skin. Heavy skillets were bludgeons. Long apron strings could serve as garrotes. Neat packages of cheesecloth might unfold into shrouds.

The store's shelves overflowed with weapons. Every aspiring chef browsing in the arsenal was a potential executioner.

She'd wait until she reached home before she called to tell Butler to look for the missing rolling pin. Her suggestion that he search for a heavy blunt instrument in a murder case wasn't likely to meet with unbridled enthusiasm. Still, he might prefer it to the object she'd insisted was a major clue to finding the first murderer she'd encountered. Although her certainty in that case had proved dangerously correct, she doubted he'd forget his scruples and make her a full partner in this investigation. More likely, he'd suggest she get out her Clue board and leave his work alone.

She didn't look forward to trying to convince him again that finding a murder victim gave her a proprietor's rights. It wasn't an argument she'd ever wanted to repeat.

A weary clerk's announcement that the store was closing sent her back into the heat empty-handed. Nothing in the store had tempted her to buy it.

The streets hadn't cooled, although the sidewalks

appeared less crowded. She started walking home, concentrating on an unhurried pace while she tried to convince herself she preferred thinking about a quick blow than the slow terror of suffocation.

It was hard not to hurry.

# Chapter Seven

Rose trudged up Houston and cut across the cacophony of Sixth, ignoring the beggars, incense sellers, and purveyors of books hawking their wares from blankets lining the avenue. Heading home on Fourth Street, she passed The Slaughtered Lamb and Jack the Ripper bars, glad that her route had avoided Jekyll and Hyde on Seventh Avenue. Realtors still called the West Village one of the city's most civilized neighborhoods.

Wasn't complaining about tasteless restaurant names an intelligent response to murder? The next place she passed would probably be called The I Did It, with the proprietor's name spelled out in big gilt letters.

The heat had melted her brain cells into slushy stupidity, but reaching the shelter of West Fourth Street's shade trees didn't make her feel any brighter. Anticipating a cool bath behind a series of locked doors propelled her along the last few blocks home. She could bring the phone into the bathroom and tilt the medicine cabinet window so that it reflected the door to her hall. Just in case the water might drown the sound of psychotic footsteps.

The sight of her building's steps postponed bath time. Nick sat on her stoop, his long legs stretching down four or five stairs. Even though his large hands cupped his head in what could have been a mourner's pose that hid his face, she recognized him immediately. Nobody else she knew had hair like his, legs so long, or shoulders that wide.

Rose studied Nick from the corner. He couldn't have seen her yet. She hesitated before moving closer. What if Butler was right? What if he really hadn't gone to Long Island City today? What if Nick meant to start a series called *Women without Faces* and wanted her for his next model?

Goddamn Frank Butler. Her lover would have her suspecting her guardian angel next. But she wouldn't, and she wouldn't suspect Nick either. He had wanted to immortalize Yvonne's face, not obliterate it. Rose could not believe that Nick would have forced that crude death mask onto the woman he'd sculpted with such love.

Nobody who had ever admired Nick's sculptures could think that Yvonne's corpse belonged to his body of work.

Rose refused to think that Nick could be guilty.

He was as innocent as she was.

She had no reason to run, and nowhere to go. Her own apartment seemed the safest place in the city.

She called Nick's name and crossed the street to stand at the bottom of the steps. He stood and stretched, standing impossibly tall above her. Impossibly tall, monumentally tall, but not ominously tall.

The very fact that he waited on her public doorstep disproved Butler's suspicions. She doubted Nick had mistaken her stoop for either a confessional or a sanctuary. The fleeting spark that had jumped between them last night didn't make her the first person he'd turn to in his grief. She couldn't believe that he meant to pursue the attraction. She didn't want to think that he didn't know about his grief yet.

Whatever emotion had brought Nick here and however wrong Butler's suspicions of his guilt, she still wanted to talk to Nick outside. Fear had nothing to do with it.

Nick didn't seem all that much shorter as he descended the steps to meet her.

Standing on the sidewalk, he looked at her face with an unease she couldn't interpret. If he didn't know about Yvonne, what was he doing here?

If he did know about Yvonne, why was a slow smile transforming his face?

He couldn't smile like that if he knew. Maybe he was in shock. This smile couldn't mask guilt. Not mask. She meant hide.

"Nick." She reached out and hugged him. He stiffened at her touch, then relaxed and held her tightly for just a moment. He stepped back when he released her.

He took another minute to speak, "Something happened between us last night, Rose, some crazy electricity. It wasn't a sleazy pass. I don't cheat, and I bet you don't either."

"Don't." She had to tell him. The words had to come out of her mouth. Stringing the perfect words together was supposed to be what she did.

He didn't give her a chance to try. "Please hear me out. I love Yvonne more than I know how to describe. We weren't big on emotional vocabulary where I grew up. But I can tell you that she's gone through too much already, and that I won't let anything bad happen to her again. No matter how obsessed I get with my work."

Oh God, he didn't know. He really didn't.

"You can't—"

"Please listen. While we were doing the dishes after you and Frank left last night, Yvonne wanted to know why I didn't have much to say about the dinner. She's always saying I should tell her how I feel and doesn't get that I grew up in a family where men didn't talk much. So I made the mistake of telling her I'd felt attracted to you for a weird minute." He shrugged those shoulders.

"What did she say?"

Nick shook his head. "She said you were too happy with Frank to play games with me, then she flipped out. She yelled that I was just trying to pay her back for, uh, for something that happened. When we started fighting again this morning, I walked out. I've wasted all day wandering around instead of doing my work. Now I feel stupid and guilty."

Rose cringed at his last word. The slow tones of his earnest confession sounded like a dirge. Hearing his scruples tortured her. She couldn't let him continue flaying himself while she dreaded cutting his heart out.

She stepped closer to hide her face against his chest for a silent minute, then drew back, sliding her hands down his arms. He pulled away, widening the distance between them until their outstretched arms looked ready for a game of London Bridge. He stared down at her without any trace of a smile. She knew he'd misinterpreted her but dreaded the moment when he'd understand what she meant. Appearing to encourage an illicit attraction seemed preferable to announcing a death.

Unready to meet his eyes or watch his face when she told him what she prayed really was news, Rose stared down at the sidewalk as if it were her cue card. Telling the nearest and dearest wasn't her job. She didn't know her lines.

She held onto his hands again after he loosened his

grip. Somebody should hold him when he heard his lover was dead.

Brakes shrieked, and a car door slammed. Concentrating on what she wanted to say, Rose didn't turn to see who was in such a hurry. She tightened her grasp on Nick's hands when he started to pull them away. It was time now.

"Forget what you just said. It doesn't matter anymore. I have to tell you something." She couldn't worry about trite phrasing now. One last deep breath. "Yvonne's dead, Nick. Somebody killed her."

"No."

"I'm sorry, but yes."

He stared at her.

"It's true. I found her."

"No."

They still stood in their silly pose, and London Bridge had fallen down.

"Why? Who? Goddamn it, I was supposed to protect her." He kept staring, as if he'd find absolution in her face.

She couldn't tolerate his dazed scrutiny another second. Rose closed her eyes, promising herself she'd return his gaze steadily after a moment's pause. She squeezed her eyes shut. He didn't need to see her tears. Dry eyes tendered more comfort.

She opened her eyes again at the sound of footsteps racing toward them. Butler appeared behind Nick.

His hand chopped at Nick's right wrist with frightening force. Nick dropped Rose's hand. Butler grabbed Nick's right arm and twisted it behind his back.

She tightened her hold on Nick's left hand. "Frank, what are you doing?"

He ignored her, speaking to Nick like a stranger. "Let go of her other hand right now."

Nick released her, pushing her away when he did. His long reach propelled her back at least a yard.

"Get out of the way, Rose." Butler's command echoed Nick's movement in a tone of cold fury.

Amazed, she watched as Butler twisted Nick's arm higher behind his back.

Nick's face twisted too. "Ease up, Frank. I'm not touching Rose now. What the fuck you doing, man? Let me go."

Butler grunted but didn't move. "Why don't you tell me why you're here? What do you want with Rose?"

She had to stop this scene now. "Frank, I just told Nick about Yvonne. Let him go now. He's in enough pain without you manhandling him."

"Manhandling? Perfect word for what I saw a minute ago. Trust you to come up with it." Butler wouldn't look at her.

"Let go of me, Frank. Why are you doing this?" Nick turned his head to try to see Butler's face.

"Don't tell me what to do here. Any questions to be asked, they'll come from me. Let's start with why you killed your girlfriend."

"What in the hell?" Nick stopped trying to look at Butler.

"You heard me. Why did you kill Yvonne?" Butler dropped Nick's arm a fraction of an inch.

Nick's arm left Butler's grasp as he wrenched himself free, whirled around, and swung at Butler. She heard a dull thump when Nick's fist hit Butler's stomach, then Butler's low groan. Butler doubled over, then straightened himself slowly.

She watched Nick struggle to control himself. He stepped toward Butler, then backed away again. He froze when Butler pulled his gun.

"Sorry, Frank. I didn't mean to do that." He stretched his right arm out. "I thought you were about to break my arm. Then I snapped when you accused me of killing Yvonne."

Butler panted as he glared at Nick. "Yeah, you snapped all right. Quite a reaction, that snap. Lot of guilty guys strike out when they're accused."

Nick took another step back. "Damn it, you can't think I'm guilty. How could I kill Yvonne? I love her."

"People kill their lovers every day. Trust me, I know. I've seen more dearly-beloved stiffs than you want to imagine."

Nick clenched his fists. "I swear I'll hit you again if you accuse me again. Use your fucking gun if you want to. Do me a favor."

Butler raised his gun. "Want and need get confused real easy in these situations. Don't make things worse for yourself."

West Fourth Street didn't show up on maps of Dodge City. She couldn't watch this anymore. She slipped between the two men, thinking what an inadequate shield her small body made for Nick's bulk. Butler's face whitened.

"Stop this, both of you." The nuns' voices had sounded stronger when they broke up schoolyard skirmishes. "Nobody's going to hit or shoot anybody. What is this macho madness?

"Damnit, Frank, you drove Nick to hit you. And Nick, you're not doing Yvonne any good acting like this. Getting yourself shot won't make your pain go away."

She kept her eyes on the gun, which seemed safer than looking at either man's face. "Frank suspects you. It's his job. Seeing us together just made him take his job too seriously for a minute there. He won't admit it for a while, but he knows it's true."

Rose didn't let Butler's snort stop her, "I don't think you killed Yvonne. He thinks you might have. So convince him you didn't. Then we can all concentrate on finding out who did." Providing the voice of cool reason left her trembling.

Butler lowered his gun and took several deep breaths. "Shit, I shouldn't have lost control like that. Nick, you're gonna have to come in to the station with me for questioning. For Yvonne's sake, I won't charge you with assaulting me right now. I ate dinner at your house last night, right? But you're still a suspect. Little Miss Peacemaker here can't change that. You ready?"

"Yeah. I'll go answer all the questions you want. Now tell me how Yvonne died." Nick stared at Butler.

"Later. You want to get in the car now?"

A squad car pulled up behind Butler's battered vehicle just as Butler unlocked his passenger's door. Neighbors in the small crowd across the street or leaning out of the windows up and down the block must have called the police, not knowing what sort of confrontation they witnessed. With Butler in plainclothes, the scene must have looked like just another tacky triangle.

Ignoring the neighbors she recognized in the crowd, Rose tried to take comfort in the uniform cops not having seen Butler's drawn gun. Hot August evenings inspired excessive force. She could survive excessive gossip. Maybe she'd avoid the block party next weekend, though.

After a quick conversation with the uniforms, Butler pointed Nick toward the squad car, walked back to her, looked over her head, and told the small crowd that everything was all right now and they could go on about their business. One of the cops stood behind him, obviously ready to echo his directions. The other cop ushered Nick into the back of the squad car. He slumped behind the grill as if he'd never sit straight again.

Too late to suggest the two men shake hands before they drove away. Western heroes didn't drive off in separate stagecoaches.

Butler walked away from her with a military posture, his body as stiff as a warning post. She recognized the stupidity of asking if she could accompany him, which would earn her at best a tirade on interfering. He hadn't addressed a word to her since she'd stepped in front of his gun. Nick wasn't the only one he accused. Her lover's sense of betrayal hung in the air. The lingering smell of the fighters' sweat sharpened the heavy atmosphere.

Both cars drove west on Eleventh Street, Butler's new windshield glittering incongruously above his car's scratched hood. Driving off into the sunset wouldn't provide the happy ending to this story. Reaching her own apartment might be as good as today would get.

It was after seven and still in the high nineties. Her mailbox contained nothing but four bills. She started up the five flights to her apartment.

Yvonne is dead. Yvonne is dead. Yvonne is dead. The steps whispered the news as she climbed.

She'd discovered a dead friend, argued with two absurd conventioneers, bungled announcing the death, angered her boyfriend more deeply than ever in their volatile affair, and missed her scheduled writing time.

Monday had punished her earlier hubris more than enough. She'd never gloat about having the day free again.

Rose wondered if peacemakers always felt so dirty, and how long it took them to stop shaking.

She also wondered where Nick had been all day.

# Chapter Eight

No calls. No calls. No calls.

Butler didn't call to apologize. Nick didn't call to say he'd established his innocence. Butler didn't call to tell her what he'd discovered. The murderer didn't call to identify himself. Butler didn't call to argue. Yvonne didn't call to laugh about the ridiculous hoax she'd perpetrated this afternoon. Butler didn't call to see how she felt. No one called to tell her the magic words that would wake her from this bad dream.

Her phone hadn't stayed so silent since the time the plug had slipped out of its wobbly jack. She stared at it like a Dorothy Parker heroine, then ignored it like a superstitious teenager.

She couldn't call Butler at work. Not tonight.

The quick temptation to call in an anonymous tip about the rolling pin vanished the second she recognized it. No need to bring crank callers into this case. She'd never been good at disguising her voice.

Rose had barricaded herself behind closed windows and a humming air-conditioner. She hadn't expected the insulation to work this well. Her apartment was an isolation tank—with squirmy creatures in the water.

Which of her friends needed a call telling of her new prowess as a corpse-finder? She couldn't think of a soul she could talk to without crying, and she couldn't bear the idea of anything wet on her face.

She put five of her oldest blues favorites in the cd player, then hit stop halfway through the first song. Moans weren't what the apartment needed to break the silence. Nothing in her music collection was. *Pace,* Bessie; another time, Dinah.

Her own manuscript taunted her from the desk with the impossibility of writing about fictional murders when another real one surrounded her. She'd never picked true crime as her genre, thank you. Writing mysteries allowed playing "what if?" Finding Yvonne dead demanded "what next?"

"Who next?" couldn't happen again.

Real corpses demanded more attention than even an obsessive writer's characters. A sick certainty that her novel wouldn't grow until Yvonne's killer was arrested kept Rose staring at her keyboard.

The keys all looked like little tombstones. Her keyboard had turned into a cemetery.

Homicide made such a novel excuse for writer's block.

Reading a book or magazine article someone else had had the equanimity to complete seemed as attractive as scheduling a dentist's appointment to distract yourself from a bad haircut.

She couldn't do a single thing except think about who had killed Yvonne. And why.

Rose had to learn more about Yvonne's life. She needed to talk to Nick. No one answered at their—his—loft. She couldn't page him at the Sixth Precinct. Suspects didn't receive switchboard privileges.

Her absolute conviction that Nick had not killed Yvonne frightened her when she imagined trying to defend it to Butler. She knew art didn't guarantee innocence as well as she knew Nick could not have defiled Yvonne's body with such ugly mockery. She prayed he'd managed to substantiate wandering around into an acceptable alibi. Realizing that Butler was the person who would judge the alibi, she tried to remember how to say an entire rosary. Sorrowful, Joyous, Glorious, they were all Mysteries.

What did she know about Yvonne? She worked at My World. Only six months ago, Rose had suspected everyone now working at the restaurant, except for the recently hired Ken and Terri, of murder. Mentally convicting your coworkers should be restricted to once a year. Or once a job.

Yvonne went to school. Rose would investigate, but she couldn't imagine any fate more threatening than boredom resulting from a study of advanced accounting. Unless studying money could mimic money itself as a motive. Baruch College still lacked the reputation as a dangerous environment.

A gorgon of an ex-husband lurked in Yvonne's past, perhaps not distantly.

All of Yvonne's life was past now.

The man troublesome enough to make Nick ask about a restraining order had already proved himself capable of abuse. Maybe he'd escalated his attacks. Nick would know more about him. Barney, she remembered his name now. Maybe Nick would know where to find Barney. What had Barney done today?

There was still no answer at the loft.

Her phone still hadn't rung.

Butler wasn't rushing to tell her everything he

discovered. He'd radiated more anger while he ignored her than she'd known he could generate, and she'd never underestimated the strength of his temper. Butler's rage had even contaminated his professional behavior. His momentary loss of control seemed a lapse he'd expect her to atone for. Bless me, Butler, for I have sinned.

Who would atone for Yvonne's death? No matter what the penance, the murderer's guilty soul shouldn't merit absolution.

She had lesser guilts to address, too. She hadn't blurted denials when Nick had acknowledged the soapish something that had surfaced between them after dinner yesterday. She'd liked the feeling of his arm around her last night. She had also touched him more today than consolation strictly demanded.

Passing attractions happened. Anyone but a dead fool would enjoy the frisson, maybe even flirt a little, without endangering her serious relationship. She'd never called Anna and Emma role models.

Nick had claimed more guilt than he needed. Nothing had happened between them last night. Not really.

Butler had never been so demonstrative at a social dinner before. He couldn't have seen Nick holding her inside the dark loft, could he? Their brief contact had remained too chaste to leave visible traces. No mussed hair, disarrayed clothes, or smudged lipstick. If Nick's t-shirt had included a collar, it would have remained innocently clean.

But Butler had seen—or sensed—something, his cop's intuition sharpening his lover's instincts. She wondered if he'd seen the embrace before it happened. He'd probably have claimed prescience, if he'd mentioned the incident at all. Instead, he'd acted determinedly affable on their way home and lavishly attentive when they'd reached her apartment. Last night's long hours of lovemaking suddenly felt different. His fierce passion, the tight grip with which he'd held her beneath him, chafed her now. She didn't want to think she'd been claimed instead of caressed. Her desires didn't include driving Butler mad with jealousy.

Be a girl, better yet a good Catholic girl. Take the blame, wear it like a scratchy wool sweater over a short-sleeved blouse. Draw your bath too hot and don't look down at your reddening body, or you'll have to sprinkle talcum powder on the water to veil yourself. Occasions of sin proliferated.

She told herself that neither she nor Nick had done anything wrong. Not last night. And not today.

No man who had just murdered his girlfriend would come running to another woman to apologize for a moment's flirtation. A killer wouldn't care about that.

By now, Nick should have described his fight with Yvonne. Maybe he'd even established witnesses to his errands today.

Rose saw Butler's skeptical expression, how his lips compressed as his eyes barely widened in a face tilted slightly to the left. She loved deciphering Butler's thoughts behind his skepticism, and she wished she could try to read his face right now. Nick wouldn't want to study the look she was enamored of; he'd probably seen more than enough of Butler's mistrust by now. Nick probably didn't give a damn about Butler's face.

She didn't know if Nick had been able to see Yvonne yet, or if anybody had. They'd remove the hideous plaster mask soon, wouldn't they? An autopsy wasn't carbon-dating. It hurt to imagine the cold hard plaster being ripped away from Yvonne. Several pairs of gloved hands would rock the mask's edges, loosening it gently, working inward until the whole hideous sculpture lifted. The plaster wouldn't separate from the skin cleanly. She wouldn't want to see the inner surface of the mask, please, or hear the sounds.

They'd have to do it that way to keep the evidence intact. Demolishing the mask, sawing it in two or breaking it into a pile of shards, could destroy evidence too. The sounds of surgical saws whirring or heavy instruments tapping might muffle a killer's careless message. Too bad the killer hadn't signed his work.

Butler might call her in for questioning as one of the victim's coworkers. He'd interrogated everyone who worked at My World when he'd investigated the deaths at the restaurant in February. All the employees there would soon be expert witnesses. Ken and Terri were the only neophytes.

Rose winced when she thought about Terri—little, sweet, saccharine, simpering Terri. While Yvonne's death trivialized jealousy, it didn't obliterate it. Butler hadn't held a monopoly on the ugly vice today.

Rose knew that hearing Terri's name had added jealousy to her anger about Butler's lateness at the loft. He'd talked with Terri rather than rushing to Rose.

All right, so she hadn't been in any immediate danger. Butler couldn't have known that absolutely. He might be used to finding dead bodies; he knew Rose wasn't.

She could picture them, Terri looking up at Butler, big baby tears welling around her Bambi eyes as she bravely batted them away with her sticky lashes while Butler's hands hovered over her shaking shoulders. Or had the situation required a comforting embrace? Terri wouldn't stiffen and protest that she was fine. No, she would nestle right into the nearest strong arms with a few delicate shudders. Butler would have had to hold Terri tighter to quiet the shaking.

Passersby would have admired the tableau as Terri's undoubtedly pastel dress contrasted beautifully with Butler's dark suit. She probably wore waterproof mascara all the time, too thoughtful to smudge or stain anyone's shirtfront. Shit, Terri probably dyed her eyelashes.

Damn. Rose looked to see if her own blunt nails had elongated into claws. Savaging Terri didn't solve anything. Terri was married, and absurdly devoted, to Ken. Her flirtations with other men were like fishermen who'd already caught their limit trolling a few lines off the side on the return to port, unconcerned with catching anything. Or anyone.

Enough of blaming Terri for Butler's transgressions. She hadn't chained him to the sidewalk outside the station, and she could not have physically detained him. He'd made his own choice. It might not have been an intellectual process.

But no intellectualizing or stern self-lectures on her part would calm jealousy's nervous turmoil. She'd tried every technique she could think of during her ex-husband's womanizing years. You couldn't think yourself back onto solid ground when the world became a funhouse walled with distorting mirrors on shaking floors. Relying on faith wasn't rational. Closing your eyes wasn't safe. Jealousy killed the soul. Again and again.

Checking the locks on her door for the third time and dragging the phone into the bedroom didn't feel like superb security measures either. Maybe the snarls of phone cord draped down the hall would trip an intruder. She wedged a book under the phone jack in the living room to make sure the plug couldn't slip out, then turned the ringer to its highest volume.

Butler had called her in the middle of the night before. Rose hoped he wouldn't worry about disturbing her rest now.

# Chapter Nine

The phone rang before nine Tuesday morning. Everyone who knew her unlisted number also knew the noon rule. No calls till the big and little hands pointed straight up, thanks. Unless Butler had worked all night and couldn't call her until now. Rose grabbed the phone and tried not to trip over its snaking cord as the stumbled into the living room to hear her machine. She placed the phone at the edge of her desk, ready to pick up the receiver at the first sound of his voice. She didn't touch the phone when Ken announced that he hadn't cancelled today's staff meeting, despite the terrible tragedy.

Trudging back to the kitchen, she cursed when she saw she'd forgotten to set up the coffee machine last night. Old grinds into the bulging bag beneath the sink, new beans into the basket, forever to run the water till it felt cold. Finally, the grinder's racket and the strong smell of French roast nudged her toward the bathroom.

She hesitated before lifting her eyes to the medicine cabinet mirror while brushing her teeth. The amount of beauty sleep she'd managed presaged a hag. Terri probably used under-eye concealer before her perfumed showers. Any woman who boasted that her husband never saw her without makeup probably owned a full range of waterproof cosmetics.

Two cups of coffee later, Rose still felt sad, worried, irrationally frightened, and no prettier. She needed cosmetics for the soul, psychic versions of before-and-after. She wanted layers of grief eraser, generosity foundation, wisdom liner, and courage blush. Or six hours of innocent sleep.

But one of the peculiar tenets of restaurant management held that employees, many who had worked past three or four in the morning, should always gather for meetings before the noon whistle blew. Wearing a nightgown wouldn't signal the good attitude Ken insisted made the number-one attribute of a good worker. Worse, it might inspire him into another fantasy about staff uniforms designed to transform My World into the Baby Doll Lounge.

A loose black cotton shell over baggy black pants mimicked pajamas' comfort; her color choice was preordained. Terri wouldn't dare mention black's depressing qualities today. And Rose wouldn't have the chance to nibble any of the cinnamon rolls Yvonne assembled at home and baked in the restaurant kitchen just before the meetings began.

The thermometer outside Rose's kitchen window offered ninety-five degrees when her watch insisted she had fifteen minutes to walk the seven blocks to My World. She hated leaving the safety of her air-conditioned apartment.

Wilted nannies and whining children filled the sandbox area of Abingdon Square Park. Old women and young men reading newspapers occupied every shaded bench, waiting for a breeze to ruffle the pages they held and the leaves above them. Talcum powder and coffee battled beer and urine in the air.

A homeless family used one of the picnic tables as a bunk bed, the parents sprawled facedown across the table while a little girl slept in a shaded nest of blankets underneath. Sleep was the most sensible activity in this heat, no matter what your options. Wishing she could tuck ice cream money into the little girl's hand without disturbing the family's rest, Rose resolved to buy them a bag of groceries at Key Foods if they hadn't been rousted before her return home. She'd get bread, sliced turkey, fruit, cheese, juice, and milk. She substituted less perishable peanut butter for the turkey and cheese on her mental list, but knew she'd risk letting a quart of ice cream melt. The little girl should have a proper picnic.

The unshaded bricks burned through her sandals' thin soles as she neared Hudson Street. Neither the sidewalk nor the nearly melting asphalt on the wide street felt any cooler. Rose jettisoned her plan for a long afternoon walk after the meeting. She didn't feel a breath of cooling river breeze as she walked west.

Ken had better have cranked up My World's air-conditioner early today, instead of waiting to cool the place until half an hour before the restaurant opened for lunch in his scheme to make customers drink more in a warmer room. Discomfort as marketing tool. She'd welcome even minimal air-conditioning after these hot blocks.

Jimmy waited just within the restaurant's front door. Dressed in pleated white slacks and a white cotton shirt, he was her negative image.

"Don't tell me you're impersonating the good humor man, Jimmy. You'll need to do something radical about the look on your face."

"No, dear, someone with your education should

know that the highly civilized East has designated white as the color of mourning. Are you all right? I wanted to call you this morning when Ken warbled the news in his absurdly early reminder call, but I thought you could use every extra second of sleep you could get. I'm worried you're overdoing. I just can't think why you needed to refine your skills at spotting dead bodies."

He lowered his voice, "Can you bear to tell me about it after this marvelous meeting concludes? Do you think Nick did it? Ken's been throwing out the sort of less than subtle hints that could engender a libel suit. And speaking of suits, wait till you see his mourning ensemble. You'll be comforted to see that black is one of the twenty or so colors on his shirt."

She scanned the room for Ken. "Maybe we can have iced coffee somewhere very cool and dark after the meeting. But I have to run an errand first. And I absolutely don't think Nick did it. Let's find chairs as far away from Ken's seat as possible and pray he doesn't attempt to eulogize Yvonne during the meeting."

Five square tables had been pushed into one long rectangle, with chairs crammed along all sides. A two-top to the left of the meeting table held styrofoam cups, two pots of coffee on a double warmer, three quarts of Tropicana orange juice, and a large pink box of donuts from Fourteenth Street. Drops of melted fat glistened in the donuts' frosting, and grease stained the sides of the box. With the Village full of excellent bakeries, Ken had walked out of his way to buy greasy donuts. She hoped he hadn't been reading articles about the nostalgic diner trend in one of his magazines. Please God, no poodle skirts.

The chef, Ward, walked out of the kitchen carrying a large platter of fruit and a basket of sliced baguettes, then centered his offerings on a side table. A busboy followed him with a tray of ceramic mugs, water glasses, a pitcher of ice water, and an empty juice carafe. Rose avoided Ward's eyes when he moved the spotted pink box and stack of styrofoam cups to a chair. The disdain on the chef's face didn't award Ken's version of a continental breakfast any stars.

Ken ignored Ward's maneuvers from his seat at the head of the table. Like a junior-high classroom, the seats at the far end of the table were full, with chairs wedged into a rough second row. Except for the chair immediately to Ken's right, where Terri's navy blue shift and sunglasses portrayed an attempt at brave dignity, the seven or eight chairs closest to Ken sat empty, reserved by consensus for late arrivals.

Excited chatter buzzed from the occupied seats. Alyse, the prep cook, and two of the waitresses, Helen and Angela, had puffy, reddened eyes broadcasting their grief. Jimmy angled his lanky body next to Rose in an obvious effort to block questions and solicitous looks from their coworkers. Given the speed of restaurant gossip, everyone at the table probably knew what nightmares she'd had last night.

Ken stood after his felt tip scratched a final notation on the yellow legal pad in front of him. The garish depictions of surfboards and palm trees mocked the black background of the shirt he wore tucked into a pair of khaki shorts. Ken had spent the first thirty-four years of his life in the mountains of Colorado and now lived in the city of Manhattan, so why did he wear clothes that suggested the last gust off the Pacific had just blown the sand from his hair?

Ken cleared his throat. "Yvonne was a great girl. No way she deserved what that big bastard did to her. But we have to dwell on the positive now. She worked hard for My World. I know she'd want us all to pull together and do our best as a team to make the place better. So let's look forward now, gang. I knew Yvonne. I'm sure she would want it that way."

She felt Jimmy's sharp elbow in her ribs as he leaned over to whisper in her ear, "Andy's fifteen minutes of fame wasn't bad enough, now Ken's changing it to fifteen seconds of grief? Is Nick the big bastard?"

"Sssh." She nudged Jimmy back.

Terri reached up and tugged Ken's elbow until he leaned over so she could whisper in his ear. He straightened with an annoyed expression on his face and cleared his throat again.

"Right. I don't mean to underestimate the tragedy we're all sharing in here. Way I see it, something like this might even bring us closer together as a team. But you all know how committed I am to open communication with you all. So if anybody has anything he wants to say about Yvonne, or feelings he needs to express, Terri and I are here to listen. The floor is open, guys."

Alyse's voice rose, "What about if any of us gals wanted to say something, Ken? Are women allowed to take the floor here, too?"

Terri answered quickly, "Now, honey, you know what Ken meant. It's just how he talks. I'm here to tell you how much Ken respects women. Everybody here is an equal member of our team."

"If they bring out the pom-poms, I'm out of here." Jimmy's comment and Rose's squelched giggle were the only response to Terri's defense.

They drew Ken's attention. "Rose, maybe after what you underwent yesterday, you'd like to share with the group."

She shook her head as an uncomfortable silence settled around the table. Maybe he expected her to stand up and introduce herself, "Hello, my name is Rose and I'm a body-finder." Or should she have brought in yesterday's ruined skirt for show-and-tell?

"Anybody else want to kick things off?" Not even a coffee cup clattered in response to Ken's question. The entire staff stared at the table in front of them in a parody of seventh-graders hoping to avoid the teacher's attention in a surprise quiz.

"Great. I think what we've had here is a kind of spontaneous minute of silence. I'm sure Yvonne would appreciate that. You guys want to go for two minutes?" Ken sounded like a coach; she hoped he wouldn't suggest a huddle next.

Ward's English accent thickened into Parliamentary tones. "Actually, I believe we'd all prefer to deal with our grief privately, Ken. Perhaps we can proceed to the business matters on your agenda. Unless anyone objects?"

Relieved denials rose around the table. Ward might mean to claim a share of control over the meeting. He'd muttered about frontier upstarts ever since Ben had installed Ken and Terri as temporary managers. Some of the staff had speculated that he'd wanted to run the place himself.

Ken gave a thumbs-up. "Good thinking, Ward. We have a pretty full agenda here anyway. My beautiful wife and I spent yesterday riding back and forth on the Staten Island Ferry. I'll be damned if it didn't fire me up. You people got a beautiful skyline here, and believe me when I say I'm gonna put my mark on your city. Improving My World is my first step, and today I'm rarin' to go."

Like a professional athlete's wife, Terri's smile stayed frozen while her husband spoke.

"First off, I want everybody to take notes at these meetings from now on. That way you guys can go over what we discuss and have more input for me at the next meeting. Hon?" Terri reached into a large canvas bag at her side and started a box of sharpened number two pencils and a sheaf of copy paper around the table, while Ken explained that he wanted everyone to start his own notebook for the meetings and those all-important staff suggestions.

As soon as Jimmy received his paper and pencil he wrote, "Mr. and Mrs. Apted's Cute Alibis?" in large letters and angled the page so Rose could read it. She shook her head and turned his paper face-down.

"So, first thing you all should notate down is that from now on we're going to have meetings every two weeks instead of every few months the way Ben did. I'd like to do it every week, but I don't want to stretch payroll too far." Ken looked surprised at the mild expletives and groans that met his announcement, "Hey, I'm paying you for these meetings, don't forget."

"But you aren't tipping, are you? I'll pay the hour's minimum wage plus twenty percent if I can stay home." All of the waiters seconded Jimmy's suggestion.

Ken glared at Jimmy. "That's not the attitude I'm looking for here. These meetings are mandatory. You miss a meeting, you miss two shifts that week. Miss two meetings, and you'll be missing your job. Got it?"

Ken rolled his shoulders and stretched his neck like a boxer between rounds. Rose watched Terri, half expecting her to jump up to massage her husband's shoulders.

Ken drummed his pen on the table in a beat Rose didn't recognize. "Okay. Let's move back on a positive note. I have some other personnel policies about tardiness and improper attire. We can talk about them next meeting after Terri gets them typed up.

"Anyway, we want to make this such a fun place to work that you all will hurry in to start your shifts. Really, I've been kind of hoping that my example might inspire everybody to dress just a little sharper, whether or not we go the uniform route."

Several staff members started to doodle.

"But hey, I'm jumping ahead of myself here." Ken looked down at his legal pad, drew an exaggerated check mark, and looked around the table before his next announcement.

"Theme nights. Hell, theme weeks. Promotions. Promotion is the key to sales, and sales is what we're here for. Ben and Tom had a decent business going here, but I know we can do better."

He stood and pumped his arms. "My goal is to break a sales record every week I'm here. So we need to make some changes. Today's marketplace, you don't change, you die. I don't think Ben or his dad, Joe, would mind coming home to a place that was pulling in twice as much money as when they left, do you guys? And you can't fry eggs without breaking them, right, Ward?"

The chef didn't answer Ken's last question, and no one else answered his first. Rose didn't know if Ken's callous reference to death offended her more because of Yvonne or because only a death in the Victors' family had given Ken a job at My World. The Victors would consider more than the numbers if they returned to a restaurant they didn't recognize.

"I'm just gonna throw some thoughts at you guys now. Nothing is finalmento, but I want you to see where my mind is going." He tapped his pen on his head this time.

"How about Sinatra nights? Go for the old-style

Italian thing. My World, My Way, get it? We play a lot of Mr. Blue Eyes on the box or maybe get someone in to do a little impersonation. Hey, any of you singers or actors here would get first shot at that. We'd feature a lot of spaghettis, excuse me, Ward, pastas. I can see red check tablecloths."

Jimmy kicked Rose, "What, with a sparkler stuck in a box of wine at each table?"

Ken continued, "The whole ethnic thing is underdone here in the city, at least in nice places. Ethnic is a big trend, and there's no reason we can't ride it. I'm thinking special menus, special music, special drinks. Maybe take a different country every day of the week. We'd call it Travelin' My World."

He raised his voice to cover Ward's cough, "Or how about My World, the Sweetest Little Place in Town? We upgrade our desserts, start carrying around a display tray after every meal. Market research says people don't drink as much after dinner as they used to, so we'll offer them a substitute they can't refuse. You people would be amazed at what selling desserts to every table could do to your check averages. Higher checks mean higher tips, right?"

No one answered. The entire staff remained silent while Ken presented his concepts for Meat Nights, which would offer customers a chance to meet each other while dining on a menu designed to highlight the neighborhood's meat market history. No one argued when he suggested more attention to sports and special game nights. And no one asked for examples of what he called the great resources of the liquor companies' promotional materials. The lack of staff input didn't seem to bother Ken.

His tone remained cheerful. "I designed this last concept just for all you New Yorkers who are always in such a hurry. Terri and I haven't been here all that long, but it didn't take me long to get that time is definitely money in this town. To cater to that, I'm talking QuickServe, a part of the menu that we can guarantee will get to your table five minutes after you order it. Quick food for quick people. Think fast, eat fast."

Ward raised his hand. "Had you considered a drive-up window, Ken? Why not capitalize on Americans' obsession with cars while you're at it? Can we expect the staff to be sporting little paper caps anytime soon?"

Ken scribbled on his pad. "Love that dry English humor, Ward. No paper caps. They're not cost-effective. But I am looking at piles of uniform catalogues. We want something cheerful in here, real upbeat, like maybe shirts in a tasteful fluorescent color. And where is it written in stone that pants have to be black? Hell, weather like this, I think we might even go with shorts. From what I've seen, nobody here has legs to be ashamed of, at least not in the front of the house."

Ward shifted his wide thighs as he scowled at Ken. The chef's black and white checked pants came from the upper range of sizes. Whoever had said it was foolish to trust a thin chef would have loaned Ward his life savings.

Ignoring the groans that met his mention of uniforms, Ken continued, "You people have to wear the uniforms, if we choose them. So I'll be expecting a lot of suggestions from you at the next meeting. Make a note of that."

Jimmy raised his hand, and Ken beamed as he acknowledged him. Jimmy spoke in the serious ex-schoolteacher's tones she knew signaled trouble. "Actually, if the mortality rate around here continues, we might move into shrouds for our new uniforms. But I want you to know I draw the line at suits without backs. I trust I'm not alone in that, no matter what you think about our physiques."

Terri interrupted the suppressed giggles around the table, "Jimmy, how could you? I thought you all were so sensitive. Yvonne's death had nothing to do with the restaurant and all that other terrible trouble earlier this year. It's just coincidence, and bad luck for Ben and Uncle Joe. I don't see anything funny about it. So show some respect, please." Terri dabbed at her eyes behind her dark glasses with a pink handkerchief she pulled from her pocket.

"Yeah, stop with the smart-ass waiter routine and show some effing respect is right. Yvonne wanted this restaurant to succeed, and so do we. Life goes on. My main goal now is to pump cash into the place. If you don't want to be part of the program here, nobody's forcing you to work for us." Ken scribbled on his yellow pad again. Maybe he'd printed Jimmy's name and drawn a black mark next to it.

Terri's almost inaudible sobs continued as Ken asked if anyone had any sensible questions. When no one responded, he concluded his meeting with the demand that everyone bring "mucho input" next time.

Although Ken thought his brief stint managing My World would help him break into the New York restaurant scene, grief must have blinded Ben and Joe when they'd left Ken to manage their business. From everything she'd seen, he'd do better in shoe sales. Casual shoes.

"I suppose we'll have to bus out to K-mart for some colorful input tote bags. How could he just prattle on like that, thinking we would all forget about Yvonne after that execrable few seconds of silence?" Jimmy crumpled his meeting notes into a tiny ball and shoved it into his pants pocket. Steering Rose toward the front door, he complained about Ken in a continuous chatter which guided her through the rest of the staff before anyone else could speak to her. As much as she appreciated his protective intentions, his tactics only delayed the inevitable.

She knew she'd have to answer everyone's questions eventually and dreaded the peculiar mix of curiosity and sympathy she anticipated. Her shift tomorrow would be time enough.

When Helen called across the room asking her to wait, Rose pantomimed looking at her watch and shook her head. Pretending not to see Ken waving from the table, she leaned closer to Jimmy, "Home, James."

She heard Ken asking the Salvadoran dishwasher if he wanted to take the box of donuts home to his bambinos as Jimmy opened the door and they left the restaurant.

By the time she dragged Jimmy to the park, the homeless family had broken up their temporary crèche and moved elsewhere.

# Chapter Ten

"Dear God, Rose, Ken wants to make more changes to our place of employment in four weeks than the Victors have seen in over forty years."

"Except for the clientele, Jimmy."

"If Ken has his way, our customer base might change again. Or disappear. That family knows better than to change what works. Ken, not so much. Did you see the look on Ward's face when Ken started the fast food pitch?"

"You'll have to forgive me if I'm not up for our usual meeting postmortem. Ken's favorite book has to be the audiotape of *How to Lose Friends and Nauseate People.* I've seen slugs with more sensitivity." Rose fanned herself with a *Post* she'd found on a bench.

Jimmy stopped to look at the menu in the window of the Paris Commune. "Then we'll postmortem Yvonne's postmortem. Audition your spiel with me before you have to give it to every ghoul in Manhattan at work tomorrow. I'll help you condense it."

He pointed to her impromptu fan, then to a nearby trash can. "Come on, I'll ape your thwarted charity and buy you lunch or at least one of those iced cappuccinos every place in town suddenly sells. You want to walk over to Vivaldi? Or I'd spring for a glass or two of premium white if it would loosen your tongue."

He might have let her keep the fan if the paper weren't a tabloid. "No, even crossing Seventh Avenue seems too much of a trek. I'll go to the Koreans on Perry and buy a dozen lemons, squeeze them all into a pitcher of ice water, and drink that while I fret for the rest of the afternoon."

"Unsweetened, I assume. Fine, go fret to your bitter little heart's content. But I'm going to call you after my nap and try to prevail upon you to join me for a light supper and some cocktails, preferably martinis. Otherwise I'll stay up all night worrying about you."

"You've been up all night for the last twenty years." His chronic insomnia made her hours look like a dairy farmer's schedule.

"Don't you even want to speculate about how slickly Ken slipped his alibi for yesterday into his pep talk, dearest?"

"No. Great alibi, real easy to establish. You don't suppose Terri will corroborate it, do you?"

"Not if she has to spell it first." Jimmy sniffed.

Jimmy walked her to the greengrocer's. She bought lemons and Scottish shortbread cookies. He dropped two bunches of watercress, canned chicken stock, and a pint of cream for what he insisted would be the perfect afternoon soup into his blue basket, then walked outside to add four bunches of iris to his purchases.

"Think of them as oversized forget-me-nots." He handed her two bunches before hailing a cab after she refused his offer of a lift home. The three blocks to her apartment wouldn't wilt either her or the flowers. Detouring the extra two blocks to Butler's office at the

Sixth Precinct on West Tenth to check his car might make her spirits droop, though.

He hadn't let so many hours pass without calling her since their first date.

There was never a cop around when you needed one. Too bad Butler didn't work foot patrol. How many times would she have to cruise the neighborhood before engineering an accidental meeting? Who's tailing whom?

Nobody waited on her doorstep. No scandals in her building today. She hurried up the five empty flights to her apartment, grateful not to encounter any neighbors curious about yesterday's excitement. Her machine hadn't taken any messages. The clock showed 2:30. Fine.

She gulped most of a quart of Pellegrino straight from the bottle, then composed herself with a cool shower and a sundress patterned on a nightgown's comfort. Resolutely halving lemons and crushing them against her old porcelain juicer, she tried to enjoy a more leisurely lemonade mood. Her tallest glasses were in the cupboard above the sink, which also served as liquor cabinet. Stepping down from the chair she'd used as stepstool, she plunked a tumbler down on the counter with a solitary thud, knowing she'd regret it if she added Jamaican rum to her tall glass of lemonade. Too hot, too upset, too long since food for an early-afternoon drink to make sense now.

But she did have more than enough worries to tempt her into a full day's fretting. Resenting Butler for not calling would waste her time and the anger she should direct toward discovering the murderer. Whenever he finally called, his reasons for his silence would undoubtedly sound perfectly reasonable. Thinking that nothing terrible would have happened if she and Butler had only gone to the peaceful Massachusetts hills on Sunday wasn't logical. Their visiting the Berkshires wouldn't have saved anyone's life.

Who would have found Yvonne if Rose hadn't? Nick seemed the most likely. She could picture him discovering the body, but refused to see anything except surprised horror on his face. She'd shift focus before the sorrow showed.

Then she could look in the mirror at the failed spinster detective. She knew absolutely nothing more about Yvonne's murderer this afternoon than she'd known yesterday. The staff meeting had yielded no clues. Everyone had been there, but no one had worn an "I'm Guilty" t-shirt. Ken's callousness and his stupid plans for the restaurant had dominated the bits of conversation she'd heard before hurrying away with Jimmy. Her own reluctance to replay the role of body-finder had eliminated any productive eavesdropping. She'd even avoided a brainstorming session with Jimmy, who loved calling himself the Deep Throat of My World and preened at the idea of donning an amateur detective's cloak.

Given the option, she'd rather collaborate with a professional than speculate with an amateur. But Butler wasn't rushing to share whatever he'd learned about the murder, although he had to expect the worried curiosity gnawing at her today. To hell with his foolish Irish pride. Or temper. She called the station and left a message asking him to call on his voice mail. She tacked "please" on at the last second.

Rose raised her second glass of lemonade to toast the hard fact she'd finally learned. Butler wasn't sitting at his desk at this moment, thus narrowing the possibilities to any activity anywhere in all of New York City. She felt tired at the prospect of guessing where he might be and what he might be doing. Yvonne wasn't his only case. Butler could be anywhere. So could Nick.

Her buzzer blared. The silly idea that she'd summoned someone by her speculations disappeared when she recognized the slim chances of either the ornery Butler or grieving Nick responding to her psychic call.

Rose asked for her visitor's identity over the intercom her landlord had finally fixed last month. She didn't hear anything except street sounds when she pushed the listen button. She asked again, checking that she really had secured all three locks to her apartment while she listened to more horns and a distant boombox. God, don't let it be somebody randomly hitting buzzers in the hopes of sneaking into the building for a warm afternoon's crime.

She started to leave her door to call the old couple who lived downstairs. Mr. Kelly insisted cross-ventilation beat air-conditioning and propped his front door so wide that an intruder could consider it an invitation. A voice squawking over the intercom drew her back.

"Is this Ms. Leary?"

She asked who wanted to know.

"It's Barney Fine. You don't know me, but poor Yvonne used to be my wife. I need to talk to you about her. Can I come up?"

"No. You're right. I don't know you." And wife-beaters don't top my favorite unexpected guests list.

"I understand. Would you come down here, then, so we can talk? Please."

She refused again and suggested that he leave and go talk to the police. He buzzed at thirty-second intervals for five minutes before she answered again.

"I'm sorry to intrude, Ms. Leary, but I feel I need to see you. Just five minutes, please. It will be better to meet face-to-face than to talk this way or over the phone. But I'll go to my car on the corner and call if you insist." He recited her phone number and begged her again to come downstairs.

How had he gotten her unlisted number? She'd make the trip downstairs just to get that question answered. Only a fool would ignore potential clues that arrived on her very doorstep. Anything Barney told her would be more than she knew now.

Rose wavered, telling herself it was broad daylight and knowing quite well that bad things didn't only happen at night. She hit the talk button again, telling him to wait on the stoop across the street because she'd run into the super's ground floor apartment and call the police if she even saw him on her side of the street, forget her vestibule.

He agreed and said he commended her caution.

Rose walked to the front window and watched a small man hurry across the street and sit on the opposite building's stoop, hands open at his sides as if for examination. She still checked the vestibule before she unlocked the inside door. She clenched her keys into a weapon as she cracked open the outer door. He hadn't moved.

She walked across the street, turning to wave and call to the super's wife sitting at the ground floor window. Let Yvonne's ex know someone was watching.

He stood and extended his right hand when she reached the sidewalk. She nodded, shoving her hands in her pockets, then saw the New Jersey driver's license he'd put on the top of the stoop's post. The little card said she was looking at Barney Fine. Mr. Fine was an organ donor.

A scrawny 5'6", he seemed an unlikely partner, much less abuser, for the robust Yvonne. Small man's complex, maybe. He wore a blue blazer with cheap shiny buttons over beige polyester slacks that wanted to be chinos when they grew up. Scuffed tan shoes showed beneath his dragging cuffs. He'd combed back his thinning light brown hair meticulously and shaved his sharp face so closely the skin gleamed. She'd smelled his heavy cologne on a magazine insert card last month.

"I understand your caution, Ms. Leary, and I'm glad you managed to overcome it. I know this appears irregular, but I've just spent my day being interrogated about poor Yvonne's death. Interrogated with my full cooperation, that is. I would have volunteered my help if the authorities hadn't requested it."

He wiped the sweat off his nose, then dried his hands on his slacks. "As I was leaving the police station, I overheard one of the cops saying Detective Butler's girlfriend worked at the bar where Yvonne did the books. He said you'd found my poor girl. Of course, your boyfriend hadn't disclosed that information. He doesn't give a whole lot away, I guess. I'm a lawyer myself, so I understand where he's coming from. But I still have some questions of my own, things I need explained so I can move into my grief stages."

She interrupted his tale of understanding, "How did you get my address and number?" Butler wouldn't have volunteered that information in gratitude to the helpful Mr. Fine.

He swabbed at his face again. "After your detective finally finished with me, I walked over to My World and talked to Ken. Under the sad circumstances, he understood and gave me your number and address. I thought I'd take my chances on seeing if you were in, since you live so close."

Ken or Barney might not understand the furious call she'd make as soon as she hurried upstairs. Every New York bartender Rose knew paid for an unlisted phone number. Too many customers misinterpreted professional cheer as an invitation to friendship, with some men wanting more than friendship. A series of torturous crank calls earlier this year had taught Rose all about protecting her privacy.

"I need to process this whole issue, and I think talking to you will help."

She wondered how Yvonne had processed the bruises Barney had given her.

He sat on the stoop and looked up at her. "Do you think Yvonne died peacefully? Did she look as if she'd had a chance to reach her higher power at the end?"

"I doubt it." Nobody could read expressions on a face buried in plaster. Barney might have designed his question to demonstrate his ignorance of the death mask.

He scrubbed at his eyes. "I can't believe she's gone. I've been trying and trying to contact her for the last month. I've joined a program to help me control my temper. I wanted to apologize to her for any harm she may have thought I'd caused her in the past. It's one of the things we do. I needed to take the step of erasing the hurt I caused Yvonne."

He'd mapped out all the steps on his psychic floor. Such a pretty little dance, with or without a willing partner.

How do you erase hurt?

"Maybe Yvonne didn't want to hear your apologies."

A sheen of sweat slicked his forehead. "She might not have known it, but she did. I can't believe that crazy artist made her happy. I hoped that once she saw how I'd changed, she might be able to admit to herself that she still loved me. I always wanted her back. I can't believe it's too late." Two tears trickled down his cheeks like condensed sweat.

Doubting Barney's crisis of faith didn't impress her. His inability to believe didn't change the facts. He'd dug his knuckles into his eyes hard enough to produce the tears.

Butler didn't hold the exclusive on blunt. "Where were you yesterday?"

Barney flicked the tears off his face as if to underline them. "In Jersey. I drove down the shore to meet a client about a case. Called him three times, but he never showed up. So I took a walk on the beach, then drove back home to Hoboken. It seemed like I was in my car most of the day. Thank God for the portable car phone. I made a lot of business calls on the road."

The cops might not thank their maker for car phones. Mobile technology turned alibis fuzzier and fuzzier.

She leaned closer and looked into his dry eyes. "Did you have lunch or buy anything at the shore?"

He stood. "You and your boyfriend certainly have a lot in common. I can't believe you're looking for an alibi too. What a cold couple. Not much point in expecting any comfort about losing my Yvonne from you two."

Rose stepped back toward the curb. "From what Yvonne said, she needed comfort while she was with you. You'll have to excuse me, but my sympathy for men who beat women is limited. Don't tell me whether anybody saw you at the shore if you don't want to. The police will know by now anyway."

His voice lowered. "You know, Ms. Leary, I understand why you're turning your grief into anger. But I also know how much damage anger can cause. You should be careful."

"Is that a threat, Mr. Fine?"

"No, just friendly advice from someone who learned the hard way and knows how to admit his mistakes. This doesn't seem like a productive conversation anymore. For my own peace of mind, I'd still like to know more about Yvonne's death. Here's my card. Call me if you feel like talking reasonably sometime. You'll feel better if you stop judging me and share your grief." His smug tone hid his own grief remarkably well. Losing Yvonne seemed secondary to his need to justify himself.

She took his card anyway. It said he specialized in personal injury cases.

"Don't sit by the phone, Mr. Fine, at home or in your car. And please don't drop by again either. I don't want to share anything with you." She ignored his outstretched hand. He'd probably hug her if she'd let him.

"You should work on your denial or it will hurt you more than feeling the grief honestly. I won't bother you at your place of residence. But you do work in an establishment open to the public. I may need to talk to more of Yvonne's friends at work, so don't over-react if you see me again. I won't be there to bother you." His soothing tone didn't match his angry eyes or the force with which he'd jammed his spurned hand into his pants pocket. Busy street or not, she didn't want to turn her back on him to unlock her building's door.

She gambled that the red Toyota with Jersey plates parked in front of the hydrant at the corner was his. "Maybe you should get back to Jersey before the traffic, Mr. Fine. I hope you find some solace there. But I don't have any to offer you."

He muttered something about the need to control as he wrenched the Toyota's door open.

She didn't cross the street to her own building until his car growled around the corner of Bleecker Street. She pulled both doors tightly closed behind her before walking upstairs.

If Barney Fine had a car phone, why had he used her buzzer instead?

# Chapter Eleven

Fifteen minutes of conversation with Barney and the five-flight climb to her apartment had soaked Rose again. Her towels still hadn't dried yet from the first shower. Tossing the sundress into the hamper, she imagined the cool green lawns and fountains around the Absokan reservoir upstate and pictured some lucky soul bicycling across the bridge watching the water's level drop the tiniest bit. August in New York didn't inspire water conservation, despite the cheery public-service ads.

Sitting around your apartment attempting to resolve who had killed your friend didn't require a major fashion statement. The extra-large man's tank top she wrestled out of the closet worked as a short dress. Loose clothes were supposed to feel cooler. Cool heads thought better.

She held that thought and, when Butler called a moment later, she agreed to his gruff suggestion that they meet for a quick dinner in a few hours. He'd be working late but wanted to eat some decent food to keep himself going.

Too bad she wasn't inspired to pack a gingham-lined picnic basket with wholesome homemade treats. He'd had peach pie for breakfast yesterday, for God's sake.

Rose sat at her desk and transcribed everything she could remember of her conversation with Barney. Then she tried to make a list of the facts she could extrapolate from his whining self-justification. It was a short list. Barney had certainly attempted to cover himself, over-explaining both his whereabouts and his motives. He just hadn't made her believe him.

She rearranged and reexamined her skimpy inventory of information, then wondered if Butler would add anything to her knowledge. Maybe she could trade him her rolling-pin clue for some alibi assessment. She might need a real rolling pin to make him tell her anything about Nick.

She didn't dare call the Sixth Precinct to see if they had allowed Nick to leave last night. No one answered when she called Nick's number. So much for going to the source.

When she started a separate page of notes on Nick, not even her authorial eye could classify its contents as objective. How could she convince Butler of Nick's innocence when she couldn't prove it? Maybe Nick's alibi had already erased him from Butler's suspect list. She needed to know.

If only during Ken's botched tribute, Yvonne had been a topic at today's staff meeting. Rose made another list of people at My World who had worked with Yvonne. While her job as bookkeeper had given her at least minimal contact with everyone on the staff, through the paychecks she wrote if nothing else, a dispute over hours worked or taxes withheld didn't seem an adequate motive for what someone had done to Yvonne.

But Yvonne had also issued the suppliers' checks and computed the profit/cost ratios for bar and food sales. Funny business wasn't limited to comedy clubs. Restaurants were rife with theft, although Rose hadn't seen signs of it at My World. Maybe Yvonne had seen something, though, something serious enough to cost her life.

Rose wanted to talk to Nick almost as much as she wanted to talk to Butler. She hoped the couple had talked about both their jobs, not just Nick's work.

"Where do you want to eat? I'll get out of here in twenty minutes." Butler's voice sounded very cool on the phone. She suggested Mitali West, and he agreed without any of their usual restaurant negotiation. Spicy food might stimulate her thought processes, although his voice had warned her not to anticipate its aphrodisiac effects tonight.

Thin-strapped sandals, a cotton bra, and a wide belt transformed her shirt into a more stylish dress. She didn't know what would transform their dinner into a pleasant meal. Maybe they should get a table for four. Nick and Terri would join them for dinner, however invisibly. But so would Yvonne, and Barney, everyone at My World, and everybody else Yvonne knew. She should have requested a banquet room.

Tourists and locals seeking relief from the heat crowded Bleecker Street. A promiscuous musk scented the humid air, as if damp sheets tented the city. Minimal clothing, slow strolling, assessing stares, and enough come-hither glances to mimic old Forty-Second Street. Sex swirled through the air. Prudent constraints melted in the heat of an August night.

She saw Butler leaning in the doorway next to Lafayette Bakery and waved while she waited to cross the street.

"Nice bra, Rose. Glad everybody in the neighborhood had a chance to admire it."

"Sorry I forgot to do a modesty check before I left the house. The armholes on this thing are pretty low, I guess. Don't worry, though, you're the only one I've bestowed my waves on tonight." She caught a slight smile as he opened the restaurant door.

They ordered vegetable samosas, chicken biryani, lamb vindaloo, pooris, raita, and mango chutney. When Butler insisted she have a glass of wine and asked for iced tea in a martyr's tone, she knew his workday hadn't ended yet. He loved beer with Indian food.

"Stop scheming how to get me to open up, please. I know we gotta talk. I have a huge caseload right now, and Yvonne is more than just another file. I even thought about giving her case to somebody else, but I can handle it, even with the personal slant. And I want to be the one to put that guy away."

"What guy?" She jumped at the opening.

"Forget the interrogation routine. It's my job, remember? We're talking about something else now."

Forget her boyfriend as willing collaborator. She wondered if piling all the hottest sauces on his plate while withholding the soothing raita would torture him into sharing what he knew.

"What have you found out so far?" She spooned more coriander chutney onto his plate.

"Go back into journalism if you want to interview somebody. I wanted to see you, not hear you examine me." He shook his head. "I guess you have a right to know, but I don't have that much to tell. Somebody whapped Yvonne on the back of her head with a piece of wood. We found some splinters. Plenty of wood in Nick's studio. It all looks clean, so the killer took the weapon out of there. You saw what he did after he hit her."

He reached for the raita. "Woman in the loft

downstairs heard Nick and Yvonne yelling at each other the night before and again on the day she died. Nick has a half-baked alibi about going out to a marble supplier in Long Island City. Claims he wandered around the yard but didn't buy anything. Guy in the office there saw him, but has no idea what time he appeared or how long he stayed."

She burned her lips on a samosa but didn't say anything to distract him.

He let his samosa cool. "Then there's Yvonne's ex, who has a story about his day more detailed than my logbook. Maybe too much detail. And we're talking to your coworkers again, but nobody's said anything interesting yet. You may see some staff turnover, though. Couple of people had the sense to start feeling nervous about working in a place where three employees died in the last year. Don't think anybody's called OSHA yet, though."

She laughed longer than the wisecrack merited— anything to encourage him into volunteering more information. Then she told him about the missing rolling pin and her visit from Barney Fine.

"Makes sense. We'll look for it, but I doubt the guy put it away in Yvonne's hope chest or took it home as a trophy. If we're lucky, he might have tossed it somewhere in the neighborhood where the garbage guys haven't gotten it yet. I'll have the empty lots and dumpsters searched; should be a real pleasure in this weather. And I'll tell Barney Fine he isn't doing himself any good by bothering you."

"I can—"

"Take care of yourself. I know, Rose, I know. But I'd tell him not to bother you even if I'd just met you on the case. He's out of line. Maybe he's more broken up behind all that psychobabble than I figured." Butler forked the last samosa onto his plate and finished it before their main course arrived. Then he served her twice as much biryani and curry as she could imagine eating, leaving too little room on her plate for the condiments she craved.

"Did they find any prints in the plaster or anywhere?"

"Creep used gloves when he applied the plaster, probably the whole time. Our prints might still show up from Sunday night, but so far the only identifiable prints belonged to Yvonne. And Nick, of course."

She spooned half of the biryani back into the serving dish and ladled raita and chutney in its place. She kept the raita bowl next to her plate. "You still suspect Nick?"

"Yeah, he seems the most likely to me. The fact that you're wild about him doesn't prove his innocence."

She dropped her fork. "Wild?"

"I'm getting to it. I admit I acted stupid yesterday. Can't just blame it on thinking you were in harm's way, either. Something else set me off when I saw him holding you." Butler pushed his plate away.

"I don't know who made me madder last night—you or my own damn self. Your stepping between the two of us lit my fuse real fast. I've decided you wanted to protect me from my own stupidity more than you wanted to protect him. I don't want to know if I'm wrong."

"You're not wrong, Frank."

He pushed the serving plates to the side of the table and grasped her hand before he told her Terri had gone to high school with his younger sisters. She'd point out the spilled chutney soaking into his shirt's cuff in a minute.

The large bite of the incendiary vindaloo she'd just eaten scorched her lips. Her whole face reddened as Butler admitted that he'd dated Terri for a while after her boyfriend entered the seminary.

The damn curry was making her eyes water. "This hurts."

"C'mon, Rose. I wouldn't call it a big romance. Long time ago now, and I wouldn't even bother to tell you except I didn't want you to hear it from anybody else."

"Does Ken know?"

"I doubt it."

"Did you two sleep together?"

"We're talking more than twenty years ago. She wouldn't sleep with me then. Give it a rest before I'm sorry I told you."

Then?

She hated thinking that Terri had known something she didn't. She hated jealousy's paranoia even more.

"What did you do, pet heavily? Did you want to sleep with her?"

"Nah, of course not. What healthy horny kid would have been interested in a sweet and gorgeous girl like Terri?"

She made herself ignore the fond description, "Why didn't you tell me before?"

"It never came up."

She hadn't asked; he hadn't told. Whom else should she have inquired about? The nuns had talked about sins of omission and sins of commission. Silence could deceive as well as words.

How many angels could lie on the head of a pin?

She shook her head when the waiter asked if they wanted anything else. Butler threw his Visa card onto the check tray and handed it back to the waiter before she could pull her purse from beneath the table.

Duty called.

Bleecker Street's languorous heat had turned oppressive. Nothing good would flourish in this humid greenhouse.

"Are you still attracted to her?" Rose watched her

self-respect puddle like a witch in Oz.

Butler's sigh imitated the first gust of a tornado. "She reminds me of being young, back when everything seemed possible. She also knows how to pour on the flattery, and who hates that?"

The person who saved her creative lying for fiction instead of bolstering some archaic male ego?

Butler rolled his shirt sleeves higher.

She hoped it wasn't a cue to admire his biceps.

"Shoot me for wanting to shield you from some ancient history, but protecting people is what I do. Except you, of course. Anybody trying to protect you needs battle gear to defend himself from your attitude. Terri's so tiny and helpless somehow next to you."

Gargantua Leary tried not to respond to the accidental insults.

"Come on, Frank, women like Terri use helplessness like terrorists use uzis."

"This isn't about knocking Terri. It ever occur to you that someone could be genuinely sweet? Not everything is some kind of scheme."

"Mr. Trust speaks."

"You want honesty? I'm giving you honesty. Remind me to do it again real soon, since you make it so rewarding. The bottom line is that I'm not with Terri. I'm with you, God help me." He steered them off Bleecker onto West Tenth. "I worry she goes through a lot more with that husband of hers than she lets on."

"What a brave soul. Amazing that she chose him over you, isn't it?"

"Stop it. There's being funny and bitchy, and there's being a plain bitch. You're treading the line lately."

August nights had their mean side.

When they turned onto West Fourth, the

comparatively deserted quiet of the tree-lined blocks leading to her apartment didn't seem any more appealing than the busier blocks had.

Being in the dark didn't guarantee romance.

# Chapter Twelve

A car turning onto Charles Street blared its horn in emphatic violation of the neighborhood's anti-noise signs. The sound punctuated Butler's last accusation as it delayed her response. Two illegally parked moving vans blocked her view of the street's traffic.

The horn's noise hid the whirlwind's approach.

Insult became injury. Hard blows hammered the small of her back. Fists pounded her from every direction. Sharp kicks hit both knees. Tough hands slammed into her head. Arms yanked at her purse. The strap hanging across her chest cut into her neck. She struggled for balance beneath the torrent of assault.

The bodies moved so fast she couldn't count their assailants. Trying to defend herself, she punched wildly with her right arm while shielding her head with her left. Every kick she delivered in her silly strapped sandals hurt more. Too many bodies moved, moved too fast. She couldn't focus on a single fighter.

Rose saw angry young faces obscured by hooded sweatshirts. She heard only her own hard breathing and the sound of blows.

Then she heard Butler's voice curse his attackers and call her name. He fought in his own vortex five or six feet ahead, separated by more bodies whirling through the shadows. One jumped onto Butler's back. He hung on like an animated gargoyle, flailing at Butler's head with his free hand. Two more bodies struggled to pin Butler's arms. The human ornament on his right arm lifted off the ground as Butler swung at the boys gyrating in front of him.

Rose hit out blindly as she struggled to stay on her feet. She'd survived all the blows so far. Seeing Butler's battle explained why. Children attacked them, perhaps an army of children. The bodies swarming over them were small ones, their strength really in their number. If she was taller than any of these little monsters, Butler was their Gulliver.

The Lilliputians found their battle cry. A thin, high-pitched chant replaced the fight's curses and grunts.

"Get his bitch. Get his bitch. Get his bitch." The slogan's low volume intensified its viciousness. The sound seemed to bounce back onto her head from the sides of the moving vans barricading them from the street.

No.

Time for her best weapon. Rose brandished her voice in a banshee's scream. Her shriek flew at the attackers and circled above them. Apartment windows opened overhead as voices from on high called down. Two couples strolling a block away ran toward them. She heard more voices approaching from behind.

Then she didn't feel a thing. The attack stopped, its absence as eerie as its onset.

The pack of boys ran away toward Eighth Avenue. They'd reach the Fourteenth Street subway in minutes. Their bodies looked small in retreat.

She stumbled toward Butler. He started to sprint after the kids, yelling at them to halt for the police. He stopped after a few unbalanced paces and grabbed his right knee with a loud groan. Then she saw him reach for his gun, hesitate, and return it to the holster under his jacket.

He turned toward her, "Jesus, I can't shoot a kid in the back. You all right?"

"I think so. Nothing broken, and tell me you don't see any blood."

A knot of curious spectators and thwarted rescuers surrounded them now. Shiner or no shiner, she'd have to start wearing dark glasses to escape her neighbors' scrutiny. An old woman leaned out of a window above them and yelled that the police were on the way. Useless to announce the police were already here.

Rose took a quick physical inventory while Butler asked the spectators to leave, assured them no one was hurt, and flashed his badge at the two men who wanted to stay until the cops arrived. She felt battered to her bones and knew multicolored bruises would appear before morning. Minor injuries, and her purse still hung at her side.

Butler cradled her head for a moment, then ran his hands up and down her body scanning for injuries.

"You're all right, Rose." His reassurance lost the intended comfort when she considered the source. Scratches striped his neck, and thin lines of blood trickled down from both eyes. When he rubbed his right hand across his face, his scraped knuckles smeared more blood across his cheek. His best summer suit was destined for the ragbag unless NYPD fashion switched to the distressed look. The kids had ripped his jacket and pants in a dozen places; she didn't want to count the stains on his shirt.

Her own face felt damp with more than sweat. She saw blood on her right hand, too.

"How many of them, Frank?"

"Thirteen or fourteen, I think."

"It seemed like thousands."

"I got so damn caught up with you that I didn't see them coming. Three or four of them shoved me ahead, then more of the little bastards surrounded me. They hung off me like rotten fruit. I couldn't get to my gun, which might at least have scared some sense into them.

"The more I tried to get back to you, the more they swarmed me. Hitting 'em didn't register. Maybe whatever drugs they'd taken protected them. Robopunks."

"So we just survived the attack of the killer brats. How old were they?" None of them had looked old enough to shave.

"They were kids, safely in the juvenile category."

"It's a blessing they weren't armed." Her minor injuries hurt more seriously now.

"Yeah, a clever blessing at that. Who's gonna call a ten-year-old's hands deadly weapons?" Butler held out his own damaged hands.

"I can't believe they didn't get my purse after all that."

"They weren't after your purse; grabbing it would have been gravy. They were following me. The one on my back kept saying it into my ear, 'Get your bitch, get your bitch, get your bitch.' Nothing random about this attack. Mr. Greene isn't a misguided prankster anymore."

"I'd forgotten him. How do you figure he sent them?" The attack Saturday night seemed months ago.

"What were they wearing? Your fine fashion eye couldn't have missed that."

"Sweatshirts too hot for this weather, baggy shorts,

and status tennis shoes that felt more like hob-nailed boots when they hit my knees." She clutched the torn neckline of her shirt.

"Don't mention knees right now. Think about what you're describing."

She couldn't believe he would question her about an attack he'd witnessed at her side. His bloody face wore that expectant look, as if he were coaching the slow student through the catechism answers. She tried to picture the kids' costumes.

They'd attacked at the darkest section of the street, just under the trees' deepest shadows. She hadn't focused on a fashion critique but remembered over-sized hooded sweatshirts, big shorts, and shoes surprisingly small for the amount of pain they'd inflicted. She'd already mentioned all that.

"I give, Frank. What? Some explanation printed on their shirts I was too busy to read?"

"If you're admitting you don't know the answer, you must be hurt worse than I thought. Want to get checked out at St. Vincent's? You have me worried now." His smile looked grotesque on his bloody face.

"It was dark. Your knee up to chasing me after I kick you until you tell me what fashion statement proclaimed Mr. Greene sent the kids? Does he have his own label now or something?"

"Good. You're not in shock. You worried me. Figured if you didn't react to my riddle you really did need to go to St. Vincent's. Maybe I had more light. The boys were all wearing Mr. Greene's colors, all different shades of green. Guess his name finally went to his head."

The war paint on Butler's face shone an odd maroon as he solved the riddle. Streetlights always distorted colors into surreal shades. Color was the detail she hadn't registered; the attack had turned the world black and white.

So much for her value as an eyewitness. The writer's eye indeed.

"What are you going to do about it?"

"I'll talk to Mr. Greene about his work with kids in the community tomorrow. The guy's gone crazy. I can't arrest him on the basis of the kids' color choice, but he won't know that. Maybe he hopes going to jail will bring him closer to his beloved."

"Chivalry at its clumsiest." She gave up and let her neckline gape open. He'd already seen her bra tonight.

"They attacked you too. That ain't chivalry."

The arrival of a patrol car seemed to be her new welcome wagon. She could replace her doorbell's chime with a siren's wail soon. Still, she didn't want to meet all her boyfriend's colleagues on the job.

Butler muttered to the two officers who'd jumped out of the patrol car while she sat on the nearest stoop. A police spokesperson said. Let him tell the story for a change. She didn't like the characters, or their motivations.

The spectators and tardy Samaritans wandered away, their comments hushed by the rumble of the squad car's radio. She wanted to ask if they'd alerted the transit police. She wouldn't bother asking what the chances of apprehending the kids were, particularly if they'd had the sense, or experience, to scatter and lose the green sweatshirts.

Rose felt cool liquid dripping down from her scalp onto her neck. The Greene boys couldn't have shifted to an aerial attack, and their noise would have scattered any pigeons. If she'd sustained a terrible head injury, wouldn't she have felt it before now?

More liquid plopped onto her head when a loud

rattle sounded above. She twisted her aching neck to look up as the straining air-conditioner in the third floor window leaked again. She closed her eyes just before the water hit. It stung when it ran down her cheek.

Enough. Her apartment waited less than a block away. It had triple locks to keep her safe, an air-conditioner that would soothe rather than assault her, and clean water to wash away tonight's battle. All the comforts of the urban home. She wanted to be there now. Right now. When Rose stood, Butler spied her over the head of the officer he'd been briefing and walked to her side.

She yanked her neckline up. "I'm going home. If your guys have any questions for me, let them ask me now. Or you can interrogate me again later.

"Every inch of my skin feels filthy. I need to get home."

"Wait. You need to give Will here a quick description of what you saw, just for the record. Only take a minute. While he talks to you, I'll finish talking to the station over the radio. Then I'll walk you home."

Best not to question the effectiveness of his protective instinct.

The short, rotund Will hurried over at Butler's order. He asked simple questions and she gave simple answers, certain she didn't provide any new information. When he told her how much he wished he'd been there earlier to apprehend the kids, she stopped herself from asking how he could have run fast enough to catch them. The interview ended quickly.

When Will strolled back to the squad car, Butler turned and called that he just needed two more minutes. Sitting on the stoop again would require her to stand again. There were some aches she could avoid.

New pains and sore spots announced themselves as

she waited for Butler. Her impatience as his two minutes stretched into ten aggravated her injuries like peroxide on scratches. She could have made it home and into a tub bubbling with aloe vera by now.

When Butler finally finished his conversations over the radio and with the officers at the scene, she wanted to run home, to sprint up the stairs and lock the door behind her. Anybody else who wanted to attack would have to catch her first. She was in better shape than some of New York's finest.

Police escort notwithstanding, she looked over her shoulder four times in the slow half block to her apartment building. Butler's grimace and the slight roll to his walk as he favored his right knee hobbled her pace more than her own aches. God forbid he admit he was hurt and request she slow down.

Almost there. She stopped herself from another paranoid backward glance. "I'm too old for ring around the rosie, especially if I'm the maypole. I wanted a hot bath, but this heat makes one redundant. Standing still out here supplies the same effect, except maybe the relaxation aspect." She saw him hesitate at her building's stairs, then turn to survey the streets in all directions.

"Your knee that bad?"

"I want to be sure Greene doesn't have any more gremlins lurking around. Just because they've been following me doesn't mean they have to know where you live. Tell me nobody's been trailing you, please."

"Not as far as I know." Her guarded denial sounded inconclusive. Too much she didn't know these days.

Anybody watching them climb the five flights to her apartment would have mistaken them for a pair of aged arthritics anyway.

He paused on the third floor landing and groaned,

"Fucking youth."

"Spare me the world-going-to-hell lecture, okay? This night's been bad enough."

"I'm not worried about the state of the world right now. I'm pissed because they won't feel a thing tomorrow while we're going to hurt like bastards."

"Or bitches." The Greene boys hadn't been the first to attack her tonight.

She'd secured the second lock on her apartment door before he spoke again, "Any ice cream left?"

"You want to eat it or use it for an ice pack? We can always run out for some if we need more."

"Run, Rose?"

"Limp, Frank?"

He didn't smile until she reminded him that plenty of delis delivered. They'd each have to pick at least two flavors to satisfy the minimum delivery charge.

"Or we could order a pint of every flavor they have and stay home until it's all gone. At least promise me we can do something boring next time I see you."

Would avoiding the topic of Terri count as boring?

She walked into the bathroom and gingerly rinsed her face and hands in cool water. She wouldn't wake up any prettier tomorrow, but she wouldn't have any permanent scars either. Smoothing aloe vera gel over her face and neck, she heard Butler splashing water in the kitchen sink. She carried the jar of gel into the kitchen. "Want some first aid?"

"Can I drink it? No bandages, please." So now he didn't plan on going back to work tonight.

Rose opened the fridge and grabbed a bottle of fume blanc as Butler reached for two wine glasses from the shelf overhead. She brandished the point of the corkscrew at him when he tried to take it. "I'm the bartender, remember?"

"So that means I'm the only detective?"

She flicked open the foil-cutter and ran her finger slowly up and down its tiny blade before opening the bottle. "Never."

He smiled broadly and held out his wineglass. "I always knew you were a dangerous woman, Rose Leary, although I wasn't thinking about brat-gang attacks."

"What were you thinking about?" She filled both glasses and gulped a decidedly undainty swallow of wine. "You going to withhold information from me on this too?"

His tone turned serious, "No."

"Too bad, I was looking forward to prying it out of you." She wiggled the corkscrew at him.

"Maybe you should examine the evidence instead. Closely."

He didn't complain when she leaned against his knees to kiss him. And he seemed quite agile when he stood to embrace her. She'd administer the aloe later.

# Chapter Thirteen

"Long sleeves in this weather? Dabbling in bad drugs again, dearest? We may all want some before closing. Ken is outdoing himself with his communication skills tonight. Even his t-shirt has a cheery message."

She'd known her long-sleeved shirt wouldn't escape Jimmy's keen fashion eye. "What does Ken's shirt say, Jimmy? And it's lovely to see you tonight too."

"'He who dies with the most toys wins.' New heights of taste, no? Not only dated, but arguably inappropriate for the employer of a murder victim. Let's pray My World isn't one of the toys he plans on taking to his—please God—imminent grave. And Terri's doing another K-mart version of a Palm Beach socialite. I feel as if I'm scouting for Mr. Blackwell here."

"Maybe Ken bought the shirt at an estate sale in Aspen." She wished the four people at Jimmy's two tables didn't appear so contented. Where were demanding customers when she wanted them?

A horde of parched and famished regulars guaranteeing fifty percent tips wouldn't have distracted Jimmy tonight. "But how are you? Were your days off peaceful and restorative? Detective Wonderful solved the case yet?"

She'd tell him about the Greene boys later. "Awful, not quite, and not to my knowledge. Laura ran off to a rehearsal the minute I appeared. It looks like she spent most of the day going over her lines instead of stocking the bar."

"Your continuing patience at Laura's incompetence astonishes me."

"It's not patience; it's resignation. What can I do about a woman who thinks it's rude to cut fruit in front of customers?" Rose had learned the futility of complaining to Laura months ago. The woman would devote hours of chatty attention to a lingering lunch customer, then act surprised that the bar hadn't miraculously stocked itself.

"Flattering character assessment aside, you know I want to talk to you about Yvonne's murder. We did so well on the last unfortunate deaths here. Even more, I want to know how you are, Rose." Jimmy picked limp lemon twists out of the garnish tray at the service station while he waited for her reply.

"I'm fine for somebody working in a madhouse, but I'm going to be pouring conceptual drinks during the dinner rush if you don't let me get ready here." The slow hours between the lunch and cocktail rushes allowed plenty of time to prepare for the busier night. Maybe Laura thought the nightshift had a prop master.

Following a day bartender who'd left her no back-up orange juice, insufficient cut fruit, and at least a dozen missing bottles of liquor for the night's business didn't produce the equanimity required to watch Jimmy align the cherries' stems so that they all pointed toward the cash register. "Please stop playing with my damn fruit. Cut me some lemon twists if you can't find anything better to do."

"Just hand me the ice pick, dearest. Then may I silently watch your bar while you do the stocking so necessary for your psychic health? Laura did seem unusually distracted today, but at least she was civil." Jimmy wiped a droplet of cherry juice off his square pewter cufflink.

"Civility didn't stock the bar. Laura's so concerned about being an actress, maybe she'd do better if we told her to act like a bartender. I'll be back in a minute." Patience indeed.

Well vodka and gin, Dewars, Myers, grenadine, three quarts of orange juice, several stacks of bevnaps, and two boxes of sip-straws. She made a mental list as she headed downstairs to the liquor and storage rooms. Add some limes and lemons, which she could grab from the kitchen. Bananas too, for the daiquiris Ken claimed made the perfect summer drink, although nobody had ordered his banana-chocolate special yet. Maybe she'd get a demerit for poor sales skills at the next staff meeting.

Guilty amusement widened her smile when she reached the open office door and saw Ken sitting at a desk heaped with restaurant marketing magazines and sloppy stacks of invoices. Jimmy hadn't mentioned that the letters on Ken's t-shirt were shiny silver or that his pants were bright yellow. Very bright.

"Sorry to disturb you, Ken, but I need the key to the liquor room. Laura—uh—I need a few things for the bar." A good team player didn't complain.

"Absolutely." He removed the key from a large ring at his waist and tossed it to her. "I'll be there in a minute in case you want help carrying anything upstairs. You go on ahead and take what you need. If I can't trust my bartenders, who can I trust, right?"

Right.

She unlocked the door to a liquor room that did not

overflow with temptation. The sparsely stocked shelves looked like a store in its last hour of business, after weeks of drastic reductions. She needed three bottles of the house vodka; the shelf held one. The rum and bourbon shelves displayed only 151-proof rum and a dusty decorative bottle of a bourbon so expensive no one without a cigar collection ever ordered it. Laura couldn't have stocked the bar out of this room even if she'd tried.

Propping the door open with a gallon jar of maraschino cherries, Rose checked the hall and delivery area for an enormous liquor order. No reassuring stack of cartons anywhere.

This futile errand had taken far too long already. Her bar could become busy while she searched for the missing bottles. She hurried back to the liquor room, determined to grab what she could and return upstairs to pour it.

Ken stood in the middle of the liquor room with a clipboard in his hand.

"Sorry about the low stock. Deliveries got, uh, delayed this week, thanks to the mess Yvonne left us in. Have a special order coming in tomorrow, though, so we'll make it. I got plenty of creme de cacao and creme de banana here. Take some extra upstairs and move some of my specials tonight. Everything's an opportunity, I always say."

"Necessity is the mother of inebriation, huh, Ken?" When he didn't reply, she started loading an empty milk crate with the few bottles she could find.

"Need help carrying that upstairs?"

"Afraid not."

He looked puzzled, then laughed. "Well, I promise you'll need some muscle tomorrow night."

She couldn't bring herself to say she hoped he was right.

"Hey, you're a creative person, right? Being a writer and all. So let's see you put some of that creativity to work for me upstairs tonight. Give 'em a few new drinks, push the stuff we have the most of. Profit is where you find it, so let's go for silver-lining time."

Better silver lining than silver script. Ken's t-shirt collection might be his own version of Bartlett's Quotations.

"I've been meaning to ask you about your writing, Rose. You do mysteries, right? Terri always tapes *Murder She Wrote*, and I sure miss that old *Columbo*, although I did think a guy in his position should dress better."

He leaned against the doorjamb. "What I wonder is where you get your ideas? You get a lot of material from the restaurant here? People tell bartenders lots of stuff, right? And that cop you date, seems like a nice guy, he tell you a lot about his cases, give you the inside dirt on things? Like, for instance, he learn anything about who killed Yvonne yet?" Ken blocked the liquor-room door while he questioned her.

She shifted the weight of the loaded milk crate while she lied, "We try to keep our private lives separate from our work. I'd love to talk with you about my writing, but I'm afraid I should hurry back to the bar now. Maybe we can chat later. Excuse me."

He looked at her a moment before stepping out of her way. "Sure, business before pleasure. It's a hard lesson, but an important one, right?"

"Very important." The box had grown heavier while she'd listened to him. But asking for help in carrying it upstairs would prolong the conversation, or interrogation. Subtlety wasn't Ken's strength. Nor was honesty hers after the egregious lie she'd manufactured about her relationship with Butler. Unless the lie was less mortal because it described what Butler wished were the truth.

Thank God he hadn't heard her little white lie.

Several customers occupied barstools when she returned to the bar. All but two of them had drinks, and even that elegant pair had bevnaps promising imminent beverages in front of them. Jimmy rushed through the dining room attempting to take care of the four tables that had arrived in her absence.

She left the crate at the service end of the bar and walked to the sixtyish couple who probably would have received their cocktails already if they'd stayed on the Upper East Side. "Sorry for the delay. What would you like?"

"That's perfectly fine, dear. The charming young man who was just here said you'd return in a moment. We'd like two old-fashioneds, please, as soon as you have the opportunity. No need to rush now."

Her quick survey of the bar while she sliced an orange and muddled bitters and sugar over the fruit showed none of My World's regulars. At least none of these strangers would have been surprised by Jimmy's special touch. Each drink he'd served rested upon an artfully arranged pair of bevnaps, with the second napkin placed over the first to form a festive eight-pointed star. The single bevnaps under the drinks she'd served earlier looked forlorn in comparison. While Jimmy might not have rung up any of the drinks, he had arranged each customer's proffered cash precisely parallel with the edge of the bar. She'd know he'd opened the register if the coins jumbled in their compartments all faced up.

He waited for her at the service end.

"Bar looks great, Jimmy, thanks. Are you slammed?"

"Not quite, but thank God I don't have to make my own drinks now. Ready?" He spieled off a long drink order, then handed her a list of what he'd served at the bar. "I didn't take any money. Didn't have the time, or the desire to go into your register. I'm awfully glad you've returned to the bar, dearest."

She shook four margaritas, mixed three seabreezes, stirred two martinis, then opened the beers and mineral waters he'd ordered.

"I'll cut you some fresher fruit as soon as I put everything away. These limes and twists look exhausted. And try to steer our guests away from vodka beverages if possible. We have a limited supply this evening."

Jimmy stopped aligning the cocktail straws into the three o'clock position.

"All vodka?"

"Just the cheap stuff." She brandished the sole bottle of well vodka she'd found downstairs.

He sniffed. "My customers don't drink cheap, darling. Premium or death."

"I love that attitude," Ken announced as he handed her a large bunch of spotted bananas. "These soft ones blend up real well in case you can move some of my specials. I call 'em chocobanos. We gotta be extra diligent about our costs here now. And I have that high-octane rum downstairs, which we could make go a long way. Guess Yvonne hadn't developed a taste for it yet."

"Excuse me, Miss? When you have a moment?" Mr. Old Fashioned summoned her with a peremptory wave. She caught Jimmy's quizzical look over Ken's shoulder before she walked to her customers.

"Sorry, dear, it's my fault for not mentioning it. But my wife and I like extra bitters in our cocktails. Good for the stomach, you know. Would you be kind enough to splash a little more in these?"

"Certainly, sir. Extra bitters." She watched Ken stroll downstairs while she remixed the drinks. His speculation about his dead employee's preference in alcohol didn't disappear with him. It hadn't sounded like an innocent remark.

Jimmy waited at the service station again. "Give me a Stoli gibson up and two bloodies, one with no salt. Then tell me what Ken meant by that little snipe."

"Stoli bloodies?"

"Certainly, although they'll never taste the difference. Why was Ken discussing Yvonne's taste in liquor?"

Rose filled a martini glass with ice and water to chill it. "Ken may have attempted subtlety. There's almost nothing in the liquor room; his desk is piled with bills; his bookkeeper is dead. I think Ken's trying to lay some financial problems at Yvonne's grave."

"You don't think she—" Jimmy fluffed the fronds on the celery stalks garnishing the bloody marys.

"No, I don't, but I think Ken wants us to suspect her of something beyond carelessness. He's dropping hints like bowling balls." She stirred the liquor in the shaker, watching the cold condensation dull the metal.

"Figures. What other sport does he base his wardrobe on? Perhaps he'll suggest league night at My World soon. But what kind of hints?" Jimmy rejected five cocktail onions before one met his standards.

"I think he's trying to accuse Yvonne of getting the restaurant into financial trouble. Liquor companies don't stop deliveries on a whim. And I know Ken placed the order this week, 'cause he asked me how long I thought it would take us to sell the five cases of white zinfandel he'd just ordered for the discount."

"I trust you told him forever and a day, dearest."

She emptied the martini glass, then strained the cocktail into it. "Right. The point is that if we didn't get a delivery it must mean that the bills weren't paid for a while. None of the distributors would stop delivery to the Victors a minute before they had to. And paying the liquor bills is a huge priority in a place like this. If the liquor bills weren't paid, what else hasn't been?"

"Payroll, such as it is, has been right on time." Jimmy slipped the chosen onion into the drink.

"So far, but there's a week and a half before the next payroll. Who's going to write those checks? Ken?" Rose checked to see if any of her customers needed anything. Spending all her time talking to Jimmy wouldn't fatten her tip jar.

"Oh dear, would the bank honor checks scrawled in crayon?"

"Depends on what the account holds. Banks don't bounce checks 'cause of bad style."

"Whyever not? Although I'm showing less than sterling waiter behavior myself right now. Better deliver these drinks before the ice melts or the vodka warms. We'll talk later." Jimmy grabbed more bevnaps and fanned them.

"I'm sure we will. Perhaps I'll chat with a few of my customers first, though. They don't tip solely on the quality of the cocktails, remember." Wondering where all the regulars were, Rose surveyed the bar and braced herself for more talk about the weather than she wanted to indulge in.

Yes, it sure was hot. And it was the humidity that got you. Infernal heat as icebreaker, a bartender's dream.

The topic's usefulness melted quickly as she mixed two more bitter old-fashioneds and listened to how ghastly and silly, really, it had been to schedule a paint job at the Rhode Island cottage for August. The appalling fumes would drive anyone away, and even Yale students didn't work as hard as they used to. Rose agreed that exploring the city in August was certainly an amusing adventure and marveled that they hadn't worn pith helmets to venture so far to the west and south. Everyone who counted must indeed have deserted the Upper East Side.

Yes, she did pride herself on her mixologist's skills, thank you. But she unfortunately didn't have the time to work private parties, sorry. Maybe that explained the dollar tip they left on a twenty-dollar bar tab before strolling off to find that cute little courtyard bar he used to take the girls to on college breaks. Despite the wretched tip, Rose hoped he'd find his initials still carved on one of Chumley's tables.

Back to meteorology. The three guys from Colorado had never experienced anything like this heat since their tours in Nam. Icy beers sure did help though.

The dining room and bar remained unusually calm for 8:00 on a Wednesday. The August heat hurt business as much as it fascinated tourists. She'd get a decent drinking crowd later, but the first two hours of her shift hadn't broken any profit records. And she'd yet to sell a chocolate-banana concoction. More black marks in the office.

Ken appeared upstairs just as Barney Fine walked into My World. Ken hurried to the bar's service end, waving at Barney to join him. "How you doing, buddy? Feeling better than the last time we talked, I hope." Ken spoke as if years, instead of a day, had elapsed. Barney shrugged, then sat on the barstool next to Ken.

"Rose, you know Mr. Barney Fine, uh, Esquire, right? Did you two get together yesterday? Let me buy poor Barney here a drink."

She couldn't refuse to serve Barney when her boss offered to host him. Probably not the best time for a tirade about giving staff phone numbers to strangers, either.

Registering her displeasure now could start an ugly scene, not what tonight's slow bar needed. Barney put the yellow legal pad he carried and a Bic pen on the bar before him as if he'd want notes on an expected argument. She couldn't decipher his tiny angular script upside down. Looked as if he wrote a lot in all caps, though.

Barney smirked when she asked what he wanted. "Seven and seven, please, Rosie. Good to see you again. You having a better day today?"

"Just fine, Mr. Fine. How's the grief process going?"

"Shit, Rose, that's not a professional bartender's attitude. Your job is to make people forget their troubles, not remind them of their problems. Make me a greyhound, top-shelf. Try to show Barney a smile." Ken didn't speak quietly.

Presto, you're a dog. Not very professional behavior for a manager, either, letting his reprimand carry halfway down the bar. She poured Ken's drink, trying to ignore her customers' curiosity and Barney's wide complacent smile, as if he could have forgotten the death of his ex-wife two days ago if only a snippy bartender hadn't reminded him of the tragedy.

Damn quick processing, that.

Rose stretched her fake smile as she listened to Ken lower his voice and apologize to Barney, entreating him to understand how everybody at the restaurant still felt shook up at losing one of the team.

"I can relate, Ken. It still hurts me too. Doesn't seem right that Yvonne should die just when I wanted to acknowledge the hurt I'd done her in the past, talk with her about a new start. Higher power time, man." Barney drained half his drink.

Just what program was he in?

"You're both right; it's a terrible loss to all of us.

Would it help you to acknowledge that hurt to us, Barney?" She softened her smile, leaned over the bar toward him, and oozed her voice into supportive and sympathetic concern. Presto again, shrew into perfect woman. Terri would have been proud.

"I knew there was a good person hiding inside that angry woman I saw yesterday. I appreciate your concern." Barney waved magnanimously toward his empty glass and Ken's half-full one.

Yessir, born to serve.

"Tell us about it if it'll help you, Barney." She'd made his second drink twice as strong as his first.

"Now that's the My World spirit." She doubted Ken meant her egregious over-pour. His obsession with new beverage concepts apparently blinded him to the actual proportions of a drink.

Barney took a fortifying gulp. "I'm in a program that helps me with my feelings now. But I will tell you that I was a very angry person when I was married to Yvonne. She didn't know how to help me with that anger, so some things happened that weren't good. I might have acted different if she'd known how to help with my problem. Instead, she always made it worse instead of better."

He was acknowledging his hurt, all right. Smug hurt. She wondered how much comfort his acknowledgments would have given Yvonne.

"Not that everything was her fault, of course. I admit to my mistakes, and I wanted Yvonne to hear that. I tried over and over to make her meet me. I really needed to see her face again. She had to want to see me, too. But the last time I talked to her, she said that bruiser she lived with didn't want her anywhere near me, as if our marriage was his business. Then the asshole hung up on me the last time I called." Barney folded his straw into a rough square.

"When was that, Barney?" She tried to inject sympathy into her voice.

"Your boyfriend's already grilled me, hon. But I don't have a problem with telling you it was Monday morning. So I didn't even have the chance to say good-bye to her, or enjoy a last slice of her perfect pie. Mr. Insecure Artist made sure of that. I wonder what else he made sure of."

"Did you call her from home or from your car?"

Ken interrupted, willing to spring for another free drink if it would encourage a Nick-bashing partner. "I never liked that bastard. Thinks he's better than everybody else. Can we get you one more, pal?"

Rose made Barney's third drink as strong as his second. She might hear something useful if she listened to them instead of defending Nick. Questioning someone else's motivations seemed preferable to examining her new protective urges.

Three new customers wanting drink suggestions took her away from the men's conversation. She hurried through the what-do-you-like routine with the newcomers until she saw Jimmy standing at the service station. He'd eavesdrop on Barney and Ken for her.

The newcomers settled on two margaritas straight up and one on the rocks. At least they all agreed when she suggested shaken not blended and Herradura tequila. The blender's roar would have interrupted Ken and Barney. In a perfect world, no bars would include blenders, no customers would request slush, and nobody would ever regret lost opportunities to eavesdrop on Ken and Barney. So much for perfection.

She made the drinks Jimmy ordered, ignoring his raised eyebrows and sidelong glance at Ken. She'd expected a more subtle signal.

Cutting lemon twists during this lull gave her an

excuse to stand near the two men without participating in their conversation. She arranged three lemons and the bar knife on the small cutting board at the service station, cut both ends off each lemon, and stood the fruit in a row on the board. She pretended not to see Barney's startled expression when she pulled the icepick out from under the bar.

# Chapter Fourteen

Sliding the point under a lemon's skin, Rose circled the pick through the white of the rind until the denuded fruit slipped out of its yellow collar. She stripped the other two lemons, sliced and flattened the three cylinders, then cut them into strips. She inhaled the sharp smell of the zest like a restorative drug.

Barney spoke more distinctly than when he'd first arrived, as if enunciation erased alcohol's effects. "Yeah, it's funny when you think how I spend my career fighting insurance companies for my clients. Much as I hate to profit from a tragedy, Yvonne and I did take out life insurance when we got married, mostly 'cause my mother wouldn't shut up until we did. I'll tell you, Ken, I'm not ashamed to admit my practice could use an infusion of cash right now."

"I hear that." Ken gestured at Rose for another round.

Barney guzzled his new drink before continuing. "So I'll call the company tomorrow, or maybe next week would be better. You don't think that damn boyfriend would have made her change the beneficiary, do you?"

"Why not, the bastard lived off her while she was alive, didn't he? Maybe he wanted a big chunk of money all at once instead. Give him more of that artistic freedom you hear about." Ken smirked

Rose couldn't stop herself. "Excuse me Ken, but didn't you know Nick worked construction every few months, then lived off the money as long as he could? He even bought all of Yvonne's books last semester. She didn't want him to, but he insisted. Textbooks aren't cheap, as I'm sure you remember."

Vodka had encouraged Ken's democratic impulses enough so that he didn't complain about her intruding on their conversation. "That doesn't make him a saint. And a couple of books isn't my idea of a good provider. Maybe you writers see that different, though."

"Or maybe the artists just stick together, huh, Ken? When I was married to Yvonne, she bitched more about the bills than books. Thanks for the information, though, Rose. Anything else you want to enlighten us on?" The anger in Barney's voice didn't indicate that the program he attended boasted a stellar success rate.

"No. Sorry, I should check on my other customers now." The ones who were actually spending money.

She refreshed a few cocktails, told the guys from Colorado to be sure to come back for a nightcap after they'd explored the Village, and saw Barney waving his credit card at her like a distress signal. When she handed Barney his check, Ken grabbed it, insisting the drinks had been his pleasure during this tough time for Barney.

Ken and Barney exchanged business cards like two prepubescents adjusting their bra straps. Neither of them soiled her bar with a tip. She didn't reply when Barney said he'd see her soon.

"Well, time for some paperwork downstairs. Buzz

me if you need me." Ken walked a very straight line to the stairs. Two customers stepped out of his way.

She hadn't finished wiping the rings from Ken and Barney's drinks off the bar before Jimmy returned to the service station.

"Need anything, handsome?"

"Not unless you want to go onto the floor and help the busser replenish everybody's water glasses for the fifteenth time. I'm going to pour ice water over the next person who asks me for more *agua*." Jimmy fussed with the garnish tray again.

"So we won't get rich tonight. What did Ken and Barney say while I was busy?"

"Busy, Rose?

"Momentarily occupied, Jimmy."

"Those two had a delightfully edifying conversation. Were you aware that Nick is a faggot artist and a fucking asshole who probably killed Yvonne in a fit of artistic temper?"

"Temperament?" Rose laughed.

"Ken selected the word temper. What did Nick ever do to those two?" Jimmy scanned the dining room, then sighed as if he'd already known none of his customers needed him.

"Well, he lived with Barney's ex and made her a lot happier than Barney did, not something many men accept gracefully. I don't know what Ken has against Nick, but he's trying hard to blame him for Yvonne's death. He wanted to question me about it downstairs, maybe hoping to enlist me in his lynch mob." She'd finally discovered a leadership role suited to Ken's talents.

"We don't see Barney running off to any grief groups, do we, Rose?"

"The bank's more likely." She told Jimmy about

Yvonne's life insurance. "I just pray Yvonne had changed her beneficiary, even though I doubt Nick would want any money from her death. Try explaining that concept to Ken."

Jimmy asked her who Butler suspected.

Maybe Rose shouldn't hope Yvonne had named Nick her beneficiary. Butler might not choose heartfelt congratulations for his first words if he heard Nick would profit from the murder.

She detested the image of Butler standing alongside Ken and Barney to accuse Nick. She knew she'd have to do something besides positive visualization to erase the picture.

Rose couldn't believe Nick was Yvonne's killer. His work convinced her of his innocence. So who was?

"Dollar for your thoughts and three Rolling Rocks. Table ten just put enough salt on everything they ordered that I might even sell them a second round if the busser doesn't replenish their water glasses every five seconds." Jimmy controlled his enthusiasm at the prospect of selling more cheap beers.

She put the Rolling Rocks in front of him. "Then deliver these right away so you don't lose your title of highest-selling waiter. Ken's probably compiling everyone's sales figures even as we speak."

Jimmy placed the beers on a tray in a perfect triangle. "Ah yes, Ken and higher mathematics. I wonder if he's sober enough to remember to carry his ones. Thanks."

Jimmy delivered the beers, smoothly cleared the half-empty water glasses off the table, and waved the busboy away when he approached with replacements. He cruised the dining room before returning to the bar. "Not a damn order from anyone. The bright side is that now you can tell me why you look so pensive."

"Just thinking that I'd rather be concentrating on plotting my new novel than planning *Finding Yvonne's Killer* as the subtitle for my *How I Spent My Summer Vacation* essay. My World may not have been the smartest choice for my plan to bartend so I'd have the time to write fiction. Don't even think about suggesting I switch to true crime, no matter how much material this place offers."

"Remember how good the money usually is here." Jimmy raised his right hand and rubbed his thumb against his first two fingers. "Is this where I ask you how your book is coming along, and then you tell me you don't want to talk about it?"

Rose nodded. She didn't like talking about a book in progress at the best of times. Not even her most creative fictional skills could portray this month as even resembling a good one. Forget best.

Proust hadn't meant the hours wasted trying to find a killer when he wrote about lost time. James hadn't searched for any culprit scarier than a misplaced comma. The dull-witted were Austen's worst villains.

"I need new role models, Jimmy." She laughed when he volunteered.

"I suppose it's out of the question for you to do your job, or jobs, and let your boyfriend do his? Not that I wouldn't adore assisting you in the amateur detective shtick again, but not if the prospect makes you look this glum. You're flirting with frown lines here. We could always let the officials pursue justice this one time."

"Are you expecting a next time?" Rose shuddered at her own question.

"No, dearest, I only meant that your boyfriend and his cohorts must possess some competence at this justice thing, so let them have at it."

"Yvonne isn't Frank's only case." She didn't know if

she meant to defend Butler or just hoard criticizing him for herself.

Jimmy's voice oozed pity. "So you're dating someone who can't do more than one thing at a time?"

"Stop. I wish you'd drop this irrational hostility." She didn't share her own very rational hostility toward Butler.

"Irrational? Just because the man treated me like a worm when I dated one of his precious officers a few times, as if it were my fault gay cops were contaminating the manly purity of New York's finest."

"Frank doesn't give a damn about the heterosexual purity of the force. Have you forgotten that what really bothered Frank was listening to the officer in question complain about his broken heart when you dropped him after the third date?"

"He wrote poetry. Bad poetry."

"Haiku." She remembered.

"Haiku, then. Bad haiku."

"You dated him."

"And I dumped him, as kindly as I could, when he started calling me every morning to read his latest work into my answering machine. Early in the morning. The one that compared me to a nightstick did it."

She giggled, asked him if he remembered the poem, and laughed again when he insisted he'd struggled to forget it. "So maybe you weren't a heartless cad after all. You want me to tell Frank what really happened?"

"God, no. There's no reason to humiliate me or my poor blue bard like that. Can't you think of something better to discuss with your inamorato?"

"I can think of a thousand topics, a million subjects." Ninety-nine percent of which Butler would refuse to discuss, of course.

"Then go to it, Ms. Scherazade. Just eliminate me

from the potential character list if you would. The detective won't even notice my absence."

"Probably not." She checked the bar again for needy customers.

"Do I detect an experienced tone? Somebody else you're not discussing with your boyfriend?"

Rose cocked her head toward the dining room. "Table ten looks thirsty. The disappearing water trick worked."

Jimmy buffed his fingernails on his shirt. "The concerned bartender routine didn't. I might have thought we were just passing the time in idle chatter if you hadn't sunk to that charmingly evasive tactic. Now I know I'm onto something. Tell."

"I'll open the beers as soon as you call the order. She shoved four more Rolling Rocks into the ice bin.

"Think about whatever you're hiding while I'm gone, Rose."

# Chapter Fifteen

Jimmy's self-image would shatter if she told him how much he sounded like Butler. He'd better change his tone before he reached his tables. "Can I get you anything?" shouldn't sound like an interrogation.

He must have dropped the serve-and-protect act in time. "Three more inexpensive beers, please. Want to tell me what your boyfriend's doing these days that's more important than finding Yvonne's killer?"

"I haven't talked to him since late last night, or early this morning. For all I know, he's busy chasing little green people around the city."

"Will you explain the green people comment or shall I just assume it's another Irish manifestation of delirium tremens? I'll return immediately, I'm afraid." He hadn't served a new table in an hour.

She described the Greene boys' attacks when Jimmy returned to the service station. His sympathy exacerbated the vague aches she'd been trying to ignore all day. Her scratches stung again at his incredulity that she hadn't mentioned the incident earlier.

"I know it only happened last night, but it feels more

like last week. I worried about wearing something to work that would hide the scratches, but I swear I haven't thought about it since I got here."

He patted her hand. "You can't pretend it didn't happen, or that it was just a nightmare."

"I know. I'm just more worried about Yvonne than I am about a gang of punks." And her bad-dreams file didn't have room for any new entries.

He stared at her. "Odd, I'm wondering if the bereaved Nick might not be the object of your worries. You certainly rushed to defend his good name. Are you sure there isn't trouble in paradise with your detective? I didn't overlook your saying that you hadn't spoken to him all day."

The prospect of confiding her recent worries to Jimmy only tempted Rose until she realized she'd have to include her embarrassing jealousy of Terri. She didn't want to see Jimmy's face if she shared that insecurity. She didn't even want to see her own face when she entertained it.

"It's his pesky job, I guess. Imagine a cop being busy in New York in August."

"So he couldn't say good-bye this morning? Since when does fighting crime eliminate a lover's delightful farewell? I thought heteros cared about that stuff."

"If he'd woken me up when he left, you'd call him inconsiderate." No need to mention the five minutes she'd wasted looking for a note. "Why don't you try to sell some desserts now? Ken would be so pleased."

If that didn't distract Jimmy, she could offer to let him pick at the thin scabs on her arms.

She'd give anything for a horde of tourists, even budget-minded tourists, now. No one had walked into the bar for the last hour, and the few customers already there wouldn't break any consumption records. She couldn't blame news of Yvonne's death for killing business like this. After poring over the *Times*, *News*, and *Post* the last two days, Rose knew Yvonne's death hadn't made the papers. Somebody would have mentioned any television coverage.

At least Ken hadn't sent out a press release. Yet.

Word of Yvonne's death might keep the regular customers away. Gossip spread quickly in the West Village, with or without media attention. But ninety percent of My World's regular customers had never met the bookkeeper. Yvonne almost never worked in the restaurant at night, and she'd spent most of her days downstairs in the office. If her friends hadn't frequented My World when Yvonne lived, they wouldn't stay away because she'd died.

It was simply a slow late-summer night. Everyone who could escape Manhattan in August did. She'd make more money tomorrow. At least the murder groupies who had descended on My World after the deaths last winter hadn't returned to besiege her again.

She hoped Ken didn't sit downstairs plotting how to use Yvonne's death for free publicity. If tonight were any indication, he'd better re-examine his marketing plans.

A group of acting students from H-B Studio came in just before 1:00 and filled up a third of the bar. Rose hadn't finished making their drinks before she overheard the prettiest of the women ask the most gorgeous of the men what he'd thought of her scene tonight. Seven or eight voices projected minireviews at a volume that made the bar seem very crowded very fast. She knew they wouldn't spend much, ordering half of another round at the most, but they didn't require any but the most basic attention from her either. Pour the drinks and let them emote.

Ken came upstairs twenty minutes after the actors' arrival, his eyes puffed with sleep and his shirt creased with a nap's lines. His musky after-shave fought the minty mouthwash he must have gargled. She'd seen the gym bag he kept next to his desk in the office and heard it clink with toiletries.

Morning, Ken.

"Sounds lively up here. Been this happening all night? I've been concentrating on my paperwork downstairs. You could have called me if you needed help. Seen Terri yet? Give me the phone, lemme see if she's coming by." He lazily surveyed the women at the end of the bar as he dialed.

Maybe he hadn't woken up enough yet to notice the empty dining room already set for tomorrow's lunch or the noises of an early breakdown coming from the kitchen. While both kitchen and dining room would stay open for business until 2:00, Jimmy had finished everything but his last-minute paperwork and sat folding napkins at one of the many empty tables. Ward had let the salad man order the kitchen-closing round of beers twenty minutes ago. The crew had probably stored all the food and scrubbed everything by now. Rose foresaw a mass staff exodus at 2:05.

She didn't relish the prospect of spending the hour-and-a-half until last call at 3:30 with no one but Ken and the actors for company. She doubted Jimmy would want to stay with her. Right, please keep me company, and please do memorize this list of off-limit topics.

Ken handed her the phone across the bar, "Funny, no answer. Ter must have headed this way already." He looked at the group of actors with regret, then announced he wanted something to eat and walked into the kitchen.

Ward's raised voice reached the bar. Ken walked out of the kitchen and sat at Jimmy's table. His elbow knocked half the napkins Jimmy had folded to the floor. Jimmy stood, retrieved the napkins, and set a place for Ken with exaggerated formality.

Ward delivered Ken's spinach salad, then came to the bar.

"Balls. Let me have a special orange juice, love."

She filled a tall glass with half orange juice and half Cuervo Gold and gave it to the angry chef. The Victors didn't want any kitchen staff drinking on duty, but Ken insisted the chef could drink whenever he wanted. The prospect of unlimited free booze didn't seem to tempt Ward, or to lessen his contempt for Ken.

"The one time I thought I could send the boys home early and get my salary costs down, this idiot decides he wants a late-night snack. Salad, and then a special pasta with cream and cheese and tomatoes and everything we've already put in the bloody walk-in, but not until he's finished with his salad, mind you. He thought it was funny to insist on eating what he called the regular American way, having his salad first." Ward gulped his drink. "The blighter actually asked me for 'that rice thing,' as if I would start risotto at this hour. Hell, it may take me as long to make his effin' pasta."

"Slow nights are always the hardest, Ward." She wouldn't want to taste anything the chef made in this mood.

"Right you are. Ever notice how slow nights always end up to be the longest ones, too? Fill this again and I'll go see if I have any bologna instead of prosciutto for his majesty."

The kitchen crew all left by the front instead of the back door five minutes later, no doubt following Ward's instructions to make their exit as obvious as possible. If the chef did wait to make Ken a special dessert, she didn't want to speculate about what ingredients he'd use.

The last customers in the dining room left, and

Jimmy escaped downstairs to finish his paperwork. She prayed Ken would stay at his table alone and that he'd chew each bite 100 times. She added a quick apology to Ward to her wish.

The nine actors wanted two more beers and eight waters. Great, more glasses to wash.

"Night, Ms. Rose. Ward said he'd clear Ken's place when he finally finished his marathon meal. I'm out of here. Sorry I couldn't sell enough to make this more." Jimmy handed her a few folded bills, the waiter's ten percent for the bartender that wouldn't amount to much tonight. His tone warned her not to ask him to stay.

Only another hour now. The thing about bartending was that you could never predict business. You could know what to expect, but never know for certain how a shift would be. A slim chance still existed that the bar would fill up with bartenders and servers from other restaurants. She could make more in tips in the last hour than she'd made all night. Maybe.

If other places in the neighborhood had suffered the same slow business as My World tonight, hordes of disheartened men and women carrying crumpled white shirts in their shoulder bags could be heading toward My World for their after-work cocktails right now, more than willing to spend their meager tips in the last hour before the bars closed.

Her bar could fill up any minute now. The Prize Patrol could also arrive to tell her the seven magazines she'd subscribed to and the thousands of stamps she'd licked had worked. She started wiping bottles and cleaning the speed racks.

Ken still hadn't finished his salad. The fuss about his meal reminded her she was hungry. She wouldn't dare ask Ward for anything and tried to remember what she had at home. She decided on Zito's whole wheat bread with fresh mozzarella from Murray's and the beefsteak tomatoes and basil from Butler's sister's garden in New Jersey. Too bad if he wasn't around to share them. He had his own kitchen.

Rose started to break down the service station. The noise of the hot water pouring into the ice bin must have covered the sound of the front door opening. She looked up when Ken's loud "God dammit" silenced the actors' chatter.

Nick stood just inside the door, paralyzed into one of his own sculptures. His big frame had lost at least ten pounds. Sleepless smudges darkened the blue of his eyes into black. Grief had etched his mouth and cheekbones into sharp relief, as if he'd taken the chisel one too many times to his face. White smears Rose didn't want to see covered his jeans. Sweat stains thickened the dirt on his work shirt.

The actors became audience as Ken threw down his napkin and stalked toward Nick.

"Ken, why don't you and Nick talk down at this end?" She'd be damned if she'd let Ken give the group another scene to criticize.

Ken glared at her and the expectant actors. "Of course I wouldn't disturb our guests, Rose."

Nick shambled down the bar to meet Ken.

"You're not welcome here, buddy. The free ride is over. You want to walk out nicely or you want me to throw you out?" Ken tried to look tough. He needed an acting coach.

Nick's shoulders tensed, but his expression didn't change as he looked down at Ken. The actors' end of the bar remained silent. Rose smelled Nick's sweat during the long moments before he replied. "I don't want any trouble, Ken. I just want to talk to Rose."

"Do it on her time, then, not mine. Out or I call the cops." Ken's stance could have been a boxer's, or he could have been standing on the tips of his toes.

Nick looked down at him for another long minute, shrugged his shoulders, and walked out.

Rose hurried toward the door. Ken blocked her way. "Don't even think about going after him. The crazy bastard might hurt you. If you go after him, I'll call the cops and tell 'em Nick is stalking you."

His bullying tone didn't cow her. She just didn't want to run after Nick quite as much as she wanted Ken to stop this scene. She didn't want Ken to call the cops. She didn't even want him to explain how she could run after someone who was stalking her.

She walked back behind the bar as Ken strolled over and apologized to the actors for the unpleasantness, addressing his explanation to the woman with the largest breasts. Terri would have hated to see her husband's cleavage-directed chivalry.

The actors left just before Ward delivered Ken's pasta. The chef ground fresh pepper onto the plate from an obsequious stance and offered to sprinkle hot sauce onto the dish from a bottle he pulled out of his pants pocket. When Ken lifted the fork to his mouth, Ward moved behind Ken and pantomimed bashing his skull in with the pepper mill.

Time to kill this night.

# Chapter Sixteen

Ken shot the bolt behind her the minute Rose closed My World's front door. She'd cleaned the bar, done her paperwork, and deposited the money before he'd finished his pasta. He hadn't argued when she'd refused his offer to escort her home as soon as he'd finished his dessert.

She hadn't left work alone in months. If Butler didn't appear just before last call, Jimmy or another waiter would linger until she could leave. If all else failed, the porter saw her safely into a cab. But Eduardo hadn't arrived yet tonight, and she couldn't bear the prospect of waiting in the empty restaurant while Ken finished his meal.

The Victors would never have watched her walk out the front door alone at 4:20 in the morning. They'd be horrified if they ever heard that Ken had. She wished again that My World's owners would hurry back from Italy. Grief wasn't an exclusively European experience.

In another hour, the block would grow busy with men unloading carcasses from meat trucks, their tan jackets quickly staining with blood in the early morning. But the street was deserted now. She'd be halfway home by the time she found a cab. She'd still grab the first one she saw.

A beer can skittered across the first loading dock she passed, clanging like little footsteps. She moved into the middle of the street. Better to be mistaken for a lunatic than a victim. She hurried toward the avenue, listening for approaching vehicles.

Any vehicles, not just Mr. Greene's mysterious brown van.

A deep glass of Pinot Grigio joined her early-morning menu. She'd ice the wine while she took a long, cool shower.

She didn't hear a car coming up behind her. She heard footsteps, heavy rushing footsteps. Rushing to overtake her. Rose started to run, too scared to look back at her pursuer.

"Wait, it's me." She didn't recognize the man's shout. Me could be anyone. She ran faster. The aches from last night's attack ran with her. So did the fear.

Her pursuer drew closer. She'd have to stand and fight in a minute. Better than suffering an attack from behind.

She breathed deeper, trying for the breath to scream.

The footsteps stopped. Or maybe her pursuer had finally matched her rhythm. Rose ran as fast as she could.

A garbage truck turned the corner and stopped at the first building. The garbage men looked at her before they threw trash bags into the truck. If she called them sanitation workers, they might help her. If she needed help.

She ran toward the rumbling truck and the men in weightlifters' belts. Her heroes.

"You okay, lady? It's too hot already to jog." A stocky redhead in a green uniform ambled toward her.

"Rose, it's Nick. Stop." She stopped, gasped that she

was fine to her would-be rescuer, and turned to look at Nick a hundred feet behind her. His long legs covered the distance in a quick walk, as if he feared running would send her sprinting off again.

The redhead crossed his arms against his chest and leaned against the truck's front bumper while his partners loaded trash. "You know this guy? He okay?"

When she answered yes to both questions, he yelled to his partners that it was just another fucking lovers' quarrel, at this hour no less. Crazy damn neighborhood.

She still felt his eyes on her back while she gasped for air and waited for Nick. She didn't waste her breath protesting Nick wasn't her lover. "Jesus, Nick, you scared me half to death."

"I didn't want to frighten you, Rose." He stopped a careful six feet away. "I need to talk to you, but I didn't mean to make Ken give you any grief."

Grief, he'd said, not trouble. It was what she saw when she looked at him. "Where have you been tonight?"

"I tried to work, once the cops let me back into my studio. Then I went to some friends' loft till about midnight and walked around, hoping that walking might make me tired enough to sleep." He spoke slowly in a flat voice, as if describing someone else's night.

"I didn't plan to end up at My World. I've been waiting for you since Ken threw me out." His gaunt face shone under the streetlamp, a thin layer of sweat emphasizing the pallor exertion hadn't banished.

Most of her breath had returned. "You're almost as scary standing here as you were thundering up behind me. Did you eat at your friends'?"

"They kept trying to feed me, but I wasn't hungry."

"Did you eat today?" Easier to question him about nutrition than to throw her arms around him in the sweaty hug he really needed.

"I didn't want anything from our kitchen. Food doesn't matter. Can we talk about Yvonne? I need to talk about her with somebody. I've been thinking all night you were the one. You were one of the last people she saw, and talked to, and then you found her." He still stood too far away.

She wanted to talk with him, but where? It was too hot for a long walk, and the park benches were occupied by people whose sleep she wouldn't disturb. Nick didn't frighten her now that her heart had almost stopping racing. She'd already learned the hard way about letting men she didn't know extremely well into her apartment.

Rose studied him while she considered alternatives. "You need food. Tiffany's is open twenty-four hours, and their air-conditioner almost makes up for the food itself."

He agreed and they walked to Sheridan Square in silence, as if they'd struck a deal not to talk without eating first. Worrying about exactly what they'd talk about mocked the concept of a companionable silence.

Neither of them offered the requisite remark about breakfast at Tiffany's as they entered the large coffee shop off Sheridan Square. The Tiffany II on West Fourth Street didn't offer any understated elegance, and its décor lacked even a hint of robin's egg blue. Bright lights ricocheted off the posters of Greece; heavy china and silver clattered; the waitresses spoke to customers in hearty tones and bellowed their orders to the kitchen. The menu offered food to fuel farmers through long days of heavy work. Most of the clientele appeared between 2:00 and 6:00 a.m.

Few of the customers looked as if their days had just begun.

No one gave Nick a second glance. Half the people in here might not have slept or eaten in days.

Technicolor pies topped with ludicrously high meringue rotated in a tall display at the end of the counter. A light snack here meant cottage cheese instead of fries.

Four giggling women left a window table, their flawless hair, impeccable makeup, and willowy figures in crisp cotton sheaths proclaiming they were en route to a fashion shoot. Their high heels tapped the floor as they swayed toward the door.

Rose didn't bother to torture herself by comparing their perfection to the disheveled reflection she'd glimpsed in an entry mirror. It was a West Village maxim. If it looked too good to be true, particularly in the late night or early morning hours, it was. Four very beautiful men had just left the restaurant.

Nick looked at the glossy menu as if it were written in Greek. He nodded when the waitress asked if they wanted coffee, then dropped the menu and told Rose nothing sounded good. The waitress sniffed as if she'd personally designed the menu and would cook the food. Rose ordered steak with three scrambled eggs, home fries, wheat toast, and a large orange juice for him, then a Greek salad with extra olives for herself. Fat and salt weren't the issues here.

"More olives cost two bucks extra, babe. It's a side order." The waitress tapped the point of her pen against her pad.

"Fine." Rose took a sip of coffee, pushed the mug away, and added an iced tea to her order.

"What do you want to ask me, Nick?" So much for small talk.

"Do you know who killed my girl?" He stared into her eyes.

Remembering the scratches on Butler's car, she flinched.

"Don't look at me like I'm a sexist dog, please. The

Guerilla Girls will vouch for me, even if I am from a Plains state. Yvonne liked it when I called her my girl. That matters more than any pc bull."

When their food arrived. Nick's hands reduced the scale of his huge breakfast platter. Her side order contained six olives.

"I don't know who killed her. I didn't see anything when I found her that told me who the murderer is, except that he's a very sick soul. Or she." Rose nibbled a precious olive.

"Your boyfriend thinks I did it. He's wrong." Nick started eating his breakfast as if a clean plate could prove innocence.

Wishing she could tell Nick he'd misjudged Butler, Rose attacked her salad, pepperoncini first. She speared feta and lettuce on her fork to soothe the pepper's bite. Criticizing Butler suddenly felt disloyal.

"So who do you think did it?" Rose covered her mug with her hand when the waitress brought more coffee.

"Did you think Ken was out of line tonight, Rose?

"Of course. Who wouldn't?"

"He hates me, you know. He's just using Yvonne's death to treat me like shit." Nick poured sugar into his coffee.

"Why does he hate you?"

"Because he knows I think he's lower than dirt. He also worries about how much Yvonne might have told me." Nick kept stirring his coffee, clinking the spoon against the thick mug.

"Told you about what?" Jesus, she was starting to sound like Butler, firing questions at every opportunity.

"Their affair." Nick almost whispered the words.

She fought to keep tea from sputtering across the table. "Yvonne and Ken? No."

"Yeah, Yvonne and Ken. We had a tough time early this summer. I got so hung up in my work, trying to get a piece into Storm King, I didn't pay her enough—shit—any attention." Nick pushed eggs around his plate.

"Ken went after Yvonne the week he and Terri came to town. He chased her like a hound dog. She let him catch her."

"I never knew. I doubt anybody at My World did." Jimmy would have mentioned it if he'd suspected.

"It didn't last long. Cheating wasn't Yvonne's style. She had to confess. She said she couldn't believe the weird relief of being with someone who only saw the surface layer of things." Nick shook his head. "Shit, that jerk probably hasn't thought about structure since tinker toys. I had the sense not to tell her that, at least."

She couldn't think of a single comforting word. Nick didn't give her long to try.

"It wasn't easy, but we got over it. Yvonne never accused me, but I knew I deserved part of the blame. I ignored her so much when I worked that I never even suspected she was having an affair till she told me. She could be gone for hours and hours and I wouldn't even ask."

"Blaming yourself won't help now." Nick's news seemed to have transformed her voice again. Her imitation of a self-help book didn't sound any better than her Butler act.

Nick rubbed his big hand across his eyes. "We were talking about getting married next year."

Easier to think of Yvonne planning a wedding than an assignation with Ken. But Yvonne had already planned another wedding, to Barney. The two men drinking together tonight had shared a bond Rose couldn't have imagined.

She hadn't known Yvonne very well. At all.

"I'm sorry, Nick. Did you tell Frank about this?"

"I couldn't. It's too private, and not fair to Yvonne." Nick pushed his plate away, as if surprised to see it empty. He'd eaten so methodically that she doubted he'd tasted anything. He shook his head when she offered him her remaining salad.

"You think I should have?"

"Yeah. The cops will look at Ken very differently if they know about the affair."

"I've thought about that. Information is their material, like stone and metal are mine. I might have told Frank tonight if we hadn't had that scene." Nick wiped his hands on his jeans.

Oh God. "What scene?"

"I told you I tried to work earlier. I found this beautiful piece of marble a few months ago. It cost way more than I could afford, but I had to have it, with no fucking idea what for. Once I lugged it home, I knew it was for Yvonne. I wanted to sculpt her, show her once and for all how beautiful she was. Damn, she'd make me so crazy sometimes, calling herself fat and talking about losing weight."

Nick scrubbed at his eyes again. "So I tried to work on it tonight, but I kept fucking up, cutting all wrong. It just looked dead to me, like something in a graveyard, some awful monument to the dead. My work looked like a tombstone.

"I lost it. Threw my chisel across the studio and attacked the piece with my hammer. That's when Frank appeared."

She considered Butler's impeccable timing as Nick described ignoring the buzzer downstairs, then hearing the elevator door clang open after Butler remembered the code and rode upstairs.

"So I ran to the door with the hammer in my hand. Frank followed me back into the studio and saw the mess. He asked me if I hadn't done enough damage already. Frank had a lot more questions, too, going over and over where I was Monday. How could I talk about something so personal with a guy who suspects every word I say is a lie?"

All she'd had to suffer through was an annoying night at work. She couldn't apologize for Butler. She wanted to defend his behavior but didn't know how.

"You have to tell Frank. Did Terri know?" If Terri did, had she already shared her sad betrayal with Butler? Did they have another secret?

"Yvonne never said. I didn't ask." He shrugged.

Would this new knowledge make Butler view Terri with more suspicion or sympathy?

"You have to tell him, Nick."

Nick looked at her pleadingly for a minute. "All right, I'll call him later today. Unless you might?"

"Nope, sorry." She didn't even try to explain what a bad idea it would be for her to deliver this news to Butler.

"Ken could have done it. Yvonne said a few things that sounded like he might have fooled around with the books. Later, she got all excited about writing a paper on small-business theft, so maybe Ken thought she'd expose him." Nick straightened his shoulders. "Or maybe Terri, if she knew Ken had betrayed her. I can't think of anybody else who'd have any reason to hurt Yvonne. I sure as hell didn't."

"I believe you, but I'm not the one you need to convince. Why don't you go sleep a few hours, then call Frank?" She'd ask him about Barney and about the books another time.

Nick insisted on paying the check, and Rose left a larger tip than the service warranted. Graveyard at Tiffany's couldn't be an easy shift.

She thanked Nick for breakfast and told him she'd walk herself home. West Fourth Street lightened with the start of another hazy, smoggy day. Determined joggers, early dog-walkers, and Wall Street-bound suits moved through the humid early-morning streets as if the day had begun bright and clear.

"It's only a few blocks. Let me walk you, then I'll go home and try to sleep." Nick looked even more exhausted outside than he had in the coffee shop's bright light.

She agreed. An argument would take longer than walking home with him.

When they reached the spot where the Greene boys had attacked, Rose shivered and whirled to look nervously behind them. Nick put his arm around her shoulder and pulled her closer. She let herself feel comforted by his protective gesture for half a block, then wiggled out of his hold when a patrol car passed. He grinned down at her, but didn't ask what crime she'd been hiding. She walked a little faster. No point in telling him about the Greene boys now.

At her building, Nick asked her to wait a minute before going upstairs. He ran halfway down the block, reached under a parked van, and returned with a bulky parcel wrapped in newspaper.

"Here. Too many flowers came today. They should be for the living, right? Yvonne would want you to enjoy these."

Thorns pricked at her hand as she unwrapped the top of the heavy bundle. She hadn't expected such a strong scent of roses. She saw at least two dozen flowers, creamy white tinged with the faintest pink, surrounded by dark green ferns.

A bride's flowers.

"Just take them, please. But let's not talk about them." Nick hesitated, then leaned down to give her a quick kiss on the forehead. "Thanks. I gotta go now. I'll call you."

He stood on the sidewalk until she closed the street door behind her. She walked upstairs slowly, tired from the long hours of a slow night, her frightened run, and their strange breakfast. The flowers felt heavier than they should.

She heard her phone ringing while she unlocked her door. Before she could reach it, the machine recorded a loud slam of the receiver as the caller's only message. A message from Butler at 4:30, a more brusque call at 5:00, and a terse "what the hell" at 6:15 all asked her to call as soon as she got in.

She put the flowers on the drainboard and unwrapped the layers of newspaper, plastic wrap, and saturated paper towels. Carefully steadying herself, she climbed on a chair to reach for her largest crystal vase, then hacked off the stems' bottoms with a carving knife, too tired to cut them properly under running water.

The bedroom clock showed 6:45 when she centered the vase on her dresser. She told herself it was too late, or early, to call Butler, but she knew it wasn't true. He'd rather have her disturb his sleep than wonder where she'd been. Or worry.

She should call.

She didn't need to hide having breakfast with Nick. She could tell Butler that Nick had more to tell him without specifying what it was. She could even mention that Nick had received so many flowers he'd given her some.

What she couldn't tell Butler was why Nick had

hidden the flowers near her house when he hadn't planned to see her tonight. Or how she still felt Nick's arm around her shoulders.

The stock from Butler had started to smell again, too.

# Chapter Seventeen

She woke to the smell of roses and a jangling phone. Her bedside clock's big hand and little hand both pointed straight up.

"Tell me you didn't go to a damn after-hours club." Butler didn't bother with a greeting.

"Morning, darling." Rose stretched and slid out of bed.

"Walk home the long way last night? The Hoboken route?"

"No, I was starving and went for some breakfast. Bad night at work." She walked into the kitchen, then described Barney's visit and his interest in Yvonne's insurance policy while she filled the coffeemaker with beans and ran the water until it chilled her wrist. She raised her voice when the grinder started.

"Jesus, you renovating the kitchen?"

"Just making coffee, which I desperately need." Probably not as much as Butler needed her to volunteer the name of her breakfast companion. She couldn't believe he hadn't asked already.

"I bet. The reason I called is to tell you I'm taking

Sunday and Monday off, even if Jack the Ripper reappears this week. You want to call Catherine and see if her guest room's free? We could leave right after you finish work Saturday, make Great Barrington in two-and-a-half hours. She's what, about twenty minutes from there?"

He didn't wait for her answer. "A couple of hours' nap, and we'll have all Sunday afternoon, Sunday night, and Monday. Gotta be back Monday night, though. Ask Catherine who's playing Tanglewood Sunday night, and we can all go. We need to get away.

He didn't have to convince her. They both needed to walk in green grass, with sunburn the only threat and squashed mosquitoes the only dead bodies for miles. They needed to banter again instead of haggling over information and real or perceived threats.

"You're a genius, Frank." Since she set her novels in the Berkshires, she could do a little surreptitious research, on atmosphere if nothing else.

"And you're a brilliant judge of intelligence, Ms. Leary."

"Smart enough to know that you remember Catherine works in her restaurant Sunday nights, since we sent your friends there last weekend.

"So you'll have to listen to music under the stars with just me. You can talk to the people on the next blanket if you get bored. We'll go to Combray after the concert."

"Combray?"

"Catherine's restaurant. First we'll have a wonderful Tanglewood picnic to get us through the dull spots in the music."

She hadn't heard Butler laugh with pleasure in too long.

"Drink your coffee and call Catherine. Your friend Nick is coming in this afternoon, said he has to tell me something important. You know anything about that?"

They couldn't talk for ten minutes anymore without somebody's secrets intruding.

Better he heard it from her. "We had breakfast this morning. He needs to talk to you."

"Did he have his hammer with him?" The long sigh preceding Butler's question stamped his lost good humor with a large red fragile sign. A voice in the background shouted he had a visitor. He told Rose he needed to get back to work.

"I'm excited about the Berkshires, Frank."

"Right." He hung up.

She considered throwing her cup on the floor, then filled it with coffee and milk instead. Damned if she'd do penance by cutting her feet on the shards of a favorite cup. Penance for what? An innocent breakfast that she hadn't even kept secret?.

She took her coffee and phone to the easy chair by the front window and called Catherine. They'd met on a red-eye flight back from California three years ago, two displaced Californians living in New York. Halfway across the country, they'd decided they were actually displaced New Yorkers mistakenly born in California.

Like good natives, Rose and Catherine had emptied cases of California wine in hundreds of lunch and late-night sessions of what Catherine called The Joyfully Tragic Women's Club. Early this spring, Catherine had moved to Massachusetts full-time to start her restaurant. Rose still missed her friend almost every day.

Not a week passed that Catherine didn't beseech Rose to move to the Berkshires and collaborate on the cookbook that would make them both rich and famous enough for apartments in the city and houses in the "godforsaken" country.

The offer tempted Rose today. Recipes seemed easier than plots.

She called Catherine, left a message asking if the open invitation still stood and outlining Butler's travel plan, then asked what inanimate objects she wanted from the city. Catherine had requested kosher chickens on Rose's last visit. Live chickens. When Rose had refused to transport them, Catherine had offered to settle for any delivery boy with downy cheeks and tight buns. Rose had hated disappointing her friend twice in one visit.

The phone rang again as soon as she clicked it off. Wasn't this a productive day? Catherine must have run in from outside just in time to hear Rose's message. Rose checked to make sure her cup held enough coffee for a long chat.

"Tell me you've been seducing the neighbor boy who mows the lawn, rubbing buttercups on all his cheeks."

"Excuse me?" Rose couldn't place the voice but blushed at knowing it wasn't Catherine's. She recognized Terri's nervous giggle a second later.

Please God, anything but an emergency staff meeting.

She hadn't meant an invitation to lunch instead, much less a ladies' lunch.

"I'm playing hookie from work this afternoon. Ken's all crazy about his liquor orders, and I'd just be in his way. So many of my old friends have moved to the suburbs, I feel like a stranger right where I grew up. Sometimes I don't even know this neighborhood any more, but you seem so at home here. When I was thinking who would be fun to hang out with, I thought of you right away."

Breakfast with Nick, lunch with Terri, maybe she should see if Ken was free for an early dinner.

She told Terri she'd planned on writing this

afternoon.

"How can you concentrate on writing with everything that's going on now? I thought you and Yvonne were friends. Let's think of our lunch as in her honor. My treat."

Guilt, bribery, and a bland refusal to acknowledge any arguments. Rose might have underestimated Terri.

They agreed on 2:15 at Da Silvano's on Sixth Avenue. Terri would reserve a table.

Rose refused to look toward the precinct house as she crossed Tenth Street at Bleecker. Butler hated the long crinkled silk dress she wore anyway, saying she drowned in its black fullness. He'd laughed at her insistence the dress was chic, saying it made her look like an ancient Eastern European widow.

When she reached the restaurant, the dress made her look like Terri's negative image. Terri sat at an outside table, her white rayon suit silhouetting her figure in the shade of a Cinzano umbrella. Tiny and perfectly put together, Terri could have modeled for a wedding cake's bridal figurine.

Standing to air kiss Rose, she tugged at the suit's short skirt, slowly smoothing it down her thighs in their pale stockings. Her high-heeled white pumps brought her to Rose's height and the waiters' certain attention.

"Let's be bad girls and have wine. You don't have to be at work for hours and either do I. This is gonna be so much fun." Her skirt rode high on Terri's thighs as she wiggled back into her chair.

"Fine, as long as I can drink a lot of Pellegrino too." Her small smile might not promise as much fun as Terri expected.

Terri ordered the water along with the Bianco della Lega recommended by the waiter. She returned his professional flirtation eagerly, listened to his recitation of today's specials with rapt attention, then asked him if the carpaccio followed by angel hair with shrimp would make her happy. He swore it would make her ecstatic, but only nodded when Rose ordered a large insalata tricolore and the caprese she'd craved last night. Maybe he didn't like her dress either.

"I love Italian men, don't you?" Terri smiled as if the waiter's attention had crowned her Miss Universe. "Sometimes I tease Ken that not being Italian is the only tiny thing that keeps him from being totally perfect."

"Really?" Rose tried to keep the disbelief out of her voice.

"Of course I don't mean it, but it's important to make him think I do."

The wine was very good. Rose drank a greater than ladylike sip. "I missed the lesson on flattery in the Perfect Woman course. Actually, I missed the course."

"Frank's right, Rose, you do have a fun sense of humor. He told me this morning you and I should get to know each other better. I think his saying I should invite you to lunch was a stroke of genius. Frank always was smart, even when we were kids." Terri let a small smile play over her precisely lined lips. "And you're so smart, and pretty, and artistic. You two make a great couple. How did you meet?"

Terri didn't restrict her flattery to men. Eyes meeting over a corpse didn't qualify as the cute story appropriate for today's lunch.

"Ask Frank some time. He tells the story better than I do."

"But you're the writer."

"The way we met is more of a cop's story." And police report.

The waiter presented their plates with a flourish,

wielding the pepper mill as if it were an extension of his most private body.

The tip of Terri's tongue protruded through her glossy lips as she cut the pink meat on her plate. "Okay, then, will it upset you if I ask about Yvonne? I need to talk about it to someone. Ken just clams up and looks mad if I even mention her name. She seemed too sweet to get killed, although sometimes now I wonder if she was as innocent as she pretended. But I still don't believe her boyfriend is the creep Ken says he is."

"Why not?" Rose assembled the perfect forkful of tomatoes, basil, and smooth cheese.

"Because whenever I saw him his eyes followed Yvonne like she was the only woman in the world. Men don't do that unless they're really in love. 'Course, even men in love don't always do it. Weren't you friends with both of them?" Terri lifted three capers with her long nails and popped them into her mouth without touching her lips.

Terri's nails reminded Rose of pincers. She didn't feel any urge to share their food the way she and Catherine always did.

"I don't know Nick that well, and now I wonder how well I knew Yvonne. We were just starting a friendship outside of work."

"I thought you knew her better. Anyway, I hope we'll be friends outside of work too, Rose. I'm only your boss for a little while, but I hope Ken and I can stay in the city a long time. I'd love it if you could kind of show me the ropes. Everything's changed so much. You think we can be friends?"

Terri's eyes begged Rose to agree, minus the fluttering-eyelashes routine she'd lavished on the waiter. An expression of naked entreaty seemed to erase Terri's layers of carefully applied makeup until Rose remembered the same serious look on Veronica Lamb's face when they'd promised to be best friends forever in fourth grade. In fifth grade, Veronica devoted herself to the other girls whose mothers bought them training bras. Rose still hated undershirts.

"Frankie said he'd like it if we were friends." Terri giggled.

"Oh, in that case." Rose raised her glass in a toast and Terri beamed as she clinked it, as if Butler's wish had clinched it. At least Veronica Lamb hadn't mentioned boys. Specifically.

Terri emptied her glass without leaving any lipstick on the rim. "Terrific. Now I can ask you like a friend, not an employee. Has Ken seemed weird to you lately?"

If Rose cut her mozzarella into pieces any smaller, it would look grated. Admitting that Terri's husband had always seemed strange might not be the first confidence her new friend expected.

Honesty versus tact. Information instead of insult.

"How do you mean?" She refilled Terri's wineglass.

"Well, moving to the city was a big adjustment for him. It's hard to be a stranger in town, 'specially when Ken's real used to knowing everybody wherever he is. We've always lived on his turf before.

"Plus, running My World is a huge responsibility. Ken says it's his shot at the big leagues. He's gotta make good here."

Terri pushed her plate away. She'd eaten exactly half of her carpaccio. "But something else must be wrong. He looks at me sometimes like he doesn't know who I am. He used to like Yvonne, and he felt sorry for her for being fat. Since she died, he doesn't have a good word to say about her. Not one."

Terri dabbed the inner corners her eyes with her napkin. "He even told me not to waste my tears on her. When I told Ken about a doctor I saw on Merv Griffin who said people can get mad at a person for dying, he looked at me like I was a monster. Then he slammed out of the house and was gone for hours. When he did come home, he slept on the couch." Terri whispered the last five words as the waiter approached with their second courses.

She thanked him as if he'd just delivered a plate of pearls, but waited until he'd walked away before she continued, "That's not like him. I make it my business to know my husband real good, and that's not Ken."

"Maybe all the pressure got to him and he took it out on you." It sounded like a good girlfriend's comment.

"Nah. I know what that's about; this is different. The other thing? He spends a whole lot of time alone now. He used to go out with the boys a lot, but suddenly he's a loner? I ask him where he's been and he says just walking around by himself, trying to learn New York." Terri picked the shrimp out of her pasta. "He's a people person. I don't get it."

Rose dipped her third piece of bread into the olive oil, then sprinkled salt onto it. "Being around people all day and all night in a restaurant can make solitude seem pretty attractive."

"Ken's been in the business for years. So why the sudden need for solitude?" Terri's tone sharpened with each question she asked.

Because his interpretation of solitude involved at least one other woman. They weren't good enough girlfriends for Rose to break the news about Ken's affair with Yvonne. Please, God, don't let Terri ask her about another woman. Or women. Rose remembered the buxom actress at My World last night.

"Listen to me, ruining our first lunch together with my complaints. I'll figure it out. I still think he's hiding something about Yvonne, but my husband doesn't keep his secrets secret for long." Terri caught the waiter's eye and asked him if he could tempt her with anything wonderful for dessert.

He tried, but both women ordered only double espressos. The waiter brought them extra biscotti.

"Ah, girls' speedballs." Rose admired the crema on her coffee, reluctant to disturb the thick golden surface.

Terri looked at her quizzically.

"Coffee and white wine. We used to call them girls' speedballs, a more delicate version of the heroin and cocaine combination." Her espresso tasted even better than it looked.

"I knew what a speedball was, Rose. A friend of Tommy's used to love them. But I like our version better."

"Tommy?"

"Didn't you know I dated Thomas Victors in high school? Uncle Joe—at least I always called him Uncle cause he was so good to me and Mom—used to joke he'd walk me down the aisle, then go sit on the groom's side."

"Were you engaged to Thomas?"

"Nah, I knew that wouldn't happen. It made more sense when he went into the Jesuits. He never really looked at me that way, ya know?" Terri still sounded surprised that any man had resisted her carefully tended charms.

The waiter brought two tiny glasses of Vin Santo with his compliments. Rose drained hers in a single ungirlish gulp. "Do you have any idea what Ken might be hiding about Yvonne? What does your wife's intuition tell you?"

Terri sipped her sweet wine, signaled for the check, and applied lipstick with a concentration that ignored Rose's question. She blotted her lips on a tissue she pulled from an embroidered packet in her white purse. "It's getting late, and we're both working women. Can I ask you something personal before we go?"

Maybe she'd needed to fortify herself with lipstick before sharing her suspicions about Yvonne and Ken. A perfect face lent strength.

Rose nodded and braced herself.

Terri lowered her voice, "Where do you shop? I know my clothes aren't right for the city anymore. What worked in Colorado looks silly here. You want to go shopping with me?" She asked it as if suggesting the ultimate intimacy.

Too relieved to think of an excuse, Rose agreed.

"Terrif. Before we go, I want to tell you how happy I am to see you and Frank together. He cares for you, really cares. I don't think I've seen him this happy since—well, in a long time." Terri beamed.

Exactly how happy had Butler seemed when talking to Terri this morning, and why he hadn't mentioned their little chat? Wasn't it supposed to have been a very long time since Butler had seen Terri before her return to New York? How many times had they talked since then?

Terri's lusty sigh interrupted her thoughts. "God, I love summer in New York."

Rose followed Terri's gaze. A trio of muscled, sweat-drenched young men carrying bats and gloves passed within yards of their table, undoubtedly leaving the large playground on the corner of Houston and Sixth. Rose waited a moment before agreeing summer wasn't so bad and joining Terri in a silly giggle. When the waiter deposited their check on the table, she noticed his eyes followed the ballplayers across Bleecker Street, too.

Terri registered his expression and halved her tip. Catherine wouldn't have done that. Rose didn't know what Veronica Lamb would have done.

# Chapter Eighteen

Rose walked into work with the souvenir headache afternoon wine always gave. The sweet Vin Santo contributed a high note to the pain in her temples.

"You girls have a nice time today? Terri just finished a nap. She'll be here as soon as she gets prettied up again. Hey, don't broadcast that you're palling around so I don't have to deal with people whining about favoritism." The wide orange and yellow stripes on Ken's shirt looked like a beach umbrella. "I thought about that before I told her to call you, but I figured you know how to be discreet. I'm gonna pick up some booze now. Back in a few."

Rose remembered Terri emphasizing that Butler had suggested their lunch. Was Ken just claiming credit for the idea, or had the two different men shared the same unlikely brainstorm? Unless Terri had simply lied, giving the girlfriends' meeting a secret agenda.

Rose wished she could eat her next several meals alone, at home, in peace, with a book her only dining companion.

"I got a callback from my audition yesterday, and I'm having dinner tonight with an unbelievably gorgeous guy

I met there. Thanks for not bitching about how I left the bar yesterday. Everything is as set as it can be tonight. If you don't see it up here, we don't have it. Prepare yourself for some creative bartending." Laura pointed to several empty spots on the back bar before she grabbed a bottle of Corona from the ice bin and hurried downstairs to cash out.

The good news was that the fruit trays overflowed; the bad news was that Rose had no backup house vodka, house gin, or several of the most popular premium brands. Maybe she could push creme de cacao and tonics, with extra lime. Ken could name that creation, too.

Her first four customers ordered vodka and tonics instead, emptying the bottles on both speedracks. She couldn't wait until their second round. "Sorry, gentlemen, we're out of vodka tonight. The bookkeeper died, and the suppliers must be in mourning. May I offer you something sweet and syrupy instead?"

She'd sell all the premium brands at well prices first. Let Ken worry about the liquor costs. At least the beer coolers were full.

"Laura already told me about our interesting alcohol offerings tonight. I'll push premium and tell people how refreshing bourbon is on a hot summer's night. It worked for Faulkner, didn't it? We're in for a busy one, too." Jimmy ordered nine cocktails and rushed off to seat the couple waiting by the door.

She poured the drinks before he returned to the bar, emptying two more bottles without replacements.

Jimmy started loading his tray, "Add two Dubonnet and sodas to my order and tell me Terri or Ken are going to surface soon to seat our guests. Helen and I can't cover the dining room and the door much longer like this."

"Ken's on an errand, and Terri's finishing her toilette

even as we speak. One or both of them should be here soon. You think we're going to have a waiting list?" Rose calculated how much premium vodka the shelves held. Not nearly enough for a busy night.

"Not within the next half hour, I pray to the gods of mismanagement." Jimmy had loaded the cocktail tray perilously full of drinks. "Thanks. I'll be back."

Tonight promised to be as busy as last night had been slow. Late-summer Thursday nights often rushed the weekend. Many offices would be deserted tomorrow, either from early closings or outbreaks of the Hamptons flu. Three tables already held customers sporting beachy clothes, all ready for an early dinner to outwait the dregs of rush hour before they escaped town.

Her curiosity about why Catherine hadn't returned her call disappeared as every seat at the bar filled within the next five minutes. Time for three aspirins and fifth gear.

Radio stations must have whispered vodka subliminally all day; every other customer wanted it. She'd exhaust the Stoli and Absolut supply soon at this rate.

Ordering liquor wasn't that complicated. My World's delivery day was Wednesday. If the liquor room's continued emptiness signaled big money trouble, why had Terri picked today to splurge on lunch and gossip?

Pouring drinks for a full bar and a nearly full dining room didn't give Rose the time to solve even that mystery. Staying too busy to think had its attractions. She cranked the jukebox volume up a notch.

Ken shouldered his way past a threesome at the front door and deposited two liquor cases on the bar.

He grabbed a pile of bevnaps from the service station and wiped his sweaty face. "Damn. That liquor store is further than I thought. This shit got heavy the last two blocks."

Jesus. The State Liquor Authority would pull My World's liquor license for buying alcohol from a retail store. Bar owners covered the infrequent shortage by borrowing from each other, with perhaps a rare discreet retail purchase. Every customer at the bar could have heard and seen Ken's delivery.

Ken wrestled two half-gallons of vodka from the first carton. The legal distributors didn't sell half-gallons to restaurants. The large bottles didn't belong anywhere near her bar.

She rushed down to the service end, stuffed the bottles back into the carton, and explained the law to Ken. No, it would not be okay just this once. She didn't bother to argue when he snarled about stupid New York laws, told her to pass him four empty house vodka bottles under the bar, and took his loot downstairs.

The authorities also frowned on decanting.

Wait till Butler heard she'd graduated from amateur detective to accessory to a crime. Maybe he'd tell her more if he thought she'd entered the big time.

Her job was to pour and stock the booze. Worrying about who supplied it didn't appear in her job description. And ignorance of the law was no excuse.

Jimmy and Helen both had drink orders up, three couples at the bar needed refills, and she still hadn't helped the foursome at the end of the bar select a bottle of wine. She made drinks and let the phone behind the bar ring. Let Ken answer the line downstairs.

When two customers pointed toward the ringing phone, she grabbed it on the tenth ring. The other line's light shone without blinking. Ken must be chatting on the office phone while he decanted. Didn't they have hold buttons in Colorado?

"Helen?"

Rose almost didn't recognize Terri's voice either. "No, it's Rose, Terri."

"You busy? Where's Ken?"

"Swamped. In the office, on the phone. Want me to buzz him?" Rose signaled the people waiting for a sommelier that she'd get to them next. The blond woman waved the wine list at her, glaring as if she assumed Rose preferred idle chit-chat to helping her select "an inexpensive, but compelling" chardonnay.

"Nah. I feel awful. I suspect the shrimp at lunch. Tell him I'm staying home, making those calls he wanted. I'll call back if there's news. Say I'm sorry, but he'll just have to handle the door himself tonight. I'll come in later if I feel better. Have a good night." Terri sounded as if she were crying.

The light on the other line blinked off. Terri hung up when Rose offered again to connect her to Ken.

Seven more people stood at the front door, waiting to be seated. Jimmy and Helen rushed around the dining room, too involved with their current customers to escort new diners to their tables. Definitely waiting-list time, if anyone could find a minute to start one.

Rose established eye contact with the new arrivals, called to them that someone would be right with them, and jabbed at the intercom button until Ken answered. Another three women at the door glared at her while she gave Ken Terri's message and asked him to hurry upstairs.

Ken had decided to cut the host's schedule to only weekend shifts on the first quiet night he worked, even though the Victors believed a staff member should greet customers at the door on even the slowest nights. Of course, the Victors also believed in providing their restaurant and bar with adequate supplies. Silly bosses.

Ken slammed four house vodka bottles on the bar, none of them completely full. Had he spilled or sipped the missing booze? She uncapped two of the bottles, inserted pour spouts, and jammed them into the speedracks before Ken finished telling the busboy to bring the rest of the liquor upstairs.

The waiters would suffer from losing their busser during this rush while she tried to stock a standing-room-only bar. What had Ken done all afternoon, waited for the neighborhood liquor store to run a happy-hour special?

He seated everyone at the door in a rush, as if the customers were playing musical chairs and should reach their tables before the jukebox changed songs. His speedy work filled the dining room in one swoop, giving each server four new tables and guaranteeing too many simultaneous orders and an infuriated chef in the kitchen. Ken had just managed to slam both the waitstaff and the kitchen, a bad move it would take hours to overcome.

Busy as Rose already was with stocking bottles at her crowded bar and the waiters' requests, the night would only get worse as new arrivals waited for tables that wouldn't turn for far too long. Rose hoped her aspirin would kick in before Madonna stopped begging Papa not to preach.

It was midnight before she appreciated that her headache had disappeared dozens of songs ago. The bar stayed busy after the dining room had finally calmed. Half of the bar customers were regulars, while the remaining drinkers had arrived in three large and self-sufficient groups.

Jimmy and Helen looked shell-shocked as they dragged around the restaurant, their professional personas battered by hours of struggling to catch up since the early rush. Both servers had requested an unprecedented number of free drinks for their tables tonight. Rose had poured them all without question. She'd scream if Ken balked at initialing anything on the comp list.

Until Ken learned to run a dining room, he could consider buying drinks for customers who'd waited forty minutes for food as part of his new public relations campaign. Damage control wasn't a buzzword in the hospitality magazines.

"How ya doing, sweetheart? Gimme a Black Label when you get a minute." The heavyset man who'd ordered peeled a hundred off a fat wad of bills. She saw his fingers strain as he forced his gold money clip back onto the thick roll before casually shoving the cash into his right jacket pocket.

That jacket was beige silk and the open shirt under it a thinner black silk. A golden shark's tooth dangled in his thick gray chest hair, his wide wedding band sparkled with diamonds large enough to excite any bride's envy, and his watch hadn't come from a sidewalk vendor.

"Something for yourself? Joe don't mind if you have one." He tapped the hundred.

"Thanks, but I try to wait till the end of the night to drink." She crossed her fingers behind her back.

His heavily hooded eyes studied her. Rose held his gaze and smiled when she finally placed him. She'd seen his eyes, his large broad nose, and the planes of his cheekbones on a fresco in Siena and remembered making the same connection the half-dozen times she'd already seen this man with Joe or Ben Victors. The Victors had always escorted him to a prime table in the rear of the dining room, without stopping at the bar.

"You sure, Rosie? It's Rose, right? Terri mentioned your name when she called tonight. I'm Enzo." He took a measured sip of his scotch. "I'd like it if you'd join me, please."

She didn't need to know his name to know that he was a gentleman of respect. Buying the bartender a drink was a ritual courtesy, directed more at the absent owners than at her.

She did the right thing—pouring herself a shot of chilled Fernet, clinking glasses, and returning his *salud*. She thanked Enzo again when she gave him his change.

He glanced at the glass she'd barely sipped from. "My pleasure. The kid around? Teresa's husband?"

She took her cue and drained the glass. "Ken just went to the office. Would you like me to buzz him?"

"I'll go down. He knows I'm coming." He gulped his drink and picked up his change. He carefully aligned the four twenties, one five, and two singles before returning the straightened bills to the bar and setting his glass on top of the money. "Thanks, hon. I gotta go take care of business now."

She told Enzo he was welcome, thanked him very much, and waited before his broad back disappeared down the stairs before she grabbed the eighty-seven dollars he'd tipped her. Over-tipping was a wiseguy's signature. Enzo's extravagance elevated him to the heights of the shadowy hierarchy.

Best not to worry about the money's source. The West Village streets and the piers of the Hudson River hid histories not included in the walking tours. Longshoremen and large trucks predated the yuppies and the promenade. Not all of the shadows disappeared when the West Side Highway collapsed under the wrecking balls.

"Did you fake nicely, or should we expect your boudoir to resemble an Equus road tour soon? I don't even want to know who that was. Tell me we're not working in a mob joint. The code of silence is not among

my aspirations, and you just don't have the moll look."
Jimmy ordered seven Coronas. "What happened to all the
new MBA types in the families I've read about? Honestly,
that man was a cartoon."

"Right, Captain Connected. Forget about it, Jimmy."

"See, you've already been corrupted. Have I been
missing something about our esteemed bosses?" Jimmy
tapped his right nostril.

"The Victors are clean. Don't ask me to draw the line
between connected and neighborhood." She decided not
to tell Jimmy about Enzo's enormous tip when he started
speculating about the skill of the witness-protection
program's plastic surgeons.

"Really, it's like a government grant for a facelift.
Oh, God, here comes il patrone. Duty calls." He balanced
a lime wedge on each bottle and waltzed away to deliver
the beers.

She waved good night to her benefactor, mouthing
a silent thank you. Enzo nodded but didn't smile as he
hurried out of the restaurant. What urgent business had
brought him to My World's office at the end of a Thursday
night?

Jimmy hurried back to the bar the minute Enzo left.
"What was he doing here? Do you think Ken's okay?"

"No, he's hanging from the office ceiling fixture,
suspended by the piano wire around his neck. Of course
he's okay. The gentleman just wanted to talk to him
privately."

"I'm worried."

"Your sudden concern for Ken's health touches me
deeply. Go downstairs and check on him if you're that
worried."

Jimmy cocked his head toward the dining room. "I
can't. Table ten has had their check for half an hour, but

I guarantee they'll be ready to pay the instant I leave the floor. The guy's been looking for something to complain about since they arrived. I've done everything perfectly, even in this madhouse. I'm not about to concede defeat now. You go, and I'll watch the bar."

"Enzo was a perfect gentleman. He bought me a drink, told me he knows the Victors, and tipped me a memorably generous amount. This is not a hit-man's profile. You have to stop watching late-late movies." She didn't specify the tip's generosity and wondered if Jimmy had counted it from across the room.

"If you don't care about Ken, at least go down to the ladies and freshen your makeup. Your mascara is rather smudged and your lipstick is quite faded."

"My hair is undoubtedly something of a mess too, right?"

"It's looked better. Might as well check on Ken after you're gorgeous again. I'm unaccountably nervous about him. Please."

Rose patted her thighs. "And if I don't go now, how long will it be before you resort to telling me descending the stairs will banish unsightly cellulite from my rear? This is going to be one of your relentless arguments, isn't it?"

"Consider going downstairs a teensy break. Please. That man scared me. Call it queer's intuition if you want."

She told Jimmy to wait, checked on her customers, and served three rounds. "Don't go behind the bar unless you have to. I'll be back in a few. This is a fool's errand. If I thought for a second that Ken had suffered anything worse than a little intimidation from our friend, I'd call the cops without worrying about the state of my makeup. Guys who are up to no good don't usually introduce themselves and then tip big enough to make sure a potential witness remembers them, silly."

Rose ducked under the service station. "Also, I don't intend to find another damaged body as long as I live."

# Chapter Nineteen

Rose hurried down the stairs, grateful for even a brief escape from the bar. Any thought of enjoying her break disappeared when she opened the women's room door. My World's female customers had left the room in a shambles again. Multicolored strands of hair festooned the sink. Water puddled on the counter, with a thin layer of powdered blush and eyeshadows staining the sink and surround. Crumpled paper towels and saturated tissues littered the floor. Clownish pink lips floating on the mirror showed a method of lipstick blotting she'd yet to read about in a fashion magazine.

The tendency of perfectly lovely and impeccably groomed ladies to trash a public restroom remained one of the mysteries of the restaurant business. Other customers, horrified by the mess, would forever condemn the restaurant they might otherwise have recommended.

An employee or manager should have checked the bathrooms several times on a night this busy. Right.

And someone else should clean the women's room now. Rose grabbed a handful of paper towels and swabbed at the counter, sink, and floor, leaving the pink kiss on the mirror for the porter. Easier to do it herself than delegate, although she wouldn't brave the men's room.

Her cursory cleaning done, Rose remembered Jimmy's critique of her appearance. Her reflection showed her hair still in its loose topknot and not a single mascara smudge. She did need lipstick and less shine. Jimmy would have pushed her down the stairs if he'd seen the sheen of sweat generated by scrubbing the stuffy bathroom.

Rose patted her forehead and blotted her lips on a rough paper towel, determined to show Jimmy a pretty face when she sent him downstairs to investigate the men's room. She'd assign him the errand as mild revenge for nagging her to visit Ken. She tried to decide which was more foolish—Jimmy's fretting over her appearance or his odd concern for Ken.

Only her promise to Jimmy propelled her toward the office door. He had to know she would have resisted his pleas forever if she'd imagined even the most minuscule chance of discovering anything more frightening than the sight of Ken tackling paperwork.

The office door opened as she approached. Ken stopped whistling "Margaritaville" when he saw her. "Perfect timing, I was just headed up to you." When he gestured with the clipboard he held to his chest, she saw a lumpy white envelope secured with a rubber band protruding from his colorful shirt's pocket like a gentleman's handkerchief fallen on desperate times.

He waggled the clipboard. "Got the liquor inventory sheets right here. I arranged for a special delivery tomorrow. Gotta call it in to a special number right now. You know anything we need off the top of your head?"

Three of the unattached papers piled on top of the inventory sheets fell to the floor. She recognized a liquor distributor's invoice when it landed on her left foot.

Rose bent quickly to retrieve the paper foot, squirming at the remembered voice of Sister Mary Damian warning about filthy-minded boys dropping pencils solely for the opportunity to peer up skirts. The black jeans she wore tonight didn't silence Sister's voice. Neither had twenty years.

She barely had time to read the large block letters of OVERDUE before Ken grabbed the invoice back. More loose papers rained from the clipboard, scattering all around them.

Rose stood and watched Ken scrabble for his papers for a moment, then bent to help again. The envelope fell from Ken's pocket when he reached for the invoices nearest her feet.

She picked it up before he ordered her not to touch it. Rose understood his urgency when she felt the contents. A thick sheaf of paper in the unmistakable shape of currency bulged beneath the rubber band. When she handed him the packet, Ken shoved it into the back pocket of his pants in a move pickpockets prayed for.

Enzo's visit made sudden sense. Liquor distributors had strict rules about timely payment. When an establishment fell too far behind on its bills, delivery stopped. The most commission-starved salesperson couldn't help a customer in deep arrears. Companies wouldn't fill an order till the bill was paid. Period.

She'd bet her rent-controlled lease that the envelope in Ken's pocket represented the c.o.d. payment for tomorrow's special delivery, including a sizeable tip for whoever he'd convinced to fill the order at the last minute. Then she remembered Enzo mentioning Terri had called him earlier tonight.

If Ken held the money Terri had requested, who did Enzo expect to repay him? His payment policies might make the liquor companies seem like charitable organizations.

"I'll make a liquor list upstairs. I don't want to leave Jimmy watching the bar for too long." She started toward the stairs.

"That's the spirit, Rose. I'll check the liquor room, then we'll put our heads together at the bar."

She had her foot on the second step when Ken called her back. "Let Jimmy watch the bar for another minute or two. Come into the liquor room with me now, please. It's a two-man job. I don't want to wait till later."

Counting the bottles on the storeroom's empty shelves shouldn't take more than a few minutes. No matter how "special" Ken's contact at the distributor was, My World's order was already late for delivery tomorrow. Imagining Friday night behind another unstocked bar convinced Rose Jimmy could handle her customers a bit longer. Sacrificing any tips she'd lose by helping Ken an extra few minutes for the chance to work a fully stocked bar tomorrow night seemed a fine bargain.

Rose followed Ken into the liquor room, trying not to show her surprise when he closed the door behind them. Air from the hallway would have relieved the heat in the small, stuffy room.

"Okay, Ken, call the brands, I'll give you a count."

He shuffled the papers on his clipboard.

She assessed the shelves. "Ken? You want to start with vodkas? We need them the most."

He leaned against the closed door and looked her up and down like a tailor's fitter. The room warmed.

"What's the first category on the list? I really should get back to the bar soon. They might be slammed up there."

He stared at her instead of his clipboard. "Don't worry about the bar, honey. I wanted to talk to you last night, but that damn Nick spoiled everything again. I know you must wonder what's been going on around here. Your boyfriend probably has his questions, too."

Honey?

He leaned against the door jamb as if he needed its support. "I hate to speak bad of the dead, but I decided I gotta tell you, if you haven't figured it out already. The awful truth is that Yvonne was stealing from us. Maybe that bastard Nick has a drug habit. I hope he didn't kill her for money."

He paused as if waiting for a reaction, then continued when she didn't respond, "So we've been short on cash and I've been doing my damnedest to keep our heads above water. I got it under control now, though. Hey, when the going gets tough, right? Terri don't know how bad the situation was. No need to get her all upset now."

Rose forgot about counting bottles. "How do you know Yvonne was stealing? Did you tell the cops?" She stopped herself from telling him she didn't believe his accusation.

"C'mon, you think I can't see what's going on in my own place? I'm waiting till I get all the paperwork together before I tell the cops. They like proof, right?"

She nodded. They certainly did. And when did My World become Ken's place?

"So you think you can keep quiet about this to your boyfriend for another day or two? He doesn't have to know everything. You're not married to the guy, right?" Ken smirked.

"We don't even live together." But Butler would know about Ken's accusations as soon as she could reach him. No divided loyalties here.

She waited, but Ken didn't demand she promise not to tell Butler. Or anybody else.

"Thanks, Rose. I guess I just needed to get it off my chest. You know what they say about lonely at the top. I figured you could handle it okay, being a writer and interested in human nature and all. You know, I dated a writer in high school, a poet. That girl could rhyme any word you thought of. She was awful sensitive, though."

"Yeah, poets are like that. I really need to get back to work now." She told herself it was melodramatic to think she was trapped.

He didn't move away from the door. "Sometimes I think you're the only gal I can depend on around here. Terri gets so emotional about her sacred Uncle Joe, she forgets we're here to do business. So maybe that's why I feel kind of close to you."

The liquor room shrunk. Ken and his confidences still blocked the door.

"Hey, don't worry. You want to go upstairs now, then stay for a few minutes after we close to help me with this? It shouldn't take long. I could run you home after. Ter's fast asleep by now. She ain't waiting up for me tonight." He winked.

Jimmy could manage the bar until last call if the alternative were staying after hours with Ken in an empty restaurant. A deserted My World would shrink the liquor room to a nightmare's cell. Melodrama might verge into gothic.

"I have a late date. Let's inventory now. Vodka first?" Rose didn't like turning her back on Ken and didn't answer when he asked if her date was with anybody exciting. She sang out the one bottle of lemon-flavored vodka on the shelf, then started counting gins aloud.

Her only answers to Ken's attempts to chat about her date were to call out the next category of liquor and tally the bottles on the shelves. Damned if she'd stoop to invoking her cop boyfriend to scare him off. Yet.

He repeated her tallies in a sluggish voice. Rose fidgeted through the pauses before his pencil scratched the entries on the inventory form. She could have written paragraphs in the time it took him to make tick marks.

"Okay, Ken. We can leave the cordials and liqueurs for next delivery, except maybe a couple of Amarettos and Sambuccas. I have to get back to the bar. They must be going crazy up there by now." Standing on an empty milk crate to see the upper shelves, she tried to pretend Ken wasn't studying her ass more than his paperwork. Her snug jeans no longer felt like protection. The nuns had warned about them too.

"Don't talk about going crazy. You've been looking real good lately, you know. I could barely concentrate on the orders with you posing there like that."

Posing? Maybe he'd seen the milk crate as her pedestal. Suddenly glad of her temporary height advantage, Rose side-stepped around the top of the crate until she faced Ken. He grabbed her arm and pulled her down just as she finished her clumsy pirouette. She lurched to the floor.

"Jesus, Ken, what—"

He yanked her to him before she could regain her balance. His clipboard squashed against the back of her neck, smashing her face into his throat. She pulled herself back to glare at him, then whipped her head to the side when he tried to kiss her. His hold loosened just as she started to raise her right knee.

The clipboard clattered to the floor when she backed away. She felt it under her feet when she took another step backward.

Rose struggled not to slap Ken. He shook his head slowly, smiling at her with a little boy's grin. She could almost see the puddled milk, broken glass, and cookie crumbs on the liquor room's floor.

"Don't take it the wrong way, huh? Just trying to show my appreciation for your help."

"A simple thank you would have been more professional." Rose stopped herself from saying anything else when she saw her bright lipstick smeared across his shirt. The dark red over his orange and yellow stripes looked like a chemical sunset.

His grin disappeared. "Touchy broad, huh? Now look at my paperwork all over the floor. Run back to your damn bar if you're in such a hurry. I got work to do here."

Ken's bad boy grin reappeared when he opened the door. "Hey, maybe I was out of line. You New Yorkers are just more formal than I'm used to. And I do think real highly of you. No big deal, okay?"

Grabbing and kissing an employee was a big deal, actually. Remembering Nick describing Ken's aggressive pursuit of Yvonne made Rose wonder if Ken had intended his kiss as a serious seduction. His affair with Yvonne might have convinced him that all the women at My World were fair game.

While Rose didn't believe Yvonne had stolen from the restaurant, she did see how attractive the dead woman could become as a scapegoat. Ken's accusation redefined kiss and tell.

Rose slammed the liquor room door behind her and started to shake with anger. Maybe she should pound on the door and threaten Ken with a harassment claim and an immediate phone call to his wife. Damn. Either an official or unofficial report would only exacerbate the current turmoil at My World, further confusing the search for Yvonne's murderer. The gush of Terri's girlish confidences would dry immediately if she saw Rose as any type of rival.

For Ken.

Returning to the bathroom, Rose saw a reflection that looked more like the victim of an attack than the instigator of a seduction. She quickly straightened her disheveled hair, ran cold water on her wrists, and reapplied her lipstick.

She stopped at the bottom of the stairs, reconsidering her decision not to threaten Ken with reporting his attack. Maybe she could add her close personal friend Enzo to the list of people she intended to tell. Even without any intention of fulfilling the threat, watching Ken squirm seemed an attractive revenge. Threatening him would also alienate him forever as a source of any further information. She abandoned the idea regretfully.

Bye-bye, threat.

On the third step, Rose hoped Ken wouldn't notice his reddened shirt before he came upstairs. He should blush dark enough to match her lipstick's deep red when he did discover the stain. Nobody who saw the smeared shirt would think she'd initiated the kiss. Ken could always change into one of the promotional t-shirts stockpiled in the office. But what would Terri think if her husband offered to take in the laundry this week?

# Chapter Twenty

The bar looked slightly calmer, and certainly neater, than she'd left it. All the customers appeared satisfied. Jimmy's relaxed posture announced he'd poured himself at least one drink.

She decided to join him in another as soon as she'd checked on her patrons. Then, if the bar didn't reek of disinfectant, she'd tell Jimmy everything, practice the story before she told it to Butler.

"A poet girlfriend in high school? I'd never have suspected Ken and I were members of the male muse club. However did you keep a straight face?"

"I tried not to imagine the poems. Then he said—"

Laura hurried into the bar and sat on the barstool nearest the service station.

"Rose? Rose, I gotta talk to you. It can't wait till tomorrow. Make me a top-shelf cosmopolitan. I gotta calm down. Hey, Jimmy."

Rose shook the vodka, lime juice, Grand Marnier, and cranberry juice, then studied Laura as she strained the cocktail into a chilled martini glass. Laura's hair was tousled out of its usual slick coiffure and her face scrubbed clean of dramatic makeup. Her eyes looked twice as big without their daily outline of kohl. A sweet pink glowed on her cheeks instead of her usual thick layer of pale foundation. Rose had never seen Laura look prettier.

Laura didn't touch her cocktail. "Can I buy you a drink?"

Rose shook her head. "Thanks anyway. Jimmy and I just had one. It's been that kind of night. What's up?"

"Remember that guy I told you about? We went out tonight and I got home about half an hour ago. I went to bed but was too excited to sleep, so I rushed over here to ask you something. I couldn't wait till tomorrow. I need a huge favor."

"What?"

"He's it, Rose. He's so beautiful. Those Calvin Klein guys should throw in their briefs. I'm in love. I swear it. And he asked me out again."

Rose smiled and nodded at Laura, wondering when she'd stop gushing and ask for the favor.

"So here's the thing. He asked me to go hear him read a scene at his class next Monday night. And I said yes, before I even thought that I work Mondays. So, I know this is huge, but would you consider trading this Saturday for Monday? You must make more on Saturday nights, so I'll even throw in some cash. Please. I'll just die if I have to call him back and say no." Laura managed to make her eyes well. "Can you imagine what kind of flake he'd think I am?"

For cancelling the date or offering to pay to keep it?

Rose couldn't resist the chance to get out of town and away from My World a day early. She and Butler would have a real, actual, American weekend in the country. The prospect of taking Saturday and Sunday off seemed somehow comforting, as if there truly were safety in numbers.

"Sure, I'll trade. Forget about the money. You can return the favor sometime. But you have to ask Ken to okay it and make sure he initials the change on the schedule. He's downstairs if you want to ask him now."

"Save my drink; I'll be right back." Laura almost skipped to the stairs.

Jimmy had heard every word. "You're going to leave me with that space cadet on a Saturday night? I'll have to call every drink my miserable tourist customers request at least three times. Honestly, I'm horrified by your lack of loyalty."

"You'll survive. It won't be that busy. Think of this as a sacrifice in the service of young love." Rose started to top off Laura's Cosmo, then drained the shaker into a rocks glass and handed it to Jimmy.

He gulped it. "Yeah, I'll be sacrificing and giving lousy service while you and the dashing detective gambol in the country. How do you expect to discover Yvonne's murderer from another state?"

"I'll come back refreshed and inspired. The thought of not seeing Ken for a few days tempts me too much. You can admit you're jealous now."

"Fine. I'll take pictures of what Ken wears every day you're gone and fax them to wherever you're staying. Do they have faxes in the wilds of Massachusetts, dearest?"

"Only in the big towns, the ones that have electricity. But you know what a romantic light kerosene lamps cast."

"Yes, Ms. Stewart, and the smell is a real aphrodisiac too. Here comes Laura. My God, she's absolutely glowing. You could run halogens off this girl. Maybe I should date again soon."

"Too bad *Poets and Writers* doesn't have personals. You want me to ask Frank if he knows anybody?"

"Perish both thoughts. I'll find my own romantic objects, thank you. Maybe someone fabulous will walk in here Saturday night, see me across the crowded dining room, and offer his undying love forever."

"And you'll reject him 'cause his shoes aren't polished to a high enough gloss."

Laura interrupted their laughter. "Ken said okay. He said you deserved a break after what's been going on around here."

"I deserved a break? Didn't you tell him the switch was your idea, Laura?"

"Yeah, I did, but he kept talking about it as if he were doing you a favor. It was weird. You know what else was weird?"

"I can't guess." Or begin to list the possibilities.

"When I walked into the office, Ken was sitting there bare-chested. But he had this wet shirt laid out on the desk under the lamp. As soon as he saw me, he pulled the shirt up and held it in front of him. He kept it like that the whole time we talked, like some little kid who was hypermodest or something. It was embarrassing. What, does he think I wanted to stare at his bare chest?" Laura's voice rose two octaves with her question.

"Ken may think most women want to see him naked." Poor Terri.

"Then he should go to the gym and get some definition. Chris has excellent definition." Laura finished her drink, thanked Rose again for switching shifts, tipped five dollars, and floated out of My World.

Jimmy sighed. "Oh dear God, I do hope she brings this Chris in to show him off before the romance ends. An actor with excellent definition is such a rare sight these days. Wasn't she in love with a musician last month?"

"Last week. But he's moving to Georgia, so they

decided to be friends." Rose thought it was Georgia.

Jimmy shrugged. "Maybe I won't date again after all. What could that shirt story mean? You think Ken was drooling while he napped in the office?"

"No, he drooled in the liquor room. It got ugly."

"Tell."

She did, describing Ken's calling Yvonne a thief, their impromptu liquor inventory, and his clumsy seduction attempt.

Jimmy didn't even laugh when she told him about her lipstick on Ken's collar. "You should have told me Ken hit on you right away, instead of joking about his poet girlfriend. You can't let him assault you that way with impunity. File a harassment claim; call Ben in Italy; tell everybody, including Terri. His arrogance appalls me. What in the world made Ken think he could hit on a woman who works here with any faint hope of success?"

She hesitated. Ken's affair with Yvonne was the obvious answer. But it wasn't her answer to give. Nick hadn't specifically asked her to keep the information about Ken and Yvonne confidential, but she couldn't imagine he'd want it broadcast in My World. Linking Yvonne with Ken would be a slur that the dead woman couldn't explain or defend herself against. But the affair could also be a factor in discovering Yvonne's murderer, and Jimmy wanted to help with that.

The line between gossip and important information blurred as she looked at Jimmy's indignant face.

Telling the truth shouldn't seem like slander.

"I don't know. But I'm not going to make a fuss about Ken hitting on me. My World is in enough of an uproar right now. Finding out who killed Yvonne seems more important than embarrassing Ken. We'll have plenty of time for that later." She didn't mention Nick.

"Probably no dearth of opportunities, either, although I do think Ken's behavior merits more than embarrassment. I'm not sure the man even has a shame threshold. He thinks blush refers to a great wine." Jimmy scanned the dining room.

"Somebody who'd make his wife ask Enzo to borrow money does have different standards." She told him about the envelope full of cash and her theory that Ken had borrowed it to pay the liquor bills.

"So now we're working in a place that's at the mercy of loan sharks? I hope Enzo and his boys are extremely clear on the concept of who exactly borrowed the money. I like my bony little kneecaps just the way they are, thank you." He smoothed the sharp creases in his pants.

"I'm sure Enzo did it as a favor to the Victors. Ken by himself wouldn't have a lot of credibility with Enzo and his friends." What had Terri said to Enzo?

"Ken's credibility is universally limited, except perhaps to his adoring wife. What else happened downstairs?"

"Mine wasn't the only virtue attacked. Ken baldly accused Yvonne of stealing. He's 'getting his paperwork together' before he offers it to the cops as proof."

"How odd that he waits until she's dead and can't defend herself to call her a thief. I can't see Yvonne as an embezzler. And if she were in fact stealing, I rather doubt she would have left a paper trail wide enough for Ken to follow."

"Or simple enough. Too bad his rhyming girlfriend isn't around:
Can you see the dead Yvonne?
Can you see the money gone?
I am Ken, I am the boss.
I won't cover up this loss."

Jimmy patted her hand. "Rose? Did the shock of Ken's advances induce a touch of brain damage? Should I call somebody?"

She laughed. "I'm sorry. Don't ask me where that came from. I'd rather not know. Ken didn't stop with accusing Yvonne. He started in on Nick, suggesting he has a drug problem and piously hoping that Nick didn't murder Yvonne for money."

"Did I miss something? Has Nick been convicted?"

"Only in Ken's mind. He'll probably get the proof on Nick together as soon as he's done cooking up the papers to damn Yvonne."

Why did it feel good to say Nick's name?

Jimmy treated Nick's name like any other word. "Are you so certain he can't find anything on Yvonne? She didn't seem like a thief to me, although I'm not sure what a thief would seem like. And God knows I've been disappointed before."

"I'm positive. Yvonne was using her job at My World for school credit. No way she would have jeopardized that by playing with the books. I still believe she was honest. She had her career and her future all planned." Rose remembered Yvonne's careful strategy for a life she'd never lead.

"Too bad her murderer didn't respect her plans. On that note, I'd better see if any of my dear diners need anything." Jimmy walked toward his tables.

When Rose surveyed the bar, she saw all her customers engaged in conversations and all their glasses at least half-full. It had felt good to offer Jimmy a rational, fact-based explanation for Yvonne's innocence. She wished she knew a twin explanation exonerating Nick to offer Butler.

She started to list the missing bar stock.

When Ken approached the bar, she wished she'd mentioned Ken asking her not to tell Butler anything about their conversation. He might not have worried that she'd run upstairs and tell Jimmy almost everything. Even though she'd never promised to honor Ken's confidences, she didn't want him to stop sharing his version of events yet.

The large smile on Jimmy's face when he walked toward Ken scared her. She knew Jimmy wouldn't mean to divulge what she'd told him; she didn't know what he might say without thinking.

Ken spoke as if he hadn't seen her since yesterday. "Rose, your friend Catherine called. I have a policy against personal phone calls at work, you know. But she sounded like a nice lady and it was long distance, so I took the message. She said she's put new candles in the guest room, and that you should come early and stay late."

He winked. "Maybe a couple of days out of town will do you some good. But the new employee manual states my policy on last-minute schedule changes in black and white. Just this once, huh?"

Did Ken think she'd asked to switch shifts with Laura, or was he trying to erase his behavior downstairs by impersonating a magnanimous boss? Who cared? Catherine had called. Rose would see her best friend day after tomorrow. With Butler. In the country.

Jimmy cleared his throat. "Ken, I simply love your shirt. There's almost a madras effect around the collar. All those colors look terrific on you. You're definitely a fall guy."

Ken could blush.

# Chapter Twenty-one

Rose sat ramrod straight to avoid contact with the vinyl seatback in this sweltering cab, but her blouse still clung. She would have felt cooler if she'd walked home. To avoid the extra few minutes circling on Perry, she had the cab stop at the corner of Bleecker and Eleventh. The driver apologized again for the broken air-conditioner, and she tipped him as if he'd driven her to Park Avenue in a stretch limo.

The prospect of a quick shower and starting her Berkshires packing list rushed her through the shadows on Eleventh. She only looked over her shoulder a few times.

Damn those kids.

And damn the nerves that sent her walking in the middle of the street when she saw a lone male turn off Fourth and hurry toward her.

She pulled her key ring out of her right pocket and twisted it so that the keys faced out. She slipped the ring back in her pocket when she recognized Butler.

"Frank? What's that smell?"

"Sssh. Wait here a second. Please don't argue." He ran to her building, trotted up the stairs, and pulled hard on the locked door. He bent to examine her stoop, then waved her up.

"Gee, thanks, but what—"

"The Greene bastards are at it again. Trashed my car right in front of my place, which means they figured out my address somehow. Doesn't mean they know yours, too, but I wanted to make sure nothing happened here. Glad I didn't have to wait till dawn again."

She ignored the reproach in "dawn again." Silly to think that Butler had used the Greene boys' work as an excuse to spy on her homecoming.

"Let's get upstairs and crank the a.c." She couldn't stand another second of this thick humidity.

She followed him up the stairs, grateful his shoes didn't leave any colorful footprints on the floor. His pants hadn't escaped green handprints, though.

He waited until they she'd clicked the last lock shut. "I don't like this, Rose."

"Really, Frank? I can't think of a better way to end a long, confusing, and generally horrendous day. You want a drink?" She opened the fridge.

"Whatever you're having."

He frowned when she poured them both tall glasses of Pellegrino. She scowled right back when the smell of the paint on his clothes and shoes grew stronger in the small kitchen.

Heat or stench? She opened the windows immediately, cursing the cool air escaping the apartment.

"Let me guess. They've graduated beyond slimy water. How much paint did they splash on your car?"

"Splash? They flooded it with enough to cover it and leave paint puddles all around." He pointed to his shoes. "The guys in the garage think they can get all the paint off the windows by tomorrow night, at least."

"But why—"

"Maybe Greene thinks this shit is enough to scare me. Damned if I know."

Damned indeed.

"What if it isn't Mr. Greene doing all this? You don't know it's him. It could be anybody. It could be Ken. Maybe he found out you and Terri used to date. After tonight, I wouldn't put anything past him."

"What happened tonight?" He emptied his glass as if the paint fumes had dehydrated him to a dangerous level.

She met his eyes. "Nothing much. Ken tried to serve retail booze, borrowed money from a loan shark, accused Yvonne of embezzling, and hit on me. Just another night."

"Slow down. Tell me what the hell you're talking about. Hit on you?"

"It gets worse." She told him about the liquor shortage, Enzo's visit, and Ken's calling Yvonne a thief.

He took a bottle of wine out of the fridge and refilled his water glass. "Yeah. Ken's thrown some pretty broad hints about Yvonne's stealing at me. Did he say anything specific to you?"

She covered her glass when he tilted the wine bottle toward it. "Just that Yvonne stole, and that's why the liquor bills weren't paid. Until Enzo came to the rescue. I doubt that Enzo would ever have lent Ken the money unless Terri asked. He said he'd spoken to her earlier. Terri arranged a loan with a wiseguy, Frank, so why do you insist on seeing her as this perpetually innocent little thing?"

"'Cause I don't think she has a clue what a slimeball her husband is. You know, love is blind."

"Blind and dumb."

Did Butler know about Ken and Yvonne now? Would he tell her if he did? She couldn't ask him without alerting him to the affair. That was Nick's job, or responsibility, or hard-earned right. Not hers. She just needed to prod Butler into telling her what he already knew.

She described Ken's clumsy advances in greater detail. Butler didn't react, although she'd hoped he'd blurt anything he already knew about Ken's real infidelities. Maybe he'd reserved his indignation for poor Terri's suffering. Rose tried to sound very wronged by Ken's advances. Her growing distress didn't help make Captain Closed Mouth share his information.

Butler poured himself more wine. "Poor Terri. Ken's an asshole. She has a lot to put up with."

Her boss hit on her, and her lover worried about how the creep's wife felt?

Wrong reaction. How did Butler know what Terri had to tolerate? Why did he keep his conversations with Terri secret? She couldn't believe he had anything more to hide about Terri, but his secrecy fueled her obstinate sense of suspicion.

"Just how often do you and Terri talk, anyway? Did you really suggest she invite me to lunch today? Funny, I don't remember your mentioning it when you and I spoke earlier."

"Not as often as you and Nick chat. He told me all about your lengthy breakfast. Why are you talking about Ken trying to fuck you but not mentioning Nick? Where'd those flowers come from?" He pointed toward the roses by her bedroom door.

She ignored the attempt to distract her. "What did Nick say when you talked to him?"

"Nothing about pacing up and down your block looking like a demented delivery boy and then hiding flowers under a car. A bored neighbor phoned that one in. Thought it might be a bomb."

"A bomb?"

He shrugged. "People get squirrely in the heat. Your neighbors may have good reason to feel nervous lately. Shit, Nick could scare anybody."

"He doesn't scare me, Frank."

"Maybe he should, Rose. He looked frightening enough when I saw him last night."

"Wasn't he calmer when you saw him today? He came in to see you, didn't he?"

"You need to know his every move these days?"

"I sure as hell don't know yours. Just how much comfort has poor little Terri needed these days? You worry more about her than you do about me."

Damn. She hadn't meant to say that.

"Maybe she makes it easier to care about her than you do."

She stared at him, biting her lip.

"Jesus, you know I don't mean that. This isn't about Terri. It's about Yvonne's murder. You want me to tell you everything I've discovered, from Nick and from everyone else. But you sure as hell won't tell me everything you know. You tried to get me mad enough to blurt out what Nick said today. Only the mad part worked,"

Their anger scared Rose tonight. Jealousy honed both their tempers into a mean sharpness that felt dangerous.

She tried to calm her voice. "Okay, you're the champ at the who-knows-what game. I concede. Now will you tell me what Nick said?"

"You won't give up, will you? Why don't you tell me what he told you?"

Rose reached for the wine bottle.

Bluff called, wine poured, decision made.

"Sorry, but I can't. Nick talked to me as a friend, and some of what he said doesn't reflect well on Yvonne.

She's dead, and it doesn't feel right for me to tell you her secrets."

"You and Nick have more in common than I thought, then. It took him forever to tell me about Yvonne's thing with Ken. Poor judgment on her part, but who knows how unhappy Nick had made her. Meeting Barney Fine already made me question her choice in men."

Rose didn't argue that Nick shouldn't take all the guilt for the affair, no matter how much he blamed himself.

"So now we have Ken calling Yvonne a thief while we all know he was sleeping with her. Gotta wonder about his motivation there. I also gotta wonder if Terri knows. It's not my business to tell her, but somebody should." He sighed again.

"Not me."

"Definitely not you. I just don't want to have to do it myself."

She refused to picture the mascara stains on his shoulder if he did. "Where does Ken say he was Monday afternoon?"

He looked grateful at the change of subject—grateful enough to answer the question directly. "Says he rode the ferry over to Staten Island and back with Terri. She wanted to repeat the trip, but he'd seen enough. A skyline's a skyline, right? So he left her on the boat and explored downtown. Real excited at seeing Wall Street for the first time, Ken was. Then he walked back to the Village, but it took a darn long time."

"I thought Terri said she was with Ken all afternoon?" Butler hadn't mentioned that little discrepancy.

He put his hands up as if to block her questions. "Stop it. Lay off Terri, please."

"Okay then, what about Nick?" She knew she was pushing her luck. She also knew he wanted to dissipate the anger between them.

He dropped his hands. "As if you didn't know. They fought, he left, but he can't prove where he was at any exact hour. Nick had time to kill her, either before or after his trip. It's a quick drive midday."

"I wish you believed him, Frank." She reached for his right hand.

He only let her hold it a second. "So do I, Rose. So do I."

She poured them both another splash of wine and told Butler about the change in her weekend work schedule. He said he'd rearrange his plans for Saturday so they could leave after her Friday night shift. He didn't tell her what those plans were. She couldn't find the energy to push him any further.

Enough. Enough of Nick, and Terri, and Ken, and this ugly jealous anger. Enough of seeing Yvonne's death mask every time she closed her eyes.

Tomorrow was another day.

They could fight about it then.

# Chapter Twenty-two

She heard the shower running in the morning, then burrowed back into a deep sleep until Butler kissed her forehead.

"I'm leaving. My damn feet are still green. Pack your stuff. I'll pick you up at work, swing by here for your bags, then we'll hit the road. You can sleep in the car if you want."

She murmured her agreement and tried to sleep again. No sex last night and none this morning. So jealousy wasn't always an aphrodisiac.

She made coffee and called Catherine, who said a trip to the country would cure all her troubles with Butler, that she shouldn't even think about packing a Tanglewood picnic when visiting a restaurateur, and that their hostess would be waiting with bloomers on for their arrival.

Catherine had also asked about Rose's novel. Rose spent four hours at her desk repositioning commas and rewriting sentences she'd written last week. When she left her desk in disgust, she had a document shorter than the chapter she'd opened. She prayed the Berkshires would inspire her.

She still hadn't bought Catherine a hostess gift. Too bad she'd been distracted at Broadway Panhandler Monday.

Rose showered and packed quickly. One of Catherine's many charms as a hostess was how she stocked her guest bathroom with all the finest toiletries and beauty products known to woman. She even provided an entire basket stuffed with every available number of sunscreen.

Rose only needed to pack clothes. She filled a medium-sized bag, hesitating barely a minute before she included her most provocative innocent white cotton nightgown.

One should wear lace in the Berkshires. Catherine's house was only a short drive away from Edith Wharton's home at the Mount, after all.

But Edith Wharton hadn't bartended. Thinking about how long she'd be wearing today's outfit, Rose tucked a boat-necked black jersey into loose black pants with plenty of pockets.

Then she called Jimmy, told him she wanted to browse the shops on Hudson, and asked if he wanted to meet for coffee before work.

"Delightful thought, Rose. But, in case you haven't ventured out yet today, let me warn you that it is revoltingly tropical out there. August at its worst. Too hot to shop, if you can believe that. But coffee somewhere dark and cool sounds lovely. With lots of ice."

She groaned at the weather report. "Where?"

"I'll make it easy for you and agree to the White Horse. They have the best air-conditioning in that back room. We can even split a shot of Sambuca in our coffees."

They agreed to meet in forty-five minutes. Jimmy's suggesting the White Horse told her how anxious he was to talk. The old place wasn't number one on his chic parade.

She put her bag by the front door, turned off her air-conditioner, and left the apartment. The dirty ugly heat slowed her steps. Nobody should have to breathe air this thick. West Fourth and Bleecker Streets were deserted for a Friday afternoon, as if anyone who didn't absolutely have to venture outside had chosen to hide from the heat.

She revised that theory when she reached Hudson Street. People weren't sheltering inside; they were stuck in traffic. Cars jammed the broad avenue as the weekend exodus started early. It would take these poor souls hours and hours to reach their destinations. She and Butler would make much better time by leaving early tomorrow morning, no matter how ridiculous his car might look.

The stalled traffic let her cross Hudson without waiting for the light to change. She darted through the cars, trying not to inhale exhaust fumes and the smell of overheated metal.

Jimmy had been right when he said it wasn't a day to wander from store to store. She ducked into Hudson Street Papers, confident she'd find something delightful. Catherine loved wearing outrageous earrings with her chef's whites. A jeweler might have designed the pair dangling tiny charms of wine bottles, grapes, and goblets just for her. Rose bought a black lacquered box and surrounded the perfect earrings with bars of California lavender soap.

She arrived at the White Horse early; Jimmy was even earlier. He'd settled in with a stack of newspapers at the corner table in the back room. The tabloid headlines all screamed about the heat, senseless violence, and flaring tempers. She didn't know reporters had covered her apartment last night.

He pushed the papers onto an empty chair. "Is there any chance at all, darling, that you and that lovely man you date would let me trail along this weekend? I could help drive, or distract the driver, and I'd certainly carry all your luggage. It would be such fun to spend time with you two together."

"I only have one bag, Frank won't let anybody else drive his car, and this trip could resemble travels with Martha and George, if last night is any indication. The heat must be getting to you if you'd even consider spending that much time with him."

Jimmy pouted and ordered two iced coffees and a single shot of Sambuca from the waitress.

She showed him Catherine's gifts, graciously accepting his praise of her shopping skills, then drank half of her coffee the minute it arrived. She covered her glass when Jimmy tried to share the Sambuca. "It's too early, and way too hot, to drink. Thanks anyway."

"You look tired. You and the darling detective spatting again?" He stirred the liqueur into his glass.

"We'll be fine. Tough night, though. So then I couldn't get any decent work done today."

"Which would you rather not talk about? No, I'll give you a break and share my dirt. Prepare yourself for another installation of Crazyhouse Theatre tonight at work."

She groaned and listened to Jimmy tell her about today's phone calls from Ken and Helen. His boss had congratulated him on his fine liquor sales, despite the "temporary difficulties" at work, and assured him he'd have "every little booze your heart desires" to sell tonight. His coworker had complained about the chaos at the restaurant last night and asked if he really thought Yvonne had stolen money.

"Ken is telling absolutely everyone at work that Yvonne stole so much she almost bankrupted My World. You were just the first witness to his slander campaign.

He's even calling the kitchen staff. At home. Ward also told Helen that Terri ran out of the restaurant in hysterics after she and Ken had a screaming fight downstairs today. Would you like to indulge in second thoughts about my offer of Sambuca now?" Jimmy smiled when the waitress looked their way.

Rose shook her head, but ordered two more iced coffees when the waitress sauntered over. She stirred a short stream of sugar into her glass. The approaching night threatened to be a long one.

"What do you suppose Ken and Terri fought about?" Jimmy floated cream into his glass off the back of his spoon.

Rose widened her eyes and threw her hands out, palms up. Concealing her knowledge of Ken and Yvonne's affair from Jimmy today seemed effortless after trying to hide it from Butler last night. Practice makes perfect.

He licked his spoon. "Well, reliable sources say Terri was screaming something about 'fucking that fat bitch,' who, incidentally, Terri also shrieked 'deserved to die.'"

The secret she'd agonized over protecting was all over town. Everybody knew now. But who had made the information public?

"And, you'll love this part. Ken has also been accusing Nick of killing Yvonne. Blatantly, according to Helen."

"Guess the wronged guy is the bad guy in Ken's mind." Did anyone believe Ken?

"You've been less than frank with me, haven't you? I hate it when you don't take me fully into your confidence." Jimmy pouted again.

"Not just with you. But I don't have anything left to hide." Before he could ask, she told him she could not and would not believe that Nick had killed Yvonne.

He crunched a coffee bean from the Sambuca glass.

"Fine. Let's stop talking about the wretched place. We have to slave there soon enough. We'll just pretend the traffic is a gorgeous river and watch it pour out of town until it's time to trudge into work. What are you two going to do in the country this weekend?"

She painted a lovely picture of hammocks swaying in the breeze, deep green lawns, Combray's simple but elegant country food, and music at Tanglewood. She didn't mention a word about arguing with Butler. An idyllic description seemed better than telling Jimmy about the Greene boys' latest sally.

They talked about places to go and things to do in the Berkshires until time for work, then trudged to My World. They both hesitated at the restaurant's doorstep, neither eager to begin the evening.

Jimmy finally opened the door. "Well, into the fray yet again. It was lovely, if too brief. Ready or not, here we come."

Rose said hello to Laura at the half-empty bar, waved off her effusive thanks for switching shifts, and went to the office for her bank.

She stopped when she saw the downstairs hallway. Cartons upon cartons of liquor lined the walls from the delivery door, past the liquor room, and halfway to the office. They made a blockade of boxes, with only a narrow pathway left to walk through.

Ken had taken advantage of every deep discount the distributors offered. Enzo must have lent him a substantial sum. She couldn't imagine what they'd do with five cases of Midori, or ten of white zinfandel. Somebody or bodies was going to have to spend several hours shelving so much booze. She wondered if it would all fit in the liquor room, or if Ken considered the open hallway secure storage.

August was always a comparatively slow month. This

huge order would inflate Ken's liquor costs unmercifully. He must have missed the chapter on cash flow in his management courses.

A closer look at the boxes showed that some of them already lacked bottles. Please God, let the missing bottles be shelved behind the bar already. They didn't need another opportunity for Ken to accuse the staff of theft.

She straightened her shoulders and knocked on the office door, determined to get her bank and hurry upstairs to the bar as soon as possible.

Laura had an erratic sense of order when shelving bottles. Rose could bear tonight's shift much better if she organized the bar before the rush started. She couldn't stand the idea of another chaotic shift.

Her determination to ignore Ken's advances last night wavered when he opened the office door. The temptation to smack the silly grin off his face made her hand itch. It was hard to be noble to the oblivious. Maybe she should hurl some accusations of her own.

No. Acknowledging his flirtation again would just complicate the mess at My World. Get the bank, count the money, hit the bar. She could be upstairs in three minutes.

"Rosie, just the person I wanted to see. I was half taking a little break from shelving that dynamite delivery and half waiting to talk to you private-like. Guess we won't hear any complaints about the booze supply tonight, huh?" He made a show of stepping a foot back.

She didn't smile. "Right. Can I have my bank, please?"

"In a minute, hon. Oops, I shouldn't call you hon, should I? Which brings me to what I want to talk about here."

He shouldn't call her Rosie, either. Not since first grade.

Ken took a deep breath. "I was outta line last night and I know it. Just 'cause I'm the boss doesn't mean I can't apologize. I've been under a lot of stress lately, not that you couldn't figure that one out yourself. Moving to the Big Apple, taking over this place, trying to keep my girl Terri happy."

Ken sighed at the challenge of his enormous responsibilities, "Damn, but she thinks working for the Victors is like working for God Almighty. Makes her all irrational and way too emotional. I could handle her way easier in Colorado."

She wouldn't react to the idea of Ken's handling Terri. The less she said, the quicker she could head upstairs.

He pointed to the mess of papers on his desk. "I won't even go into the shock of discovering that Yvonne was stealing here, or how hard I've worked to get everything straightened out. Never mind managing a team of people who've just lost someone they thought was their friend. But we're back on track now. Time for a clean slate."

"Some of us still think Yvonne was our friend." She couldn't stop herself.

His voice hardened. "Hey, if your delusions make you happy, keep 'em. Me, I think someone who puts the place where you work in big trouble is less than a pal. Maybe we define friendship differently where I come from."

Maybe they did.

"Anyway, part of my clean slate is to tell you I'm sorry I overstepped my boundaries last night. All the stress, and you looking so cute up on that box, and the way you seem so sympathetic sometimes." He tried a big grin. She didn't smile back.

"But you already have a boyfriend, a cop no less. I should have respected that. What was I thinking, hitting on a cop's girl? Did you happen to mention it to him?"

"I try not to upset Frank more than necessary." Necessity was open to many interpretations. So was an apology that worried more about insulting her boyfriend than offending her girlish self.

"I wish Terri had your smarts. She's making a damn career out of upsetting things lately.

"Anyways, I'm sorry I overstepped last night. Doesn't mean I'm not still attracted to you, but I shouldn't have acted it out, what with you working here and being involved already and all. So, you accept my apology? Even the boss has to admit his mistakes."

Not a word about the fact that he was married. A better boss might see his real mistakes.

"Don't worry about it." She looked at her watch again. "Shift's about to change. Think I can get my bank now?"

First Barney, now Ken. She wished she could hear some genuine remorse in this new apologies trend. So far, she didn't believe either of them regretted a single stupid mistake.

"Sure thing. But there's one more thing I want to mention to you. Stay away from Nick. He's real bad news. Forget that you're both artistic types. I hate the idea that he was killing Yvonne right while I was out exploring this great town. Hey, as a writer, you can probably understand why it bothers me that I was walking by a real old graveyard when somebody, even somebody who wasn't how she appeared to be, was getting killed. What do you call it, irony?" He finally handed her the bank.

"That could be ironic, Ken." It could also be a pretty clumsy way of telling her his alibi and trying to focus the blame on Nick again.

She started counting her bank.

She was halfway through the singles when he

interrupted, "I should finish putting our big delivery away. Close the office door behind you when you're through counting. Even after Yvonne, I gotta start trusting you all again. Can't let one rotten apple spoil the whole bunch, right?"

Ken whistled as he left the office.

Rose sighed as she walked up the stairs. She should tell Jimmy about Ken's confidences and warnings. Later.

The backbar was fully stocked, well organized, and clean. Switching shifts with Laura offered more advantages than an extra day in the country. The surface of the bar itself was cluttered, however.

"Ken try to make you wear one of those stupid t-shirts?" Laura wiped down the service area. She'd crammed so much fruit into the garnish trays that cherry juice stained the sides of the container.

"What t-shirts?" Rose ducked under the service bar and waited for Laura to leave.

Laura pulled her cash drawer from the register, then explained that two cartons of promotional materials had arrived with the liquor delivery today. "Ken wanted me to wear a shirt that said "HOT STUFF" across the chest. What am I, a billboard? Besides, who in the hell wants to drink some spicy cinnamon shit in August? I said no. He seemed annoyed, but there was too much going on around here today for him to insist. Check out the bevnaps and the rest of the promo crap, too."

A dozen piles of garishly patterned napkins advertising several obscure liqueurs replaced the usual plain white bevnaps. New stacks of oddly shaped beer coasters also cluttered the bar. Tented triangles of bright cardboard blared more strange drink suggestions.

The bar looked like a small highway littered with too many miniature billboards. All these materials promoting new cocktails didn't leave much room for actual glasses filled with real drinks. Customers shouldn't be assaulted by advertising while they tried to relax.

Laura lingered at the service station. "It could have been worse. Ken tried to put posters for melonritas on the mirror behind the bar, but Terri came in right then. They went downstairs to yell and scream at each other. Terri ran out of here crying so hard she grabbed a bunch of napkins on her way out. I hid the posters before Ken came upstairs again."

"Well done. At least Terri took some of the napkins. What happened to the regular bevnaps?" Rose started removing the garish coasters.

"Ken said they were boring and took them down to the liquor room. As if they'll fit in there with all the shit he got delivered today. He wanted me to leave the bar to help him put the booze away. Luckily the architects from around the corner came in then and kept me busy at the bar. That room's a tight fit for two people anyway."

Tighter than Laura knew.

"Serving drinks amongst all this clutter will be tight too, if it gets busy." Rose cleared half the mess off the bar and shoved it into the back cupboard. When Laura warned her that Ken might get angry, Rose said she'd take the risk.

As Laura left the bar with more effusive thanks for the switched shifts, Jimmy approached. "Well, time for the drinks of our lives. This place resembles a bad soap opera more every day. I'd fire the set decorator on this one, though. Your bar looks ghastly."

"You should have seen it before I cleared away half of Ken's promotional materials. Go bother your customers, or I'll tell Ken you want to wear one of the t-shirts Laura said he's pushing." Ken hadn't extended his promotional efforts into the dining room, but she didn't suggest Jimmy take any coasters for his tables.

"You were once a pleasant person, Rose."

"I once worked in a pleasant place, Jimmy."

"Cheer up, darling. You have plenty of booze to sell, you're leaving town in a few short hours, and tonight feels as if it will be busy. Things could be worse."

Things could also be better. Yvonne could still be alive.

# Chapter Twenty-three

The terrible traffic doubled My World's early business. The first five people who sat at the bar said they'd decided to postpone leaving town till it took less than four light changes to move one block. Two more foursomes, each with one designated driver who ordered mineral water in a martyred tone, added that the radio said traffic leaving town was as bad as it got. Three couples who'd just driven in from Long Island for a night on the town joked about going against the tide. Familiar faces from the neighborhood, people whose weekend plans wouldn't take them outside of their usual ten-block radius, joined the travelers. A group of six businessmen craving martinis were more interested in cursing the Yankees than in traffic patterns. Within half an hour, all the barstools and most of the standing room at the bar had filled.

Customers seemed in a leisurely mood tonight, lingering over a drink at the bar before even asking about a table. Ken appeared at the host's station wearing a HOT STUFF t-shirt. Perhaps inspired by his shirt's slogan, he sat the dining room systematically, alternating tables between the servers according to plan.

Happily busy, Rose stirred and shook and poured. The heat, and the weekend's arrival, boosted liquor sales more than any scheme Ken could design. She refused to feel grateful for having everything she needed to mix the drinks her customers and the waiters ordered. Some standards had to be maintained.

Dave, Chris, and Greg, three neighborhood regulars whom she hadn't seen in weeks, wanted dinner at the bar. She moved more promo junk away to give them room to eat, then told them she didn't have any news about the search for Yvonne's killer. Yes, she missed Joe and Ben Victors, too, but no, she didn't think the place would change permanently. She bought the three a round when one of them, Dave, unfolded a table tent and started to sketch on its blank lining. She admired his sketch, too.

Rose waved Jimmy over to take the trio's food order, sorry she hadn't checked tonight's menu yet. Jimmy recited tonight's specials, all salads except for the pasta, which also featured more vegetables than a farmers' market. It seemed an odd selection, even for an August evening. Ward usually offered a balanced specials list.

When Jimmy delivered the dinners to the bar, Dave and his friends raved about the size of their salads. My World always served generous portions, but the mounds of greens on these plates almost doubled the normal serving. Any one of these salads could have fed at least two people.

Ward came up to the bar and ordered a special juice half an hour later. The chef looked at the three customers still gamely working on their salads. "Your people have done better than most tonight. Buy them a glass of wine on me to help them get through their dinners. I've seen more food thrown away at the bus station tonight. Still, better the customers get a chance at it than to see it go straight to the trash bin." He gulped his drink.

"What's with the gargantuan servings tonight, Chef? The salads look beautiful, but I couldn't help noticing how, um, generous they are." Best not to test Ward's good humor by mentioning the lopsided selection of specials.

"Call me Chef bloody Goldilocks, luv. Yesterday my salads were too small, and today they're too big. I haven't lost my eye, mind you, just any control over the deliveries. Couldn't get any produce at all yesterday, then today a double order arrived. C.O.D., no less. The idiots simply added the old order to the new, without a thought that they're delivering perishables. I couldn't vet the delivery when it arrived, because the bloody liquor truck blocked the door. Ken was checking in the liquor and told me he'd check the produce delivery too." Ward finished his drink.

The chef chewed half the ice in his glass with loud crunches. "The fool let my food sit out in the heat while the liquor truck unloaded. My prep cooks had to help carry it in from the sidewalk, but I should have set up a soup kitchen right there. The supplier wouldn't take any of it back. Ken had already signed off on the order and paid the driver without even seeing what he paid for."

Rose knew how meticulously Ward vetted his deliveries. The chef would open crates to examine individual fruits and vegetables. He still bragged about catching the dairy vendor selling five-pound boxes of butter that actually weighed four pounds and twelve ounces. He regularly haggled with the seafood supplier over the freshness of the fish and refused deliveries that didn't meet his standards at least once a month.

Ward shook his glass at her. "Kind of you not to mention how salads dominated the specials tonight, sweets. Managing this kitchen is like juggling black holes these days. I knew I was in for trouble when Ken took over the food ordering." He fished the last piece of ice out of the glass with two broad fingers.

"Since the damned fool got me twice as much produce as I could use and then mistreated the food, I decided to pass the bonus onto our customers. I doubt Ken even notices the new portions. Now watch my food costs soar through the roof. I'll relish explaining the reason to Ben upon his return, however."

Ward thanked her for his juice, asked her to put a few extra beers on ice for the kitchen crew, then lumbered back into the kitchen. He might have run back to his domain if she'd told him where Ken had gotten the cash for today's deliveries.

Jimmy took Ward's place at the service station and ordered six black russians. "Too bad we're running low on desserts tonight. Grazing their way through Ward's fields of greens leaves our guests with the desire to end their meals on a sweet note. Chef tell you about the fucked up deliveries?"

"Eloquently. First we don't have enough of anything, then we have too much. God, am I glad to be getting away from here for a few days." She looked at her watch again.

"Braggart." Jimmy took his drinks and left the bar before she could tell him about her conversation with Ken. The dining room and bar were slowing down. They'd have time to talk later.

Jimmy always made time to talk.

Dave declared tonight Bonus Night when she offered his trio the wine Ward had sponsored. With the wine's help, Dave and Greg finished their salads, but Chris pushed his unemptied plate away. "Can't remember the last time I couldn't finish a dinner. Hope this doesn't ruin my reputation as a starving artist."

Rose promised she wouldn't tell anyone. When Chris asked how her work was going, she answered with more questions about his search for a gallery. Bad enough many of the regulars had learned she was writing a novel. The grapevine didn't have to know how poorly her manuscript grew these days.

She didn't ask if Chris or his friends knew Nick. All the artists in Manhattan weren't acquainted, despite Ken's assertions.

A large and complicated drink order from Helen distracted her from wondering where Nick was tonight.

Rose hadn't had time to notice Terri's absence till she walked into the restaurant shortly after midnight. Ken had done a good job running the floor alone all night. Perhaps there was more to promotional slogans than she'd thought.

Terri's appearance advertised a different mood. She'd arranged her hair into new heights and plastered on enough makeup for a drag beauty pageant. Her frilly blouse hung off her shoulders, revealing a surprising amount of cleavage produced by the miraculous wonders of a pushup bra. Terri's very tight, very short, very red skirt lengthened her legs down into red sandals with three-inch spike heels. Rose couldn't imagine walking across her bedroom in such shoes, much less around the restaurant. Forget the streets.

Terri sashayed past the bar without her usual cheery hello, spotted Ken in the dining room, and teetered up to him. The eyes of most of the men in the place followed her. Ken smiled broadly when he saw his wife, then pursed his lips into a wolf whistle not often heard indoors. Terri's skirt rose even higher when she threw her arms around Ken's neck and kissed him with a starlet's enthusiasm.

Her garter belt was red too.

One of the men at the bar groaned. His friends shook their heads in sympathy and ordered another round.

Helen waited at the service station. "Sorry, but I need four brandy alexanders. Everybody's jonesing for sweets tonight. I'll wait here for them without even looking at the fucking freak show in the dining room. Terri looks like a Ninth Avenue hooker, and all the assholes in the place are eating her up. Just when I had a nice flirtation going with the blonde at table seven, the slut goddess arrived. He's history after the way he drooled over her."

Rose filled four birdbaths with the foamy drink, then poured an extra two inches into a rocks glass for Helen. "Drink up. It'll give you energy. And maybe patience."

"Fuck patience. I'm here for the money." Helen lifted her glass in a salute before she emptied it. She swaggered slightly as she delivered the drinks to table eight, rocking her hips in a dancer's practiced strut. Rose wondered if anybody would appreciate Helen's choreographed mockery.

Not Ken. His eyes never left Terri's ass as she sauntered to the bar. The three women at table five giggled as he stood next to them, still clutching the check he'd meant to deliver. One of the women finally grabbed it out of his hand. Then she offered him her napkin and mimed wiping the lipstick off his face.

The jukebox paused between songs, and the sound of Terri's heels clattered across the dining room in a deliberate cadence, as if she'd discovered the Morse code for lust. Four male customers rose to offer her their barstools. She shook her head and smiled prettily at all of them, then stood at the end of the bar.

"Hi, Rose. Hon, that outfit you're wearing isn't one of your most flattering. Makes you look like you're trying to hide some extra weight. You and Frank been hitting the ice cream a teensy bit too often these days? Not that Frankie ever gains an ounce, of course."

Rose might find some small comfort in the fact that Terri didn't know about Butler's softening middle. Maybe. And Butler could have loved ice cream as a teenager, too. Probably.

Her waistband wasn't the slightest bit tight. No need at all to worry about what the summer's first bathing suit might reveal tomorrow. "Sorry you don't like the outfit, Terri. I was going for comfort." And resolutely ignoring the insult.

"I'll talk to Ken about hurrying to get the new uniforms in here. Don't worry, they'll be comfortable. But they'll also be cute. They'll even look good on less-than-perfect shapes."

Rose ignored this implied insult, too, and asked Terri what she wanted to drink.

"How about a blended iced cappuccino, with lots of foam on top and just a touch of Amaretto? Not too much, though. Some of us still worry about our figures."

Strike three.

# Chapter Twenty-four

The drink order itself might have been Terri's cruelest blow of all. Every bartender Rose knew wanted to kill whoever had first suggested putting an espresso machine behind the bar. Making a single cappuccino took longer than pouring a dozen cocktails. She also had to turn her back to the bar while she made it, ignoring her customers and the wait staff. A series of multiple coffee orders from the floor could disrupt the best bartender's whole rhythm.

Terri only wanted one cappuccino. She also wanted it blended. Rose had just changed the water in the wash sink after cleaning the blender from the brandy alexanders. She'd have to change it again right after she washed the blender this time, too, to get rid of another milky residue.

Terri probably hadn't meant to order such a labor intensive drink. Maybe not.

Rose made the coffee, winced while the blender shrieked, and served Terri the concoction. She washed the blender and started to drain the sink again.

Terri clicked her glittery nails on the bar to get Rose's attention. "Scrumptious, hon, but it needs just a teense more Amaretto. Blend it again, please, so it stays nice and thick. Maybe Ken will want one when he gets a break, too."

"I could make it for him now." Or spend the rest of her life washing blenders and scalding her fingers in newly poured hot water.

"No, you and I need to have a little talk private-like before he joins us. Trust me, he won't come to the bar for a few minutes." Terri pronounced the second version of her drink "perfecto."

A busy bar didn't offer the best place for a private talk. Rose hoped the topic wouldn't be clothes again. Or weight. Or Butler. She couldn't think of a topic she did want to discuss with Terri at the moment.

"Check your bar and see if the waiters need anything. I want your total attention when I talk to you." Terri's new look had inspired a more commanding tone than Rose had ever heard before. Maybe she and Ken had been renting dominance videos.

Rose did as she'd been told, disappointed at the lack of drink orders from her customers or the dining room, then poured herself a large mineral water. She sucked in her stomach when she stood in front of Terri again.

"It's about Ken. I'm going to say this as nice as I can, and I'm only going to say it once. Uncle Joe speaks real highly of you, and I'd hate to have to do anything drastic. But I will if I have to." Terri beckoned Rose closer with nails louder than her garter belt.

"Leave Ken alone. You flirt with him anymore, I'll fire you, no matter how good you are at your job. Uncle Joe would understand anything I have to do to protect my marriage. You've got Frank for now. Leave my husband alone."

For now? Rose cleared her throat and told Terri that she'd never flirted with her husband. Never even thought about it.

"Don't deny it. He told me all about how you throw yourself at him. Your performance last night embarrassed him so much that he needed to talk about it. A good marriage is based on communication." Terri spoke the platitude as if she'd just invented the concept.

"I know how attractive Ken is, and I can't really blame you for wanting him. But he's mine. So stay away. I still want you and me to be friends. I can forgive you for losing your head one time, but not twice."

"Terri, you can't—"

"The topic is closed. Now, I think the gentlemen at the end of the bar need their cocktails refreshed." Terri fluffed her hair and gave Rose a smile colder than the ice bin.

Seething, Rose walked to the far end of the bar. She asked the four remaining businessmen, now on their fifth martinis, if they wanted refills. She refilled the water glasses they'd alternated with their cocktails, then she slowly and methodically chilled new glasses and more vodka, acting too engrossed in her task to chat with the group. The men were holding their liquor well, but her mood could extinguish a dozen martinis' mellow glow.

Terri's warning had left Rose as close to speechless as she could imagine. The mouse had roared. Terri's aggressive approach, Ken's reversing the roles in last night's come-on, the threat of being fired, and the very idea that she found Ken attractive—she didn't know which was more ludicrous, or more infuriating.

A flurry of orders from Jimmy and Helen gave her a few minutes to calm herself, even if half of them were for espressos and lattes. Turning her back to Terri at the bar seemed a wise move now.

As soon as the steam's racket quieted, Terri waved

Rose back again. "Okay, hon, I'm glad we had our little talk. I'm going back to the kitchen to tell Ward to make me a little snack now. I'll have another of these scrumptious concoctions when I'm through." Terri flounced across the dining room on her way to the kitchen, her body again a magnet for the male eyes in the restaurant.

Little talk? No point in explaining the difference between dialogue and monologue, as if defining literary terms in a madhouse could prove sanity. Terri's tone had forbidden any response when she'd pronounced the topic closed. Her diminutive temporary boss had shown more than her legs tonight.

"You and Ter have a nice little chat? I'm not supposed to ask what you talked about. Gimme one of those things she was drinking, heavy on the Amaretto." Ken didn't meet her eyes once as he spoke.

"Maybe you and I need to talk, Ken." She substituted brewed coffee for the cappuccino in his drink.

"Hey, I'm busy. Quit looking like you're pissed and give the customers some smiles. Let's see a more professional attitude, huh?"

A professional bartender would not throw a full blender at her boss. Rose held the handle of the blender cup very tightly as she poured Ken's drink. She put the cup on the drainboard without washing it, certain that Terri would want another frothy concoction soon.

Past 1:00. Barely three more hours to work, and then she'd have all weekend to think about the implications of Terri's speech. Or not think about them, if she wanted to enjoy the trip.

Leaving Manhattan had never seemed a more pleasant prospect. Catherine's idea of collaborating on a cookbook held a new appeal.

Dave and his friends left, thanking Rose profusely

for the free drinks and tipping more than thirty percent. Three new couples arrived, ordered a round of seabreezes, and started to discuss their sailing vacation next week. Their happy plans didn't need Rose's attention. Just when she wanted the distraction of idle barchat, nobody wanted to talk to the bartender.

Helen apologized when she ordered another round of brandy alexanders. Rose washed the blender cup and made the drinks, hating feeling more like a soda jerk than a bartender.

Fifteen minutes later, Jimmy ordered a glass of red wine for Terri, who sat at a table in the back with a large salad in front of her. "I suppose she's ordering red to match that outfit, which I categorically refuse to discuss. Life is too short, and beauty is too precious. What time will you and Butler arrive in the Berkshires?"

As if conjured by Jimmy's question, Butler walked in the door and up to the bar. "Don't give me that look. I know it's early, but I reached a point where I could either leave work right then or stay another six hours if I opened one more folder. Wouldn't mind eating something before the drive, either. Don't worry, I won't sit here."

He waved to Terri at her table. Rose watched Terri crook her finger and beckon Butler to join her. Her nails looked like tiny red signal flags on the Good Ship Slut.

"Matter of fact, maybe I'll go eat with Terri over there. That way you can't complain about me waiting at your bar too long. See you later."

Butler went to join Terri before Rose could tell him that she'd welcome his company at the bar tonight. Terri stood, smoothed her skirt so that the fabric outlined her garter belt, and gave Butler a welcoming hug.

Rose wished she could see Butler's face. She watched his back instead, trying to read his reaction to Terri's outfit

232 Maureen Anne Jennings

in his body language. She'd memorized the wrinkles across his shoulders before the hug ended.

Ken hurried over and shook Butler's hand, then rested both hands on Terri's shoulders in a gesture that screamed private property. He eventually handed Butler a menu, talked a moment longer, then walked to the kitchen, waving Jimmy away when he approached Terri's table. Ken must have wanted to place Butler's food order himself, something he never did. Just another irrational glitch in the evening.

Rose told herself she wasn't sending a glass of wine to Butler's table because he had to drive. It had nothing to do with the way he leaned over the table toward Terri.

She watched Jimmy bring Butler a cup of house coffee, then waved him over to the bar. "Could you hear what they're talking about?"

"Trust is so important in a relationship, isn't it, Rose? I tried my best to drop some eaves, but they both pasted smiles on their faces and stopped talking when I approached. I'll try again, of course."

"Thanks. I wish I could read lips better." She tried to smile.

"Difficult when they're both eating, darling. Wonder what Ken ordered for your boyfriend's dinner."

"You think I should worry about it? Maybe he told Ward to poison Frank." Or to give him a small salad.

"You and I both know that, should the urge to poison hit Ward, he'd be much more likely to add special spices to Ken's plate. Chef hasn't stopped bitching about the food deliveries all night. Let me go check my tables. I'll linger near Terri and her dinner date too, see if they're whispering sweet nothings to each other."

Rose glared at Jimmy.

"Save the ugly look for the *tete a tete* table, please.

I'm certainly not flirting with your boyfriend."

"You're a wise man."

"With good taste, too. And more grace than to even consider flirting with someone you're attached to, even if he weren't so resolutely heterosexual."

Terri could use some of Jimmy's grace tonight. Rose had seen her lean across the table and put her hand on Butler's arm twice already. "Go spy now. Come back and tell me what they're talking about."

Jimmy saluted and left the bar. He grabbed a coffee pot from the bus station on his way to Terri's table. Rose watched both Butler and Terri stop speaking while Jimmy approached the table and refilled Butler's coffee cup. Then Terri said something Rose couldn't even guess at to Jimmy. The restaurant was too loud and the table too far away.

Butler and Terri's loud laughter carried over to the bar when Jimmy left their table. No way in hell they had laughed about Rose gaining weight, of course.

Jimmy marched back to the bar. "Terri wants another scrumptious drinkypoo. I swear that's what she said, or slightly slurred. She also wants to treat your boyfriend to a virgin version of the same thing. 'Virgin version' was quite a challenge to her pronunciation skills tonight. I assume you remember what the drinkypoo is?"

"All too well. It'll take a few minutes to make their drinks, if you need to check your other tables." Terri was watching her, so she had to produce the damn cappuccino.

Butler always refused Ken's offers of a drink on the house. Why would he accept Terri's?

Rose didn't like any of the answers that occurred to her while she made the drinks. None at all.

Nor did she like how tonight reversed the roles in her relationship with Butler. She'd asked him not to spend hours at My World during her shifts to prevent his jealousy, not hers. It was too easy to misinterpret the attention she paid her male customers as motivated by more than the desire for a good tip. She'd never considered worrying about his flirting while she worked. Until tonight.

It was an ugly variation on the theme, made even worse by Terri's little speech earlier. Leave my husband alone. Now watch while I flirt with your boyfriend. Fatso.

Rose did watch, relieved when she saw Butler lean back in his chair, pulling his arm away from Terri's descending hand. If Terri were engaging in some sort of revenge flirtation, who did she want to suffer more? Rose? Or Ken?

She looked for Ken in the dining room, then remembered seeing him go downstairs a while ago. He hadn't stayed to watch his wife and Butler. He hadn't approached Rose again either. Maybe Terri had told him to stay away from her, too.

All she needed now was for Nick to walk in. But he wouldn't.

Jimmy waved to Rose from across the dining room, pulled on his ear in a wiseguy's gesture, and shook his head no.

Rose refused to watch Terri's table any longer.

The businessmen at the end of the bar wanted just one more martini, and several other customers said yes when she asked if they wanted refills. Nothing like an attack of jealousy to boost her sales skills.

She'd made herself too busy to notice Butler standing at the end of the bar. "I may never eat another piece of lettuce as long as I live. You should be out of here in, what, an hour? Think you could trust me with your apartment keys long enough for me to swing by for your bags? That way we can get right on the road when you're done."

Rose agreed, told him her bag waited by her hall door, and fished her keys out of her purse behind the bar.

She handed him the key ring. "What did you and Terri talk about for so long?"

"Nothing much, mostly memories. She's in some weird mood tonight, though. I'll wait in the car out front after I get your stuff. Maybe I'll even catnap till you're done."

"After all that coffee?"

He smiled. "I didn't know you were watching so closely. Slow night at the bar?"

"Not bad, but I did have time to watch the floor show." She didn't smile back.

He laughed, patted her cheek, and walked out the door.

She started the first stages of cleaning the bar, anxious to leave town as soon as possible after last call.

She wouldn't let herself think about Butler alone in her apartment. Could he resist the temptation to spy?

# Chapter Twenty-five

Rose didn't see Butler's battered Bonneville when she finally left work. He'd had more than enough time to drive to her apartment and back, even allowing for a slow climb up the stairs. And a quick look around, if he thought the court of true love issued search warrants.

She walked to the near corner and peered up the street. No Bonneville. Humidity blurred the streetlamps in a sickly yellow fog. Nothing looked right, and nothing looked like Butler's car. She wiped the sweat off her face, retraced her steps, and checked the far corner. Still no Bonneville.

Thirty-five minutes past four on a Saturday morning wasn't a safe time to search for a missing ride. A car with Jersey plates slowed, and the boisterous young men inside offered her a ride anywhere she wanted to go. She refused, glad to see an approaching cab. The Jerseyites pulled away when she waved to the taxi. Despite its shining on-duty light, the cab already carried a full load of passengers. It sped by. The street seemed too quiet again.

Butler's car was impossible to miss, even before the Greene boys' attack. She looked again anyway. He could have fallen asleep inside and not seen her searching for him. But she would still see him, if only he were here.

A few more cars cruised by, slowing at the sight of a woman walking alone on a deserted street. None of the drivers bothered her, but such luck wouldn't hold. It was too late on a hot weekend night, too close to the hookers' blocks, with too many of the men heading home after long nights of drinking.

Rose retreated to My World's doorway, hoping its shelter would make her less of a target. She'd already waited outside over fifteen minutes. Terri and Ken would walk out through this same doorway soon. The prospect of seeing those two again tonight seemed worse than the street's dangers.

She cursed Butler, searching the street as if his Bonneville would magically appear in a spot she'd already passed. Where could he be and what could have kept him? She couldn't reconcile his absence with the protective instincts she usually complained about. Some protection.

After five more minutes, she started to worry. Anything could have happened. He could have passed a robbery in progress, stopped to intervene, and been shot like that cop last month. He could have fallen and not been able to get up. He could have abandoned her forever and decided to run away with Terri.

Not until Terri left the restaurant, though. She and Ken would appear any minute, and Rose did not want to listen to Terri gloat her syrupy pity at Butler's lateness.

Men were probably never late for Terri.

Ten more minutes and no Butler. Rose started to walk to the corner, hoping to find an empty cab this time. Whatever his explanation, he could call her with it at home. She tried not to think he might be unable to call.

A black Cadillac approached, honked, and pulled

over next to her. She quickened her pace, not looking at the driver. Damn Butler.

The driver honked again. She walked faster, almost ready to run.

Another honk.

"It's me. Get in. Sorry I'm late."

"A Cadillac, Frank? What took you so long?" The car's air-conditioning felt like jumping into a cool lake.

"I didn't want to embarrass you with the Bonneville, so I rented this today. They didn't have anything else left. Your phone rang just as I unlocked your door, and I couldn't help but hear Catherine saying she'd love a dozen loaves of semolina bread, if you could find any at this hour. So I swung by Zito's and talked them into an early sale. We have a baker's dozen, in case you want one on the way up."

Catherine would have preferred the battered Bonneville to the ostentatious Cadillac, but Rose appreciated his wanting to rent something more presentable. And his extravagance. Summer weekend car rentals didn't offer any bargains.

"No wonder it smells so good in here. You just bought yourself a place on Catherine's good side." Once she got over her shock at seeing Rose arrive in a cashmobile, of course.

It took him a minute to find the switch for the headlights. "Why didn't you wait for me inside? You're crazy to wander around alone at this hour of night."

She didn't point out that the high beams were on. "Not as crazy as I'd have been if I'd gone back inside that madhouse. I had more than enough of the place tonight, thank you."

"Yeah, I couldn't wait to get out of there myself earlier. I've never seen Terri so wound up." He adjusted the lights.

She grunted, refraining from mentioning how very much of Terri everyone had seen tonight. The sweet yeasty smell of the bread filled the car in luscious contrast to the welcome chill of the air-conditioner. She reached into the back and pulled a golden loaf out of the tall brown paper bag. The bread was still warm.

Rose relaxed into her seat, fiddling with the controls until she'd stretched into the most comfortable position. Compared to the Bonneville, the Caddy's seat seemed like the most luxurious of armchairs. "This feels lovely. Thanks."

She nibbled on the bread, passed him a hunk, and hoped they could drive away from all tonight's troubles.

Rose snuggled deeper into her seat, relishing feeling almost too cold. Butler played with the radio until mellow jazz filled the car. Too bad they couldn't extend the two hours to the Berkshires into a cross-county trek, driving far enough so that the radio would only play corny country stations with livestock reports. Maybe they could just keep going north, to the continent's edge.

"Sorry I snapped at you about being late. But it was spooky looking for you on the street." Spooky seemed miles behind them now.

"I figured, worst that could happen, you'd have to listen to Ken and Terri for another ten minutes. I wouldn't have bothered with the bread if I'd thought you'd leave My World before I got back."

"It doesn't matter now. You know, I think this strange sensation I'm experiencing is a sense of absolute safety. We're not even out of Yonkers yet, and the city seems miles behind us already. You're a genius, darling."

Flattery seemed easier in a luxury car. She could ask Catherine why later.

Or Terri.

# Chapter Twenty-six

Rose stirred when the car slowed to exit the Taconic Parkway. She'd fallen into an exhausted half-sleep, lulled by the smooth motion and soft music, but never able to fully silence her thoughts. She remembered confused images of pie crusts and torn drink coasters, not the stuff that dreams were made of.

A soft morning light misted the hills. Butler smiled when she stretched and asked if she needed to stop for coffee or anything.

She bought a glazed donut and two styrofoam coffees at the gas station in Hillsdale. Her face looked pale and wrinkled in the unlocked bathroom's harsh light. Cold water hadn't helped; coffee might.

Rose handed Butler the donut, swearing it wasn't a cop joke. They groaned simultaneously when they tasted their bitter brew, which must have languished on a burner all night. That shared reaction seemed a good omen for the rest of the weekend. They needed to enjoy each other's company again.

Butler refused her offer to drive, saying the coffee

had more than perked him up. Rose ignored the pun, determined to enjoy the last part of the trip.

Even the Bickersons would enjoy this ride. Sleepy small towns floated by, not yet crammed with the traffic that would clog them by noon. She saw more birds than cars.

And heard more birds, too, when they rolled down the windows to enjoy what her mother had called good clean country air. The sounds of chirping and peeping welcomed them.

"It smells so good, Frank. Let's stay forever."

"Forever and a day, Rose."

She marveled at the thousand shades of green on the lawns, bushes, and trees lining the road. The verdant bounty of an east coast summer still surprised her Californian's eyes. The greens were so lush, deepening into the woods in tangled shades. These were colors to submerge in, to lose yourself in, to forget everything. She could swim in these greens.

"The greens are so amazing."

He patted her hand. "Don't worry; we'll stop them soon."

"I meant the colors outside, the ones found in nature."

Butler finished his donut and brushed at the flakes of hardened sugar on his shirt. "Welcome to Massachusetts."

He put the largest flake of frosting on her lips. His eyes finally left the road when she started to massage his thigh. After half a mile, he firmly placed her hand back in her own lap.

Happy Saturday.

Great Barrington hadn't woken up yet. No early-morning joggers cruised its empty streets, and no tourists clustered outside its closed shoppes.

The soft curves of the Berkshires rose around them as they drove toward Stockbridge. Several trees on the side of the road were already tipped with gold, previewing the fall palette's extravaganza. If the country continued to work its soothing magic, she might even suggest she and Butler plan a return trip to admire those colors.

They hadn't argued in several hours now. Maybe she could stop keeping count soon.

Stockbridge waited, frozen in its perpetual postcard perfection, Main Street lacking only a freckle-faced kid delivering papers on a battered Schwinn. Rose wished their rented car were an actual carriage.

When they passed the old graveyard, she asked Butler if he'd walk back into town with her later to read the headstones. He muttered something about a busman's holiday and promised they could do whatever she wanted after a long nap.

"Now that you've brought up your job, let's make a pact. I'll swear not to talk about Yvonne or the craziness at my work if you'll promise not to talk about the case while we're up here. We need a break from the ugly."

"Done." He dropped his right hand from the wheel and reached to shake hers. "Best idea you've had all year."

Another mile out of town and they reached Catherine's. Rose felt the familiar bite of envy when she saw the three-story white house. Built in 1865, the house had four bedrooms, seven fireplaces, two parlors, a dining room, a library, an enormous kitchen, and a separate pantry bigger than most Manhattan bedrooms. Catherine used half the rooms and joked about starting an underground railroad for New York refugees in the others.

Butler groaned when he saw the note on the front door announcing the lock was stuck and directing them to make noise and come in through the mudroom. He stopped complaining about stupid risks when he heard Bergdorf and Bendel, Catherine's two Great Danes. The dogs' ferocious barking silenced his questions about crime rate in the country.

Rose hurried around the side of the house, calling to the dogs. Their slobber smeared the small paned windows lining the mud room, and their barking sounded loud enough to shatter the glass. Butler looked shocked when she ordered the dogs to charge, then tried to hide his relief when she explained that was Catherine's command code to quiet her animals. He still hung back a few steps when she opened the mudroom door.

Rose hadn't finished telling the dogs what good puppies they were and scratching behind their ears when Catherine's voice called from upstairs. "Rose? Let the little darlings out, tell that gorgeous boyfriend I spied from my window to relax, and get your butt upstairs now."

The gorgeous boyfriend offered to carry in the bags and make friends with the beasts. Sight unseen, he'd joined Catherine's fan club.

Rose raced up the steep narrow staircase.

Catherine met her in the hall, dressed in a brightly embroidered kimono that fell open to reveal the blue silk boxers underneath. Just an inch short of six feet, Catherine had a '50s pinup's figure she called Barbie plus. Her hair was dark brown this month, cut close to her scalp in a convict's cut. The contrast between her lush body and severe hair worked, even before coffee. As soon as they stopped giggling and hugging each other, Rose would tell her so.

Catherine stretched in a pose Vargas would have painted. "It's almost seven. So much for my plans to make the kitchen smell like bread before you arrived. You or that man hungry?"

"No, we're probably too tired to eat."

"Perfect. I have gallons of fresh tomato juice just dying to become bloody marys. No vodka in mine, but I want that man to have his first impression of me softened by booze."

Rose told Catherine not to worry about meeting Butler and told herself that these two people she loved would certainly love each other. Of course they would. Her sudden attack of nervousness about how Butler and Catherine would get along owed more to memories of other bad combinations than to these two personalities. Of course it did.

Catherine hurried into a quick shower, and Rose walked downstairs.

Butler waited in the kitchen, a room half the size of Rose's entire apartment. Morning sun poured in through the wall of windows above the table, and the room smelled better than bread, some mix of spices Rose couldn't identify.

Catherine appeared in white leggings and a snug shirt announcing that women were waitresses at the banquet of life, one of her inexhaustible collection of acerbic shirts. She'd explained years ago that if men were going to stare at her chest anyway, they might as well learn something. Butler looked like an appreciative pupil as he stood to shake Catherine's hand.

He turned into an honor student when Catherine ignored his hand, hugged him, and told him her house was his. She grated fresh horseradish into a pitcher of spiced tomato juice, poured three tall glasses, and added vodka from the freezer to two.

"Don't argue; a drink will put you both to sleep. God help me, Rose, this tomato juice is an offshoot of last week's canning. Kill me if I start to make dried flower wreaths."

Catherine drank half her juice in one long swallow. "Mmmm. Better than coffee. I want to get into work while it's still cool. You two can tour the, um, grounds, after your power nap. Plenty of snacks in the fridge, and pick whatever you want from the garden. Your dinner reservation is at whatever time you arrive tonight. If the new kid works out, I may even be able to sit with you by then. Sorry I have to run."

Butler offered to walk Catherine to her car. When she told him she didn't need an escort in her own driveway, he reminded her about the semolina bread.

"You found it? How resourceful. He's a keeper, Rose. I like him already."

"Me too, Cath." Rose sipped her drink while she watched Butler and Catherine chat their way out to the cars and Butler transfer the big bread bag to Catherine's Volvo. She'd never had vodka at 7:30 in the morning before. It was perfect after the long drive, much more restorative than coffee.

"I thought your friend was crazy when she suggested these drinks, but they're exactly right. So much for good clean country living." Butler poured himself another glass of juice, sans vodka.

"We're on vacation now."

"And we have your friend's gorgeous estate all to ourselves for several hours. Should we frolic on the lawn or something?" He raised his eyebrows and tried to wiggle them. "How the hell do you frolic anyway?"

"I'm sure the retired minister across the road would love it if we did. How about a walk instead? I can show you a pretty pond less than a mile away."

"Less than a mile?" His eyebrows lowered.

"Think of it as ten blocks. I want to stretch out after the drive up here. We can take the dogs for protection, officer."

He agreed only after she promised a swim in the pond.

They walked up the dirt road behind Catherine's house. When Rose angled into the woods, Butler stopped still. "Where are you taking me? First an unpaved road, now an unmarked path. Where are the sidewalks?"

"I know the way. Trust me. The dogs will lead us back if we get lost."

"Just where is this pond?"

She pointed ahead. "On the other side of this hill. We can walk straight up, or circle around. It's two miles if we take the easy way."

"How can the easy way be longer? What are you, some crazed girl scout all of a sudden?" He shuffled his loafers.

She promised the climb would be worth it and started scrambling up the hill. Her memories of the path had described a gentler slope. Her memories were also two years old, and her city shoes had slick soles.

They stopped to rest at the top. Butler leaned against a white birch. She reached around him and peeled off a long strip of bark. "People used to write on this. I've always loved that idea."

"If we have to make ink out of nuts and berries, I'm outta here."

"Sssh. Look."

They stood in second-growth woods. Sunlight dappled through the canopy of leaves. Tall grasses and infant saplings grew around their knees. There wasn't a bare patch of ground to be seen.

The birds that had stilled as they crashed through the underbrush resumed their songs over the quiet buzz of insects. The woods seemed more alive than the city ever had.

She held a finger to her lips, then pointed to the small pond in the valley below. A breeze rippled the water's surface, which sparkled in the morning light like a natural neon.

Butler shouted that the last one in the water would be a big loser and rushed down the hill, his knees rejuvenated by his taunt. She raced after him, yelling cautions about the pond's depth. A granite outcropping submerged along one side of the pond could break a diver's neck.

She ran faster when she realized she'd never seen Butler dive or swim. They'd never been in the woods together before, either. Except for one blissfully snowbound weekend in Bearsville, they'd played out their affair within Manhattan's embrace.

Butler's pants and shirt already hung from a tree branch when she reached the pond. He waited for her to strip, then took her hand and led her over the mossy rocks into the water. They walked further into the pool. Mud squelched between her toes and tiny fish bit her knees.

Splashing and playing like ten-year-olds, they swam into the pond's deep center. She guided Butler to the submerged granite, where the water was only shoulder-deep. He lifted her to his waist. Their play turned more adult.

She floated on her back when they finished, watching the leaves dance on the trees circling the pond. The long trip, the longer day, and Catherine's relaxing cocktails made her wish she could sleep in the water. Butler waded onto the bank and sprawled on a patch of moss. "Get out of there before you doze off and drown, please. I wouldn't have the energy to play lifeguard."

She joined him and collapsed onto the soft moss.

He slicked his hair back. "Nature girl forget towel?"

"We'll drip dry."

He slipped an arm under her neck to pillow her head, and the springy moss cushioned her back. They lay so quietly she could almost feel each drop of water evaporate from her skin. She closed her eyes against the sun and watched the little dots jitterbug inside her eyelids.

A cold spray of water and loud barking woke her. The dogs had left the pond to shake their coats dry a foot away from her and Butler. He groaned and clenched his eyes more tightly. "Damn animals. I could have slept here all day."

She pressed her forefinger into his pinkened chest. Only the faintest white mark remained when she lifted her hand. "You may owe them a bone or two, Frank. Catherine must have trained the dogs for sunburn patrol. The sun's climbed a lot higher since we dozed off."

"Then where are the flasks of sunscreen around their necks? You trying to tell me I'm not responsible for your rosy glow?" He grabbed his shirt off the tree branch and tossed it to her. "Dry the dogs' spray off yourself and let's get going. It's a long walk back."

She threw the shirt back to him. "But think of the big bed waiting for us in Catherine's guest room."

He raised his right arm and bellowed for a taxi.

# Chapter Twenty-seven

They climbed the stairs to the guest room. Small-paned windows along the top halves of three walls looked into the maples. The view into the gently moving branches and the leaves brushing against the windows reminded Rose of her childhood treehouse. The trees cradled the room and anyone in it.

Butler seemed more intrigued by the tall antique armoire which Catherine had added to the room since Rose's last visit. He opened it and admired the workmanship of its interior. Then he angled the door so its mirror reflected the bed.

"Cute trick, Frank. Look at all the treats Catherine left us." She showed him the bowl of fruit, tin of shortbread, and piles of new books on the bedside tables.

"Hey, I thought admiring antiques was a required activity in the Berkshires. How rude would we look if we stayed in this room the whole weekend?"

"Too rude. But we do have the whole afternoon." When she pulled back the coverlet, a faint scent of lavender rose from the bed. The cool cotton sheets felt as silky as pond water against her skin. Their reflections in the old mirror wavered as if they were still underwater. They swam in the glass for a long time before sleeping.

Butler only snored when he was very tired. The volume racketing from the next pillow attested to his exhaustion.

Then she heard the dogs barking downstairs. So much for a quiet country nap. She slipped out of bed to investigate. Catherine's car had returned.

Fearful of waking Butler by rummaging through her luggage but unwilling to put on yesterday's bar-scented clothes, she tiptoed naked down the hall and grabbed one of the several kimonos that hung on the back of Catherine's bathroom door. She belted the kimono and admired its embroidered hem puddling around her feet, then hoisted the material up so she wouldn't kill herself walking downstairs.

She followed the sound of coffee grinding back to the kitchen. The rhinestone cat clock next to the fridge said it was 2:15. An extravagant arrangement of lilies, Queen Anne's lace, and peonies dominated the kitchen table. Catherine carried in another large vase filled with heirloom roses and plopped it on the kitchen counter. "Did we wake you? Did you get any sleep? Coffee?"

"No. Some. Yes, please." Rose buried her nose in the heirlooms. "This smell reminds me of reading in my grandmother's back yard during summer vacations. She had rose bushes tall enough for me to crawl under. I see you haven't lost your touch."

"I didn't grow these." Catherine handed Rose a delicate china cup and saucer.

"Nobody thought you had. New admirer?"

"Yeah, some Manhattan shrink who Augusts up here. That's what he calls it, Augusting. But he's more in love with my food than with me. Wait till you see what else

I have."

Catherine ran outside and returned carrying a flat of deep red strawberries. She pulled a big foil-wrapped lump out of her shoulder bag. "Let's make tarts while we gossip. Tarts by tarts, if you will. The dough's all ready. Frank gonna sleep awhile?"

"Forever, from the sound of it. This good clean country air has exhausted him."

"From the beardburn on your face, I'd guess Mother Nature had an accomplice in wearing him out."

Rose covered her chin with her hand and considered claiming a sunburn, but Catherine knew her, and her skin, too well.

"So, Rose, is this the real thing? Is he a keeper?"

"Sometimes I think yes, sometimes I don't know. It's been real tough at work lately. Tough with him, too."

Catherine rinsed the strawberries and handed Rose the colander, a paring knife, and a big white ceramic bowl. She rummaged in her kitchen drawers while she instructed Rose to hull the berries over the bowl so as not to lose any of the precious juice. Rose stiffened when Catherine found the rolling pin and reminded her guest to look for bruises.

"Forget work. You can tell me about that when he's listening. I want to hear about your love life. God knows you've listened to enough installments of mine over the years." Catherine leaned over Rose and picked out a handful of perfect berries for garnish.

Rose twisted the paring knife around another starry stem. "My personal life and work are too intertwined these days. My World is hell, and Frank's involved professionally. That affects us personally."

"I knew by the tone of your last message that you weren't telling me something. Spill." Catherine sat on the kitchen counter, her hands for once idle.

Rose told Catherine about Yvonne's murder, about Nick, and about Terri and Ken. Then she told her about the Greene boys.

The clock said 3:15 when Rose finished, "So, there's a homicidal maniac running around the restaurant again, my male boss is a cheater at best, I'm strongly attracted to someone my boyfriend thinks is a murderer, and said boyfriend seems a little too sympathetic to my female boss. Watch for me on afternoon television soon."

"As the amazing woman who tells all on only one cup of coffee?" Catherine refilled both their cups. "What bothers you most about all this?"

"Aside from the fact that these nasty real life murders keep getting in the way of the ones I want to write about? We won't even talk about how astoundingly unproductive I've been since Yvonne's death." Rose picked a fleck of green stem out of the berry bowl.

"You'll get back to work soon. You always do. Excuse my back." Catherine started to roll out the dough and line the tart shells.

Rose made herself ignore the flour that had fallen onto Catherine's pants.

"Why can't you just concentrate on your work and let Frank do his?" Catherine turned around and watched Rose's face.

"It's my insatiable need to know, a hunger more consuming than my desire for one of these tarts when they're finished. Melodrama aside, I need to know who killed Yvonne. Wrong. I have to convince Frank that Nick didn't. Wait, that's wrong, too. Damned if I know exactly what's right."

How could she explain to Catherine what she didn't understand herself?

"Frank seems like a pretty competent guy to me. You

sure your belief in Nick's innocence is unbiased? Just how attracted are you to this poor bereaved artist?" Catherine sat across the table.

"More than I want to be. I haven't felt this electricity for anyone else since Frank and I first got together. I don't think I want to feel it now." Rose searched for more green in the berries' red.

Catherine grinned. "You're in a relationship, not dead. I fall in lust at least five times a day, and that's the days I don't go anywhere. Don't be so hard on yourself."

"I'm trying to make it easy on myself. One man at a time is more than enough trouble for me, thanks."

Catherine stood and added sugar, a splash of balsamic vinegar, and cornstarch to the hulled berries, then carefully stirred the mixture. "That's where you and I differ, as always. I say the more the merrier."

"Even these days?"

"Yes, even in these benighted times. I don't sleep with every man I'm attracted to, honey, but I still run on the kind of electricity you try to avoid." Catherine smelled the berries and added one more drop of balsamic.

"The restaurant takes a lot of the attention I used to give my love life. It's hard to feel sexy when sweat plasters the hair to my head and my chef's pants make my butt look like an aerial view of Nebraska."

Rose had seen too many men admire Catherine's figure to listen to her self-deprecation. "Nebraska's too flat for your butt."

"How would you know?" Catherine ground black pepper into the bowl.

"I drove through it once. Are you actually claiming that you're putting your work before men?"

"Hell, no. But the restaurant is doing so well that most nights I'm more interested in putting my feet than my libido up. And I have improved, Rose. Haven't slept with a married man since I moved up here." Catherine licked her finger and crossed her heart.

Rose laughed. "Why not? Is the town too small?"

Catherine craned her head over her shoulder as she rolled out the dough. "No town's that small. But I've been good. Nothing past a little innocent flirtation with anyone wearing a ring or driving a station wagon." Catherine started filling the tarts.

Rose laughed. "You mean you still flirt with married men? I knew this new reformation was too good to be true."

Catherine looked indignant. "I flirt with all my customers, even the old women. Flirting makes me feel more alive. Them too."

Rose heard noises upstairs, then decided she'd heard a squirrel running across the roof.

"Then Frank must be feeling pretty damn vital these days. Terri coos like a dove on a goddamn Valentine's Day card every time she sees him."

Catherine slid the first batch of tarts into the oven and sat again. "Coos like a card, honey? This bitch must be getting to you way more than you've admitted."

"Maybe. I can't imagine how to compete with someone who probably includes the eyelashes on the smiley faces that dot her i's. How much of a threat can a woman who voluntarily married an ass like Ken be?"

"Are we forgetting our exes? Remember that book we meant to write, *Smart Women, Stupid Husbands*?"

"Yeah, until we decided to opt for emotional amnesia instead. Damn it, after my divorce I swore I'd never feel jealous again. But now Frank's reaction to Terri drives me crazy. He denies it, but he flirts back with her. And worse."

Rose told Catherine about Butler's history with

Terri, and how he'd lingered with her instead of rushing to Rose at Yvonne's loft.

"You can't persecute the guy for what he did in high school. At least he wasn't wasting his time with crushes on teachers, the way we did." Catherine checked the tarts.

"I'm pouring more creative energy into paranoid suspicions than my work these days. The worst of it is that I don't know if I'm angrier at him or at myself for reverting to feeling so jealous." She'd mention Butler's jealousy later.

Catherine refilled Rose's coffee. "Unless you've undergone some wondrous personality change, you're undoubtedly far angrier at yourself. It's easy to feel jealous when you love somebody. Not that I've heard you use the l-word yet. Why can't you just admit you love the man?"

Rose watched the branches of the large willow sway on the lawn and wished she were hidden up on one of its gnarled branches, listening to nothing more insistent than the wind whispering through the leaves.

Catherine tapped her on the shoulder. "Cut the pensive nature-girl act. You can't climb the tree and read a book to get out of this question. Do you or do you not love Frank?"

She never should have told Catherine about those long childhood afternoons in the backyard. She probably shouldn't have brought Butler to meet Catherine, either. A little semolina bread, and her best friend suddenly decided he was the perfect man.

Loyalty was as reliable as yeast.

Rose smiled as she slowly nodded her head. Catherine cupped her hand behind her ear and widened her eyes. "Say it. I won't believe you till you do."

"Christ, Cath. You recording this for posterity or something?"

"Nah, I won't bring out the camera till I try on the bridesmaid's dress. Promise it won't be pink."

Rose laughed nervously. "Shocking pink, if anybody had ever mentioned a wedding. With ruffles. Okay, I love him and, to forestall your next question, he loves me. Words have been spoken."

Catherine jumped up and hugged Rose. "I knew it. So what's the problem?"

"Beside these pesky murders I keep discovering and he keeps having to solve? I want to help with finding Yvonne's killer, and he wants me out of that picture. I'm not supposed to interfere with his job, but he's allowed to investigate mine. A gang of juvenile hooligans attacks me, and I'm supposed to wait patiently for the big strong detective who's their real target to catch them. Not a short problem list."

Catherine dabbed her finger on a small drift of sugar she'd spilled on the table. "How much would this be bothering you if your writing were going well? You didn't sign up at the police-force table at the school job fair. He did."

Rose sighed. "It's more than that. We're torturing each other these days. The way Frank acts with Terri drives me crazy, and he's sure I only think Nick's innocent 'cause he tempts me. He's probably worried I'll be writing mash notes to guys on death row next."

A sweet late-summer smell filled the kitchen. Catherine sniffed, nodded, and started a fresh pot of coffee. Then she took the first dozen tarts out of the oven and put the second batch in.

"How'd you do that without a timer?"

Catherine wrinkled her nose and sniffed loudly as she slid a tart onto Rose's plate. "My schnozz beats any timer."

Rose bit into the buttery crust and perfumed berries. "Forget the bridesmaid's dress. I should marry you."

Catherine laughed and wiped the crumbs off her chin. "Not in this lifetime, I'm afraid."

Catherine offered Rose another tart and pouted when Rose refused. "Fine, we'll just serve you two at dinner. Now, back to Frank."

Rose groaned and reached for the tart while Catherine continued her interrogation. "So now that we know you love him, do you trust him?"

Rose bisected the tart and slid half onto Catherine's saucer. "I'd like to say it's impossible to really love someone without trusting him completely, but you and I both know better. One of the best things about our relationship, up till now, has been that I never worried about Frank cheating."

"Do you now?"

Rose poured more coffee. "Yes. No. I don't know. Maybe I'll just keep eating these until I'm a big enough woman not to worry about it."

"Sounds as if your jealousy has more than a splash of guilt." Catherine pointed at the red rhinestone cat clock. "I hate to, but I have to go. I left your Tanglewood picnic in the garage fridge. Nothing substantial, just snacks to tide you over till midnight supper."

Catherine's idea of snacks could probably feed half the orchestra. Rose asked if she still kept condoms tucked into one of the silverware packets in her picnic basket.

"Do you plan to need them this evening?" Catherine laughed, then told Rose about a promising silent auction at the Berkshire Garden Center while she packed the tarts onto two sheet pans. She'd already bid on a couple of silver platters.

Seeing the tarts about to leave felt like watching a jewel thief. Rose offered to check Catherine's bids at the auction.

"Nah, Dr. August will be there, probably looking for further ways to buy my heart. He's in the shower-her-with-gifts stage. At least the money goes to a good cause." Catherine covered the trays with plastic wrap from the industrial-sized roll on the counter.

"Who would make the more difficult partner, a shrink or a cop?"

"Why don't we find ourselves a couple of Jesuits and ask them, Rose? Think about what I said. See you later."

When Catherine drove away, Rose tiptoed upstairs, bunching the kimono up with one hand. Butler's snores echoed down the narrow staircase. She stood in the bedroom door, admiring his black hair and pink face against the embroidered white pillowcase and wondering why men always got the longest, darkest eyelashes.

The bedroom held other temptations, too. One nightstand held hardcovers of *The Beet Queen*, *Kate Valden*, *The Handmaid's Tale*, *Roger's Version*, and *Drunk with Love*, while the other held *The Prince of Tides*, *A Perfect Spy*, *The Bourne Supremacy*, and *It*. All the books still wore their dustcovers, boasting sharper and brighter colors than anything else in the room. Rose chose Ellen Gilchrist's story collection from the stack on the nearer nightstand, then tiptoed downstairs and onto the lawn. She sprawled on a wicker chaise and opened the book. Two pages into the book, she remembered Catherine's hammock.

Suspended between two huge willow trees, the hammock swayed behind a curtain of drooping branches. Rose stilled it and wriggled in. It felt like being in a small room, with walls of narrow leaves moving in the breeze. She experimented until she found the precise hip movement required to maintain the hammock's gentle sway.

The strawberry juice had stained her fingers the faintest red, and she could still smell the sweet fruit. A thin line of darker red rimmed her fingernails. Out, out, damn juice. She'd have to scrub her hands later with one of Catherine's extravagant soaps.

Strawberry tarts, a picnic, and then a midnight supper. She and Butler really should take a long walk this afternoon. A visit to Catherine always threatened to send her home with a few extra pounds, pounds Terri would notice.

Rose opened the book. Butler obviously needed his rest. They could walk to town tomorrow. The graveyard wasn't going anywhere.

# Chapter Twenty-eight

Rose stepped delicately across Tanglewood's Great Lawn three hours later, wearing a vintage silk dress—okay, slip—and delicate Peter Fox shoes. Their slim heels aerated the grass in a manner certain to horrify the groundskeepers. She held Butler's hand and tried to put more weight on the balls of her feet.

They'd barely unfurled the blanket and unpacked the extravagant picnic before dark fell.

The six votives from the basket cast a soft glow over Catherine's sumptuous picnic. Her linen-lined wicker basket held two Waterford flutes and tumblers, a bottle of Schramsberg, and a pair of Pellegrinos. Rose unpacked plates of smoked trout sandwiched with pear slices, thick tomato wedges buried in julienned basil, roasted asparagus, tiny potatoes in crème fraiche and dill, a small St. Andre surrounded by figs, fresh corn salad, and a Cornish hen with burnished skin. Catherine had provisioned them for several symphonies.

Rose had forgotten about dark in the country, real dark. The lights of the Shed shone like an ocean liner in the distance, while other picnickers' candles scattered flickering islands around the lawn. One or two tall candelabras acted as landlocked lighthouses.

The lights in the Shed flashed three times. Rose slipped off her shoes when the music started. Copeland embraced her as she leaned against the basket and studied constellations she never saw in the city. Butler's chest replaced the basket behind her during the third movement. The crescent moon moved across the sky.

When the orchestra stopped playing, Rose wanted to shout "no" instead of "bravo." She took her time repacking the basket, trying to avoid the parking-lot traffic jam. They saw enough traffic in the city.

"How we supposed to eat dinner after that feast?" Butler patted his stomach.

She sucked hers in. "I don't know, Frank, but Catherine expects us, so we should at least show up for dessert."

Rose squirmed in the front seat of the car while Butler tried to remember the shortcut Catherine had described. They toured dark country roads for almost an hour in what should have been a twenty-minute drive. When they finally reached Housatonic, Rose didn't mention that they'd somehow ended up entering from the wrong side of town.

Butler braked hard when a gaunt mutt appeared in front of the car at the sharp curve next to the old mill building. This dark stretch of road under an old bridge always spooked Rose, made her wonder if Mr. King might move his settings south. She didn't share her irrational fears with Butler, though. They didn't need to talk about haunting topics tonight. Not discussing Yvonne's death at all didn't mean they'd stopped thinking about it.

Butler edged the car around the mutt, which bared its teeth. "Damn, it seems so late. Wonder if Catherine will still be open."

"The after-Tanglewood suppers bring in a lot of business." She checked the rearview mirror. The dog hadn't moved.

"Her place is the only sign of life for miles." Butler parked at the end of a long line of Mercedes and Volvos, muttering about buying American.

"Or renting."

Butler waited till the waiter had seated them at the only free table in the restaurant to tell her he'd be happy anywhere with her. The waiter grinned as he poured the champagne waiting in an ice bucket, then told them they wouldn't need menus. Rose requested a large bottle of mineral water and looked around the busy dining room.

Catherine had designed Combray's simple decor scheme to flatter her customers as much as her food. She'd chosen soft colors, smart lighting, and dozens of small antique mirrors for the dining room, telling Rose that she'd learned a lot from cruel dressing rooms. She'd scoured every flea market between Maine and Delaware to amass an eclectic collection of plates, glasses, and flatware. Nothing ever matched; everything always looked gorgeous. Customers often asked if they could purchase their table settings along with their meals.

"Not seeing a menu scares me. How much more can we eat? Or drink? I still have to drive us back to Catherine's."

"Brace yourself, and loosen your belt. Catherine's idea of a midnight snack is at least four courses. I don't think she's ever quite considered champagne booze, either. In her mind, it's just special water."

"Tell that to my blood count." Butler groaned and scooped all of the green gazpacho out of his bowl. Then he scraped the lobster creme fraiche off his plate with the last scrap of corn cake. He polished off the scallops in vanilla sauce and the warm pickled green beans, too.

"Will dessert count as four? I don't want to offend our hostess, but I'm reaching my limit here."

Rose saw Catherine sashaying across the dining room, stopping at every other table to chat. "Here she comes. Ask her yourself."

Catherine apologized for not joining them earlier as she plopped into the chair Butler rose to pull out for her. She chugged two glasses of mineral water, then gloated that nights like this would carry her through the winter. Butler swore he'd drive through any blizzard for food as fine as hers.

Then he devoured both of his strawberry tarts to prove it. Gallant to the end, he ate another while they waited for Catherine to close the restaurant. He refused her offers of a lovely late-harvest Muscat to complement his dessert, insisting he'd wait till her lawn for a nightcap.

"Perfect. We can sit on the lawn and watch fireflies."

Catherine patted Butler on the head, promised she'd be ready to leave in five minutes, and strolled back to her kitchen.

When Butler asked for the check, the waiter shook his head, displayed his empty palms, and pointed toward the kitchen. Butler tried to argue, but the waiter told him it would be worth his life to ignore the boss lady's orders.

Butler left a fifty under his water glass, then asked Rose if she'd like to try the hammock tonight.

Catherine appeared at the table before Rose could describe how unsexy she found mosquitoes.

They followed Catherine's speeding car down small country roads and what seemed to be part of a private lane, a route Butler swore he'd remember.

Catherine and Rose hurried upstairs to change into

kimonos, although Butler refused to join their tradition. When Rose walked downstairs, Catherine and Butler had already sprawled on pillows piled onto a quilt on the lawn. Butler's white shirt glowed in the moonlight.

Drops of moisture beaded the tiny glasses of chilled Muscat Catherine had poured, precursors to the gathering dew. The fireflies glimmered down the lawn, their lights brighter after Catherine extinguished her citronella candle. Butler's arms tightened around Rose. Catherine started a detailed description of tonight's best-looking customer, his face, his clothes, and his dinner choices.

Butler's arms loosened and his breath slowed into a deep, regular, pattern. Rose and Catherine talked softly till all the fireflies disappeared.

Nobody mentioned jealousy again.

# Chapter Twenty-nine

Returning to the city Sunday night, Rose wished she'd memorized all the moments on all the lawns they'd visited, etched all the images onto her eyes. Returning to New York felt like entering a different country. The two-hour crawl down the West Side Highway seemed longer than the weekend at Catherine's. She wished their Manhattan visas had expired.

"I'll drop you and my bag at your place, take back the rental, and see you in a while. Let's take a walk, have a drink, readjust to the big city." Butler ran the red light at Abingdon Square and veered down Bleecker. "They won't charge for another day if I get the car back by eleven."

"A walk and drink sound good after the long drive. I'll reserve judgment on readjusting to the big city. I miss the country already."

"The grass is always greener, Rose." Butler double-parked in front of her apartment. "I'll walk you up."

"Don't bother, Frank."

"It'll take you four trips to lug the bags and loot from

Catherine by yourself." Butler flicked on the hazard lights.

"I don't mind. Just leave everything in the vestibule and return the car in time." He wasn't worried about her carrying too much upstairs; he just wanted to do a quick security check on her apartment. Did he think the clean Berkshires air had washed all her city smarts away?

Pop goes the idyll.

Rose followed Butler up the stairs, deciding whether she dared suggest he go to his own apartment after returning the car. They'd had a lovely weekend together, enjoyed themselves and each other thoroughly. But she'd assumed the weekend ended Sunday night and had anticipated a few quiet hours to herself. He'd assumed otherwise, apparently not believing in too much of a good thing this week. Or, maybe he'd rather go home alone, too, but didn't want to hurt her feelings by dumping her on the doorstep for a quick escape?

Maybe she'd buy him a watch chain for Christmas, right after she cut her hair. At least she'd have time to unpack while he returned the rental. Unpack, display Catherine's gifts, reclaim her apartment.

The landing outside Rose's apartment felt very crowded as she juggled two sacks of garden bounty and a big bunch of delphiniums while she unlocked her apartment door. She'd just deposited the bags on the kitchen counter when the phone shrilled.

"Damn. Whoever that is can wait until tomorrow. I can't think of a soul I want to talk to tonight."

Butler raised an eyebrow.

"Except you, of course, pond man."

The phone stopped ringing just as the machine played her outgoing message. It started again the second Butler kissed Rose. This time, the caller waited to leave a message. Butler stopped the kiss, his curiosity about the caller's identity overwhelming his passion.

Rose listened for a moment before she recognized the voice whining into her living room as Terri's. Butler gestured at her to stop when she moved to mute the volume.

"I don't want to talk to her tonight, Frank. We're both off-duty, remember?"

"Ssshhh, let's hear what she has to say."

Sobs interrupted Terri's voice as she begged Rose to pick up the phone. Rose shook her head, refusing to answer. Butler stepped in front of her and reached for the phone. Furious, she grabbed his arm. Terri sobbed through three broken efforts to recite her home number.

"Answer it, please. She sounds in real bad shape."

"That would be a first, huh? Should we pronounce the weekend officially over now?"

She could have sworn Butler quietly called her a bitch again when she said a sharp hello to Terri.

Bye-bye, Berkshires. Hello, hysterics.

"Oh, thank Jesus you're there, hon. Ken's gone. He's missing, disappeared. He didn't come home last night. I've looked everywhere. Where's Frank? I've called his house a hundred times, but he's not there, or at his office. Please tell me where to find him, so he can find Ken." Terri's sobs leaked out of the receiver. "I need my Frankie, Rose."

No point in her trying to soothe Terri. "It's for you, Frankie."

She stood next to him, damned if she'd worry about eavesdropping in her own apartment. He turned the machine off, as if she'd want a recording of this melodrama.

Butler didn't give her much to listen to. He asked Terri four questions, told her to calm down three times, assured her everything would be fine twice, then promised he'd rush right over.

He only called her sweetheart once.

Rose didn't hear him ask Terri for her address. She didn't bother asking him how Terri had his home number, the unlisted number he'd told her less than twenty people in the world knew, since anyone who wanted to hear his voice could always reach him at work.

"I gotta go. She's hysterical."

"I gathered that, Frankie. Thanks again for a lovely weekend. Let's chat again soon about the importance of keeping our work and personal lives separate. So glad Terri called my home to locate you. Always glad to serve as your answering service."

"The woman's husband is missing."

"Losing Ken doesn't strike me as the worst of fates."

No doubt about it this time. He did call her a bitch, right before he stormed out. Captain Security didn't even stop to close her front door safely behind him. She kicked his bag into the hall closet and snapped all three locks closed.

Rose fumed while she put the delphiniums into a vase and Catherine's tomatoes into the blue pottery bowl they'd bought in Sheffield this afternoon. She shoved the greens, herbs, cucumbers, and beans from Catherine's garden into her fridge without bothering to wash anything first. The vegetables would all taste bitter now.

She'd almost enjoyed the luxury of her ambivalence about spending tonight with Butler, but she hated how quickly Terri's call had resolved the question. Just because she didn't know if she wanted to be with him tonight didn't mean she wanted him to rush to another woman's aid. Or arms, since Terri would undoubtedly demand at least one comforting hug. At the address he already knew. By heart.

Talking with Catherine had almost convinced Rose she had nothing to feel jealous about. Except maybe more secrets.

The quiet apartment she'd craved started to feel like solitary confinement. Suspicion and anger weren't boon companions. A walk suddenly seemed much more appealing. Plenty of people would still be out enjoying this late Sunday night. She'd be perfectly safe. Alone.

Rose rooted through her bag, tossing her dress and all its other contents onto the floor before she found the rose geranium soap Catherine had given her. She showered quickly, then dabbed the tea rose perfume Butler hated on her pulse points. He didn't like the loose linen pants and tank top she pulled out of her closet, either. Who knew what he thought about the heeled sandals she slipped on?

She turned the answering machine back on before she left. Let it ring. Or not.

Where to walk? Automatically avoiding West Fourth, Rose strolled down Bleecker, then cut over to Hudson when the third tourist couple blocked her path to admire something "cute" in a shop window. By the time she'd crossed Grove Street, she'd calmed down enough to begin wondering about Ken's disappearance.

Next came a twinge of unwilling pity for Terri. Despite Rose's firm belief that losing Ken permanently could only improve his wife's life, Terri had sounded absolutely miserable. Inexplicable as it was, Terri idolized Ken. Rose didn't want to think about how much her tastes in men differed from Terri's. That mismatch might lead to comparing Ken and Butler's taste in women. Not a good direction tonight.

Ken. She should make herself think about Ken. She didn't have to miss him to wonder why he'd gone missing.

A Saturday night that lasted too long? Ken often drank more than he could handle, but he didn't seem a candidate for a lost weekend. She doubted he'd established a rapport with anyone who ran one of the neighborhood bars. She couldn't imagine him venturing into a seedy after-hours club or making it past the doorman at an elegant one.

If Ken wanted to binge, he probably would have stayed at My World and drunk for free.

Given Ken's recent infidelity, perhaps he'd just shacked up with some poor unsuspecting soul. But Terri's hysteria at his not coming home proved that he'd at least had the grace, or survival sense, to hide his cheating so far. Nobody at My World seemed to have discovered his affair with Yvonne. Rose knew she hadn't suspected it. Hard to guess what Terri had chosen not to see.

Rose closed her own eyes to any image of Butler comforting Terri.

Then she pictured the envelope stuffed with cash Enzo had given Ken Thursday night. Too bad she hadn't managed to see the denominations of the thick stack of bills. Friday's mammoth liquor delivery must have required a hefty payment, but Enzo could have lent Ken five times that amount. Had Ken decided to keep the change? Add the cash from Friday and Saturday nights' business, and Ken could have put his hands on a tempting sum.

Nick said Yvonne had hinted that Ken might be skimming or playing with the books. Mismanaging the place as badly as he did approached a sort of theft in itself. But to actually put money in his pockets and run away? From his wife, his job, and—perhaps more dangerous— the Victors and their friends? He couldn't run far enough, or find an island sufficiently remote. He might not understand that, though.

Just how stupid could Ken be? Rose giggled aloud at the idea that she could have underestimated his intelligence. A man strolling behind her beseeched her to share the joke. She told him to get lost.

All the best people were doing it these days.

Wine, women, and stolen cash. None of them seemed like a plausible explanation for Ken's disappearance. Rose didn't want to consider foul play for someone who worked at My World.

Not again.

# Chapter Thirty

Rose couldn't remember the last time she'd visited the Ear Inn. She'd continued walking down Hudson until Spring Street, where she felt tired, thirsty, and far too frustrated to face Soho crowds. She turned west and, a few blocks later, settled gratefully at a table in the back room of the old bar. The Ear was the perfect place for a solitary Sunday night drink.

She'd adorned a fair portion of the butcher paper covering the table with blue interlocking triangles before a waiter appeared to take her order of mineral water and wine, separately, thanks. When he brought the drinks, she switched to a red crayon from the jar on the table and shaded in her doodles. Five Talking Heads songs later, she started with black borders.

Her decorative efforts were a kindergartner's compared to the usual tabletop sketches in this artists' and musicians' haunt. But she found the repetitive patterns soothing. Anything to avoid the temptation to start inscribing her thoughts. In crayon.

Butler probably hadn't known the Ear existed, although the bar claimed to be the second oldest in

New York City. Nick would know the story that erased the vertical lines in the illegal "Bar" sign to rename the establishment. She wondered if he and Yvonne had ever visited here together. Then she remembered Nick joking about his Ear buddies at dinner last week. Their conversation hadn't influenced her choice of bars tonight; she'd simply followed her tired feet as they tried to escape her thoughts.

She stared at the phone booth in the corner, knowing she couldn't call Butler and shouldn't call Nick. Jimmy, of course, would rush downtown if she called him. She reached into her pocket for change, but pulled her hand out empty. Jimmy would insist on hours of speculation about Ken's disappearance, right after he demanded a full description of her lovely weekend in the country with the man she wasn't speaking to now. She wouldn't be able to sidetrack him by praising the Ear's charms, either. Jimmy constantly disparaged her choice of boîtes and would dismiss the Ear's cozy dive charm before he found her table.

Two hours ago, she'd bemoaned the lack of solitude. Now she wanted another voice to distract her. Rose appraised the various solitary male drinkers at the bar. Most of them would probably be happy to chat; several of them were very attractive. Getting a male artist or musician to talk about himself wouldn't require too much effort on her part.

There were some kinds of trouble she could avoid. Maybe a fourth color would help her doodles. Aquamarine looked good.

Where in the hell could Ken have disappeared? How far would Butler take his pledge to serve and protect with Terri quivering in front of him? Why had their lovely weekend turned into a door-slamming fight? Just how much trouble could a simple drink with an attractive man engender? She knew the answer to one out of four.

Time for a fifth color. Anything but green.

Rose concentrated on her doodling, watching her triangles shrink tighter and tighter. The most doting mother wouldn't post this on the fridge.

She didn't know what bothered her more—the thought of Butler abandoning her and rushing to Terri's side, or her suspicions about the sort of comfort Terri might provoke.

Their brief escape into the country might as well have never happened. The willow tree had provided only the most temporary of shelter.

Jealousy gnawed at her again. She should be bigger than this nasty emotion.

"A piece of flourless chocolate cake, please."

She'd check her messages while she waited for dessert. Rose slid the door of the battered old phone booth closed, comforted by the protection the cubicle seemed to offer. Better than a bell jar, anytime. She could barely hear the Blondie song that a moment ago had taunted her.

I'm going to be your only one, indeed.

Butler and Terri probably preferred Tony Bennett. For whatever they were doing.

Rose pushed a quarter in the slot and called her own number, praying as she punched in her code that a message from Butler would prove all her suspicions silly. He might have a perfectly innocent explanation for knowing Terri's home address. Rose swore to herself that she'd accept any apologies he might make without reproach. She'd invite him to join her at the Ear. They could share the flourless cake.

They'd enjoyed themselves too much this weekend to let a little thing like Terri ruin it.

She should have cleared her machine before she left the apartment. Rose fumbled for more change when she heard she had fourteen messages. Terri's quavering voice filled nine of them. Her repeated requests to talk to "my Frankie" infuriated Rose again, the possessive pronoun erasing any sympathy for Terri's panic. She almost hung up after the fifth "my Frankie," but forced herself to keep listening. She didn't want to miss the message Butler should have left by now.

Should have, but hadn't.

No word from Butler, obviously too engrossed in Terri's needs to worry about Rose. The only male voice belonged to Nick, who'd left two messages begging her to call him back immediately. He had something very important he needed to tell her. Rose grabbed the pen hanging off the little shelf attached to the old phone and scribbled his number on her hand.

She'd run out of change. But maybe she would invite someone else to join her at the Ear.

Rose returned to her table and traced triangles on the cake's frosting with the tines of her fork while she waited for the waiter. Only a spoiled teenager would call Nick because Butler had deserted her. A mature and curious woman, however, could call him to learn whatever information he wanted to share. Maybe he'd discovered Yvonne's killer. Maybe he knew Ken's whereabouts. Maybe he'd want some flourless cake.

Rose took a stack of quarters from the waiter and ordered another glass of wine. She waited for a woman in dark grey Norma Kamali to finish a conversation punctuated by dramatic arm-waving that rattled the phone booth's doors.

She memorized the number she'd scrawled on her wrist and tried to translate the numbers into letters and a word. Concentrating on the code wouldn't let her reconsider the wisdom of calling Nick. Too bad innocent had eight letters, one too many for a phone number.

Rose carried her wine into the phone booth as soon as the fashion plate stormed out, took a deep breath, and called Butler. His machine answered at his apartment. The deskman at the precinct hadn't seen him all night. No message, thanks. Damned if she'd call Terri's apartment.

Instead, she called Nick. He answered on the second ring and said she had to see what he'd found in the loft this morning.

She'd seen enough surprises in his loft, thanks. Nothing could entice her into that space again. She hesitated, unsure how to tell someone that his home struck her as a chamber of horrors.

"Do you want me to come to your place instead, Rose?"

So whatever he'd found was portable. "I'm at the Ear."

"We can still meet at your house. We could both get there in about twenty minutes. I'll wait for you downstairs if I'm there first."

She didn't want anybody lingering in front of her apartment again and wasn't sure she wanted Nick in her home tonight. She told him she felt like staying out, adding that she'd just ordered food. He didn't say anything for a moment, then agreed to meet her at the Ear in twenty-five minutes.

She detoured to the spacious ladies' room, which seemed bigger than the Ear's kitchen, on her way back to the table. After five minutes reading the witty and even literate graffiti, she slicked on more lipstick and tossed her hair free of its topknot. Her eyes looked very bright in the wavy mirror. She wasn't primping for Nick. Any self-respecting woman would freshen up after a long walk on an August night.

When she returned to her table, the waiter delivered another glass of wine "on the gentlemen at the bar." So much for the need to freshen up. Still, delivering a sponsored drink to a woman without asking if she wanted to accept it violated good bar etiquette. Too many men thought buying a beverage also bought conversation, if not more. She'd just started to tell the waiter no thanks when she recognized Dave and Chris, two of My World's regulars, waving to her from the bar. Manhattan was a smaller town than most people understood.

She raised her glass and smiled. Dave and Chris took the smile as invitation and ambled over to her table. They told her they'd missed her Saturday night and that Laura had struggled with a very busy bar, so busy that Ken had insisted on helping her serve drinks.

"All I wanted was a glass of red, and that bozo just kept pushing what he called his specialities. He told me real men drank cocktails, with this sick pause that broke cocktail into two words. And he kept bumping into Laura in a way that didn't look accidental. I couldn't stand it and went to the Horse instead." Chris wasn't too indignant to signal the waiter for another round.

God only knew how many other customers Ken had managed to alienate.

Dave laughed. "You forgetting to mention how smashed Ken was? Pathetic, man."

"He was drunk behind the bar?" Ken fumbled so much bartending even while sober that she couldn't imagine the chaos he'd cause drunk.

"Yeah, he told everybody his old lady had ridden his last nerve and he needed to unwind. Not pretty." Chris sat in the chair across from Rose. "He dissed Yvonne every chance he got, too."

"What did he say about Yvonne?"

Chris grimaced, "You don't want to hear it. Real ugly bullshit. Don't repeat it, Dave."

Dave pulled an empty chair from the adjoining table and squeezed in next to her. "Don't worry. Good thing Nick wasn't there to hear Ken diss his old lady like that. The big guy would have killed Ken. Talk about ugly."

"I'm glad I missed it."

When they asked her where she'd been Saturday night, she just said she'd visited a friend in the country, not mentioning Butler or how she felt as if their trip had happened a century ago. If it had happened at all.

The table felt crowded with Dave and Chris. Condensation from the men's beer glasses blurred her doodling, and the table rocked on the uneven floor whenever one of them moved a glass. The two-top wasn't big enough for three, much less four.

How would Nick fit in?

# Chapter Thirty-one

"Speak of the devil," Chris cocked his head toward Nick standing in the doorway. Nick scanned the room. He didn't smile when he spotted her sitting with the two men, although he did grin at three women sitting at a table in the far corner.

She didn't want her new drinking buddies to know that she'd expected Nick. However innocently they'd planned it, her meeting him didn't need to hit the My World grapevine. Or Butler's radar.

Nick walked to the bar, rolling the file folder he carried into a tight cylinder. He turned his back on the room and spoke to the bartender.

"Poor Nick. Maybe we should ask him to join us. I don't believe any of Ken's crap about the big guy being an evil murderer." Chris shoved back his chair and strolled to the bar.

She watched Nick shake his head, Chris talk more, and finally Nick pick up his beer and walk toward their table.

"Dave, Rose," he hovered above them until Chris grabbed an empty chair and crowded it in across from

Rose, although there'd been more space to her right.

Should she pretend to be surprised? Nick hadn't indicated he'd expected to see her. For all she knew, the three men might meet here regularly.

If they did, they didn't seem to remember the casual-banter aspect of barroom behavior. Nick fidgeted with his rolled up file, Chris seemed suddenly fascinated by the head on his beer, and Dave tilted his chair back and stared at the tin ceiling. In a minute, she'd start talking about sports, kicking into bartending mode even on her night off.

Nick lifted his glass, "Damn, this is awkward. Scott wouldn't take my money, said my drink was in honor of Yvonne. He meant well, but I don't need free drinks to honor her."

Dave and Chris muttered their own awkward condolences, which Nick accepted with equally awkward thanks. When Chris asked if the police had any leads yet, Nick shook his head and studied the abstract oil hanging above their table as if he'd never seen such work.

Chris took the silent cue and started a detailed critique of the painting and its artist's entire oeuvre. Dave defended the use of color but said the artist was a real prick.

Rose didn't contribute to the discussion. Neither did Nick.

A tall blonde in a '60s ruffled pink prom dress finally shut the two up when she walked to the table to tell Nick how sorry she was to hear about Yvonne and how much she'd miss her. She treated them all to a detailed description of just how horrible she'd felt when she'd heard the news, so bad she'd missed two openings that night. Dave offered her condolences, too, this time with more eye contact. The blonde appraised Rose coolly, told

Nick to call her anytime, then returned to her friends' table.

Nick then sat stoically through five more condolence calls from other patrons. He shook everyone's hands, dodging two women's attempts at sympathy kisses. He didn't introduce Rose to anyone.

Dave and Chris seemed to know most of the visitors by name but didn't prolong any of the conversations. They looked like two schoolboys kept inside on the first day of baseball season to practice cursive, right after the teacher had suggested they use their own blood as ink. So much sympathy made them squirm, but neither of them made any move to leave. They barely brightened at the free round of drinks the waiter delivered "from the three ladies."

If she drank this next glass of wine, Nick's big news would be lost on her, whenever he finally disclosed it. Rose waited, hoping the table had received its last sympathy visitor. The four of them sat silently for a few minutes. She tried to think of a way to get rid of Chris and Dave, sure that they were just as eager to extricate themselves.

Saved by the blonde. The prom queen and her friends stopped on their way out to announce that they were headed to Puffy's and ask if anyone wanted to join. Chris and Dave accepted the invitation with big smiles. Nick said no thanks. None of the women waited to hear Rose answer. Chris did invite her but didn't look disappointed when she said the Ear was her last stop tonight.

"That was rough. I knew meeting you here might be. Yvonne had lots of friends here." Nick surveyed the room as if checking that the sympathy visits had finished.

Rose wished Butler could have seen the warm comfort Nick's community had offered him. Nobody here had studied Nick suspiciously.

"Yvonne was such a homebody; we didn't go out much. We mostly came here when we did." He searched the room as if he hoped to see Yvonne.

His reluctance to come to the Ear made sense now. She regretted insisting they meet here. She hadn't wanted their rendezvous to pain Nick.

He stopped looking at whatever he'd been seeing in the room and focused on Rose. She waited, hoping he'd start talking about his discovery. Interrogating a man who had just blinked away tears wasn't in her repertoire.

Nick unrolled the folder he'd been holding in his lap. "This is it, Rose. This proves that my girl wasn't a thief. And that Ken is."

He opened the folder and passed her a sheaf of papers. "Remember I told you Yvonne said she suspected Ken was stealing from My World? This proves it. I wish she'd shown it to me." Nick's voice sounded as if he blamed himself for Yvonne's reticence.

She read the title on the pale blue cover sheet, "The Progressive Consequences of Embezzlement on a Small Business Structure and a Method for Discovery." Scratched out and inserted words showed the many revisions Yvonne had made to the title. Rose wondered if this would have been her final version and started to consider another rewrite.

Stop. Nick hadn't handed her a novel, and nobody had asked her to edit. She turned the pages, skimming over Yvonne's introduction and the development of her argument. The paper referred to "a temporary manager" in a "small, family-owned, establishment purveying primarily perishables within a cash-intensive structure." Yvonne presented a precise description of the bookkeeping systems, with numbing details about ledgers and cross-check systems. Then the examples started.

Yvonne had used daily, weekly, and monthly records to illustrate the slow seep of cash from the business Rose recognized as My World. One or two orders on the waiters' checks voided by Ken, a missing check or two every few nights. He'd started slowly. Then entire checks were voided and several more disappeared from the numerical sequence each waiter used daily. The kitchen's and bar's dupes vanished from the daily paperwork system.

Receipts from food purveyors the restaurant had never used before appeared in the ledgers, all marked "cash payment." The names of vendors who had received weekly checks for years disappeared from the register. Many checks were written to "cash." The bank charged for overdrafts. A previously small category for petty cash grew to surpass the kitchen staff's weekly payroll. What had been a system of daily bank deposits dwindled to two or three a week. The deposit amounts suggested a restaurant that catered solely to anorexics on strict budgets.

Monthly profit/cost reports stopped, disappeared entirely from the official books. But Yvonne had calculated them anyway, and the cost percentages were four or five times the norm. No wonder Ken had erased them.

He would have burned the other reports Yvonne had run, if he'd ever seen them. She'd managed to grab several weeks' worth of kitchen dupes, probably with Ward's help. The actual amount of food served dwarfed the sales Ken had reported. Yvonne had used the bartenders' pull sheets to show an even larger discrepancy in the liquor sales. Yvonne had attempted her own version of the double ledger system, but this time for truth instead of tax evasion.

Rose read quickly and knew she'd missed some details. But Yvonne's paper condemned Ken with enough proof to convince a jury of spendthrifts.

While the Victors were in Italy mourning a death in the family, Ken had been burying their restaurant.

She aligned the edges of the pages while she tried to think how to phrase her question, how to ask a grieving man if the woman he'd loved had participated in embezzlement. Yvonne had discovered Ken's theft; why hadn't she exposed it?

"I know what you're thinking, Rose. Why didn't Yvonne tell somebody, try to stop it?"

"Ken did a lot of damage to My World. I don't know why she let that happen."

"She tried to stop him. Look." Nick pulled a single sheet of paper from his shirt pocket. Someone had folded the paper into the size of a business card. He smoothed it out before he handed it to her.

Yvonne had phrased the letter of resignation she'd addressed to Ken as if she'd expected lawyers to examine it. She itemized a series of memos by date, noting that she'd kept duplicates of all their past correspondence. Yvonne also listed a set of reports that she'd mailed to the Italian address Ken had given her for Joe Victors, then wrote that all that correspondence had been returned as undeliverable.

At the bottom left of the letter, Yvonne had written that she'd sent copies to Joe and Ben Victors in New York, her ex-husband Barney, and to another Esquire whose name Rose didn't recognize. She'd also sent a copy to Terri at her home address.

The letter was dated three days before Yvonne died.

Yvonne's letter gave Ken a laundry list of motives for her murder.

She hadn't meant it as a suicide note.

Had Terri received the copy Yvonne had sent, or had Ken managed to intercept it? If Terri had seen the letter, where would her loyalties lie?

"You have to show this to Frank."

"Yeah, he'll love asking me why Yvonne didn't show it to me before she sent it. He'll have a field day with that one."

She couldn't assure him that Butler would be gentle. Or considerate of his bruised feelings.

"It was hard enough telling Frank about our problems with Ken once. I don't know if I could take him grilling me about that affair again. He acts as if I'm the one who fucked up."

"You're not the one who cheated."

"No, but I am the one who made Yvonne feel she could never mention Ken's name. I can't believe she worked so hard on this without sharing it with me. I let her down."

"She'd have shown it to you eventually, I'm sure." Yvonne would have had to explain leaving My World somehow.

"But she didn't get the chance, did she? I could kill that bastard Ken for what he stole from us. Then Frank could accuse me of double homicide." Nick rolled the paper and folder back into a tight cylinder.

"You'd have to find him first." She told Nick about Ken's disappearance and Terri's frantic calls.

"I hope he's rotting somewhere. I hope somebody hurt him the way he hurt us."

Nick's large hands tightened on the rolled folder as if he wanted to strangle its contents out of existence.

# Chapter Thirty-two

"It's been a long day, Nick." Catherine's verdant lawns seemed years away.

"Every day seems too long now, Rose." The bruised shadows under Nick's blue eyes agreed.

"I need to get home. I still have to unpack from the weekend." She caught the waiter's eye and motioned for her check.

"Sorry. I didn't even ask you how your time away was."

"Good. Beautiful. Gone." She wished she could walk out of the Ear's door and back onto a peaceful Berkshires lawn. Instead, she paid the check and wondered how long it would take to find a cab.

The night had turned cooler, with a welcome breeze off the river. Spring Street didn't smell like the country, but it didn't smell like garbage either. Or exhaust. They waited on the corner of Spring and Greenwich Streets for ten minutes without spotting a cab.

"Can you walk in those things?"

"I didn't fly down here. The heels are barely two inches." And the sandals' soft straps didn't threaten blisters. Walking to Hudson Street would triple their chances of spotting a cab.

"I guess I always think of you as delicate. I feel like such a hulk next to you, like I could break something if I wasn't careful."

Even in the heels, she didn't reach Nick's shoulder. She told herself to consider his size as protective instead of threatening on the quiet street. This wasn't the first time they'd been alone in the early morning hours in a deserted neighborhood. Despite Butler's disapproval, she felt safe with Nick. Very safe.

Too safe?

They walked without talking, as if their earlier conversation had exhausted them. When Rose's heel caught on a cobblestone, Nick grabbed her arm to steady her. She heard a smart snap and felt her right foot collapse. Another favorite shoe ruined by the quaint streets so favored by historical walking tours. In sensible shoes.

Rose arched her right foot to compensate for the missing heel. She started a familiar teetering limp. Click. Shuffle. Click. Shuffle. Another pair ruined.

Since the walk home would take longer now, she'd have plenty of time to convince Nick to show Butler Yvonne's papers. She tucked her arm under Nick's, using him as her human crutch.

"I could carry you." He tensed the muscles in his forearm.

She shook her head at the image of herself swept up in Nick's arms. "I'll manage. This is the third damn pair this year." Click. Shuffle. Click. Shuffle.

"If I didn't have sisters, I'd ask you why you keep buying shoes you know might break. Your legs don't need heels to look good."

"I like feeling taller. I also hate looking up to my

inferiors." She clenched her right foot into a taut arch to keep the shoe from slipping off.

Nick laughed and pulled her arm next to his body. She leaned in a little closer, telling herself it was only for the sake of balance. Neither of them waved when four taxis swarmed up Hudson Street at Barrow.

She felt Nick's warm breath ruffle her hair.

"Where's Frank? Why aren't you with him tonight?"

"Terri needed him. He couldn't resist her pleas for help." She didn't want to talk about how much help Terri might have requested.

"Do you think she knows she married a cheating thief? Maybe she finally got smart and dumped Ken."

"I don't know. You can ask Frank all about what Terri does and doesn't know when you call him tomorrow. He should be an expert on the subject by then." Pain jabbed the muscles in her right calf.

Nick didn't argue with her assumption that he'd call Butler tomorrow. Or ask if she planned on calling him first. They walked past Christopher Street without speaking again. Two more cabs sailed by.

"It's my fault." Nick stopped under a streetlamp that illuminated the sorrow on his face like stage lighting. "Yvonne wouldn't have died if only she'd felt able to talk to me about this mess. She shouldn't have sent that letter without me knowing. I could have protected her."

"Oh, Nick." She didn't know how to comfort him. Or ask him to comfort her for the bitter taste that lingered after she'd talked about Butler.

She teetered on her left foot, wriggling the toes she'd cramped as she'd tried to keep the broken sandal on. When Nick moved his arms around her waist, she leaned onto his chest. He moved his right hand up to her face and cradled her jaw, tilting her head back to stare into her eyes. She looked back for a long moment, watching her own desire reflected on his face. Rose slid her hands up Nick's great arms, slowing at his Sandburg shoulders, then rested them around his thick column of a neck. Neither of her shoes touched the pavement when they kissed.

She tasted salt on Nick's lips, then a deep sweetness. Her own hunger amazed her, as if all the weekend's passion with Butler had only primed her for Nick. He lifted her higher, his lips never leaving hers. She felt him harden. She wanted to grasp his neck more tightly and squirm her body onto his. For a minute, she thought about raising her legs around his waist, clasping onto him completely. Her broken sandal clattered onto the sidewalk.

"Jesus." She slid her arms off his neck, regained her footing, and backed away.

"Rose—" He leaned toward her.

"No. We can't." She raised her hands to ward him off.

"I didn't mean—" He picked up her fallen shoe and handed it to her, careful not to step any closer.

"Stop. Neither of us did." She wiggled her foot back into the sandal and started walking away, this time without his support.

After half a block, she turned to look at Nick. He slumped motionless against the streetlamp, until she thought his big shoulders shuddered.

She would have rushed away if he'd attempted to follow her. But she couldn't abandon him as he stood alone and so bereft. She held out one hand, as if to a child. He walked quickly, but didn't run, toward her.

"You should go home now."

"I can't." He turned away from her for a second, wiping his face with both hands.

"Please." She hated the tremor she heard in her

voice.

"I won't leave you alone on the streets at this hour. It's not safe." His deep voice didn't shake at all.

"I wouldn't describe what just happened as safe, either. Maybe we should try for a cab again." Why hadn't they taken one earlier?

"Where I grew up, the back seat of a car was considered dangerous."

She laughed, wishing she still had teenage hormones to blame for their embrace.

He grinned and offered her his arm at an exaggerated distance. "We might as well walk until a cab shows up. We're close to your apartment anyway."

Her calf and foot hurt. Standing here arguing seemed stupid. She knew Nick would follow her if she walked away again. Stopping him would take more cruelty than she could muster.

Rose stepped off the curb carefully, then tried to hurry across the intersection.

Nick told her to slow down or she'd twist her ankle. She hastened her pace, not explaining that they'd just embraced on the corner of Hudson and Tenth. If Butler had managed to tear himself away from Terri and appear at work, the Sixth Precinct was just down the block.

She hurried them to Perry Street, then insisted they cut across to West Fourth. Butler was less likely to take this route on his way to or from work.

Nick didn't argue about her directions. Maybe he thought she possessed a superior knowledge of the Village's serpentine streets. Or maybe he found the quieter side streets more appealing too.

She wondered if he could feel Butler following them, see their chaperoning escort. Butler walked the street arm-in-arm too, with guilt as his companion. Rose peered behind them again. Butler wasn't really there. Guilt was. Remorse shadowed her footsteps like a grown-up Peter Pan.

So she found Nick attractive. She'd known that since the first time she'd seen him. His grief seemed to have heightened his appeal. Add some wine, more anger at Butler, and a heightened sensual state she could blame on visiting the country. Kissing Nick wasn't a mortal sin. She'd stopped in time.

What Butler didn't know couldn't hurt him. But what she knew about how good Nick's kisses felt might.

She didn't need to turn around again to know that guilt still strolled right behind her.

When they reached her building, she sat on the front steps and kicked both shoes off. She wouldn't wobble in front of Nick for this discussion, wouldn't lose her balance again.

He sat a few steps below her, so that their heads were almost level and yet a safe distance apart. Had his artist's eye arranged a good composition for even this difficult scene?

Rose took a deep breath and started to explain herself. The kiss had been a mistake; things were rough with Butler right now; she'd had too much wine; the long day had exhausted her, clouded her judgment. It could never happen again. She didn't tell Nick she'd felt sorry for him. She also didn't mention her self-loathing paranoia about Butler's interest in Terri and how she might have wanted a tit for Butler's potential tat. Or maybe a preemptive strike in the battle their affair now felt like.

"Stop. I get it. I won't lie and say I wish it hadn't happened. You don't have to explain any more. You're Frank's girl. I respect that."

She didn't clarify either her girlhood or Butler's

possession.

"What about Yvonne?"

He flinched. "Did you think I forgot about her? God. I loved her. I still do. She'll always be with me."

"I know. I could see that whenever I saw you two together." For a second, she envied his certainty that Yvonne would somehow stay with him. She couldn't say the same thing about Butler right now. She shivered even in the night's warm air as she stood.

"Wait, Rose. I need a big favor."

"What?"

"Please don't make me go home to that empty loft alone. I'm losing it there. I can't make myself walk into the kitchen."

"I can't—"

"I'll be a perfect gentleman, I promise. You have a couch, right?" He gave her his most boyish grin.

"It's more like a loveseat, too short for you. And I'm not sure it's a good idea anyway."

"I can manage. Please? As a friend?" He stood too, although even the few steps' difference couldn't hide his height.

"Is this where we say 'just friends,' like in high school?" The thought of having company, even in the living room, seemed strangely attractive. She still hesitated. She knew that all the rationales she'd just trotted out to excuse their kiss hadn't erased her attraction to Nick.

"I have another reason for asking. I'm worried about Ken. I have a bad feeling about him tonight."

Surprised to hear that he'd care anything about Ken, except for wanting him in jail, she asked Nick what he meant.

He explained that he was worried about her safety as long as nobody knew Ken's whereabouts.

"That bastard killed Yvonne. I don't want him hurting you, too. If you don't let me come upstairs, I swear I'll sit on your front stairs all night. Ken could be anywhere, the desperate shit." Nick climbed to her step, folding his arms like a Russian dancer's as he approached. "What if he thinks you know what he's done?"

"Don't be silly. I can take care of myself." It was a familiar refrain, even if Butler didn't hear it this time. If the professional guardian Butler worried more tonight about Terri's emotional well-being than Rose's safety, she couldn't be in any real danger. From Ken.

"Your call. I'm staying." Nick sat again.

Five minutes of hushed arguing about her safety, arguments that never included Butler's name, didn't convince Nick. Please don't let any of the neighbors be watching tonight's installment of front-stoop theater. She finally gave up and trudged upstairs, watching the hem of her pants sweep her bare feet and the dirty floors.

After checking that her apartment looked exactly as she'd left it, Rose peeked out her window. Nick still sat on her stoop.

She scrubbed her filthy feet in the bathtub and changed into a billowing cotton nightgown. Nick hadn't moved.

She hauled all Catherine's garden bounty out of the fridge, swished it around in a sink of cold water, and mummied it into paper towels for the produce drawer. When she looked outside again, a patrol car cruised her block. The driver slowed to check Nick out but didn't stop the car. She hoped the officer hadn't used his radio. Nick needed to prepare for his next visit to the precinct, not get hauled in without warning again.

Rose pried her front window open and hissed Nick's name. When he looked up, she beckoned, then went to buzz him in. She heard his heavy tread plodding up the stairs, surprised at his slow pace.

Exasperated and totally exhausted, she ushered Nick into the apartment. He thanked her and said he'd hated seeing the patrol car.

"All of a sudden I wondered if maybe Frank would try to blame me for Ken too." He hovered over her.

"We don't know that Ken is dead. He could have slimed off to any of a million places. I'm too tired to worry about harboring a fugitive from justice tonight."

She showed him the couch, kicked Butler's bag as she pulled linens out of the hall closet, and tried not to smirk at the foot-and-a-half gap between her couch's length and Nick's height. She didn't offer him anything to eat. She didn't encourage him to speculate about Ken's location. She didn't stay in the same room with him another five minutes.

When she'd closed her bedroom door so hard that three scarves fell off the hooks on its back, she remembered that she also hadn't checked her phone machine. Much as she wanted to know if Butler—or anyone else—had called, she didn't want Nick to hear her messages. Particularly not tonight, when sweet nothings probably didn't fill the tape.

Hoping Nick was an early riser, Rose propped herself up in bed with *The Portrait of a Lady*. She could hear Nick trying to fit himself onto her couch and thought she heard him curse. Twenty slow pages later, she didn't hear anything from the living room.

She'd never sleep until she knew if Butler had called.

Damning her curiosity and her insomnia, she tiptoed down the hall. When she approached the living room, Nick's soft snores signaled that he'd stopped his vigil.

She lifted the hem of her white nightgown, grateful

that the cotton didn't rustle, and took slow quiet steps toward her machine. She still couldn't see its signal buttons. She stopped for a moment, caught by her reflection in the antique mirror over the couch. Her long white gown made a ghostly figure in the old glass. She wondered what Nick would think if he awoke to the sight and tried to believe that she couldn't haunt herself.

Nick stirred. She froze. He flailed around on the too-short couch, and she prayed he wouldn't waken. When his snores resumed their rhythm, she tiptoed to her desk. No blinks interrupted its steady glow. The constant red light shone like a clown's pursed neon mouth. Nobody had called since the last time she'd checked her machine from the Ear. Nobody.

She tried to tell herself that Terri's slew of messages had filled her machine to capacity but knew it wasn't true. The last message left on her machine tonight had come from the man now sleeping an innocent few feet away.

Rose shifted her gaze away from the mean red light and studied Nick. The streetlight shining in through the windows traced his strong cheekbones and outlined the big shoulders stretching above her blue flowered sheets. The tendons on his neck and upper arms seemed to glow. The light made his head's silvery stubble into a luxurious velvet her fingers ached to touch.

When she looked into the mirror above the couch again, her own eyes seemed bigger.

Rose clenched her own fists, gathering her nightgown closer to her body. Then she walked back to bed, slapping the soles of her feet in a slow cadence to match Nick's breathing.

Her hallway had never seemed longer.

# Chapter Thirty-three

Rose woke Monday morning with her nightgown curled around her legs. Groggy from hours of twisting and turning, she didn't know when she'd fallen asleep. As she wriggled to disentangle herself, she saw that her bed testified to a night no one could call peaceful. She straightened the offending sheets and quilt, relieved that only one pillow needed plumping.

No freshly brewed coffee waited for her in the kitchen. She'd forgotten to set up the machine again. She hesitated before she hit the on button, but better that Nick woke to the grinder's noise than her voice. She ducked into the bathroom, splashed cold water on her face, smoothed her hair, and scrambled into the outfit she'd tossed on the hamper last night. She wadded her crumpled nightgown into a tight ball and crammed it into the basket full of dirty laundry.

Ignoring the twinges in her calf, she stomped her bare feet as hard as she could as she walked into the quiet living room. The empty living room. Nick had folded his sheets into perfect rectangles and piled them at one end of the couch. She didn't see a note.

The mirror over the couch looked dusty in the morning light.

The message light on her answering machine still shone balefully steady.

She'd wasted her worries about disturbing anyone.

While she waited for the coffee to brew, Rose removed the meager traces of Nick's stay. The sheets wouldn't fit in her laundry hamper, so she bundled them into his pillowcase. Reaching into the hall closet to find the old duffle she used for extra laundry, she stubbed her toe on Butler's bag.

She pulled it out of the closet and set it by her front door. A couple of airport baggage claims still hung around the handle. She read Florida and Bonaire on the tags, but didn't see the Happy Land of Long Ago label the bag should have sported.

Rose remembered reading somewhere that objects left behind signaled the owner's desire to return. She hoped that had been Butler's unconscious intent last night and tried to remember where she'd read the statement. The vicious voice he'd used to call her a bitch before he rushed off to comfort Terri might negate that theory.

Pouring a large cup of coffee, Rose groaned when she remembered that she had to work tonight in exchange for swapping shifts with Laura. An unwelcome night at My World would destroy the Monday she usually treasured as a full writing day. She didn't even know if Ken had surfaced, or if she should expect to walk into a bar once again drowning in rumor.

Rose rushed back into the living room and searched to see if Nick had forgotten Yvonne's paper. She stopped speculating about his motives when she found herself face to face with the dust bunnies under the couch.

After a very long and very cool shower, Rose spent

another five minutes at the sink scrubbing the ghost of Nick's number off her wrist with water so hot her whole body warmed. She didn't need to wear those scrawled digits as a souvenir.

She put on a knee-length black linen shift and chunky black sandals, deciding to take the pair she'd broken last night to the cobbler on Grove Street. While she was out, she might as well drop Butler's bag at the front desk at the precinct.

She didn't want it in her apartment any more, didn't want his clothes in her closet now. She doubted he'd remember she had to work tonight and hoped he wouldn't show up at My World if he did. Whatever reconciliation they might attempt shouldn't be staged at the bar. Or anywhere that might include Terri.

She couldn't walk fast enough in the heavy heat to stretch out the tight ache in her right calf. Too bad it didn't hurt badly enough to give her an excuse to miss work. Butler's bag felt heavier than it had last night.

She didn't see his car when she checked the precinct parking lot on Charles. Wiping the sweat off her forehead, she walked on to Tenth and into the station.

A middle-aged tourist in a polyester sundress who'd had her fanny pack grabbed off the bench in Washington Square Park where she'd left it for "just the teensiest minute" argued with the officer at the desk. Why did they call them New York's finest if they couldn't protect visitors? Nobody at home would suggest she go searching through garbage to recover stolen property. She didn't think the cops gave a good gosh darn.

The desk man wrote the woman's hotel and home addresses down, as if he'd make sending officers out to search for a missing fanny pack a top priority on this sweltering August day. Rose waited while the woman corrected the spelling of her hometown in Wisconsin and promised she'd call in an hour to see if they'd found it yet.

"Next," the man at the desk studied the bag Rose carried as if he suspected it might hold a severed head.

"Hi. I need to leave this for Detective Frank Butler, please."

"What's in it?"

"His clothes and dopp kit." She tried to hand him the bag.

He held up his hand. "Wait a minute. You got stuff belongs to Mr. Popularity, you can leave it in his office. I look like a coat-check girl to you?"

She assured him he didn't and asked in her sweetest voice if he wouldn't please hold the bag for Butler.

"Who knows when he'll show his face to get it? He interviewed some geek for about an hour this morning. I ain't seen or heard from him since. Wait here till I get someone to escort you back to his desk."

"I know where it is, thanks." When she asked if she could go to Butler's office on her own, he thought for a moment, as if assessing the damage she could do in a precinct full of armed officers.

He looked her up and down until she fought the urge to tug at her hem. "G'ahead, then. I know who you are. Your address, too, what with all the manpower going your way lately." He cocked his thumb over his shoulder

Rose surveyed Butler's cluttered desk for a place to put his bag without causing stacks of paper to cascade onto the floor. Without rifling through them, she tried to see if any of those stacks included Yvonne's paper, but she couldn't spot the pale blue Yvonne had used for her cover sheet.

Maybe she should write a note, if she could decide what a note should say. She didn't want to apologize or beg him to call her. Let the bag speak for itself. She had better things to write.

Standing here looking at the mess that was Butler's work life wouldn't add a damn page to her manuscript. She had her own desk to deal with at home. And five more hours before her shift at My World started.

His desk was so damn cluttered she'd leave his bag on the chair. No way he could miss it there. She pictured him leaning back in the old naugahyde chair to interrogate her when they'd first met, remembering the way he'd slammed it upright when she answered his questions with her own. Some courtship. She walked around his desk, pulled the chair out, and started to drop his bag onto it.

His chair wasn't empty. Someone else had left Butler a reminder today. A small white cardboard pastry box tied with red and white string sat in the seat. It looked like a box from from Rocco's, the bakery on Bleecker, except Rocco's boxes were usually plain. Rose leaned over to read the loopy script written in a hot pink felt tip that decorated this box.

> *Frankie,*
> *Thanks for every preshus hour*
> *last night. Your the best.*
> *XOXOXO*
> *Allways,*
> *Terri*

Rose read the message three times, torturing herself more with each repetition. She'd memorized the coy words the first time.

Every precious hour? Butler had been giving Terri precious hours while Rose agonized over kissing Nick for a few seconds? Her stomach felt as if she'd swallowed every ton of flour Rocco's had used this year.

All her suspicions screamed truth in hideous

hot pink. She looked at the message one last time and recognized she'd been wrong about something else. Terri didn't dot her I's with a smiley face. She used a daisy— complete with stem and leaves.

Rose held Butler's bag over his chair, directly above the pastry box. Then she released her grip on the handles and watched the bag drop onto the box. The scent of hazelnut filled the office. She knew cyanide smelled like bitter almonds but didn't know what to call the cloying poison she'd just discovered. Smashing Terri's gift hadn't banished her presence.

Butler wouldn't need a trail of cookie crumbs to read this message.

Rose bent over and wiped her face with the hem of her dress, telling herself that sweat was the only moisture dampening her face. She stood, smoothed her dress as far down her legs as it would reach, and wished for six-inch heels. She lifted her head and straightened her back, then walked away from Butler's office.

The officer at the desk stopped her when she tried to walk past him. "Find everything okay, Ms. Leary? You took so long back there, I started to worry."

While she couldn't tell if he'd taken the time to escort Terri to Butler's office himself, she knew he'd definitely read Terri's message. The smirk on his pudgy face announced the pleasure the pink letters had given him.

Rose didn't even miss the precinct's air-conditioning as she walked down Bleecker to discover the cobbler had a closed-for-vacation sign in his window. She tried to think of where to find the nearest shoe-repair shop. Once found on every few blocks, cobblers now seemed yet another endangered small-business species. The heat didn't tempt her to wander around looking, so she shoved the broken sandal into her purse and walked to Vivaldi's.

Rose gulped her first iced latte the minute the waitress delivered it and sipped her second. She'd insisted the waitress remove the biscotti from both saucers at once, as if she had a fatal allergy to pastry.

She tried to pretend that caffeine motivated the slight shake in her hands and pressed the backs of both hands firmly onto the table to steady herself. The skin where she'd scrubbed Nick's number off her wrist looked pink now.

Rose ordered another latte, this one hot. The waitress giggled and said she didn't have to worry about any nasty cookies this time. Rose sighed but didn't explain how very wrong the waitress was. Then she dug in her purse for a pen and notebook to start the note she hadn't written in Butler's office.

Two hours and enough caffeine to fuel a swing shift later, Terri's word count for the day still beat Rose's. She'd slashed out everything she'd written, too angry to form coherent thoughts, much less well-written ones. Blue ink smudged her hands and up her arms. A paler blue tint on a paper napkin showed that the pen she'd sucked on had leaked, too. Five crumpled sheets of paper surrounded her cup.

Since she couldn't find the words to tell Butler how she felt, she started a list. Abandoned. Betrayed. Confused. Desolate. Rejecting her new alphabet of sorrow, she crumpled that sheet too. She threw all the pages she'd scribbled on into her purse, paid her check, and walked slowly home by way of West Fourth Street, avoiding the precinct again.

She didn't know how she could face work tonight. Or what she might do at the sight of Terri's simpering face

Rose had better luck drafting her letter of resignation

to My World as she walked home. But she knew she couldn't turn it in until she'd proved Nick's innocence and discovered Yvonne's killer. Quitting My World now would kill her.

# Chapter Thirty-four

After another long shower and the smallest of salads from Catherine's garden, Rose changed into a sleeveless white cotton blouse and a short navy skirt. She gave the skirt the bend-over test in her bedroom's full-length mirror, checking to confirm that she could reach even the lowest bar shelf without giving the customers a show. She hoped the slight golden glow on her legs would last longer than her fond thoughts of the weekend with Butler had. The constant red light on her answering machine proved he didn't want to share any memories today, either. At least not with her.

Rose trudged to My World, dreading her shift. She still didn't know if Ken had surfaced, or how she could bear seeing Terri.

Since their schedules didn't coincide, Rose barely knew Liz, the woman standing behind the empty bar. But Liz called her name with a big smile as she started toward the stairs to get her bank from the office.

"Save yourself a trip, Rose. Terri left your bank with me. She's been running in and out of here all day, said she had to talk to the cops, go to the bank, buy some new mascara." Liz reached into the cooler and pulled out the night-shift cash drawer.

"Is she here now?" Rose stepped behind the bar, relieved that she didn't have to see Terri before her shift started and wondering whose shirt Terri's old mascara had stained.

"Who knows? She said she had a lot of paperwork to go through. I thought she was still out a few hours ago, but she must have snuck by me without even saying hi, 'cause all of a sudden she waltzed up the stairs wearing one of those awful promo shirts of Ken's. It hung down to her knees."

Liz counted her tips, grimacing at the small stack of bills. "When I asked her what she'd spilled on herself, she just giggled. Then she left again, I guess to change. It's taking her long enough."

Liz shook her head when Rose asked if Ken had reappeared. "Maybe that's why Terri's acting so squirrelly. Take my advice and don't ask her about Ken, though, unless you want to listen to her emote for half an hour. Be fine with me if the horny bastard never showed his face again." She pulled her drawer out of the register and handed Rose the night bank.

Rose waited till Liz had left the bar to unfold the piece of paper tucked on top of the tens. She recognized the wretched hot pink script.

> *Have a great shift.*
> *See you later.*
> *Thanks for shareing your*
> *boyfreind with me last night.*
> *He took good care of me.*

Along with the requisite daisies over her I's, Terri had added a big smiley face under her good wishes. Yes, with eyelashes.

Rose refolded the paper and shoved it into her skirt pocket, wishing it were a rock she could throw at Terri's face instead. Liz had left the bar perfectly set up, so Rose started polishing liquor bottles with more force than the busywork required.

She almost dropped the Dewars when Jimmy walked in. "Stop gawking; you'll get frown lines. You smudged a spot on the Myers bottle. I'd like a greyhound, please. Tall."

She loaded a collins glass with ice. "What are you doing here? I thought you had a strict policy of never drinking where you work on your free nights."

"Desperate times, dearest. I couldn't wait to hear about your bucolic weekend. Or to tell you about the insanity you so cleverly missed around here."

She gave him his drink, knocking her fingers on his twenty to signal it was on the house.

"Thank you. After the torturous weekend here, the minimum this establishment can do is sponsor me in a restorative cocktail. We'll get to the grisly details soon enough. First, I want to hear every delicious detail of your weekend away in Paradise. I kept thinking about you, hoping you were adoring every second." Jimmy removed the fat red straw from his drink as if it were a snakeskin.

"The weekend was fine, thanks." When he insisted on details, she gave a cursory description of Tanglewood and Combray, then relented and described both menus. She didn't mention the pond. Or the fireflies.

"I heard Laura got slammed Saturday night." She hoped Jimmy wouldn't ask for her source.

"Slammed? Battered would be a better vocabulary choice. We got extraordinarily busy very early. Laura did her limited best, but she fell behind before 9:00. Her incompetence, however, was the least of the problems plaguing My World that sad night." He paused to align his bevnap with the edge of the bar.

When she asked him what the other problems had been, Jimmy launched into a description of Ken's drunkenness much crueler than what Chris had described. Jimmy reported that Ken had even stumbled behind the bar, grabbing at Laura for balance. He'd also told anyone who would listen that Yvonne had stolen the restaurant blind.

"It was an absolute train wreck. Even Terri had to recognize what an absolute fool her beloved was making of himself. Not that she had a clue how to stop him. When she finally quavered that he might want a break, he grabbed a fistful of bills from the register and stormed out the door."

She poured Jimmy another drink in a fresh glass and asked if he remembered what time Ken had left.

"Not a clue. I didn't have the time to worry about that. Impossible as it is to pretend I miss the lout, I do wonder what rock he's climbed under." Jimmy pushed his twenty toward her and pointed toward the register. "Now you must promise never ever to leave me again on a Saturday night."

The arrival of a group of guys from one of the neighborhood's meat wholesalers saved Rose from answering. She poured their shots and beers, chatting until a game of liars' dice engrossed them.

Promise avoided, she spent the next twenty minutes speculating with Jimmy about Ken's whereabouts and tending to the customers slowly filling the bar.

Ward waited at the service end, holding a white plastic measuring cup. "Since the liquor room is locked, and neither Terri or Ken is to be found, I fear I must beg some white vermouth from you, Rose. Two cups will bathe my mussels in the nectar they deserve. I'll square it with our bloody MIA bosses later."

Rose poured Ward the vermouth and told him she'd note it on her comp sheet. After reading Yvonne's paper, she wondered if the chef really thought they needed to worry about recording where a pint of cheap vermouth went.

Ward held the cup up to his nose and inhaled deeply. "Thanks, love. This smells lovely. I took a bag of trash down with me when I tried the liquor room. It's hell in the back. Stinks to high heaven. Bags and bags of garbage."

"Didn't the haulers pick up this morning?" Jimmy joined the conversation.

Ward shook his head. "Perhaps it's yet another bill Ken hasn't paid. The bloody back door was unlocked again, too. I of course locked it, but I don't know if even that thick metal can keep the stench out of downstairs much longer. Don't venture down there unless you have to, kiddoes."

When Jimmy suggested that Ken might have reduced the garbage pick-up schedule to cut costs, Ward groaned. "The health department may cut our operating hours to zero soon if he did. I'd love to watch Ken explain his budgetary theories to them."

"I'd love to hear Ken defend his budgetary theories to anyone," Rose studied Ward's face, but he didn't react.

Jimmy pushed his glass toward Rose for a refill. "Wait. How much trash could there be? Joe bought those enormous industrial cans back in April when the recycling law went into effect. We've never come close to filling them all."

Ward assured them that not only did the large cans overflow, but that excess bagged garbage surrounded them. "And I can't imagine how the area will look after tonight. But now I have mussels to kill slowly and gently. Ta-ta."

Jimmy waited until Ward had walked back to the kitchen whistling Roberta Flack. "My, my. Did you notice how oddly cheerful Ward seemed? He's so fastidious, I'd think the overflowing garbage would infuriate him, rather than turn him into a happy, albeit oversized, elf."

Hearing Jimmy criticize Ward's fastidiousness was like listening to Reggie Jackson talk about hubris. "Maybe he's just glad Ken's gone."

"Wouldn't it be divine if he were gone forever? And if Terri disappeared too? You and I could run this place so much better than the Bobbsey Twins." Jimmy's third quick drink raised his voice.

Rose hissed at him to shut up, then adjusted her mouth into a welcoming smile as Enzo approached the bar. Jimmy paled when Enzo sat next to him, then pretended to be engrossed by the dinner specials on the blackboard behind the bar.

"Hey, Rosie, how you doing?" Enzo's tan had deepened since the last time she'd seen him.

Rose reached for the Black Label bottle.

"Nah. Too hot for scotch. Give me a Stoly screw, lots of juice, and get yourself and your friend here something."

Jimmy demurred, thanking Enzo extravagantly, but insisting he had a date uptown. Rose poured herself a Dubonnet and soda, clinked glasses, and took a deep swallow. She and Enzo both wished Jimmy a pleasant evening.

"Terri around?" Enzo pointed at the floor.

"No, I haven't seen her since my shift started."

Enzo lowered his voice, "Poor little thing been calling me all day. Said she needed a special favor. You know what she meant?"

Rose told Enzo she didn't, resisting the urge to suggest he call Butler for an update on Terri's needs. She blushed when he asked to borrow the phone, then polished glasses at the other end of the bar until he finished his brief call and pushed the phone away.

"It better not be another favor that jerk she married put her up to. You know what I mean?" Enzo put a hundred-dollar bill on the bar.

Rose assured him she did but wondered exactly how much he thought she knew about the last favor Terri had requested. Enzo didn't seem to know Ken had disappeared. Before she shared the news, though, she wanted to be absolutely sure Ken hadn't surfaced. Maybe he and Terri were having a passionate reunion somewhere right now.

If only.

When she gave Enzo his change, he added another hundred to the stack of bills next to his drink.

If he wanted to bribe her, she couldn't imagine what info he might want from her. Then Enzo explained that he'd run into a nephew and some buddies on their way to play softball on Leroy Street earlier. He'd told them to meet him at My World after the game. They should show up any minute.

"Let's get some money into Joe's register tonight, huh, hon? Waste of talent having you behind the bar on a Monday. The Colorado Kid doin' the schedule now?" Enzo motioned for another drink.

Before she could answer, a boisterous team of sweaty softball players wearing Formerly Joe's t-shirts came in the front door. Another group wearing shirts from The Front joined them. Then The Buffalo Roadhouse and Chumley's teams jostled up to the bar. More than fifty hot and tired customers wanted drinks at once. Right now.

Thank God right now translated into "when you get a chance, please" with this crowd. No need to worry about any impatient attitudes in this crowd, since every one of them worked as bartenders, waiters, bussers, cooks, or managers in Village bars. Rose knew many of them by name, and almost all of them by face. Professional courtesy would prevail, along with significant overtipping, as they celebrated the Monday that started many of their weekends.

She threw Enzo a grateful smile, then threw herself into the graceful dance of high bartending mode. This group guaranteed a far better night than she'd anticipated. Bartenders dreamed of crowds like this.

# Chapter Thirty-five

If anyone were keeping real records, her sales tonight might break them in the Monday category. The softball players ordered round after round. Rose had to beg the busboy for extra ice three times. If Jimmy had stayed, she would have drafted him as her barback.

Enzo gave her a thumbs-up as he stood to leave. She rushed down to thank him again, even before she'd seen the fifty dollars he'd left under his glass.

Shortly after midnight, Ward walked up to the bar carrying three enormous platters of French fries. "You're doing all the business here tonight, my pet. Dining room's been dead, if you've had a minute to notice. I'm sending everybody home early."

He handed her the first platter, cautioning her to use a towel to take it. "Hot plate to keep the frites hotter longer. Give these to your customers with our compliments. Then refuse to divulge my special seasoning mixture when they ask. No ketchup, no matter how they beg." He winked. "Oceans of salt, cayenne, and vinegar. They'll keep drinking a while longer on these."

Rose thanked him profusely and distributed the fries

along the bar, surrounding each platter with tall stacks of promotional bevnaps. Four people wanted to send drinks back to the chef. She took their money, promising Ward would appreciate the beverages soon. Even his Cuervo would be paid for tonight.

Pouring herself a tall pint of water, Rose took her first break in hours, figuring she'd only have a few minutes before the cayenne and salt inspired more drink orders. She'd deal with the dirty glassware covering both sides of the drainboard later. She gulped her entire glass and poured a second, then took it to stand in front of a middle-aged man in a mechanic's coveralls who'd been nursing a Courvoisier and coke alone for the last hour. He'd shaken his head when she'd offered him fries.

"Can I get you anything?" She pointed to his empty glass.

"One more, please, ma'am." He took a deep breath. "Then I'd be grateful if you could spare me a minute to talk."

She poured his drink, apologizing that the large group had monopolized her for so long.

"You been busy, I saw that, " He didn't touch his refill. "I'm sorry to bother you at work, but I wouldn't dare go to your house. I'm here to apologize to you."

"For what?" She poured herself more water.

"For being the biggest fool uptown, shooting my damn mouth off, and bringing trouble to your door." He pointed to an oval label on his uniform, which identified him as Abe Greene.

She stepped back, suddenly grateful for tonight's crowd for another reason.

He winced. "Guess I can't blame you for that. But please hear me out. I came down here to tell you that I've put a stop to all that bullshit, excuse me. It wasn't me causing the trouble. My damn fool nephew heard me bitching about what the police did to my girl. He decided to take things into his own dumb hands, said he would avenge his auntie. Thought he'd make a name for himself. I swear I didn't know what the fool was doing until the detective tracked me down last night."

"What detective?"

"Detective Butler. He wanted to throw my ass in jail too. Man seemed like he wanted to execute anybody who ever bothered you. Took me hours to make him see I didn't do anything bad. But he hung in till we tracked my nephew down and got the bragging truth out of him. Now I got two family members in jail." Abe Greene's voice sunk on his last line, then rose again. "But please hear me when I tell you how sorry I am for what those punk kids did. Anything I can do to make it up to you, you just ask."

Rose assured him his apology was more than enough and thanked him for his efforts. Then she tried very hard to help him to remember exactly when and for how long he'd been with Butler last night.

He looked at her quizzically, but didn't question her prodding, "Seemed like most of the night, and early this morning too. Sorry, ma'am, but I didn't note the hours." Abe Greene swallowed his drink quickly and stood to leave. "You can rest easy tonight, ma'am. I promise you that. No more trouble coming your way."

She wanted to hug Abe Greene. Butler hadn't spent the night with Terri. He'd left Terri, presumably alone, to catch someone who had threatened Rose's safety. While she'd maligned and cursed him, Butler had spent a sleepless night trying to help her.

Ward's spice mixture started to work. All the ballplayers wanted refills. Rose rushed to pour several dozen more drinks, unable to remove the goofy smile from her face.

The smile slipped off her face when she remembered kissing Nick. Just kissing him.

She wished she had the time now to call and check her machine to see if Butler had discovered the bag she'd left in his office. Or Terri's pastries.

The softball players, who seemed in training for the World Series of alcohol consumption, wanted more drinks. For the first time since they'd arrived, she accepted their constant offer to buy her one, too.

She raised her glass in a toast to the group at large, imagining Butler standing among them.

Ward had changed out of his whites into a Sex Pistols XXL t-shirt and madras bermudas before he joined the revelers at the bar. "I've closed the kitchen, Rose. Daresay you'll want to keep this bar going for a while, though. I'll stay for a bit, but I'm too beat to make the duration. If Terri hasn't appeared before last call, will you be okay closing on your own?"

She assured Ward she would, figuring she could get Rick or Max, who'd stuck to soda all night, to stay and see her safely out the door. But what should she do with tonight's full cash drawer if Terri didn't show up to unlock the office?

The restaurant's only safe was in the office downstairs. Terri and Ken had the only keys.

Where the hell were they, anyway?

Rose finally stole a minute to call their apartment. She felt a moment's relief when she heard Ken's voice shout, "Hello, hello, speak up," then realized that was his idea of a clever greeting. She waited till he'd wished her a "fantabulous" day before leaving a message asking someone to call her at the bar the minute they got this.

Maybe Terri was clattering her dainty way back to

My World by now.

Half an hour later, Ward finished his fifth Cuervo and orange juice, thanked the softball players effusively, and called it a night. He scrawled his home number on a bevnap and told Rose to call him if she had any problems closing up. She assured him she'd be fine.

She hadn't noticed her empty ice bin until after Ward left. Telling everyone she'd be back in a second, she locked the register and hurried to the kitchen for two more buckets of ice. Dammit. The busboy had forgotten to put the clear plastic scoop on top of the ice machine. Rose wasted five minutes scrabbling through the top layer of cubes to find it and fill her buckets.

When she left the kitchen, Hank, who tended bar at Chumley's, rushed to take the buckets out of her hands, chastising her for not drafting him to fetch the ice. He staggered slightly as he passed the pails over the bar. His friend Rick, one of the two who'd stayed sober all night, ambled up to steady him.

Rick grinned at Rose, threw his arm around Hank's shoulders, and suggested they call it a night since he had an early audition in the morning. Hank smiled beatifically and agreed. As Rick guided Hank to the front door, Rose looked for Max at the bar. His friends said he'd left just a few minutes ago. The ten-dollar bill under his soda glass signaled that he didn't plan to return tonight.

Surveying the drinkers left at the bar, Rose decided most of them might be more hindrance than help at closing time.

Without access to the safe, she'd have to think of a clever hiding place for tonight's cash. Although she knew many of the remaining customers casually, she couldn't write character references for any of them. Rose resigned herself to closing the bar solo, suddenly missing San

Francisco, where you could call and order a cab after work the way New Yorkers ordered take-out.

Nobody at the bar passed up last call. As she made the final rounds of drinks, Rose saw that cleaning the bar might keep her here till the day shift arrived anyway. For the first time in years, she'd let dirty glasses pile up in revolting ranks. Both the trash cans behind the bar overflowed, and the bottle recycling crates under the bar had reached their limit hours ago. She'd have to bag up the extra empties crammed under the bar.

Even if she had found someone she trusted to close My World with her, asking him to wait through this massive cleanup would have asked too much. She wished again that Jimmy hadn't left so early. He actually enjoyed cleaning.

Twenty minutes later, Rose locked the door behind the last customer. She turned off all the dining room lights and raised the bar lights to their brightest, making the bar look like an operating room. Groaning when she saw the full extent of the mess, she grabbed a few bills out of her overflowing tip cup and played every Eurythmics song on the jukebox. She turned the volume up too.

The two cups of coffee left in the pot had thickened into late-night sludge. Rose poured it over ice, added simple syrup, and gulped it. The nasty road-trip caffeine did its job.

After an hour's hard work, the bar looked respectable.

She'd saved counting her tips and reconciling the register till last. Rose looked at the bar with new affection after she'd exchanged the crumpled bills she'd gathered from the crowd of restaurant workers for twenty-three crisp twenties. Laura would be crushed she'd missed this shift.

Rose folded the bills and tucked them into her left

shoe, then remembered the fifty from Enzo and tucked it into her right. She always kept some money in her purse, but hid any significant sums in her shoes after work. She'd yet to hear of a mugger desperate enough to look under the socks of someone who'd just worked nine hours on her feet.

Her own money safely stashed, she still had to decide where to leave the register's cash. No point in calling Terri again. If Terri had heard Rose's earlier message, she would have returned the call. Wouldn't she?

Joe or Bob Victors would never have made a bartender responsible for securing a cash drawer. Or allowed a bartender to walk out of the restaurant alone after closing. Rose didn't want to think about the hard way the Victors had learned that lesson.

Rose surveyed the bar again, looking for possible hiding spaces. Any potential thief would look in the register drawer first. Bottles and glasses crowded all the shelf space. Damn, she'd forgotten to pack duct tape into her purse tonight, so she'd couldn't tape the cash underneath the bar. The floor mats, even if she'd dared to lift them, were comprised of interlocking circles that cushioned the feet but wouldn't hide anything from curious eyes.

The coolers seemed her best option. Tonight's crowd had almost exhausted her stock of imported beer, and she didn't envy whoever had to stock tomorrow. Kneeling on the grimy mat to reach far back into the cooler, Rose pulled out three rows of Coronas, stuck the cash she'd wrapped in a bar towel onto the shelf, and blocked it with the beers. Shit. The clear bottles of pale beer didn't completely hide the cash bundle.

She could feel the floor mats imprinting little circles on her knees as she removed the Coronas and cash, then returned the Coronas to their original rows on the shelf.

Resting back on her heels, Rose judged the selection of beers with a new eye. Dos Equiis won. A woman with more subterfuge experience would have started with the dark beer in its brown bottles. Rose knelt forward again to move the Dos Equiis bottles. She pulled four rows out this time and stashed the cash far back in the cooler. She'd stagger the rows in front of the money to eliminate any glimpse of its location.

Just as she finished returning the second row to the cooler, Rose thought she heard the phone ring over the loud hum of the compressor thrumming inches from her head. She kicked over one of the bottles on the floor and almost tripped over the dozen more that fell like dominoes. She reached the phone, but nobody answered.

"Hello, hello? Is anybody there?"

"Hello?"

# Chapter Thirty-six

Rose hung up when she heard the dial tone, hoping the caller had just disconnected a second too soon and would call back. She waited for the phone to ring again. Maybe Terri wanted to announce her imminent arrival, and Rose had wasted her time rearranging all that beer. Ken might have surfaced and hoped to get his hands on tonight's cash. Ward could have called to check up on her, although all the tequila he'd drunk had probably put him into a snoring sleep by now.

Or Butler. Butler might have decided he finally wanted to hear her voice again.

Looking down at her knees, imprinted with the floor mat's pattern like crude fishnets, Rose decided she didn't regret not seeing Butler tonight. Thank God she hadn't left a note with his bag at the precinct. Attacking him for spending the night with Terri when he'd actually been working to stop the Greene madness would have been a hard mistake to erase. If Butler hadn't realized she'd seen Terri's missive on the pastry box, the churly desk officer would have smirked that update. She didn't want to think about the desk guy reading the note from Terri.

Now that she'd safely hidden tonight's cash, Rose needed to inform Terri where to find it tomorrow. No telling which officer might respond to a complaint about missing cash at My World. She called Terri and Ken's number again, hanging up when she heard his giddy message. Only a fool would announce the location of a significant amount of cash when she didn't know who could hear the message.

She'd been here too long, too late, by herself already. The normal noises of compressors turning on and off started to take on an ominous rhythm.

One good note deserved another. She scribbled a quick note to Terri, telling her that she'd hidden tonight's cash somewhere safe and that she should call to find out where. Rose used blue ink and unadorned letters. Her only artistic touch was to underline "anytime" with three bold strokes.

Deciding where to leave the note took longer than writing it. Rose finally settled on slipping it under the office door. If she had to walk downstairs anyway, she might as well haul some of tonight's extra trash with her. Rose dumped the bar trash cans into a big plastic sack, then put as many surplus empty bottles as she could carry into another. She tucked the note into her shirt pocket, hefted the two sacks, and walked to the stairs.

She stopped at the top of the stairs to fumble for the light switch, then carefully slung the sack with the bottles over her shoulder, feeling like the Santa Claus of recycling. She tightened her grip on the other sack and started down the stairs. The weight on her back threw her off balance, and she hobbled a little on the treads.

She couldn't hear anything except the empty bottles clinking behind her. She wished she could race down the stairs instead of mistrusting every next step.

Her relief at stepping into the hallway vanished when Rose saw the restroom doors. She'd broken a universal restaurant rule.

Someone should have checked both bathrooms at closing time.

She knew better than to lock the front door before establishing that no one lurked downstairs.

How could she have been so stupid?

Her relief at knowing Butler's whereabouts last night had erased this essential step on her mental checklist. He'd kill her if he knew.

If anyone had hidden, better he think she wasn't alone in the closed restaurant. Rose shouted to an imaginary pal to come down and help her with the trash.

Nobody answered.

The only other noise she heard was the sound of the trash settling as she put the sacks on the floor and rummaged for the Galliano bottle she'd emptied for rounds of wallbangers.

Rose raised the long bottle over her shoulder like a club and opened the door to the women's room. She peered under both stall doors before slowly pushing them open. Nothing scarier than empty toilet paper rolls and stained tissues skulked behind the doors.

Yelling again to her phantom friend, she pushed the door to the men's room open until it swung back against the wall. Nobody crouched on the urinals. The room's sole stall didn't hide anything worse than smutty graffiti. She waited till she stepped back into the hall to take a deep breath.

Adrenaline married caffeine, and she carried both big bags to the delivery entrance as if they held nothing heavier than sweet dreams. Dropping the sacks by the door, she walked back to the office. When she bent to shove her note under the door, she saw a thin line of light shining into the hall.

No one answered her knocks.

She'd have to dump the trash outside by herself.

When Rose opened the heavy delivery door, the heat and stench poured into the hallway. She checked twice to make sure that she'd latched the door open before she carried the first bag into the loading area. Ward hadn't exaggerated: it reeked like a landfill on an August afternoon. The thick heat magnified the stink.

Extra bags of trash huddled in an ugly mountain she didn't want to climb. Even in the dim light from the one bulb in a metal cage, she could see scattered pieces of garbage and the lid to the biggest can lying on the ground. Fat black flies swarmed above the trash, their low buzzing seeming to rise and fall as she moved.

She picked up the lid and returned it to the biggest can, surprised to see that it still had some empty space. Trying not to breathe in the stink, she shoved down with all her strength so she could fit a sack into the can. She batted away the cloud of flies that flew up to meet her in what would have seemed a banquet to Renfield. When her efforts forced her to inhale the stench, she wondered what Ward had butchered today. Nobody who smelled this would mistake My World for a vegetarian establishment tonight.

Dante would have moved into double digits to describe this scene

Something rustled behind the can. Rustled, not clinked like settling bottles. Rose hated rats. She closed her eyes and stood on tiptoe as she leaned into the can to push again, trying not to think what would happen if she fell in. She hoped the dampness spreading up her arms was nothing worse than fruit juice.

She couldn't do it, couldn't make enough room in the can for her sack. Cursing at the wasted effort, she leaned her sack against the can and dragged the bag of bottles over to the recycling bin. They jangled into a chorus of ugly giggles. Enough.

Rose rushed back into the hall and slammed the delivery door behind her. She checked twice to make sure that the lock had caught. Then she saw the splotchy fingerprints her hands had stamped on the dull metal door.

# Chapter Thirty-seven

Rose stared at her hands and arms in the bright hallway light, refusing to name the red that covered her. This wasn't grenadine, or tomato juice, or even any mess Ward might have produced in the kitchen today.

Rose knew this color. Rose knew this metallic smell. Her senses announced the truth her mind wanted to deny. She had just covered herself in blood, blood that felt warm on her hands and up her arms.

What if the sound she'd heard had come from inside the can, instead of outside? What if the bleeding hadn't stopped, and someone was still alive in the can? Whose blood was she wearing?

Just whose blood was it, anyway?

Rose unlocked the door and ran back to the trash cans, almost slipping on the littered ground. She couldn't make herself reach in there again. She shoved against the can to tip it over, but it stayed upright, stubborn like an inflatable clown doll. The can shouldn't feel this heavy. Shaking off the flies that tried to settle on her hands and arms like hideous opera gloves, Rose shoved and pushed until the can teetered over.

She rolled the can slowly until it rested in the light coming from the hallway. The flies' shadows dappled everything she saw in a crazed moving mosaic. Rose crouched over to peer inside the can. The bad bright red glimmered through kitchen scraps and bits of crumpled paper. She grabbed an empty Stoli bottle and used the neck to move the rotten lettuces and dirty paper aside. The bottle kept hitting something solid under the scrim of trash. Solid, but motionless.

Rose leaned a few inches to the left so that her shadow wouldn't block the hallway light. She made herself look into the can again. She saw two cheap brown shoes that didn't shine anymore, pink socks, and spattered canary yellow pants. Rose pulled on the shoes. She struggled against the weight until the body lay on the filthy floor in front of her, its torso still folded at the waist.

Rose ripped a trash sack apart and sheathed her hands in slimy black. She pushed on the body's shoulders until it lay straight, then knelt next to it, trying not to think what might leave traces on her knees this time.

A bullet hole had dyed Ken's orange shirt a deep red over his belly. His paunch didn't hang over his belt anymore. His eyes stared up at her as if surprised she'd bothered to extricate him. Slimy lettuces and breadcrumbs had caught in his hair. Something Rose hoped was lipstick covered his still mouth. Nothing she could pretend was breath stirred his gaudy chest.

Ken hadn't made whatever noise she might have heard. She couldn't do a damn thing to help Ken now.

Clenching her lips tightly against the swarming flies and the shriek she shouldn't release, Rose stood, stripped the plastic from her hands, and swatted at the gunk on her knees. She peered around the gloomy scene, telling herself no creature larger than a rodent could hide in these shadows.

When she backed toward the delivery door, she almost lost her balance when her foot hit an empty bottle. The idea of falling onto the filthy ground that held Ken scared her so that she peered once more into the dark, then turned and ran to the door.

As she slammed and locked the door behind herself, she saw that its surface held two perfectly delineated fingerprints amidst the splotchy marks. Her fingerprints, stamped in Ken's blood.

A horde of flies pursued her into the hallway.

She stopped for a second outside the ladies' room door, craving the sensation of soap and hot water. If only she hadn't become a walking exhibit in this crime scene. The cops would have their own procedures for removing all the evidence, including the awful substances on her skin. They could keep her clothes if they wanted, too.

Rose rushed upstairs and watched her fingers stain the handset of the host station's phone as she called 911. The dispatcher asked her three times if she felt safe "at her present location" and if anyone else might be in the building with her. Looking around the dim dining room and beyond into the dark kitchen, Rose tried to steady her voice as she answered that she thought she was alone. She couldn't answer the question about feeling safe.

Several flies had followed her upstairs.

The dispatcher insisted Rose stay on the line until the first squad car arrived. She asked Rose to describe the "situation" again. Rose heard her own voice fall into a dull monotone as she repeated what she'd found. Her hand started to feel sticky where her fingers touched the receiver.

It felt as if the humid stench had created a horrid film that clung to her whole body.

She stared out at the street, praying to see revolving blue lights.

A few minutes later, she winced at the floodlights pouring in the windows to illuminate the dining room. She put the phone down, held her arms above her head the way the dispatcher had instructed, and walked slowly to the entrance. The blue lights flickered in the dark street when she opened the door and waited. She didn't drop her hands until an officer said she should.

Rose recognized Will from the night on West Fourth Street. She told him she was fine, just fine, and slumped onto the chair he pulled away from a table. She described what she'd found and told Will where he could find it too. Then she pointed out the light switches for the dining room and asked if they could kill the floodlights.

More squad cars screeched outside. Rose looked up each time another cop entered My World, but she didn't see the face she wanted. She tried not to let her hands touch the table's white cloth. More officers thumped down the stairs, but she couldn't hear anything from the delivery area.

After what seemed like a very long time, Will returned to hover above her. He spoke gently when he told her he'd left urgent messages for Butler everywhere he could think of and knew they'd hear from him soon. With formal courtesy, he told her the techs needed to take some samples from her and suggested she ride with him to the precinct for "a few more questions."

Rose agreed and followed him to his squad car. Grateful that no curious onlookers had gathered yet, she ducked into the back seat and sat up very straight all the way to the precinct.

She felt a ridiculous relief when she saw that the shift change had put a new man on the front desk. A female officer took Rose into a chilly room and scraped samples of gunk off her skin and clothes. Then the woman took her into a bathroom and stood outside the door while Rose scrubbed at herself with granular soap and scratchy paper towels. Waiting on the bench the woman then escorted her to, Rose wondered if she'd ever feel clean again.

Five minutes later, Rose followed Will back to an office she'd never seen and answered questions from a man she didn't know. Rose described everything she could remember since her arrival at My World tonight. She apologized that she didn't know anything useful about Ken's disappearance and bit her lip instead of suggesting they ask Butler for the details. She recounted everything Liz had told her about Terri's whereabouts during the day.

"Detective Roberts, you do know that a woman who worked at My World was murdered last week, don't you?" As she spoke, Rose realized Yvonne had died last Monday. A murder a week.

The detective stared at her with a deadpan look that made Butler's usual expression look like the Good Humor man. "We're apprised of that fact. File says you found the deceased that time, too."

Rose nodded, fighting the urge to defend herself, as if she'd deliberately combed Manhattan for dead bodies. He couldn't think she'd done more than find the bodies.

Roberts asked her more questions, several rephrasing what he'd already asked. She answered each question carefully, hoping she wouldn't contradict herself. When the interrogation finally stopped, she suddenly felt so tired she wanted to put her head down on Robert's desk for a nap. She probably wouldn't wake up to milk and cookies, though.

Yawning, Rose asked if she could leave yet. Roberts nodded. She'd almost reached the door when he called her back, "Just one more thing. We need a list of every customer at the bar tonight. Any contact info for them, too." He handed her a yellow legal pad and a cheap ballpoint.

"This will take hours. I told you how busy it was tonight. Can't I do this tomorrow? Please?"

Roberts shook his head and offered to get her coffee. Rose accepted and hunched over the pad, realizing that she hadn't mentioned Abe Greene's visit yet. She sighed with exhaustion at the thought of describing the Greene saga to Roberts. Maybe Butler could fill him in on that aspect, at least.

She'd never get her assignment done and see her apartment again if she allowed herself to speculate about why Butler hadn't responded to any of Will's messages.

By the time Roberts returned, she'd almost finished the second page of names. She'd drawn big sloppy brackets around some of the groups and scrawled the places where they worked in larger letters next to the brackets. Relieved that she couldn't provide any more detailed contact info for most of tonight's customers, Rose had hesitated when she'd written Enzo's name. She didn't have a clue where the cops could find Enzo.

Rose thanked Roberts for the styrofoam cup of lukewarm coffee but almost gagged when she took the first sip. She put the cup down on the desk, wanting to wash again. Dried blood had outlined her fingernails against the white styrofoam when she lifted the cup to her lips. The taste of rusty metal filled her mouth now. She pushed the cup as far away as the desk allowed, then bent over her list again.

"That bad, huh?" Roberts reached into his pocket

and brought out a lumpy paper napkin. "Here, I found these by the coffee machine. Maybe they'll help you keep your strength up."

Rose didn't touch the hazelnut biscotti Roberts put on the desk in front of her.

# Chapter Thirty-eight

Rose accepted Will's offer of a ride home. Much as she'd prefer walking, her stained clothing might attract yet more trouble in the bright morning light now filling the streets. He let her sit in the front seat. She couldn't muster the energy to argue when he insisted on walking her upstairs.

Double-locking her door, Rose stripped off the ruined clothes in her apartment's hallway. She cinched a Gristede's bag around her panties, bra, skirt, blouse, and shoes, determined to throw everything the cops didn't want away.

Then she stood under the shower for half an hour. She used her nailbrush to wash her entire body, then scrubbed her short nails again and again with it. Her skin looked lobster-red against the long white nightgown she finally slipped over her wet head. She tossed the towels she'd used on top of the Gristede's bag, just in case.

Walking into the kitchen, Rose doubted she'd ever want to drink coffee again. Wine at eight in the morning seemed obscene. Peppermint tea's warmth might remind her of the coffee at the precinct.

She pulled a liter of Pellegrino out of the fridge and drank half of it before she walked into the living room. The blinking light on her machine announced she'd finally received at least one message.

Rose hesitated, unsure if she even wanted to hear what Butler had to say at this late hour. Where the hell had he been all night and into the morning? Maybe Mr. Greene's explanation hadn't offered as much hope as she'd thought. She didn't know if hearing Butler's voice now would make her feel better or worse.

Her finger snuck down and pushed play before she'd decided. Butler hadn't called; Nick had. Twice.

His first message begged her to call him immediately because he needed to talk to her about last night. Rose started, then realized he meant Sunday night. Nick couldn't know she'd found Ken tonight, could he? Last night, by now.

Every day seemed like a morning after now. A bad one.

Nick pleaded with her to call again in his second message. He also told her he'd kept his word and showed Butler Yvonne's paper. He described his trip to the precinct as a waste of time and complained about the shit Butler had given him. Nick finished with another entreaty to call immediately.

She'd heard street noises in the background on both Nick's calls. If Nick was so frantic to hear from her, how did he expect her to reach him when she didn't know where he was?

Rose lifted the receiver, hesitated, and returned it to the cradle. After all the repetitions of the story she'd given at the precinct, she couldn't stand to tell Nick about finding Ken. She shouldn't turn to Nick for comfort right now, either. Shaken and exhausted, she longed to have his strong sculptor's arms wrapped around her in a protective shield. The image of herself in Nick's arms appealed so much it scared her. Rose gulped the rest of her Pellegrino.

Had the cops informed Terri of her husband's demise yet, and which particular officer might have assumed that duty? The desk man at the precinct probably wouldn't tell her if she called to ask.

Her watch volunteered information more readily, announcing she'd now been up for more than twenty-four hours. Her body felt every second.

She turned her air-conditioner to max cool and went to bed, wishing she could apply the machine's white-noise hum to her brain.

Loud pounding on her apartment door woke her around noon from nightmares she didn't want to remember. Struggling up from a restless sleep, she might have incorporated the pounding into her last bad dream.

She couldn't guess when she'd finally fallen asleep.

Rose tip-toed to the door and peered through the peephole at the funhouse image of Butler's face. She smoothed her hair for a minute, watching the way her view of him wavered when he pounded on the door, then yelled at him to relax as she unlocked the top lock.

He stopped pounding when he heard her voice.

She felt him rattling the knob the second she turned the bottom lock's button and stepped out of the way in anticipation of his swinging the door open. His face didn't look distorted when he grabbed her and held her close. She clung to him. These arms had been worth waiting for.

These arms.

His stubble scratched her skin when he kissed her. He held her another long moment without speaking, then drew back, "Jesus, Rose, I'm so sorry."

"Sorry for what?"

"For not being there when you needed me last night. I went home for a power nap yesterday afternoon and passed out. Didn't wake up till this morning. You wore me out this weekend, darling."

"The weekend ended two days ago." She walked to the sink, hoping her own coffee could erase the memory of the precinct's.

"Yeah. But I didn't get any sleep at all Sunday night, and you might remember that Saturday night was a long one, too." Butler collapsed into a chair at the kitchen table, as if talking about missing sleep had tired him again.

She turned her back on him to start the coffee brewing, "Why didn't you get any sleep Sunday? Guilty conscience, maybe?"

"Don't start that crap now, please. I only stayed at Terri's a little while, trying to calm the poor kid down. Then I had some—uh—business."

Why didn't he mention Abe Greene?

And what else he might be trying to hide?

Butler took the coffee mug she handed him, "Forget Sunday. I'm here about last night. We can't pretend you adored Ken, but you shouldn't have had to dig his corpse out of the trash. Are you okay? Roberts said he gave you the kid-gloves treatment."

"It felt more like the golden gloves. Will was very sweet, though. When did you talk to Roberts?" She took an experimental sip of her coffee, admiring her clean short nails against the blue china.

"As soon as I woke up. We're going to get that bastard real soon." He reached for the coffee pot and refilled both their cups.

"You know who did it already?"

Butler admitted they weren't quite ready to make an arrest, but said they would be very soon. Then he outlined his case against Nick, insisting that he was the obvious suspect. Butler poured sugar onto the table and traced a triangle in it, then pointed to the three sides as he named them. Yvonne. Ken. Nick. He erased the lines representing Yvonne and Ken and fingered the remaining line with a smug look.

Did he think the horror of finding Ken's body had turned her into a simpleton? Rose grabbed a sponge from the drainboard and wiped away his infantile diagram. "I'll get you a pen and pencil. You need to draw some more triangles, give your third-party theory a real workout."

He laughed and asked her what she meant.

"What about Barney? He'd threatened Yvonne before, and he still sounded possessive about her. Not to mention that life insurance policy."

"Near as the tech guys can tell, the phone calls Barney made the day Yvonne died kept him in Jersey long enough to take him off the hook. No word on the insurance yet."

"I've heard more convincing faith in modern technology. But forget Barney for now, let's move onto triangle three."

"Three triangles?"

"Terri. You could easily substitute Terri for Nick in your original triangle theory. The same relationships apply. Only the name changes. Once Terri saw the paper Yvonne wrote, she had more than love as a motive to kill Ken."

"The paper? Who knows if Yvonne ever mailed it? I think Nick's using that paper to take the heat off himself. Terri didn't mention it, not to me and not to Roberts."

When had Roberts talked to Terri? How could she convince Butler that Nick couldn't have killed Yvonne? Just why did he insist on championing Terri's innocence?

High school romances only went so far.

Rose decided not to tell Butler that she could vouch for Nick's whereabouts for most of Sunday night and Monday morning until she knew if he needed the information or not. Instead, she told him again how she suspected Terri had killed Ken.

"For God's sake, Terri was busy all day Monday. Working, running errands, going to the bank, even the precinct." Butler poured more sugar into his coffee.

"Don't forget the bakery."

"Stop. Terri knows how much I love those cookies. We used to buy them after Mass every week." His voice hardened, "Cute trick with the bag yesterday. I swore I wouldn't bring the cookies up now. But you couldn't let it slide, could you?"

Was he going on the offense because he felt defensive?

He didn't give her the chance to ask, "Think you could accept that as an alibi all right? Woman visiting cop house miraculously kills husband by astral projection. You should spend less time reading in checkout lines."

"Does that mean you know the exact time of death already? How can you know she didn't do it?" He still hadn't told her anything that proved Terri's innocence.

He shook his head, "You expect too much. There just aren't all that many cases where the suspect is photographed sitting under a big clock casually holding a newspaper." He reached across the table and clasped her hand, "Damnit, I came over here because I love you, but all you can do is argue. I wanted to apologize for calling you a bitch Sunday night, not feel tempted to do it again."

He released her hand and stood. "Fuck it. I gotta go now."

Nonapology not accepted, "Another house call? The poor kid need you again?"

He didn't call her a bitch again. He didn't say a single

word as he slammed out of her apartment.

Rose hurried to the front window and watched Butler drive away, wondering if they would ever heal this rift, if she could stop this wretched mistrust. She curled into her chair and listened to the water dripping from her air-conditioner. She didn't pick up the phone when Nick called again. Or even when Catherine called and left a message describing the special desserts she'd just introduced on her menu. For once, Rose wanted to think instead of talk.

Mass. Mass. Mass.

She hurried into the kitchen, found the phone book, and called Rocco's to ask about hazelnut biscotti. The cheerful woman at the bakery gave her the answer she'd expected. Terri had not only given Butler a box of stale treats, she'd also lied about when she'd bought them.

Terri's stories didn't include madeleines.

The next time Rose saw Butler, she'd tell him that Rocco's only made the hazelnut biscotti on the weekends. Then she'd tell him that he should follow the crooked trail of stale crumbs. All the way back to the witch's house.

# Chapter Thirty-nine

Rose did pick up the phone when Ward called a few minutes later. He apologized for leaving her to close alone last night, didn't ask for any gory details, and announced that the restaurant was closed until further notice. He wanted to make sure someone let her know. She should call him if she needed anything at all. He'd bring some leek soup if she fancied it.

Rose wondered how long Jimmy would wait to call. She didn't want to think how much time might elapse before the next time Butler dialed her number.

She stared out the window again. The leaves on the trees across the street moved in the wind. Opening the living room windows let the warm breeze in to air the room. What was good for her apartment should be good for its occupant. Freed from My World for the night, a long walk had more appeal than another shift of phone-sitting.

Rose shrugged on a white linen sundress so long she needed heels. The fabric seemed too sheer today. She added a vintage blouse she'd stalked for months at Victoria Falls before she found a way to justify the purchase. The hand-stitched pintucks, tiny mother-of-pearl buttons, and fine lace trim on the delicate lawn fabric made it a collector's item. She wanted to wear it for years.

It draped beautifully over the sundress, once she tied the thin ribbons at the drawstring waist into a demure bow. A perfect light summer jacket.

The shoes she'd worn at Tanglewood still lay on the closet floor. Their graceful heels seemed more appropriate than clunky Korkies. She wouldn't have to worry about aerating the sidewalks, either. Graceful, nimble footsteps would sound better than a Frankenstein plod.

She slicked on mascara and lipstick, then locked the door and clattered down the stairs as if monsters followed right behind her.

Rose stood in front of her building for a minute. Which way should she walk? A breeze ruffled her hair, so she headed west on Eleventh Street toward the water. Even the turgid Hudson River might soothe her today, and none of the seagulls would ask her about discovering Ken's corpse last night. She turned right when she reached Hudson Street, hoping the Jane Street pier might be less crowded than the piers to the south.

The sight of Butler's car parked on Jane two doors in from Hudson stopped her stroll. Rose looked at the tall building on the corner. She knew Terri and Ken had moved into a sublet at 61 Jane Street when they'd arrived in the city. She also knew that she'd just stalked Frank Butler. Successfully.

Rose felt a hot blush creep up her neck as she hurried toward the river. After half a block, the blush had fueled an anger that made her wheel around. Forget pride. She wanted to see the look on Butler's face when she proved Terri had lied about buying the biscotti yesterday. Then she wanted to see Terri's sweet little features twist as she tried to explain her lie away.

Apted didn't appear on the list next to the buzzers in the vestibule, but the super's name did. A quick description of Terri and twenty dollars later, Rose knew which buzzer to press. She pressed three times before anyone answered. The intercom transmitted Terri's giggle with perfect clarity. Sounding as delighted as if she'd craved a visit from Rose for months, Terri told her to turn left, then right, when she got off the elevator.

Terri stood in the apartment doorway, her hair looking even more tousled than usual. The grieving widow tightened the belt of a short peach robe over her tiny waist just after Rose glimpsed the sheer ballerina gown underneath.

"Wow, Rose, you look like you just made your first Holy Communion or something. How was confession?" Terri smiled brightly at Rose and gestured her into the apartment.

The living room reeked of the perfume Chantilly that classmates had coveted as the height of sophistication in junior high. Bouquets of bright yellow and orange gerbera daisies wreathed with baby's breath perched on the mirrored side tables bracketing the tawny ultrasuede couch. Rose didn't see Butler in the living room or in the open kitchen.

"What can I fix you to drink, hon?" Terri giggled again. "Sit down and get comfy. Isn't it fun that I get to serve you a drink for a change?"

"Where's Frank, Terri?" Rose didn't sit.

"Oh, he's gone." Terri tossed her head. "You're too late. But he talked about you so much, all about how he loved you. Frankie really loved you."

Rose didn't want to reveal what the biscotti's delivery date meant until Butler could hear her discovery too. Not a smart move to accuse Terri of murder with nobody else around. She'd pretend this was a condolence call and leave within a few minutes. "Listen—"

"Oh stop looking so grim. I know you hated Ken, so you can't be sorry he's dead. Have a seat." Terri pointed toward the couch. She'd lost the fake nail from her right forefinger, which looked stubby and more bereft than its owner. "If you won't tell me what you want, I'll bring you one of what I'm having."

Rose sat, hoping that sharing a drink with Terri would let her escape faster than wasting more time arguing. Maybe she could trick Terri into sharing some info with the beverages.

"Here, yummy," Terri put a clear cocktail garnished with cherries impaled on a frilled yellow toothpick onto the glass coffee table. Rose couldn't guess what Terri had used to make the drink, but she smelled something far sweeter than vodka.

Terri giggled again and raised her glass. When Rose raised hers in return, Terri clinked her glass against Rose's so hard that part of the drink splashed down Rose's front.

"Damn it," Rose jumped up, pulling her dress away from her chest as the icy liquid hit her breasts.

"Oopsie. Clumsy me. Such a pretty blouse, too. Is that lace handmade?" Terri pointed to the stained threads over Rose's breasts.

When Rose told Terri she didn't know and said she had to leave, Terri insisted she change into dry clothes. "There must be something in my closet you can squeeze into. You can't walk home with your nipples sticking out like that."

A quick glance down at herself forced Rose to accept Terri's offer. She headed down the short hall Terri said led to the master.

"Take anything you want to in there, hon," Terri's

giggle followed Rose into the bedroom. The room reeked of Chantilly, as if Terri had doused the walls with it.

Rose stopped wondering why Terri had giggled so much when she saw the disheveled king-size bed. The tiger-print sheets looked as if larger mammals had attacked them. A hot-pink nail on one of the oversized pillows lay over dark hairs on the pillowcase, hairs Rose recognized.

Rose stood frozen, reading all the jealousy she'd cursed herself for feeling writ large on the bed.

Trying not to cry, she took deep breaths. In. Out. In. Out. She'd pass out if she inhaled another molecule of the sickly sweet perfume. Rose gasped when she recognized the mantra could apply to more activities than breathing. She heard what seemed like a mocking groan in reply. She wheeled toward the doorway and saw Terri still lounging on the couch.

She was alone in Terri's bedroom, and Terri had wanted her to see this. Little Terri let the bed do her boasting. Rose stopped herself from picturing Butler's betrayal. She'd have plenty of time to torture herself with details later. She'd never forget this room.

Was that another moan? No, she was just imagining the ghosts of lovers past in this hellhole. Rose slid open the mirrored closet doors and rifled through the hangers for something to hide her wet clothes so she could get the hell out of here. Terri was right again: she shouldn't walk home with her nipples revealed this way. She'd kill the first fool who commented. Right after she concocted a slow and miserable death for the cheating bastard Butler.

Another loud groan. A real one. Someone was in the room with her. Rose walked around the large bed and saw a big pile of sateen quilts on the floor. The quilts stirred. She heard the rasps of labored breathing.

She didn't want to touch whatever the quilts held.

Her hands might never feel clean again.

Rose balanced on her left leg and twisted her right until she could use the heel on her right shoe to pull the quilts back.

Inch by inch, her heel unveiled Butler. He lay on his stomach, his back and shoulders streaked with scratches Rose knew her short nails had never made. The passionate graffiti on Butler's body repeated the message she'd read in the sheets. She hated this script.

Forget her nipples. She wanted to get out of here before she started to kick her exhausted ex-lover until he stopped his satisfied groans. Or used her short nails to scratch her ex-boss' eyes out. Maybe both.

Or she could just throttle Terri so she'd never have to hear her giggle again.

Too late. Rose heard the same maddening laugh trill behind her.

"Hon? You weren't supposed to see that. No fair snooping."

Rose turned toward the sound of Terri's voice. Little Terri crouched in the bedroom doorway. Little Terri held a very big gun in both hands. Little Terri pointed the big barrel of the gun straight at Rose's head.

# Chapter Forty

"Frank always talks about how smart you are, Rose. But coming here today seems pretty stupid to me. Why couldn't you leave well enough alone? Does every bitch who works at My World have to ruin everything?" Terri didn't giggle after these questions.

Rose asked Terri what she meant, sinking slowly to a sitting position in front of the mirrored closet as she spoke. The gun's barrel followed her head's descent.

"Ken told me how every girl there threw herself at him all the time. I even believed him till Enzo told me the truth about Ken and Yvonne and showed me the fat bitch's letter. I showed that to Ken the night he disappeared."

Terri perched on the end of the bed as if settling in for a good session of girl-talk. "I figured it was good riddance till Ken called me at dawn Monday. Big man was so scared. He thought people were following him." Terri mimed looking over her shoulder, but whipped her head back before Rose could move.

"Ken begged me to bring him money so he could leave town. He promised he'd send for me, of course. Like I didn't already know he'd cleaned out our bank account, didn't even leave enough for a PATH ride to Hoboken," Terri sighed. "Ken wanted me to take the cash from the bar safe instead of depositing it Monday."

Rose blurted it out without thinking, "Had you taken money from the bar like that before?"

Terri tossed her hair, "Of course not. How can you accuse me of something like that when I'm sharing my feelings with you?"

Rose apologized, determined to keep Terri talking as long as possible. She hadn't heard Butler groan for several minutes. Was he listening to their conversation, hoping to hear clues instead of pillow talk?

She didn't dare look in his direction. Why had Terri left him under that pile of quilts? On the floor?

Did his groans signal something besides satisfied passion? Why wasn't he moving? Or talking?

Terri giggled again, "Where was I? Right. I told Ken I'd be his dirty little girl and meet him out by the garbage where nobody would see us. I wasn't going to give him the whole deposit, just enough to get him out of town."

Rose nodded in a rhythm she hoped looked sympathetic. The gun's barrel tracked her head's movements.

"My dear hubby musta forgot about the gun Uncle Joe keeps in the safe. That gun told me what Uncle Joe would want me to do. Ken was stealing from me, me and my family, my real family." Terri touched her thumb to her lips and then her chest as if in quick prayer.

"Ken wrote his own death warrant the day he had that idea. I would have been humiliated in front of everyone."

Rose tsked like a girlfriend who understood. She didn't ask if killing your husband to avenge your honor was something that would make the Christmas letter.

Why was Terri confessing all of this with Butler a few

feet away? Why wasn't Butler interrupting her confession with his infernal questions?

Rose started to inch the shoe off her right foot when Terri started talking again.

"When Ken showed up, I told him I wouldn't give him a cent until he told me how Yvonne died when he killed her to cover his own ass. He just laughed and said the only reason he'd ever screwed Yvonne was so she might help him skim money. When he needed to kill her to keep his secrets safe, he decided to make it look like a crazy art thing. He bragged about that, although we don't see that big Nick in jail, do we? Then he grabbed me and kissed me real hard. He messed my lipstick up something awful. I shot him."

Rose cried out when Terri pantomimed firing the gun.

Terri shushed Rose, "He looked messy afterward, so I hid him in the garbage where he belonged. I felt stronger than I ever did before. Guess the aerobics have paid off. That Jane may be a commie bitch, but she knows how to shake it."

She lowered her voice to a confiding tone, "Please don't tell anyone, but Enzo really let me down this time. He should have helped me when I needed him. If he'd taken that trash away, you wouldn't have found Ken and ended up here."

"I didn't come here because I found Ken." Rose slipped her right hand under the hem of her dress and gripped her sandal. "I came because of Frank."

"Your boyfriend pretended he'd come to thank me for the cookies. They sure did come in handy." Terri licked her lips when she said "come."

"Who knew when I bought them after Mass Sunday that I could use them to throw the cops off the trail? Men."

Terri giggled again. "But now I need to ask you a big favor."

Rose asked Terri what she needed.

"Could you move away from the mirror? I don't want to mess it up. I have too much to clean away in here already."

Rose tilted her head to see Butler when she heard his breathing change into a ragged gasping. She didn't have to look at the scratches on his back anymore. He'd managed to turn himself over. He was still naked, though. The blood slowly seeping out of the hole in his chest didn't look like any kind of clothing.

Blood puddled around his torso, staining the beige rug. Too much blood. Too red.

She had to help Butler. Now.

# Chapter Forty-one

Rose started to stand, but Terri stopped her. "Wait. Isn't it weird how long it's taking Frankie to die? Ken was way quicker."

Rose answered by hurling her shoe at Terri's head, hoping the sharp heel would hit first. Terri's hands flew up to protect her face. The gun fell to the thick carpet. It bounced twice, then thudded to a stop. The barrel pointed at Rose.

Without waiting to see what damage her shoe had done, Rose threw herself at the gun. She landed on top of it and prayed it wouldn't fire as she felt metal poke into her pelvis. Terri screeched and jumped on top of Rose. She used her plastic nails to attack, gouging Rose's left check, her arms, and her hands.

Rose hoped the blood dripping into her hair was Terri's. She couldn't lift her head to see.

She heard Butler's breath wheezing. He shouldn't breathe so fast.

"Frank, are you okay? Say something."

He didn't answer.

She had to stop Terri and help Butler. No matter

what he'd done, she couldn't let him die. Not here.

Terri's hard nails kept clawing until Rose felt rivulets of blood creeping down her cheek and arms. She clinched her eyes shut so tight that little lightning bolts exploded in the dark. One of those dagger nails could blind her if Terri aimed right.

Rose bucked and twisted. She couldn't dislodge Terri from her back. The gun hurt her every time she moved on it. God, don't let her jouncing make it hurt her more.

Rose tried to thrust her hand under herself to reach the gun. She couldn't raise her torso enough. Terri's surprising weight stopped her.

Jesus, the shoe. Terri hadn't thought of the shoe yet. Rose couldn't give her the chance to wield that weapon.

Rose lifted her head an inch off the carpet and opened her eyes. Her shoe lay only a few inches away. The wet leather felt slick when she grabbed it. She rotated the sole until the heel pointed up and tightened her grip. Rose tilted her head and exposed the right side of her face to Terri's claws. She felt stiff hair brush her neck when Terri leaned closer to attack the fresh uncovered skin. Rose counted three deep gouges before she lifted the shoe and flailed blindly behind and above herself.

She clenched her fingers around the arch and swung. Her elbow hurt from the odd angle. Rose twisted her arm and swung again.

Terri howled when the shoe made contact. She crumpled and slid off Rose's back. Rose lifted her torso, grabbed the gun, and dragged herself upright. A glimpse at the mirror showed the ribbons of blood trailing down her face and arms.

She blinked blood out of her right eye and looked down. Terri slumped against the closet, whimpering. Her brown eyes fluttered open, then closed. The red third eye the shoe had left in the middle of her forehead stayed open.

Rose pointed the gun at Terri's head and backed toward Butler. Terri didn't move. Rose kept the gun trained on Terri as she looked at Butler.

"Can you hear me, Frank?" Rose found the bedside phone and called 911. She told the dispatcher an officer had been shot in the chest and gave the address, then hung up and crouched over Butler.

He nodded his head and tried to speak. His breath whistled a tune she hated. Pain twisted his mouth, but he didn't say anything.

"Hang on, Frank. Please hang on." She twirled to check on Terri, who stirred but still hadn't opened her eyes.

"Don't move. I'll shoot you and your damn mirror. Why in hell—?"

"Frankie made me. Nothing worked. Not my nails, not the mirror, not the 'ludes in his drink." Terri sucked on her fingerless nail. "He wouldn't do it right."

"He wouldn't—"

Rose heard Butler groan again. She'd misread the whole situation, accused him of betraying her after he'd resisted Terri's entire arsenal of tacky seduction.

Terri leaned into the mirror and scrubbed at her bloody cheeks with the hem of her robe. Then she fluffed her hair. "Frankie was more fun in high school. Do you think I need more highlights, hon?"

Rose pictured a bullet hitting the mirror and shards of glass glistening on Terri's head. Her fingers tightened on the gun.

"Shut up and don't move. I could kill you for what you did. I still might. Stay very still now."

Sirens screamed outside. Sirens had heralded his arrival in her life, serenaded the first time she saw him.

She wouldn't let them signal the end.

Butler's fingers closed on her empty hand. His grasp had never felt so weak, and his face had never looked so pale.

She bent closer, watching his lips form words she couldn't hear. The sirens screeched in her head like banshees announcing the dead.

Butler's eyes closed.

"Talk to me, Frank. Please talk." She hovered above him, willing him to look at her again.

He pulled their clasped hands to his chest, just above the wound, then tapped them above his heart.

He stared at her.

"I love you, too, Frank."

He pushed her palm flat against his chest and held it there as if he wanted them to pledge allegiance.

"Save your strength. I know you love me."

He shook his head, tapped her hand on his chest again, then pointed to the quilt bunched under him.

Blood covered her fingers. Again.

Oh.

Rose yanked a zebra-patterned throw pillow off the bed and held it against Butler's wound. Her bloody hand sunk into the foam, which soaked into a red sponge so squishy she couldn't press it down with enough force. The slippery synthetic bedspread wouldn't give her more traction.

Rose ripped her blouse off and bunched it over his wound. It went from pale pink to crimson to bright, bright red in seconds, but the antique fabric seemed to staunch his bleeding. It held.

Butler mouthed a thank-you, and his breath sounded easier. She willed his pallor to reclaim some of the color they'd brought back from the Berkshires.

Rose watched her tears plop onto his face, but she couldn't lift her hand to wipe her face. He didn't seem to notice.

She dropped the gun when a gang of cops and paramedics rushed into the room.

Terri smiled when one of the cops started to haul Rose to her feet.

Rose fought to keep her hold on the fabric pressed over the wound until Butler moved her hand away and gestured that she should stand now. Two cops hauled Rose up and wrestled her hands behind her back.

Butler raised his head and gestured at Terri. He struggled for a few deep breaths before he spoke, "Cuff the blond bitch."

The cops loosened their hold on Rose, and she moved back toward Butler.

"Please, save your breath. I can explain everything to your colleagues here. Right after I tell you how sorry—"

Butler interrupted to give the officers another order, "And leave my girl alone."

# About the author

Maureen Anne Jennings has worn the hats of a journalist, copywriter, editor, publishing consultant, media relations manager, book festival director, and Fillmore East staffer. She owns more than 100 hats, not all of them work related. After the obligatory waitressing during college, she squandered a few years behind the bar at various dives in lower Manhattan. She also owned and operated a pub in northern California. Be careful what you write about.

# Connect

Email: toughprose@gmail.com
Twitter: @toughprose, @maureenjennings
Facebook: Tough Prose Press, Maureen Jennings
LinkedIn: Maureen Anne Jennings
Google+: +Maureen Jennings,
+Tough Prose Press
Web: ToughProse.com


Some new platform, coming soon.